THE
COLLABORATOR

THE COLLABORATOR

BY

S.L. STEBEL

RANDOM HOUSE / NEW YORK

For my parents, Abe and Anna, and for my wife, Jan

THE
COLLABORATOR

1

HE STOOD APART FROM ALL THE OTH-
ers. The others all had wives, children, brothers,
sisters, cousins, friends, subordinates from their depart-
ments, and of course, inevitably, the newspaper reporters,
swarming about them.

But Ernst Gottliebsohn stood alone. He was a graying,
stolid man in his middle forties, though he looked somewhat
older; neatly, if nondescriptly dressed, except for new gloves
and hat; wearing the badge of the devoted civil servant
(starched collar and plain tie); carrying himself with a certain dignity, watching, without seeming to, the sentimental
leave-takings of the others. He finally averted his eyes, but
whether from pain or embarrassment he did not know himself.

The bedlam was curiously subdued. Ordinarily, depar-
tures from the diplomatic corridors of Lod airport outside
Jerusalem were boisterous affairs. But now even the reporters, normally strident, seemed almost shamefaced as
they pursued their questioning in damped tones.

They ignored him because he seemed unimportant;
though he was listed as a full-fledged member of the mission, his secondary ranking, and his specialty, logistical
economist, were not conducive to the kind of sensational
statements their readers wanted.

Thus he was apprehensive when he saw the Associate

Chief of Mission Auerbach, a former Rumanian who everyone said had his eventual eye on the Prime Ministership itself, approaching him with the reporters in tow. It was Auerbach who had gotten him, against his wishes, assigned to the mission.

"Statistics are as emotionless as our friend Gottliebsohn here," Auerbach announced to the trailing reporters as he stopped in front of Gottliebsohn. "Perhaps one gets that way working with figures. Figures have no memories, no hates, no axes to grind. The figures, Gottliebsohn's figures, show that trade with Germany will have enormous benefits. What we want, they have, and vice versa. Those other countries of whom the same might be said do not have the same, shall we say, *incentives* to trade with us. Incentives are the political, emotional side of our mission. Incentives I and the others worry about. Gottliebsohn is involved with the logistics, which, after all, is the more important in terms of our ultimate survival. Gentlemen, it is because of Gottliebsohn's planning that our economy is in as healthy a state as it is."

They looked him over and were no more impressed than he would have been himself.

A reporter asked, "Your statistics indicate that we should increase our trade with Germany?"

"Yes," he answered, in his flat, slightly nasal, colorless voice.

"Isn't it true that statistics must be *interpreted*?"

Clutching his brief case, avoiding Auerbach's ambitious, encouraging eye, he launched into the same evaluation of the current export-import situation vis-à-vis Germany which had finally brought the Cabinet around, after an extraordinarily heated session, to authorizing the mission.

The reporters impatiently waited him out.

"You are German?" one of them asked when he had finished.

"Jew," he corrected, flustered.

"Born in Germany," Auerbach explained for him. "Yes."

"And you yourself personally feel that we should become ever more closely involved with the Germans?"

He saw now what they were after. There had been an inevitable public outcry when the mission had been announced, not so much over the trade aspects, which could have been considered temporary and just, a small return for material confiscation (and how do you put a price on human life?). But when it became known that they were also on a diplomatic mission to work out means of increasing the political accommodation, that was another story. A closer relationship with Germany? It was like asking people to sever moral nerves, an amputation of conscience that left them awkward and misguided as spastics.

He had not wanted this assignment. His hatred of the Germans was violent, beyond reason, coming, as it did, after the fact, by hearsay, as it were, and should have been as abstract and cold as the statistics with which he worked. The idea of returning to his homeland, a homeland that was shrouded in the fog that passed for his memory, congealed his insides. He had offered every conceivable excuse for not going. All had been rejected.

Now he said sorrowfully, "My figures show me that it is inevitable."

They left him, finally, alone again.

He would have been the last one on the plane had not Auerbach, during the final good-byes, come and chivvied him aboard.

"Didn't you bring your cameras?" Auerbach asked, looking him over as he took the seat beside him.

"There is nothing in Germany I want pictures of," Gottliebsohn said. But this was only part of the truth. After the uproar in the office over his taking of candid snapshots, in which a committee from his section had protested to the bureau chief himself, he had lost interest. Not that he blamed them. He could see their point. His pictures showed them in a much different light than they pictured themselves. But that was what fascinated him, trying to capture that moment when they were off guard, when, so to speak, the mask had slipped.

"It is difficult for you, I know," Auerbach said. "But think of it this way. Without your objective, rational, on-the-spot analysis, this mission would be impossible."

He wondered whether Auerbach was sincere, or whether it was not more likely that the edge to the other's voice revealed a cynicism that was soul-deep, the malaise of the times.

The plane taxied out on the tarmac, rolling at a good speed to the takeoff runway. The engines howled and the ship and those within it shuddered, in anticipation of the coming flight, when suddenly the great plane settled back. The motors stopped. Gottliebsohn, who had never been on a jet before, looked about him in confusion. What was the trouble? No one seemed to know. He craned his head to peer out the tiny window. An official car had come wheeling out of the customs shed, and was heading for the plane.

A steward unlocked the passenger door. There was a murmured consultation with whoever was outside and then the steward came back for Auerbach and the elderly ex-Pole Hortsky, who had once been an aide to Herzl, an early settler in Palestine, a former high-ranking Cabinet member, and was now ostensibly the mission chief.

A makeshift ladder was lowered. The two men clambered down out of sight. An excited buzz traveled the plane, diminishing briefly as the pilot announced that the flight was to be delayed, then rising again.

They became quiet when Auerbach came back aboard the plane alone. He stopped at Gottliebsohn's seat. He was pale, and his eyes burned as he studied the bewildered man.

"Come with me," he said, and turned on his heel. When they stepped to the runway, Auerbach grasped Gottliebsohn's arm so hard that he was certain the bone had been bruised. "I hope you can deny everything," Auerbach said fiercely. Then he got into the back seat of the waiting car beside Hortsky and another man. Gottliebsohn got in beside the driver, catching his breath as he saw that the third man was the Foreign Secretary.

From the way they looked at him, he knew something was terribly wrong. His first thought was there must have been some enormous error in his calculations. But a statistical error coud be adjusted, compensated for. No, there was something personal about this. Had they found out about his weekly visits to the Arab quarter? But certainly those trips, potentially scandalous as they were, could not be thought important enough to call a halt to their flight.

Gottliebsohn began to sweat. It was a strange, cold sweat, one that he had never before experienced in his waking hours. He found his handkerchief, wiped his face and neck like a guilty man, and wondered whether his nightmare had finally become a reality.

The Interior Minister and another man, whom Gottliebsohn did not recognize, were waiting in the diplomats' lounge.

"You are Gottliebsohn?" the Interior Minister asked. The Minister was a stocky, florid man, whose responsibility for the security of an insecure nation had obviously done terrible things to his nerves. How was it he could so readily identify the accused? Gottliebsohn realized he still held the handkerchief. He stuffed it hastily into a pocket, then reluctantly nodded.

"Please remember he is responsible to me," the Foreign Secretary said. He was a tall, gaunt, handsome fellow, a Sephardi, whose baldness gave him an impressive forehead, but whose renowned urbanity was denied by the manner in which he was worrying an unlit cigar.

"That jurisdiction can be changed," the other Minister snapped, and then Hortsky intervened.

"Perhaps we could all calm ourselves?" the old Zionist asked. "Let us all sit down, like gentlemen." Immediately they were deferential. "Ernst," he said to Gottliebsohn, "an accusation has been made against you. We have been delayed until you have a chance to answer it, for your answer can indeed have bearing on the success or failure of our mission. Would you care to be more specific with Mr. Gottliebsohn, Captain?"

The other man stepped forward.

A captain? Gottliebsohn wondered. Then why was he in civilian clothes? A moment later the answer burned in him: the sandy-haired, freckled, sour fellow was a ranking officer in the Intelligence Department. What branch? Military? Counterespionage? Internal security? The list tumbled through his mind, but since none of the categories fit himself, he could not identify the captain with any of them, either. At least he was not one of those young hot-eyed types who were vastly unsympathetic to the weaknesses of older men.

"There is no formal charge," the captain said. "The accusation against you has not even been recorded yet. However, if you admit guilt, we are prepared to take an official statement."

"Skip the formalities, Captain," the Interior Minister said. "Tell the man the charge."

"You have been accused of collaboration with the Nazis," the captain said, after an infuriated glance at his superior.

Gottliebsohn stared unbelievingly around the group. He even attempted a smile, to show them how ridiculous he thought the whole thing was. He was almost relieved, guessing now that this was the work of some monstrous crank whom he had somehow inadvertently offended. But what kind of person would attempt such an incredible revenge?

"Well?" the Interior Minister said.

Gottliebsohn looked for support to his own superiors. "It's apparent they don't know my record," he said, shrugging self-deprecatingly.

But they continued to stare as if waiting for some further reply. What was the matter with them? He had fled Germany in 1939, before the onset of the war, gone to England, volunteered as an interpreter in the special-assault units, distinguished himself in action; and if he had, technically, deserted the British army in Palestine, it was to join up with the resistance. Auerbach and Hortsky both knew the record almost as well as he did. Why didn't they speak up?

"I couldn't have collaborated with the Nazis," he said finally, patiently, "if I was on duty with my British unit all that time, could I?"

"All what time, Gottliebsohn?" the captain asked then, coldly polite.

"Why, from 1940 on," he said.

The captain pulled out a little calfskin notebook. He opened it to the first page. "The collaboration took place in July to August 1939, in Cologne. Were you not in Cologne at that time?"

Gottliebsohn wondered if he would ever be able to breathe again.

They brought him a chair and a glass of water. The captain was very efficient—taking the pillbox from his shaking hand, he gave the contents a moment's close scrutiny, held up one tablet and then another, and pushed both between Gottliebsohn's trembling lips, followed by the water.

Gottliebsohn gagged, swallowed, gagged again; the others never turned their eyes away.

"This is a frequent occurrence?" the captain asked,

when Gottliebsohn seemed to have settled down.

"Ever since the war," Gottliebsohn said. In moments of stress or shock an enormous giddiness swept over him, followed by nausea, which took all of his strength, and the pills, to fight down. The doctors attributed it to an imbalance in his inner ear, which they said was probably the result of concussion.

Suddenly Gottliebsohn remembered what had caused this attack. *"What do you know?"* he demanded, leaning forward so far he almost lost his balance again.

"You *were* in Cologne at that time?" the captain asked.

"I'm not sure," Gottliebsohn said.

"You're not sure?" Auerbach asked, incredulously.

"Please," the Interior Minister said to his colleague. "He's under your jurisdiction, isn't he? Can't you keep him out of this?"

But Gottliebsohn was talking to Auerbach now, the only one who might conceivably listen. "What is the data they have?" he asked. "What do they say about me? What records do they have? *I must know!*" he cried.

Auerbach backed away from the other's vehemence. "I don't understand."

Gottliebsohn pounded his temples—a gesture so obviously out of character that they were all taken aback, as though they were confronted by a lunatic.

"I have no prior memory!" Gottliebsohn shouted.

They looked blankly at him. Slowly, the force went out of Gottliebsohn. He looked hopelessly back at them. "I remember nothing previous to my escape from Germany."

"Very convenient," the Interior Minister said at last.

But Gottliebsohn was watching the captain. The man was noncommittal: he took nothing at face value, but if his experience taught him to be suspicious, he had also learned to be patient—the truth was never easily come by. Gottliebsohn quailed inwardly at something else, however: the man was not completely objective. Not quite hidden beneath the impassivity, the man hated, too.

"You deny the charge of collaboration?" the captain asked.

Gottliebsohn became sullen. They refused to understand. "Of course I deny it," he said.

"But you have no proof," the captain said.

"You have proof?" Hortsky then asked.

The captain was silent.

"Come, come, Captain," Hortsky said. "You surely don't think to trick this man into a confession?"

The captain shrugged and looked to his chief. The Interior Minister stepped forward. "He has been denounced by a citizen whose sincerity is unquestioned."

"But?" Hortsky pursued.

The Interior Minister shrugged. "So far we only have hearsay evidence. The man has all the facts—times and places and people—but he did not personally witness details of the collaboration."

"Where is he now?" the Foreign Secretary demanded, throwing away the shreds of his cigar.

"In protective custody," the other said. He avoided their startled glances. "We asked for a pledge of secrecy. He would not give it to us. He is opposed to the purposes of the mission, he says."

"Great God!" the Foreign Secretary cried. "If the opposition party gets hold of this they'll murder us. The government could fall."

"Will fall," the Interior Minister corrected him.

"You must let the man go," Hortsky said.

"Then I'll need Gottliebsohn in his place," the Interior Minister said.

Auerbach swore under his breath. "If Gottliebsohn doesn't go with us," he said, "the mission is doomed."

"Can one man be that important?" the Interior Minister said.

"The reporters interviewed him," Auerbach said. "Gottliebsohn has been singled out as responsible for the statistical reasoning. They will use his figures for their stories. The international press was there, too. The Germans will pick it up, come to interview him after we arrive. And if he isn't there, the whole thing will break wide open . . ."

They all looked distastefully at the seated man. Gottliebsohn shifted uneasily.

"What a hell of a mess," the Foreign Secretary said.

"And whose fault is that?" the Interior Minister demanded. "It is *your* people who said it was time for a rapprochement with the Germans. Twenty years, you say, is long enough for hate. I say twenty years is just a beginning."

"There is another generation now," Hortsky interrupted.

"It is we who have suffered," the Interior Minister cried.

"We have a responsibility to the next generation," Hortsky said patiently.

"Precisely," the Interior Minister said. "It is a matter of security. We must search out all our guilty ones."

"How does it make us secure to be bound by the past?" the Foreign Secretary asked. "We must deal with the world as it exists today."

"I am familiar with your arguments," the Interior Minister said. "I heard them at great length in the Cabinet."

"And is it not the will of the Cabinet—the almost unanimous will—that this mission be sent to Germany?"

"Go to Germany then!" the other burst out. "Am I keeping you now? If you must embrace the devil, hop to it! Just don't expect my good wishes!"

"You will release Gottliebsohn then?" the Foreign Secretary asked.

"Gottliebsohn stays," the Interior Minister said, "until we have pursued our investigations."

"I could not have been a collaborator," Gottliebsohn muttered, reminding them that he was there.

"But you don't know that," the Interior Minister said sarcastically, turning on him. "Do you? You have told us that you are without memory."

"I was a Jew on the run in 1939," Gottliebsohn said desperately. "It would have been impossible for me to collaborate."

"Not impossible," the Interior Minister said contemptuously. "There have been too many cases where Jews have collaborated."

"But with what motive?" Gottliebsohn begged.

The captain shrugged angrily. "What difference what motive? Our concern is with what a man does, not with why he does it."

"Captain Kohn," Hortsky said reprovingly.

Gottliebsohn started up from his chair. Kohn? The revengeful tracker of fugitive Nazis? The man who had engineered abductions of Nazis out of foreign lands back to Israel for trial? The man of whom it was rumored that he had killed—assassinated—how many whom he said it was impossible to bring back? Why was he involved in a case of such minor consequence? Gottliebsohn started to sweat again. This whole thing was going too far. He had long been afraid that there had been an enormous guilt in his past, but whether it was the private misdeed of his nightmare, or this monstrous behavior they were accusing him of now, he did not know. But he could not tell them anything. If they searched his past for one, they might find the other.

"I have only my feelings to depend on," he said, "but I tell you I know it would have been impossible for me to have had anything to do with the Germans!"

The Interior Minister looked at him bitterly. "It is a different matter now, though."

"I did not want this assignment," Gottliebsohn said, after a quick glance at Auerbach.

"Oh?" the Interior Minister said. "Then why . . . ?"

"You can read the interview in the afternoon papers," Auerbach said.

"How dare you?" the Interior Minister said.

"Auerbach," the Foreign Secretary said warningly.

"Look here," Auerbach said vehemently, "our plane sits there grounded, while we are engaged in interminable discussions about the past of a single man. Is it so important? Every minute that plane waits is that much more chance that the mission goes down to failure. While we worry about the past, we lose the future."

"Whose future are you worried about?" the Interior Minister asked. "Israel's—or your own?"

"Furthermore," said Auerbach, ignoring the thrust, "here we have a man whose whole record since the alleged collaboration has been that of a courageous, patriotic individual, who has risked his life many times over for the founding of our state, whose entire public career has been devoted toward serving that state."

"Save it for the stump," the Interior Minister said.

Auerbach reddened and fell silent.

"He is quite right," Hortsky interceded.

"With all respect, sir," the Interior Minister said, "you have been in Palestine since 1919, and have since brought your family here. You suffered no personal atrocities!"

"I grieve for your dead," Hortsky said. "But our obligation is to the living. I sympathize with your position—but I do not agree with it. You are not after security, my friend, but revenge. If this man's guilt is in a forgotten past, then let us forget it, too. He has atoned for any possible wrong many times over, since."

"If he is telling the truth," the captain said.

Hortsky addressed himself to Gottliebsohn. "You remember nothing?" he asked gently.

Gottliebsohn looked fearfully at the old patriarch, wondering how powerful he could be after the months of retirement. "There are some dim recollections," he admitted finally. "A search, cattle cars, the rain . . ." His words trailed off, as meaningless to them as the memory was to himself.

"What about your family?" Hortsky asked.

Gottliebsohn shrugged heavily. "They are killed, I think."

"How do you know that?" the captain asked sharply.

"I checked with the Office of Survivors," Gottliebsohn said wearily, remembering the hopelessness of the long search, with him unable to offer anything in the way of assistance except for his name and his village of origin, taken from his German national identity card. They had traced him back to a family—a mother, a father, a younger sister—but there the trail had stopped. "They have no records of any of my family since the war."

"You didn't look for them yourself?" the captain asked.

"Where would I look?" Gottliebsohn said hopelessly.

"Retrace your steps," the captain said. "Go back to where your memory stopped, look for clues, follow them down—"

"I didn't want to go back to Germany," Gottliebsohn said.

They fell silent.

"Well?" Hortsky said.

"I *cannot* let him go without investigation," the Interior Minister said.

Auerbach looked at him thoughtfully. "Why can't the investigation proceed, in any case?" he asked.

"Let him go loose, out of the country?" the Interior Minister asked. "And if we find that he *is* guilty?"

"I would not attempt to find sanctuary there," Gottliebsohn said.

"Sanctuary?" the Interior Minister said, pretending to be

amused. "The Germans would like nothing better than to try one of our people for a change!"

"Look!" Auerbach said. "Assign Captain Kohn to the mission. While you're checking Gottliebsohn's record out here, he can pursue the matter en route. Besides, having the chief investigator of our War Crimes Bureau along is not a bad idea in itself! What a dandy way to pressure the Germans! Think of their reaction if we threaten to bring him to the bargaining table!"

The assembled men thought about the German reaction: some with enthusiasm, some with disgust.

"Captain?" the Interior Minister said finally.

"I would prefer not to be assigned to this case," the captain said.

"The issues are not clear-cut enough for you, are they, Captain?" Auerbach said. "You would prefer something more heroic, would you not?"

The captain did not answer.

"It *would* be a solution," the Foreign Secretary pressed, "if by some unfortunate circumstance the denouncement and that 'protective custody' were to get out, we could cover ourselves by pointing to the presence of the captain as the investigator, on scene."

The Interior Minister nodded slowly. "I am sorry, Captain," he said finally. "I know how you feel, but I am afraid we are left with no choice."

"Good," the Foreign Secretary said enthusiastically. "Then we can assume the matter is in good hands."

"I am not sure I like any of this," Hortsky said. "Kohn part of the mission? It smacks of blackmail."

Auerbach flushed. "Blackmail? A harsh term, is it not? We are only reminding the Germans, after all."

"And ourselves, too, are we not?" Hortsky asked.

"We will not use Kohn unless the need arises," Auerbach said. "And then only for Gottliebsohn's case."

"And then it will be a vendetta," Hortsky said. "The Jews revenging themselves on one of their own."

"Strong words, my dear Hortsky," the Interior Minister said. "There are good psychological reasons for revenge. The Jewish psyche must be cleared of the least hint of past corruption. Captain," he snapped, "that will be your responsibility. Clear?"

"Quite clear," the captain said.

"Hortsky?" the Foreign Secretary asked.

"I will accept the captain," the old man said slowly, "on one condition. In the event there is publicity, in the event the case is brought to trial, Auerbach must agree to act as Gottliebsohn's lawyer."

"Well, Auerbach?" the Foreign Secretary said, breaking the lengthening silence.

Auerbach was stunned. The old fox. If it turned out that this melancholy, self-effacing individual *had* been a collaborator, and that he not only had chosen him for the mission, but also agreed to act as his lawyer, his own career would be jeopardized.

"Of course," Auerbach finally said. What else could he do? Perhaps there would be compensations, he told himself ironically. If it did come to public trial, and Gottliebsohn was innocent, he would come to a quicker national prominence. He looked at his client, trying to catch his eye, trying to guess if it held guilt or innocence.

But Gottliebsohn was not listening. He was looking at the captain. And as the shiver roughed his skin, he understood for the first time in his remembered life how bitter, and yet how almost sweet, is the taste of fear.

2

THE CAPTAIN SAT NEXT TO GOTTLIEB-
sohn during the flight. He got aboard without luggage,
without even an attaché or brief case.

When the word was passed as to who he was, an excited
murmur ran down the aisle. He did not look at all as they
had imagined, this heroic avenger of theirs. The stories of
his exploits had made him seem larger than life, and to see
him thus, sandy-haired where he was not balding, freckled,
and delicate in his movements as a bantam cock, was disap-
pointing. There had never been any published pictures, and
the more cynical thought it not so much that the government was afraid it would ruin his effectiveness as an undercover man as that it would spoil his image as an authentic
hero.

Auerbach also passed the word that the captain had
been assigned to the mission by the Prime Minister himself.
To all questions as to his purpose on a mission of this hopefully healing nature, Auerbach had one answer: he was to
be their trump card in case the Germans were finally reluctant to meet their terms.

An argument broke out as to the moral merit of such a
presence, but strangely enough Auerbach, notoriously a
highly verbal man, took no part.

He had taken the seat behind Gottliebsohn so that he
might be handy in case the other needed him. But since

neither Gottliebsohn nor the captain said anything in the first thirty minutes, he settled back, and exhausted by the strain of getting the mission off, lulled by the muted roar of the engines, he soon fell into a nervous sleep.

A pretty little stewardess passed with an offer of coffee, which both the captain and Gottliebsohn refused. Then Kohn took out his notebook, thumbed past Gottliebsohn's denouncement, and taking out a handsome gold pencil, prepared to interrogate his companion.

"Shall we begin?"

"Begin?"

"With what you do remember."

Gottliebsohn shrugged uneasily. "Nothing. I told you."

There were many reasons why Kohn had not wanted this assignment, but the strongest was a premonition that it would turn out badly. He had always before enjoyed the hunt. Those he pursued were obvious scum, whose capture or liquidation served a higher purpose. He had right on his side—all the power of the just cause—and when he struck, he struck a mighty blow against evil. The captain was not religious, but at the successful close of his previous cases he always experienced an exaltation that brought him to the seeming brink of a miraculous revelation.

Here, though, he was confronted with a situation where if it turned out that this blank-eyed, haunted fellow was guilty, there would be the usual blather about extenuating circumstance, sophistries of legal and moral argument which confused the captain, leaving nothing specific to which or to whom he might direct his anger. Not the least of the captain's dismay was that he had been assigned to one of his own people, a situation he had managed to avoid throughout his spectacular career.

"Now look here," he said, attempting to be reasonable, "if you're lying, you won't get away with it for long. Our bureau people are checking you out right now, and I'm not to leave you alone for an instant. I've had experience in these matters, and you'll slip, you're bound to, they all do. If you're really an amnesiac, however, and you're not afraid of the truth, maybe I can help. But you've got to cooperate."

Gottliebsohn did not respond. He knew this man's reputation. He had thrilled with the rest to each exploit, shrugging away the whispered echoes in the official corridors that the captain killed not out of anger or circumstance, but out of personal need. If that was true, it was a need all of them felt, and they cheered him on, as Spaniards in the arena cheered the bullfighter.

But now he himself was the beast being harassed, and there was dust in his nostrils and the taste of blood in his throat, and this deceptively fragile elegant was attempting to flag him across the ring to the hidden sword, and he trembled, though admittedly as much with anticipation as with fear.

"Well?" the captain asked. "Why don't you speak?"

"I am afraid," Gottliebsohn said.

"Of what?"

"Of you," Gottliebsohn said. "I think that you are my enemy."

"I am not your friend," the captain said honestly. "But I am not your enemy, either. I have been assigned to get whatever facts out of you I can. That is all I am interested in. You personally mean nothing to me."

Gottliebsohn wanted to believe him. But the dammed-up emotion he had felt in Kohn was not so remote as the other would have him believe.

For the moment, though, he might be safe. And if his track did not hold the spoor of a collaborator—as he devoutly hoped it could not—and even if instead they found a more spectacular though less heinous crime, this hunter would not be required, by the habit of an aging passion, to kill him.

"Very well," Gottliebsohn said reluctantly. "How do we start?"

"It's always easier," Kohn said, relieved, "to start with simple everyday facts, like your name, your occupation, where you live, what time you get up in the morning, and so forth. It warms us both up, like a game of catch, you know? So that when an important question is thrown, you can throw the answer back. You don't get a cramp and throw short and stop the game."

"My name you know," Gottliebsohn said. "I live in the central city, on Haneviim Street."

"The Arab quarter?" Kohn asked, surprised.

"Not quite; it's a perimeter street," Gottliebsohn explained nervously. "The rent is very cheap, I have a spacious apartment and it's a short walk to work."

"You live alone?" Kohn asked, though not quite satisfied with the answer.

"Alone."

"No housekeeper, no girl companions?"

"None," said Gottliebsohn, missing the point. "The land-lord sends a maid in once a week to clean."

"Ever been married?" Kohn asked.

"Never," Gottliebsohn said. "So far as I know." He was irritated when the other shrugged as if it were unlikely or it did not matter.

"What about your friends?" Kohn asked.

There was an uncomfortable silence. "I have none," Gottliebsohn answered finally.

"None that you would call close?"

"None whatsoever."

It had been easier for him to bear his loneliness than to go through the pain of having to reveal a blank past. After the war he had joined several veterans' groups. But the veterans invariably got onto how things had been in the old days, in Europe, pre-Hitler, leaving him at loose ends, feeling an outcast, as if he were in fact a leper, equally loath-some, though of a social kind. He could not blame them for not warming to one with such a melancholy nature.

At the office, too, his seeming aridity, his aloof manner, his unfailing pedantry, repelled his fellow workers. His statistical brilliance was of the kind that cheered superiors and awed subordinates, but never encouraged anyone to want to know him better.

A few plain women made some tentative advances, but he had so obviously been unaware of them that even they had given up in order to keep their pride.

He told no one about the children's institute, feeling it would be difficult to explain that he felt like an orphan of sorts himself, and not wanting to appear mawkish over something that gave him so much quiet satisfaction.

"What do you do," the captain asked then, "for recreation?"

"I walk a great deal," Gottliebsohn said, deciding it would serve no purpose to tell him about the soccer.

"In the countryside, on hikes?" the captain asked.

"About the city, mostly," Gottliebsohn said. And then,

sensing a skepticism in the glance the other gave his rather elegant shoes, "I was not planning to go walking in Germany," he explained.

"How is walking recreation?" the captain asked.

Gottliebsohn did not answer. The fact was, he walked in search of his memory, hoping, in that pedestrian exercise, to emulate the search of that awful night he so dimly remembered, so he might further break the debris-ridden dam which clogged his mind. Through the years bits and pieces had worked free. He had examined them, turning them over and over again in the turgid surface of his mind, but what they revealed was of such a frightening and misleading character that he had not dared tell anyone. How could he tell the captain now? He had to be very cautious. He had to sort out only those things which would not prematurely affect the captain's judgment. He did not want to be condemned for something completely beside the point!

"I do remember something," Gottliebsohn said reluctantly. "But it is all so vague."

The captain urged him on with an encouraging glance.

"I remember going to the railway station on a rainy night."

"What is it, man?" the captain asked. "You're trembling."

Of course he trembled, Gottliebsohn thought angrily. How could he say aloud that which he tried not even to think in his waking moments? Every time he remembered the rain he became terribly confused. What was real and what was hallucination? Why would he remember the stink of wet wool when the clothes he wore were cotton shreds? Was that hate, or remorse, he felt in his heart? Was he being stalked by a Nazi for personal reasons, or did the fear of such an encounter replace the reality in his mind? And how could he, a Jew, only recently arrived in Cologne, have managed so to offend a Nazi that he was, or imagined he was, being followed along the slippery cobblestones, down drenched back streets, dodging with that specter out of the way of the patrolling Black Shirts, as if both were breakers of curfew, until finally, at a dead-end corner, to stand terrorized, as his shadowy follower came bounding forward, jackboots sloshing through ankle-deep puddles, to engage him in a nightmarish struggle to the death.

It was impossible for that to be real. After the struggle

(if there had been a struggle) he had found himself (seemingly bereft of all reason, unable to remember anything) huddled in an alley behind a rubbish pail, its cover askew, a marauding cat screeching off into the distance like a soul leaving its body, him shivering with the wet and the cold and with something else, until finally, looking through his wallet with hands that would not stop trembling, and eyesight which alternately blurred with rain or tears, he found his temporary residence card, and remembered that he had been rushing about forbidden streets until fear and hallucination overcame him. Getting up, stiff and sore, as if he had been crouching there for hours instead of what could only have been a few minutes, he stumbled to the nearest lighted street and thrust the card into the hands of the first passer-by he met. Though looked at askance, he had been directed to the dilapidated old apartment house in slum town. Not a light showed anywhere through the drizzle. *Mongrel Jew* was scrawled in yellow chalk across the entry door. At the sight of those words, even in his memory, his flesh crawled.

Inside, he flew up three flights of slanted stairs, the worn boards groaning under his anxious feet, and because the hallway bulb was out, he spent precious time trying to strike a light with soggy matches. Eventually he found the apartment. There was no answer to his pounding, or to his pleading breath through the keyhole.

The neighbors across the hall would not answer their door at first.

Finally, when it became apparent that his pounding would not stop, the door edged open to the width of the chain lock.

"My family?" he begged of the frightened eyes.

"Who are your family?" the other asked, blinking to see him in the damp gloom.

"The Gottliebsohns!" he cried. "I am Ernst, their son!"

The other seemed even more frightened than before. And why had he not been recognized? They had apparently moved in too recently to be well known. He himself was confused by his recent terror. He could not remember where he had lived. The loss of his memory might have frightened him more had he not been so concerned about his family.

"But didn't you know?" the shadowy face asked. "They

have been taken to the railroad station."

That "didn't you know" haunted him. It could have been a normal question to ask of a son in those fear-ridden times, but somehow his imagination put more meaning into it, even an accusation. But of what? Of being absent when his family needed him? Or something more horrifying?

He did not ask, thinking to come back later to deny whatever it might be. He rushed down the stairs, and because it was dark and his boots were slippery, he missed the second landing and took a nasty fall. The fall slowed him, his bruised ankle making it impossible to run.

When he finally reached the station, hobbling down back streets and littered alleys, he saw that a passenger train was just pulling out. He was too late—or was he? A train was in the station, a long freight train, cattle cars stretching unendingly past the blurred station lights and on into the rain-soaked darkness, and somehow he guessed, or knew, what was in those sealed cars! Was it the sound like lowing cattle that raised his hair on end, once he realized that it was human? Or was it some dreadful prior knowledge?

He went from car to car, pounding on the doors, calling his family's name, identifying himself, begging to be let in. Some station guards, hearing the commotion, found him. They laughed at his pleadings, joked with each other about how lucky for him the cars were sealed, and his name not on a manifest—didn't he know how carefully organized the whole thing was?—and then they dragged him inside, where he stood, clothes plastered to his skin, shivering with that something other than cold, while the officer, a thick-lipped bully who couldn't think for himself, called central headquarters.

Then they let him go! He was dragged to the station entrance and booted out into the rain again. They were making a terrible mistake—but he knew better than to plead any more. He slipped around the enclosed yards, found an untended gate, scuttled along the fencing until the station and the train looked like a toy in the distance. The train had picked up a good speed by the time it got to him, but he managed to grab hold of the third ladder he tried for, and he clung to it for many miles.

Eventually he found the strength to clamber to the top.

There he lay sideways, head down to the first opening, trying to make himself heard to those within over the noise of the racketing wheels. It was impossible. He sobbed with frustration—and somehow, incredibly, he dozed off and his hands loosed their clutch; as the train rounded a curve he was slung off.

He came to in midflight through the streaming darkness and before he could remember who or what or where he was, he had hit an embankment, and his body being loose as some scarecrow, he came out of it without any more harm than some deep scratches and a hurt shoulder that bothered him somewhat to this day.

From there, walking only at night in a direction perpendicular to the tracks, he came to the Belgian border. He sought sanctuary in a convent; the nuns were puzzled and a bit frightened by his peculiar behavior, but they fed him, let him sleep on an old mattress in the milking shed, and awakened him at midnight to send him on.

"The nuns were very kind," Gottliebsohn said. "Do you imagine they helped many Jews?"

"Yes, of course," the captain said impatiently. "But I am more interested in what happened in Cologne."

"I found my family being shipped out on a cattle train," Gottliebsohn said. "Imagine, the brutes, a cattle train!" His voice shook.

"You found them?" the captain asked.

"They had to've been on that train!" Gottliebsohn said. "At the apartment house a neighbor told me they were."

"What apartment house?" the captain asked.

"The one we moved to from our village," Gottliebsohn said. "Just before my parents were shipped out."

"You remember the date you moved there?"

"No," Gottliebsohn said.

"Then why do you assume the move was recent?"

"The neighbors did not recognize me," Gottliebsohn said.

"Not so unusual," the captain said. "In those days people kept to themselves. Do you remember the address?"

"I have it among my papers, back at my flat," Gottliebsohn said.

"They will be picked up," the captain said. "Then perhaps we'll pay a visit to Cologne, you and I."

"What good would that do?" Gottliebsohn demanded. "You surely don't expect to find any Jews there now?"

"I like the beer there," the captain said. "And the girls are big and buxom—big tits, big bellies, big rumps—something a man can get hold of."

Gottliebsohn was shocked and offended. How could Kohn be so frivolous in front of a man whose very existence was being called into question?

The captain became aware of the expression on Gottliebsohn's face. "Don't be a fool, man," he said. "We'll go to the apartment house and re-create the action, so to speak. You haven't done that, you say, and maybe that's one reason your memory is stuck. We'll try and jog it loose. The head-knockers have nothing on us, eh? At the same time, we'll publish the address in the German newspapers and those in Israel, asking for whoever lived there to come forward, on a matter of the utmost importance. All right? That business about the beer and the girls—well, I'm not celibate or a teetotaler, and I don't care who knows it." He shut his notebook with a snap. He thought longingly of his other cases where he had been, for all practical purposes, a free agent, operating without restraint either as to procedure or goal and able, along the way, to take advantage of whatever "cultural" opportunities the countryside provided. This situation, hemmed in by officialdom all around, was not at all to his taste. If he hadn't committed the best years of his life to the service, he was damned if he wasn't tempted to resign on the spot.

On the other hand, he thought then, he wasn't young any more, and this might be a good time to look for a spot to settle into by cultivating Auerbach. It was not inconceivable that he could wind up in a top post in some future government. He might even take his present chief's job. He could see where maybe the future belonged to those who professed more flexibility. He could see too where a heroic figure like himself, professing the new attitude, could do wonders in bridging the gap between the old school and the new. It was no good to pretend to be dumb or to be chained by old habits and loyalties. A man had to take his opportunity where he found it.

He got up, smiled benevolently at Gottliebsohn, and

went back to sit beside Auerbach. The other had just awakened and was somewhat out of sorts until he heard the captain's first words.

"I thought you might be interested in the progress that's being made with your client," the captain said.

Auerbach looked at him thoughtfully. He rang for the stewardess and asked for tea with lemon and cube sugar. "What about you?" he asked.

"No, thanks," Kohn said. "It's a bit bland for me."

They did not speak again until the tea was brought. Auerbach had had too much experience to jump too soon; too premature a move could scare the other off.

Kohn's instincts were similar. They cautioned him to wait for a response before making clear what he was about. If he miscalculated his man, it would not look too good for him back in the department, hero or no hero.

"My client, you say?" Auerbach commented finally, soaking the sugar cube in the tea and sucking it noisily. "That sounds a bit ominous, Captain. He becomes my client only if he is brought to trial. Surely you haven't gotten the kind of information in that brief interrogation that will stand up in court?"

"Not at all," Kohn said easily. "Quite the opposite."

"How is that?" Auerbach demanded, pressing now.

"You know that if this case were being conducted according to the rules," Kohn said, evading him, "I couldn't give you advance information. You'd have to wait until the prosecution people got their chance at it—and then likely most of it you'd hear for the first time in court."

"Yes, yes, I know—I have been a practicing attorney," Auerbach said testily.

"But it seems to me," Kohn continued, "that it's in Israel's best interests for all concerned to work together."

"I quite agree," Auerbach began; but Kohn was not finished.

"But the fact is, my own Minister may not see it that way."

Auerbach nodded. "Anything you tell me will be kept in complete confidence."

"That may be," Kohn said. "But if the case doesn't turn out well from my superior's standpoint, my name will still be mud. Quite frankly, I think he's wrong. But I have my own future to think about, and, well—"

"I understand perfectly, Captain," Auerbach said, smiling to himself. "You need not worry about your position with us. We need men in the government whose vision is not blinded by the past."

"It's not my present position so much I was thinking about," Kohn mused aloud. "My job's practically obsolete now, wouldn't you say? It's time I was thinking of putting my talents to other tasks. Perhaps even to an administrative job."

"Did you have anything particular in mind?" Auerbach asked, taking care not to sound cynical.

"I would think the foreign service might be right for me," the captain said. "I've traveled practically everywhere, speak many languages, and in certain countries, where it would be bound to get out what my past was—even if we had to leak it ourselves, know what I mean?—I would think I could do a good job in fund-raising."

"That's not a bad idea," Auerbach said noncommittally.

"I suppose, too, with all the experience I've had in my own department, it wouldn't be too difficult for me to take that job on, either."

"You don't have small ideas, do you, Captain?" Auerbach asked.

"Do you?" Kohn asked softly.

Auerbach pursed his mouth. "It's a bargain that's good for the country, I suppose," he said. The captain decided that he would take this grudging acceptance as commitment toward his future, like (better than!) money in the bank. "Well then, what progress?" Auerbach asked, finally impatient.

"He claims his family was shipped out to a camp," the captain said. "If that is true, I would think the case against him collapses. The accusation says his family was saved in place of others. Or had you read the full accusation yet, Associate Director Auerbach?"

Auerbach felt the pinch of his shirt collar, as he did whenever his neck swelled with anger. For one of the few times in his life, however, it was directed at himself. He wondered, too, whether he had not underestimated this dapper little beady-eyed man.

"It is only his word," Auerbach said, as if he might be the prosecutor.

"Against another man's, reputable, like the Interior Minister says, but not a hero like our Gottliebsohn."

"The Nazis may have reneged," Auerbach said.

"You are grasping at straws," the captain said. "Who will testify to that? Do you think you can get a German today to admit membership in the party?"

Auerbach sipped his tea, thinking about it. It was too easy. If they closed the case now, even on the excellent grounds of lack of evidence, lack of motive, there would remain a suspicion, not so much directed at Gottliebsohn as at himself, the perpetrator of the controversial mission. A speck a gnat would not blink at could tilt the scales against him, against the mission, against the future. He shook his head.

"What's the matter?" Kohn asked, irritated. "Isn't it enough for you?"

"For me, yes," Auerbach said. "Not for our purposes. Your chief has put a free citizen in 'protective custody'; there'll be hell to pay when the man gets out. The opposition party, their newspapers, will murder us. You think they'll be satisfied with this preliminary?"

"Oh, if that's what's worrying you," the captain said, "they'll be raking it over very thoroughly back home; the Interior Minister'll see to that. But what can they find? It's in Germany that his past is buried, and it's probably buried so deep in the rubble that it would take three generations to dig out—if the third generation gave a damn about it. Believe me, Auerbach, the chances are excellent that nothing whatsoever will turn up."

"What if Gottliebsohn is lying?" Auerbach asked.

"He probably is, a bit," the captain acknowledged cheerfully. "Everyone does when they're accused of something. It's a natural reaction, isn't it? No one likes strangers, particularly official strangers, poking around. But the man isn't a collaborator; I'd stake my reputation on it."

"You may have to, Captain," Auerbach said. Kohn winced, then shrugged, like a gambler. He'd made his choice, he'd stick by it—at least as long as all other factors remained equal. "You think he has no memory then?" Auerbach asked.

"I'd better warn you about something," Kohn said. "What I think about *that* doesn't matter. The I.M.'s very modern in his approach to the criminal mind. He'll put a headknocker on this, get an official certification, and all the rest of it."

"A court psychiatrist?" Auerbach asked.

"Most likely," Kohn said.

Auerbach brooded over this. It just wouldn't do, he thought. "Captain," he said abruptly. "We have to somehow *prove* that Gottliebsohn couldn't have been a collaborator. We have to exonerate him."

"But," the captain protested, "I just got through explaining how impossible—"

"I tell you nothing less will satisfy the people," said Auerbach. He paused when he saw how Kohn was regarding him. "Think of it, man," he said then, changing his tone. "To resurrect the past, to actually prove a man *innocent*, instead of guilty, would cap your whole career. If you can bring this off, people who call you a one-noter will have something new to chew on—and would never question your getting a top job."

Kohn was disturbed. On the one hand, he was being told things he was well aware of, but that he did not like others to point out, just the same. On the other hand, he was being carroted, as though the man truly believed him capable of such a superhuman task. Hurt, insulted, flattered, suspicious, Kohn frowned to hide his feelings, then got up and went to the bathroom.

Auerbach went up front to the little compartment that had been set up for Hortsky. He knocked, and the old man bid him enter.

"You seem agitated," Hortsky said, laying aside a book.

Auerbach noted the title: *The Politics of Unreason*—an advance copy of his own book. He was momentarily flattered, until he realized the old man could have been reading it out of suspicion as well as curiosity. "I've had a talk with our captain," he said. "Kohn says the Interior Minister will unquestionably put a psychiatrist on the case."

"Yes," the old man said, nodding, "I can see where he

would want to do that. You couldn't have an objection, could you?"

"I could, and do," Auerbach said. "He'll put one of his people on it, a criminally oriented man."

"I suppose he would," Hortsky agreed. "But if Gottliebsohn is not a criminal, what's the harm?"

"I want a man who's sympathetic," Auerbach said. "Now wait, hear me out," he continued, as the other began to object. "Given Gottliebsohn's medical history, and from what Kohn tells me, I'm pretty well convinced he does have amnesia. I need a man who'll dig in and try to reconstruct Gottliebsohn's memory. Feeling as we both do about Gottliebsohn's record, I don't think we should entrust that record to an Israeli prosecution-oriented psychiatrist. Every psychiatrist in our country that I know about has had a bad personal experience with the Germans. I don't think we can trust them, however professionally objective they may try to keep their attitude, with the possibility that our man may have been guilty. That's why I say we need a sympathetic man."

"You want to go that far with it?" Hortsky asked.

"We have to," Auerbach said. "It's too touchy a situation politically—we'd be accused of a whitewash."

The old man looked at the book he was reading. "You are as cynical as your writings then," he said dryly.

"Not cynical," Auerbach said. "Realistic. It is all in the title. The electorate is never reasonable. On any issue which has emotional undercurrents, they can be swayed *either way* by the least thing. I don't want that to happen here."

The old man nodded thoughtfully. "What do you want me to do?"

"Use your influence," Auerbach said. "Get us a man who can do this job for us."

"I'm not sure I can," Hortsky said. "To go outside the country for this sort of investigation . . . but I will make inquiries. The dean of the Jerusalem Psychiatric Institute is an old friend. I will ask his opinion on a man."

3

ISAAC WOLFE, EMERITUS DEAN OF PSY-
chiatric studies at the Jerusalem Psychiatric Institute,
folded his arthritic hands and gazed as benevolently as he
was able at the younger man.

Norman Glass, M.D., Ph.D., looking more like a student
with his cropped hair and his athletic frame than the professor he was, had been struck dumb by the proposal. But the
dean thought it unlikely that the American would be able to
refuse him. Broached by his former teacher and analyst,
whom Glass had come seeking in his latest emotional crisis,
he would find it difficult, if not impossible, to turn him
down. Furthermore, the dean knew quite well the imposing
figure he himself cut, with his shaggy tobacco-stained
goatee, his pince-nez and his towering reputation—all so
overwhelming to that essentially unsophisticated (equate:
so far uncorrupted) mind.

"You are that rarest of human beings," the dean continued, "a true *neutral*. You have no feelings one way or
another about being a Jew—you have told me that how
many times yourself? Yes, yes, I know, it is precisely because
you have no feelings in that area that you have come to
Israel. Looking for your 'psychic roots,' I believe you said?
Well, let me tell you, Norman, traitorous as it may seem to
our rather special relationship, in my opinion you will learn

more about yourself in the pursuit of this man's memory than in one hundred hours of analysis with me."

Norman Glass stirred uneasily. He was not sure the old man did not mock him. But then, did he not deserve to be mocked? He had written requesting the exchange professorship, in reaction to the taunts of his estranged wife, Estelle, who had accused him of fearing an identification with the Jews. What better way to test himself, he had reasoned, than to finally surround himself with Jewishness?

"Look at it from our point of view," the dean said. "It would be difficult, if not impossible, to find a psychiatrist in Israel who does not have personal feelings about collaboration so strong they would color his attitude toward this accused man. It is difficult, if not impossible, to be objective when one has himself suffered from the things this man is alleged to have participated in. But you do not have this problem."

Glass moved restlessly under the force of the argument. As a second-generation American, a small-town boy, a born Jew, a Unitarian with a gentile wife, he had assimilated insofar as the society would allow, and he had indeed been far removed, geographically and in point of time, from the problems of the European Jew. Was the dean mildly remonstrating with him for this situation?

The dean, though he looked at the other impassively, stroking his beard in that immemorial gesture of wisdom, recognized the other's uneasiness. He was momentarily tempted to confide his own misgivings. He knew what it was like to be alien to his own people. A year in Israel had been enough to show him how much he missed his charming whipped-cream-and-chocolate Vienna, and even that small fish-reeking New England college town with its brown-sugared salt pork and beans. More important, oh, much more important indeed, in this country created by Jews, he had discovered how much he had cherished being an outsider.

In the past, in Austria or Massachusetts, he could always stop a conversation or an idea by calling attention to his own uniqueness, by referring to the fact that he was Jewish, a product of an exotic culture. Here, with the common religion but an uncommon diversity of background, even his intellectual achievements gave him no special place. He

would have left long ago if the desert sun were not so soothing to his old bones, and if those like Hortsky were not so
persuasive in their arguments that men like himself, who
had been blind to the meaning of Hitler, owed something to
the survivors of that racial holocaust. Hortsky had never
been truly European himself, and thus could not understand
his longing for the old life, the pleasure he had had in his
very rootlessness, with no allegiances except to ideas.

It was all very amusing, if one cared for that sort of
humor. Here he was, a displaced person in the ultimate
sense, assigning a man with no sense of self to search out the
self of another, a fellow who, out of God knew what pressure of guilt, had blanked out his past, and all in the name of
a nation still in the process of defining its own character.

And what a curious unstable person this Norman Glass
was—the dean remembered him as a thin, intense, highly
strung young man. Had Glass not possessed an almost
supernatural intuition in matters of mental aberration, he
would certainly have suggested that he take up a different
specialty—gynecology, perhaps. But he had discovered that
the other had a real feel for analytic relationship, even if he
invariably became too personally involved with his patients,
going so far as to adopt their more obvious characteristics,
as if he were experimenting on himself.

The dean's own analysis of Glass had not been successful. But then he should never have taken him on in the first
place. They shared nothing in common. Glass was from the
midwestern United States (where they grew corn which
they fed to pigs, for goodness' sake!), his little knowledge of
Jewish culture gotten from books—probably the encyclo-
pedia and an illustrated version of the Old Testament. How
could he, a refugee, a highly sophisticated, urbanized,
somewhat corruptible, already aging man, recognize any of
the problems that his student had? Glass had no church and
no God, no ritual or tradition, no family background to which
he might cling in moments of need. The fellow was like a
castaway. His parents, immigrants, had done everything
possible to obscure their origins. By fleeing the city for a
small town, they had been enormously successful, leaving
their children a heritage almost primitive in its meagerness.
But perhaps this would all work to Glass's advantage.
Glass's eagerness to learn, to absorb whatever he could from

other backgrounds, might enable him to flesh out the bare bones of Gottliebsohn's memory.

"Let's come down to cases," the dean said. "Your experience in veterans' hospitals with battle fatigue, shock and so on makes you particularly well qualified on a professional level. Even if my friend Hortsky had not indicated the various *political* ramifications—"

"Those are precisely what disturb me," Glass interrupted. "I may be looking for my Jewish soul, but I have no wish to get mixed up in this country's political affairs."

"Even if Hortsky had not mentioned politics," the dean continued patiently, "I can see where you are perhaps the only psychiatrist in the country who can give this poor fellow a fighting chance."

"I appreciate your confidence in me," Glass said, "but surely one of your own colleagues in Europe, or the United States—"

This time the dean interrupted. "We don't have *time*," he said.

Glass sighed. "I had hoped we would be able to begin our own sessions before now . . ."

"Soon enough for that," the dean said, "after we see how you have handled yourself in this matter."

Glass raised his eyebrows at this. He had suspected the old man didn't want to get involved in a doctor-patient relationship again with him, but to use it as blackmail . . . it did indicate, however, how important it must be to all concerned.

"Very well," Glass said finally, his heart sinking at what he might be letting himself in for, "give me the details."

"This may be as good an introduction as any," the dean said, and handed him a newspaper. It was the morning edition, and Glass had picked up enough Hebrew to see that the headline story dealt with the mission to Bonn. A column of type had been outlined with heavy black crayon. "Gottliebsohn," the dean said, indicating a photograph within the story.

Glass studied the picture. An ordinary face looked shyly into the camera. His shoulders seemed raised the merest bit— "Why would you want *my* picture?" he seemed to be saying.

"Here's the translation," the dean said, and handed him a

typewritten sheet. DIPLOMAT WITHOUT MEMORY, the headline said. The story told of Gottliebsohn's loss of memory as of 1939 in Cologne, Germany. His war record, and his subsequent career in the Economics Ministry, were dwelt upon at some length. His participation in the mission was passed over rather quickly. The story ended with the suggestion that anyone who may have had any knowledge of him or his family, no matter how remote, should come forward. The address given was that of the Institute.

"Very cleverly done, *hein?*" the dean said. "This way there is no hint of any kind of 'official' investigation—as psychiatrists, it seems perfectly in order that we would want such information. Unfortunately, it is not a very good photo. But then it's not likely that anyone would recognize him after so many years in any case. Here, look at these," the dean continued, handing him a photo album. "They're all we've been able to unearth so far. They're not much better. But here's something for you to chew on: the only photographs the man seems to have taken are those needed for official documents. No portraits, no snapshots, nothing else, and yet his one hobby is photography."

Glass leafed through the album. Neatly arranged in chronological order, flat, dark, grainy, were photographs from military identification cards, driver's licenses, passports, and so on. The only interesting one was Gottliebsohn in uniform—being decorated for his services in the Palestine uprising, according to the caption.

"Anything else on him?" Glass asked.

"There's some rather fascinating material—interrogations of people who know Gottliebsohn now—that you will be permitted to read. They were done by a man named Levin, a trained trial lawyer, skilled in cross-examination, whose technique I think you will find interesting. He's rather good at working people into emotional corners. Also, at my suggestion, an idea I got from our man's hobby, we took secret, candid photographs of those who were being interrogated, particularly for your benefit. It will give you a *feeling* about their testimony. What people say and how they look when saying it is often contradictory. Yet quite as often revealing. People are what they look like—if you can read the signs."

Glass stirred uneasily. He could not help wondering if the old man was getting senile. The dean sighed. He guessed more or less what the other was thinking, and it sad-dened him that young men were convinced that wisdom must be found in complex obscurities, that anything pun-gent, direct and seemingly simple should be dismissed as the working of a childlike mind. Why did it take a lifetime to learn that truths about the human condition were summed up in clichés?

"When will I see this material?" Glass asked.

"Levin is on his way here to meet with you now," the dean said, looking at his watch. "He'll see that you get to the airport, too."

"When is my flight?" he asked.

"You're booked out at 2 P.M."

Had they been so sure of him then? Glass wondered.

"It wasn't possible for you to have refused us," the dean went on apologetically.

"I suppose I ought to see where the man lives," Glass said, putting his mind to the task ahead.

"Good idea," the dean said. "You can tell a lot about a man from what he puts around himself."

"Have you arrived at any judgments?"

"None that I would care to offer," the dean said. "For me to offer opinions now would not only be premature, but would have questionable validity. Let us not forget that you were chosen for this assignment because of your neutrality."

"But surely you—" Glass began.

"No, not even me," the dean said.

"You have become emotionally involved?" Glass said.

"Politically involved," the dean said.

"I would not have believed that if I heard it from anyone else," Glass said.

"In my lifetime," the old man said, beginning to tremble with the feeling which never lay far below the surface any more, "I have seen men capable of behavior that would turn the stomach of a cannibal. We smear culture over us like butter, disguise our environment, prattle about need for love—but strip a man to his soul, and you find a need for evil. Or is evil too conditioned a word? All men have a capacity for madness. Society strait-jackets them. It is all that saves us. Governments call those strait jackets 'laws.' Laws are made by politics. I am involved here in pulling the straps tight on an individual who may have been mad once, and if he was, politics say keep him in a jacket."

"Even if he is presently sane?" Glass said.

"The government's motives are different from those of individuals. There are men in this country, as in all countries, who choose to attribute human motives to the behavior of their government, with standards of morality, and so on, when in fact governments have neither conscience nor ethics but act only to survive."

"What are you saying?" Glass demanded, remembering that this old man had once held a contrary view.

The dean stared at the younger man. How could he explain his position, which would force him, an elder of the tribe, to make his judgments when the time came on what was best for the long term? "I am saying," the dean said, "for you not to get involved in future judgments, as I will not be involved in current ones. Your task is straightforward, and simply professional: to discover if the man is telling the truth, and if so, to track down what is behind the amnesia."

"And if he *is* guilty?" Glass asked.

The dean shrugged. "It depends on the government's situation at that time."

"And what about the man's—Gottliebsohn's?"

"You are his physician," the dean said. "It will be up to you to report his situation."

Glass nodded uneasily. It was a responsibility he did not have to take. But it had been left there for him, if he should want it.

Glass was driven to Gottliebsohn's apartment by Levin, the attorney whom the dean had mentioned. Levin was a balding, portly, middle-aged man with thick horn-rimmed glasses which made his eyes seem grotesquely large. Glass could imagine how they could intimidate a witness, particularly when coupled with that hoarse, sarcastic voice, sounding as though he not only doubted what you were saying, but your motives in saying it as well.

"You're an American, I understand?" Levin said.

Glass nodded.

"And you volunteered for the case," Levin said.

"I was asked to take it," Glass said.

"Is that so?"

"I've had experience with war-induced-amnesia victims," Glass said.

"There're no Israeli psychiatrists with that experience?"

"I was asked to take it," Glass said, refusing to be baited into a revealing explanation. Levin smiled and concentrated on his driving. Glass, looking at the city he had not even had time to familiarize himself with, became aware of the rapidly changing nature of the sections through which they drove. The street grew increasingly narrow and the shopfronts changed from ornate, glassed-in stores to stalls on the sidewalks piled high with jumbled piles of merchandise. The character of the people changed too, he noticed. They were shabbily dressed, and quite a few Arabs were among them.

"Are there many Arabs in Jerusalem?" Glass asked.

"We're approaching the Arab quarter," Levin said.

"Gottliebsohn lived among Arabs?" Glass asked, surprised.

"Not among them," Levin said. "As close as you can get without joining them, though."

The apartment building was old, and looked as if it were part of the original city. But the inside was immaculate. Glass sniffed the air, a habit he had picked up through varied, and distasteful, experiences with crowded apartment houses.

"No smells?" he said.

"No Arabs," Levin said. "No Orientals. No kids. No old folks. No cabbage."

They climbed stairs to the second floor. Gottliebsohn's apartment was at the rear. Levin had a key.

The inside was quite small. The furniture seemed too large, crowding the place, but at the same time the apartment had a curiously sparse atmosphere. Glass stood stock still in the middle of the front room, trying to track down the source of this feeling. Gradually, as his vision narrowed, focusing in on tabletops, he saw what it was. There were no personal items in sight: no photographs, no pipe racks or cigar humidor, no candy dishes, souvenir ashtrays or matchbooks—nothing by which he might get a clue to the man's personal habits.

A battered secretary stood in a corner. Glass began

searching the drawers. All were empty except one, which held a large manila envelope. Opening it, Glass found a few documents: Gottliebsohn's army discharge, his citation for heroic conduct, a letter commending his government service, citizenship papers and a membership card, since expired, of a veterans' group. All except the latter were photostatic copies.

"Do you have the originals?" Glass asked.

"They're in the Hall of Records," Levin said.

"I guess he didn't want to chance losing those," Glass said. "If they're all he has left."

"If," Levin agreed.

The kitchen was small and spotless. Opening the cupboard, Glass noted the sparsity of dishware—barely enough to keep one man fed, let alone entertain guests. The pantry held a few cans of soup, a tin of tea, a package of breakfast cereal, some sugar and salt. In the refrigerator were the remains of a carton of milk. It was soured.

"He ate most of his meals out," Levin said.

The bathroom was as meagerly supplied as the rest of the house. A few plain towels, a bar of deodorant soap, some squeezed-out tubes of medicated salve, were all they found. If Gottliebsohn used shaving lotion or other personal toiletries, he had apparently taken them along to Germany. On the back top of the water closet, they found the only reading material in the apartment: a well-thumbed book of Hebrew grammar and a children's simplified *History of the Jews*. Apparently he studied his country's language, Glass thought.

In the bedroom Glass made his first discoveries. At first it seemed as barren of meaning as the other rooms: the only picture on the wall a nondescript landscape of a hillside outside Jerusalem, a few articles of clothing in the drawers, a patched jacket and a baggy sweater.

But the closet contained photographic equipment— cameras, a slide and a film projector, extra lenses, mostly telescopic, and a rolled-up screen. Piled in a small box were hundreds of photographs. Most of them were loose, though there were a few trays of colored slides. The slides were of the city: buildings, streets and panoramic views. The photographs, however, were of people, none of whom apparently realized they were having their pictures taken.

"These must be what got him into hot water at the bureau," Levin said. "They're not bad, hm? His mistake was showing them. Look at this one, the old rogue, peeking into the top of that young girl's blouse; and this—what do you suppose she's thinking about? A real sourpuss. His desk was in a corner, and with that telescopic lens, he could shoot them without anyone being the wiser. But he was proud of them—naïve, wouldn't you say?—and wanted his subjects to appreciate them as he did."

"They're really very good," Glass said, intrigued and somewhat surprised. Nothing he had heard about Gottliebsohn thus far indicated this kind of sensitivity. "He seems to have an instinct for the right moment. Look here. You can tell how pleased this man is with himself."

The man in question was lighting a cigar, a small man with a large cigar, and his sucked-in cheeks, the match flame leaning to the tip, and the delicacy with which he held that fat cigar to his circled lips combined to give a portrait of vast self-importance.

"He's really a kind of artist," Glass said.

"But he's given it all up," Levin said. "Is that an artist? A bit of criticism, and he just doesn't stop taking pictures in the office, he crams all his paraphernalia into the closet and forgets about it."

"He's a portraitist," Glass said. "Obviously scenics do not interest him."

"More than portraits, Doctor," Levin said. "Candids. There's a difference. Catching people with their pants down."

"Not quite," Glass said, somewhat offended by the other's tone. "He's after character. And you said yourself he was proud of them, showed them to his subjects."

Levin smiled slightly. "I'm just trying to keep you straight, Doctor," he said. "A court can be influenced by what you call a man. I don't believe the evidence is sufficient for you to call him an artist."

Glass did not answer. They continued the search. And the bedside table drawer yielded a medicine bottle with two tablets still in it. They looked like chlorpromazine hydrochloride, Glass thought, a particularly potent tranquilizer.

But why were they kept here? The table held a water pitcher, half full, and a glass whose coating of sediment suggested frequent use. Did the man wake up in the middle of the night in such frantic need of his pills that he could not take time to walk to the bathroom for them?

"Is there a medical history?" Glass asked.

"Of course," Levin said. "You'll find that we're very thorough. Those pills are for insomnia." He reached in his brief case, which he had been carrying under his arm, and produced a thick document bound within plastic covers. "This is everything we've got on our man so far, excluding whatever Kohn may have gotten."

"Kohn?" Glass asked.

Levin looked sharply at him. "No one's briefed you about Kohn?" Glass shook his head. "He's assigned to watch Gottliebsohn. And to run down anything he can on Gottliebsohn's background in Germany. You'll work closely with him, I imagine. As either of you discovers anything, it should help the other find something else."

He was leaving something out, Glass thought. But he did not pursue the matter. "Do you mind if I read this now?" he asked, anxious to get to the material.

"Good idea," Levin said as they walked back into the front room. "You might be able to absorb more while you're sitting in his own lair, so to speak."

Glass looked about him. "But there's not a whole lot here, is there?"

"It depends on how you look at it," Levin said, shrugging. "Sometimes you can tell more by what's left out than what's right in front of you."

"Well, what's left out, in your opinion?" Glass asked.

"A life," Levin said sharply. "The man hasn't put any roots down. He's living here like a transient."

"So?"

"Transients are always running from something. Or they're up to no good. There's a reason why communities have laws regarding transients."

"Insecure communities, perhaps," Glass said. "Don't you have anything more specific?"

Levin looked irritated. "When a man's own residence, his supposed private place, doesn't have much of anything personal, you can bet your balalaika that bird's got another nest somewhere. A place for his droppings—psychologically speaking."

Glass was annoyed by the sneering tone. "You are against psychology?"

"On the contrary, Doctor," Levin said. "I believe that everyone has a need for dirt, whether it's soiled under-drawers, unwashed feet, pornographic books, a dirty comb or automobile, a messy closet—and that's not here, is it? Well, we looked for it other places. And we found it, as you shall see."

"You sound like you're building a case," Glass said.

"It's the only way I know how to work," Levin replied.

"It's in the dossier?" Glass asked.

"You go ahead and read," Levin said. "I'll make us some tea."

The accusation against Ernst Gottliebsohn had been originally made before the desk sergeant of the Talbiah Tahanah, on October 3, by Jacob Eisenberg, resident of Jerusalem, citizen of Israel, a former German national. Subsequently a statement was taken and signed before a city magistrate.

"I accuse Ernst Gottliebsohn, Director of the Bureau of Economics in the Ministry of Commerce, of collaboration with the Nazis during the summer months of 1939, in Cologne, Germany. In return for this collaboration he received many personal gratuities and favors, including safe conduct for himself and his family out of Germany at the expense of the well-being, and frequently the lives, of many other Jews."

A photograph of Eisenberg was attached. He was a famine-eyed man who looked so much older than his stated age that Glass wondered if there had not been some mistake. Then he remembered photos taken during the liberation of concentration camps; he saw what had led to this mummified creature who stared so hotly out of the page at him.

On the next page Levin's interrogation began:

Q. Why did you wait so many years to make this accusation?

A. I didn't know he was even here, in this country. I saw

his name listed among those who had been appointed to the mission.

Q. How do you know it is the same Ernst Gottliebsohn?

A. I went to the Bureau he is in charge of. I made some private inquiries. He is the same man.

Q. You know for a fact that he collaborated with the Nazis?

A. Everyone knew it.

Q. Tell me what everyone knew.

A. In the summer of thirty-nine we—all Jews in Cologne —were forbidden to do business. We were forced to move into flats which already had three and four families in them, and yet when the Gottliebsohn family came in from the village of Warsfeld, they were given an apartment all to themselves. We soon heard what the reason for that privilege was—their son, Ernst, was working for the Nazis.

Q. You know that for a fact.

A. How else would his family have been given privileged status?

Q. Tell me other facts.

A. We were all restricted to the block. He came and went as he pleased, even at night.

Q. What about the rest of his family?

A. They never left the apartment. They kept to themselves. They opened their door to no one.

Q. No one met them?

A. My wife. She needed sugar. They didn't want to let her in. But she insisted. They hadn't even unpacked their baggage. They knew they were going to ship out, you see. In spite of all that, my wife took a liking to them. It was her feeling that they would not talk to anyone because they were so ashamed of their son.

Q. May we have a statement from your wife about this?

A. She is dead.

Q. How did you meet the son—Ernst Gottliebsohn?

A. He came to my apartment, looking for his family.

Q. He didn't know they had gone away? But I thought you stated that he collaborated in return for their freedom— strange, why wouldn't he know—

A. What's so strange? It happened all the time. They probably wanted to use him on other matters. Or he may have failed to include his own freedom in the bargain, an oversight that the Nazis with their peculiar sense of humor would have leaped on.

Q. Describe what happened when he came to your place.

A. There was this pounding at the door, see? In the middle of the night. We were terror-stricken. We'd heard that a trainload of political undesirables was coming through that night for Sachsenhausen, and for all we knew they were going to add a few carloads of us from the quarter. They knew a lot of us were Social Democrats—a few Communists, too, for that matter. At first I wouldn't answer and he went away, though not far. We could hear him pounding on other doors. Then he returned. By this time he was making such a racket I was afraid he'd bring a Black Shirt patrol into the building so I went to see what he wanted. He shouldered the door so hard I got a nasty crack on the head—but luckily I had the chain in place and it wouldn't open far enough for him to get more than his nose in. He was a sight, believe me. He was soaking wet and his face was scratched and swollen, like he had been in a fight . . .

Q. Had the Nazis roughed him up?

A. They wouldn't have let him go. More likely he had been in a street fight.

Q. Please continue.

A. He asked about his family. I asked who he was—

Q. You didn't know him?

A. I told you that he came and went only at night. He identified himself. I immediately told him that if he didn't know where his family was, no one else would.

Q. Well, go on.

A. That was all. He had no answer for that.

Q. You said nothing more to each other?

A. Hardly anything.

Q. I think we should hear it all.

A. I don't remember exactly.

Q. Your memory has been remarkable thus far. Strange that it should fail you now.

A. I'm not sure I understand your attitude. Is this how you treat a citizen trying to do his duty?

Q. What else was said between you and Ernst Gottliebsohn?

A. I asked if he couldn't use his influence to get *my* family out.

Q. I see.

A. You don't see. I said it sarcastically. It wasn't influence we needed, but money. I suggested that if we hurried, we could all get on the same train for the border his family was on. I wanted him to realize that we—all of us—knew quite well what he had been up to.

Q. And did he realize this?

A. For all I know, he believed me. No matter how desperately I wanted my family saved I wouldn't have collaborated for it.

Q. But you were willing for Gottliebsohn to do it for you?

A. Go to hell.

Q. Accusations like yours must be thoroughly checked out. We cannot ruin a man's life on hearsay evidence.

A. Hearsay? His family getting away scot-free? Doesn't that prove something?

Q. Did you see them get on the train?

A. Others did.

Q. Why don't they come forward?

A. They are dead.

Q. That will be all for now. You understand that we must keep you for a few more days? We don't want to chance anyone getting wind of this before we check the facts a little further.

A. Go to hell.

Q. Take him out.

Glass took a long breath. It was a nasty business—citizens in a democracy being held "protectively." Yet he could not bring himself to blame those in authority. They had too much at stake to risk it over such an ambiguous accusation. It looked as if Gottliebsohn had been up to something, all right, but whether his nocturnal activity had something to do with the Nazis was a long way from being proven. The man resented Gottliebsohn bitterly because he had been brought to asking help for his own family. Those were terrible times; the guilt was confused and rode heavily down through the years.

Glass turned the page. The photo was of a man in his middle fifties whose clipped mustache and haughty way of holding his head gave him the look of an aristocrat. But his drooping polka-dotted bow tie made him look more rakish than elegant.

.　　.　　.

Q. You own the building at Haneviim Street in the Arab quarter?

A. It's a block this side of the quarter.

Q. You manage the building yourself?

A. Only in the larger sense. I have underlings handling the details.

Q. But you collect the rent.

A. I find it better not to put temptation in the way of—

Q. Underlings. Very good. And so you know each of your tenants personally.

A. Know them? It's not good policy for a landlord to become familiar with his tenants, not when he lives in the same building. No, I keep a proper distance, you might say an unbridgeable chasm, between us.

Q. I didn't mean you chummed around with them. But you interested yourself in their lives.

A. I resent that statement, sir. I believe that everyone is entitled to privacy. I am jealous of my own and—

Q. But surely you must safeguard your building by making sure their behavior is proper.

A. What is the purpose of this questioning? Whom are you interested in?

Q. Ernst Gottliebsohn.

A. Second floor, rear. What do you accuse him of?

Q. Have you ever seen any evidence that would indicate he is a man of erratic behavior?

A. He has always behaved with absolute propriety.

Q. Nothing strange about him at all, then.

A. He is regular as clockwork. He leaves for work at a certain hour, arrives home at a certain hour, goes to the café on the corner for his supper at a certain hour, always sits at the same table, always takes an evening walk.

Q. Ever follow him?

A. How dare you?

Q. You never chanced across him at the café, sat with him at supper, accompanied him on his evening stroll?

A. I hardly know the man. What do you accuse him of?

Q. It's a matter of state security. If you don't tell us what you know, you're liable to be in the dock with him.

A. How can I be implicated in what one of my tenants does?

Q. (*Silence*)

A. I have noticed one thing.

Q. (*Silence*)

A. He never used his apartment weekends.

Q. Go on.

A. He always left Saturday afternoon and came home on Sunday. He wasn't on a timetable like during the week. But that's understandable, I would think. When you're on your own time, it's best to relax and let time run on as it may.

Q. Where do you think he went?

A. It's not my business, after all.

Q. You do have an idea about it?

A. Perhaps he visited some girl?

Q. How did he look, coming home?

A. What do you mean?

Q. Was he disheveled, did he have a growth of beard, did he look like he'd been on a tear?

A. He was just as neatly dressed as when he left. Clean-shaven, too. That would indicate that he still behaved well no matter where he went, wouldn't you say?

Q. Did he carry his shaving kit with him?

A. I don't know.

Q. Think. Did you ever see him carry anything with him—a bundle, a sack, a package of any kind?

A. You think he's a black marketer? He carried nothing with him, I distinctly remember.

Q. That's a pretty wild assumption you're making then, when he looked exactly the same coming as going.

A. (*Silence*)

Q. Well?

A. Not exactly the same. He was clean-shaven, true, but his face was puffy, as if he hadn't had a lot of sleep.

Q. (*Silence*)

A. I *did* bump into him once in the foyer, and he had the smell of a woman on him.

Q. What kind of smell is that?

A. Don't you know?

Q. What kind of smell?

A. Sweet-sour. Like plum sauce in a Chinese restaurant. Like wine herring in sour cream. Like red cabbage—

Q. That will do.

A. He reeked of it.

Q. That is all for the moment. This interview will be typed in transcript form. Read it over carefully, make any corrections you care to, then sign.

The interview had ended. Glass looked up. Levin was sitting in the chair across from him. When Glass met his eye, he handed him tea in a thick mug.

"There's no glasses, no lemon," Levin said, "and the only sugar's granulated."

"So?" Glass said.

"It's a barbaric way to drink tea," Levin said. "I grew up in Poland—we suck tea through sugar cubes. You can see what it does to the teeth." A gold filling half-mooned his front teeth. "We didn't have much candy," he explained. "How about you?"

"Plenty of candy," Glass said shortly.

"Something troubling you?"

"You're rough on people, aren't you?" Glass asked. "Treat them like they were criminal."

"I've learned one thing in my career: if you're going to get at the truth and get at it quickly, you hammer your witness," Levin said. "You know why it works, Mr. Psychiatrist? Because we all feel like criminals deep inside, we're all worried sick that we're going to be found out. As soon as they discover you're not after *them*, after *their* secret, it's amazing how fast they'll tell you anything else you want to know."

Glass, disconcerted by the other's vehemence, took a larger sip of the tea than he had intended and recoiled as the liquid scalded his mouth.

"Sorry," Levin said quietly. "I'm used to the cube of sugar, as I said. By the time the tea reaches your mouth that way it's only lukewarm."

Glass bent to the dossier again. The next interview was brief; a boy from a school identified by Levin as an orphanage, originally for children who had somehow survived the holocaust, now used as a vocational training institute. The photo showed a good-natured face, probably North European descent, by the nose and straight blond hair—about fifteen, Glass guessed.

Q. You have known Mr. Gottliebsohn a long while?

A. He has always been here, the older boys say. As long as anyone remembers.

Q. In what capacity?

A. Once a week he comes to coach us in soccer. He was a

terrific player himself once, you can tell. Even at his age, he can still run very fast.

Q. He plays with you himself?

A. Oh, yes. It's the way he teaches. He doesn't talk at us much.

Q. And do the boys like him?

A. (*Hesitates*) I guess so. He is so quiet and . . . and . . .

Q. Reserved?

A. That is so.

Q. Is he hard to please?

A. He is very quiet. But he is very patient with us. He will go over and over the same thing with a boy until he gets it. Those who are awkward he even spends extra time with.

Q. You don't know a boy who is closer to him than the others?

A. No, we are all the same to him. We elect a captain every term. The captain is who Mr. Gottliebsohn deals with when he wants us to practice something during the week, before he comes.

Q. Why did no one see him off on his trip?

A. The captain was to have gone, but he would not allow it.

Q. Thank you for your help.

A. Is anything wrong? Is Mr. Gottliebsohn sick . . . or anything?

Q. Not at all. Mr. Gottliebsohn is up for an important promotion, a very sensitive position, and the examining board wishes to have a rather complete character analysis.

A. He is a patient man.

Q. Thank you for your help.

Glass looked up at Levin. "What did you hope to find out from the boy?" he asked.

Levin shrugged. "No one seems to know a whole lot about Mr. Gottliebsohn. We are trying to put together what we can. I am also anticipating his defense. When hard evidence is lacking, there is always a parade of character witnesses. It is best that we know in advance what they will say."

"This one works against your 'case' though, doesn't it?" Glass asked.

"Does it?" Levin asked in turn. "As a psychiatrist, would you say that this—shall we call it philanthropy?—proves he is a 'good' person? Or could it prove that he only involves himself in those relationships where few demands are made upon him for background? In my experience, those with past guilts shun the company of others. Read on, you will see how few truly social relationships he has."

Glass decided that Levin would be easy to dislike. He returned to the dossier. The next interview was with a co-worker at Gottliebsohn's office, Esther Gronski. She appeared to be in her late thirties, with a pinched nose and pursed mouth that gave her a spinsterish look. An attempt, evidently homemade, at curling her hair, gave her an oddly old-fashioned appearance, as if the photo had been taken a generation ago instead of only this week.

Q. You are not married, Miss Gronski?

A. You are taking a good deal for granted, are you not?

Q. You wear no rings.

A. Perhaps rings cause my skin to itch, and break out in terrible hives.

Q. Are you married?

A. No.

Q. Have you ever been?

A. I don't believe that is any of your affair.

Q. I tell you that it is.

A. You've found out already, haven't you?

Q. I must have your statement for the record.

A. I've never been married.

Q. When did you first become interested in Gottliebsohn?

A. What do you mean, *interested*?

Q. You know perfectly well what is meant, Miss Gronski.

A. Well I'm afraid I do not. If you want answers to questions like those, you will have to be more clear.

Q. What is your job, Miss Gronski?

A. I am in the executive stenographic pool on the fifth floor of the Bureau of Economics.

Q. Would you tell us how the pool works? How you are assigned to your executives?

A. We take the jobs as they come up, in rotation.

Q. It's interesting how frequently you worked for Gott-liebsohn.

A. I don't believe it was any more often than any of the other girls.

Q. Don't you, Miss Gronski?

A. No.

Q. The other girls think it was more often.

A. They are mistaken.

Q. According to these time sheets you are the one who is mistaken, Miss Gronski.

A. Mrs. Brache keeps sloppy records. They are undependable.

Q. Did you ever go out with Gottliebsohn?

A. He used to ask me out quite a bit. But I never went.

Q. Used to?

A. He got tired of being turned down, I suppose. I never cared for the man. I always had the feeling, no matter that everyone around the office considered him harmless, that he may have been something of a lecher.

Q. Did you?

A. Yes.

Q. So you turned him down when he asked you out?

A. Yes.

Q. Isn't it a fact, Miss Gronski, that you were the one who did the asking, not Gottliebsohn?

A. (*Silence*)

Q. Do you know the penalty for slander, Miss Gronski?

A. Everything I have told you is the truth. The man is a lecher. And of the worst kind. There is nothing at which he would draw the line.

Q. Now how do you *know* that, Miss Gronski?

A. Believe me, I know.

Q. If we are to believe you, Miss Gronski, and if you are not to find yourself this afternoon in the municipal court, accused by Gottliebsohn's representatives of slander, you had better be specific.

A. He lies down with Arab women.

Q. You've seen him with Arab women?

A. (*Silence*)

Q. Miss Gronski?

A. He goes to Arab brothels.

Q. Tell us how you know that, Miss Gronski.

A. I saw him go in one.

Q. You saw him?

A. (*Silence*)

Q. Miss Gronski?

A. I followed him.

Q. How did you happen to do that?

A. He said he never went anywhere weekends. He said he

didn't go to dances because he couldn't dance. He said he
didn't care for cards. He said he wasn't a very good mixer.
He said he *liked* to be alone, imagine, it didn't bother *him*,
he read and listened to music and kept his weekends free
because he liked to read and listen to music so much. I
didn't believe him. I went over there late one Saturday afternoon just to see if he was lying. He was dressed to kill.
He pretended he wasn't going out, of course, and he was
very polite—he has the best manners of anyone in the Bureau, everyone says so, but I have always been able to see
through him, and in spite of his manners he would not accept my (*Pause*) present. Is that good manners?

Q. Present?

A. I needed an excuse to drop in on him, didn't I? He has
no phone.

Q. What kind of present?

A. A casserole. I made a French chicken, a coq au vin.

Q. And he would not accept it?

A. No.

Q. Did he give a reason why not?

A. He said he was not feeling well and since he could not,
feeling as he did, ask me to stay, he could not take my
supper, either. I didn't believe him. I felt something funny
was going on. I went into the café across the street for some
tea—you can imagine how upset I was—and it wasn't five
minutes before he came out, peeped up and down the street
to make sure I was gone, and went down that little side
street in the direction of the Arab quarter. When I saw that,
I went back outside and followed him. I was so upset I even
forgot the casserole. I hope someone enjoyed it.

Q. You followed him?

A. I saw where he went. I saw him go in.

Q. Could you find it again, Miss Gronski?

A. I will never forget that place. It is burned in my memory, like acid.

Q. You will take us there.

A. Now?

Q. Now.

The interview ended abruptly. On the following page
there was a notation:

Witness took us to the Talbiah, identifying house as the
one accused was seen entering. Police records show house

licensed as a rooming house. But there are no permanent residents except for the owner and several servants.

The next photo was of an elderly Arab whose face was as shriveled and impassive as a dried fig.

Q. Are you running a brothel here?

A. A rooming house.

Q. Yet you rent your rooms only for one night, and only to women.

A. I had not noticed.

Q. You're not very curious, are you?

A. I'm an old man. What the women do is their business.

Q. Do you know this man? (*Showed witness photo of accused*)

A. No.

Q. Look again. We have information that not only says he has been here, but that he has been here frequently.

A. I'm not sure; perhaps. My eyes are not what they once were. And I try not to look too closely at visitors.

Q. You have a lot of non-Arab clientele?

A. Hardly any.

Q. I suggest you cooperate with us. If you do not, we will have you shut down.

A. He looks like the man who comes here.

Q. How often?

A. Every week.

Q. Ever cause any trouble?

A. Never. He took his woman and that was the end of it.

Q. Please sign the statement in triplicate.

Glass looked up at Levin. "That's all the information you got at the brothel?"

Levin looked at him coldly. "I'm only interested in a certain kind of information. Where he went, what his acquaintances thought of him, and so on. The details of his sex life do not concern me."

"It's my concern," Glass said. "That falls into the category of information *I* am interested in."

"You'll have to get it yourself, then," Levin said. "I wouldn't be good at asking that kind of question."

"I'm surprised at you," Glass said. "I wouldn't have thought a man of your wide experience would be so fastidious."

"It's enough that I know there's dirt there," Levin said. "I don't feel it's necessary to examine it, speck by speck."

"I do," Glass said.

Levin looked at his watch.

"We'll have to take the time," Glass said.

"Very well," Levin said, shrugging.

He locked the apartment, and led the way to the car. They drove for about ten minutes. The road ended at the wall to an inner city. "We'll have to walk the rest of the way," Levin said.

Almost everyone on these crowded narrow streets was Arab. Glass was somewhat nervous at this proximity to those whose economic and political situation made them seem natural enemies, but the casual attitude of his guide soon reassured him. They came onto a street of residences where the shutters were drawn and the gates were all locked.

"It's early yet," Levin said at Glass's inquisitive glance. Then, stopping in front of a shabby house at the end of the block, he yanked the bell heavily. From somewhere deep inside they heard the muffled clang. After a long wait, Glass became aware that someone looked them over from the window. Levin held his wallet up, indicating an official identification. A few moments later the gate was opened by an Arab boy.

"We want to see the owner," Levin said. They followed the boy into the house.

Glass was fascinated. In that perfumed gloom he could make out two huge figured vases, elaborate drapery, a multitude of brightly colored cushions and, underneath a few scattered striped rugs, a polished floor. The effect was not Arab, but rather *Arabian Nights'*, and he wondered if it was a reflection of the owner's taste or a reproduction from some Moorish text. They remained standing until the old Arab of the photograph came into the room and motioned them to sit on the leather-cushioned hassocks nearby. The boy who had let them in squatted by his master's feet.

"We are here to ask more questions about this man," Levin said, showing him a picture of Gottliebsohn.

The boy interpreted for the old man. "I have told you all I know," he finally replied.

"I would like to talk to a woman who knew him," Glass said.

There was a conversation between the boy and the old man. Then the boy got to his feet, bowed, somewhat ironically, Glass thought, and left the room. He was gone some time. When he finally returned, he came in first, then beckoned to the shadows behind him. An Arab woman came into the room. She was veiled.

"Do they keep the veils on where they do their business?" Glass asked Levin.

The boy answered. "She must wear it to walk our quarter streets. But part of the appeal to an Arab man is the veil coming off."

And to Gottliebsohn, too? Glass wondered, but said nothing.

Levin handed her the picture. The boy spoke to her rapidly in Arabic. She glanced quickly over at them, but spoke directly to the boy.

"She is not sure she knows this man," the boy said.

"We don't have a lot of time," Levin said. "We are not after her—tell her that, and that it will go better for her the next time she is picked up if she answers this man's questions now."

The boy handed her the picture again. She nodded slowly. "I was with the man twice," she said.

"What was he like?" Glass asked.

"A man," she said, shrugging.

"Describe what the evening was like," Glass said. "Start at the beginning. How he greeted you, did he undo his clothes immediately, and so on."

The old man looked up briefly from the floor and gave Glass a searching glance. The boy smiled. Levin shifted in his chair and muttered something.

The woman spoke. "Both times it was exactly the same," the boy translated. "He was very courteous. He would send out for a bottle of arrack and two glasses. He would sit on the chair, and I on the bed, and he would toast me with every glass. Then, when both of us were very drunk, he would ask me to take off my veil. He would say yes, I looked like an Arab girl, but it wasn't possible to be sure—and he would ask me if I minded taking off the rest of my clothes. Then he would undress, and he would pull me in front of the mirror, and point out how much darker I was than him. Then he would laugh and say it was obvious that we could not be related."

Glass looked up from his notes. "There was no sex?"

"Of course," the girl said, raising her head proudly.

"Was it"—Glass hesitated, looking for the word—"straightforward, normal?"

"He was like a bull," the girl said. "Very strong. Always two times during the night."

"Never anything . . . weird?" Glass asked.

The girl shook her head.

Glass consulted his notes. "Sometimes he would get back to his apartment very late on Sunday. The times you were with him—what times did he leave?"

"He was always sick," the girl said hesitantly, as if not sure she should tell them.

"Sick?" Glass asked. "How?"

"He would vomit," the girl said. "When his stomach was back in place again he would wash himself all over, slick his hair down, and then go. But sometimes it took him a long while to get himself in order again."

There was a silence while Glass scribbled. "How did he choose his women?" he asked finally.

The old Arab answered. "He wanted only full-blooded Arab women," he said.

"Perhaps I should interview another of his women," Glass said.

"We don't have a lot of time," Levin said.

The boy was watching Glass closely. He murmured something to the girl and waited for her answer. "She says all the girls had the same thing with him."

The boy followed them to the door. "You are American, or English?" he asked Glass.

"American," Glass said.

"A Jew," Levin said before the boy might speak again. The boy bowed very respectfully to Levin, but it seemed to Glass that the door was closed a little too hard behind them.

"How did you know he was going to ask that?" Glass said.

"It's what they ask of every tourist," Levin said. "They feel trapped here, the poor beggars. The older ones, who've lived under Arab rule and know what it's like, they're very happy to be in Israel. But the young ones, those who are bright, they burn to be among their own kind. They can't help but feel alien here, trapped among the infidels. The fact is, they're a lot better off; as citizens of Israel they have the same rights as any of us."

"Do you really believe that?" Glass asked.

"It's true," Levin insisted, and the subject was dropped.

Back at his own apartment, Glass did not take long to pack. The sparseness of his traveling wardrobe was indicative of a desire to get the job over with quickly, even though Gottliebsohn's personality, or lack of it, was beginning to fascinate him.

"Do you know Gottliebsohn?" he asked Levin on the way to the airport.

"No," the other said. "I'd never even heard of him before."

"But you did most of the investigative work here on him?"

Levin nodded.

"There anything that sticks in your mind as being of any particular significance? I don't mean the obvious things, like his periodic visits to the Arabs. That might be explained as a not overly unusual sexual aberration having to do with color." Glass kept to himself the curiosity about that word "related" that Gottliebsohn had used to the prostitute. "I mean something that might ordinarily seem insignificant, but that keeps niggling away at your mind."

Levin thought about it. "The fact that he deserted from the British army," he said finally. "I know from our country's point of view he's a hero—but the fact he deserted sticks in my craw."

Glass was disappointed. He had hoped to be given a psychiatric observation, and instead he had been given an aberrant thought.

Levin smiled slightly, as if he guessed the other's reaction. "You didn't notice anything unusual about the flat, I take it," he said.

"Nothing we haven't talked about," Glass said.

"That Arab woman's mentioning the mirror reminded me," Levin said. "Not that *I* think it's particularly significant, but you might. There are no mirrors in his apartment."

Glass thought back and remembered that in a drawer—

"That's right," Levin said, watching his face. "A hand mirror in a drawer that he probably used to shave with. Very inconvenient; you can only see a little part of your face at a time."

"But what about the medicine cabinet?" Glass asked, frowning.

"There had been a mirror in it once," Levin agreed. "Probably it broke, and our man simply never got around to replacing it. At any rate, one can't call him vain."

They rode the rest of the way in silence. "What do you think about him so far?" Levin asked when they arrived at the airport. "Think he's faking it? Think he's guilty of collaboration?"

"I don't have nearly enough data yet," Glass said.

"But surely you have a feeling about him?" Levin pressed.

"I think he's hiding something, all right," Glass said, impatient now to be away from the other. "That's what amnesia is usually all about. But whether it's a political guilt or a personal one, or even no more than an understandable desire to forget a rather dreadful past, is certainly too early to tell."

"A *political* guilt?" the other said, incredulous. "You call collaboration with the Germans *political?*"

"Look here," Glass said angrily, "it's my job and my profession to be objective. I'm not supposed to judge what he's done, only to find out if he's done it."

"You're not much of a Jew," Levin said.

"I'm not a Jew at all," Glass said. "Hadn't you heard? I'm a neutral—that's why they picked me for the job." And taking his suitcase from the other's hand, he strode across the terminal toward the gate where his plane was waiting.

4

IT WAS DUSK WHEN THE ISRAELI DELE-
gation landed at Bonn. The airport for the West German
capital was crowded. Giant planes, with the markings of almost every nation in the world big enough to afford an airline, were lined up alongside the squat, modernistic buildings. Everyone, it seemed, had an interest in the resurgent
Germans, whether for trade, or for fear of their increasing
strength, or for their usefulness in the various military alli-
ances. The Israelis, being heavy on the German conscience,
were accorded top priority, and it had taken a great deal of
argument on the parts of Hortsky and Auerbach to keep the
Germans from making a ritualistic ceremony of welcoming
them at the airport itself.

Gottliebsohn was grateful that the formal greetings were
to be delayed. His feelings at stepping, after all these years,
onto German soil, lay smothered under a blanket of shock.
He felt numbed, half awake, dream-like, confused and bewildered by all that had happened and by dread of what lay
in store for him. This fear was reinforced by the sight of the
customs officials, whose uniforms caused him to cringe with
an emotion he could not quite identify.

Going through the line in which their visas were to be
validated, Gottliebsohn was preceded by Auerbach, followed by the captain.

"Welcome to Germany," a uniformed official murmured blandly, and stamping their passports, handed them back with a curt little bow which seemed to their aroused sensibilities to contain a hint of mockery.

The official hesitated over Gottliebsohn's passport. Then he looked intently into Gottliebsohn's face. "Forgive me," he murmured, closing the passport and handing it back.

"What is it?" Auerbach asked.

"I thought I recognized this gentleman," the official said ingratiatingly. "But I see now that it is impossible."

"Why impossible?" the captain asked, pushing forward. "He is a former German national."

The official was a heavyset individual whose uniform seemed too tight; the buttoned collar kept his neck and chin very high, the visored cap seemed too small for the large head. Pale eyes and colorless lashes created a zombie-like effect, enhanced by the spots of dried blood where a razor had torn the parchment-like skin.

"But a Jew, *nicht?*" the official inquired, raising his thinned eyebrows.

"So?" the captain asked.

"You must pardon me," the official said. "But I have never had the honor of numbering Jews among my acquaintances. I grew up in a small town—by the time I went to the city, they were all . . . gone." And he raised incongruously feminine hands in a helpless gesture.

They were horrified, the three Israelis and the German official caught, seemingly frozen, in a situation that could go on forever. They were rescued at last by Hortsky, who was anxious to get them into the waiting limousines.

Auerbach, the captain, and Gottliebsohn got into the lead automobile, a black Mercedes-Benz, with the old man.

"The question about Kohn has already come up," Hortsky said. Auerbach and the captain stiffened; Gottliebsohn only half listened, staring out the window at the passing scenery, catching glimpses of German faces, enough to hypnotize him with the possibility that among them was someone recognizable.

"They had a cable from the Foreign Office questioning his presence," Hortsky continued. "I told them he was here unofficially, as an observer solely. But they are quite suspicious, not to say uncomfortable. They are bringing their own man in to balance Kohn."

"Of course, we should have anticipated that," Auerbach said.

"Who is that?" Kohn asked.

"The head of their War Crimes Bureau," Hortsky said. "You'll have to be very circumspect, Captain. The Bonn government is extremely touchy just now about how to handle war crimes—with their people anxious to bury the past, and the rest of the world equally anxious to keep the matter open, they're not eager for any 'situation' to develop."

"We don't want them to know what you're really up to, Captain," Auerbach cautioned. "If they find out, it may complicate matters for us."

"Don't worry," Kohn said. "I can cover this business all right." But when he put his lighter's flame to a small cigar, they could see that his hands trembled.

They rode the rest of the long way to Bad Godesberg, a suburb of Bonn, in silence. In the ornate lobby of the Dressen Hotel, Hortsky and the mission secretary, a plumpish elderly woman, took care of the registration details.

They put Kohn in with Gottliebsohn. The secretary seemed surprised, but Hortsky ignored her quizzical glance. Part of the agreement between the two Cabinet Ministers had been to have Kohn guarding Gottliebsohn, and Hortsky thought it unwise, in spite of mission curiosity, to change it.

Once in their room, the two men had little to say to each other. They took turns in the bath, and Gottliebsohn, as a mark of courtesy to the captain, who had no clothes other than those he was wearing, put back on the same clothing he had traveled in, changing only his shirt and undergarments.

But if Kohn noticed he gave no sign. "Do you drink?" he asked when he came out of the bathroom, buttoning his wilted collar.

"Some," Gottliebsohn said.

"Carry it with you?"

Hesitating only a moment, Gottliebsohn went to his valise, and shielding its meager interior from the captain's inquisitive gaze, took out the flask he was never without.

"I got a taste for it in England, during the war," he said, handing it to the other.

"Black and White?" Kohn asked, handing the flask back after a healthy swig and a polite little cough.

"A lesser brand," Gottliebsohn said, looking apologetic as he wiped the neck with his handerchief before drinking himself.

"Made by the same people, I'd bet," Kohn said. He eyed the flask again and Gottliebsohn handed it over.

"I'm not used to this sort of affair," the captain said, after the same little cough. "Drinks give me courage."

"I'd never heard that you drank," Gottliebsohn said.

"Hadn't you?" the captain said. Gottliebsohn, instead of putting the flask back in the valise, placed it on the bedside stand so the other would not think him inhospitable. But the captain seemed unaware of the gesture, and waited impatiently by the door.

In the elevator going down to the reception, they stood in almost identical postures, hands clasped behind them, eyes lifting and dropping as each floor slid past. Gottliebsohn, at Kohn's curt nod, got out first.

The meeting was subdued. German and Jew stood awkwardly about, wearing stiff little smiles, making ineffectual attempts at conversation. Hortsky and Bettmann, head of the German delegation, worked very hard at getting their people talking to each other. They themselves were old acquaintances, though Bettmann was a good deal younger, having met during the days when Socialists were having international conferences; it helped that Bettmann had gone into exile immediately after Hitler had come into power. He was free of any taint of complicity in the Nazi regime.

The other members of the German delegation had been as carefully picked, but since very few Germans had fled, it was difficult to find experts who had not also worked for the Nazis.

Gottliebsohn's opposite was a member of Germany's now discredited aristocracy: Baron von Haupt, a brilliant economist who had, it was said, quietly opposed Hitler even after the early days.

"We are agreed, it seems, on the necessity for this agreement," Von Haupt said, shaking hands.

"We must use every available means to survive," Gottliebsohn said. "No matter how distasteful it might seem."

"Quite so," Von Haupt said, his face whitening under the insult, unintended though it had been. He stopped a passing waiter and saw to it that Gottliebsohn took his drink first.

Kohn's opposite, a goateed scholarly-looking man, Gottfried Schenke, Director of the War Crimes Bureau, was incongruously dressed in tails. He had been intending to go to the opera, he explained, when he was informed of the captain's unexpected arrival, and it had been too late for him to change.

"But I'm afraid I don't quite understand what you are doing here," he continued apologetically.

Kohn accepted a glass of champagne from an offered tray and took an adequate sip before answering.

"They are grooming me for a diplomatic post," he said, sighing over the wonderful taste. No two ways about it, the Germans had a way with white wines. "When the mission was just about to depart, my superiors had an afterthought and sent me along to observe. They thought it a perfect opportunity for me to get my feet wet."

"You mean you are leaving investigative work?" Schenke asked doubtfully. "After all your experience?"

"My experience is no longer quite so necessary," Kohn said. "Wouldn't you agree? With both governments apparently willing to let bygones be bygones?"

"I did not realize you were a facetious man, Captain," the other said stiffly. "No matter what you may think, we Germans are quite aware of our guilt and we will never rest until we have brought to justice everyone who was responsible. It is the only way we can atone for our great sins. But we prefer to mete out our own punishment."

"Believe me," Kohn said as earnestly as he was able, "I'm no longer interested in your war criminals."

"Even if that is true," the professor said, "perhaps you will visit our War Crimes Bureau during your stay. I may be able to show you some interesting cases that are in process."

"Yes, I would enjoy that," Kohn said, and feigning a great fatigue, managed to fend off any further questioning.

The orchestra at the other end of the reception hall stopped playing. Its valiant attempts to be cheerful seemed rather pathetic in the chilly atmosphere. Its repertoire also, through an overcautious official instruction, was limited to only recent postwar tunes, and being little known to its audience, the music seemed curiously harsh and unfeeling.

Long before the end of the hour which had been planned, the two delegations, by a kind of unspoken mutual consent, bowed and went their separate ways.

Gottliebsohn wandered from the hall into the lobby and eventually found himself standing in front of the plate-glass windows, looking out into the street. He did not yet feel that he was in Germany. The encounter at customs and the reception later, though it had put him face to face with Germans, had been so official in character that he was still left with the feeling that he had not quite arrived.

"Thinking about going outside?" Kohn asked, coming up from behind him.

"Not really," Gottliebsohn said, startled.

"Why not?" Kohn asked. "You said you liked to walk. I wouldn't mind a legstretch myself."

"I don't know," Gottliebsohn said, suddenly reluctant to walk a German street. If he remained inside the hotel and only attended the conferences, he might well leave Germany without having really visited it. He shrank from the thought of mingling with, being confronted by the people whom he detested so violently, having to remain silent and orderly when what he felt like doing was to run amuck, shouting accusations at the top of his voice.

"Come on," Kohn said. "It'll do you good. And who knows —looking at street signs and listening to that hawk-and-spit language all around us might just shake something important loose from that blocked memory of yours." Kohn was anxious to see the city. He could not go without Gottliebsohn. "Come on," he urged, as Gottliebsohn stood shivering, his eyes half closed. Obediently Gottliebsohn turned and followed the smaller man through the double doors. He was apparently headed for a lighted main street that was several blocks away. When they drew near, they saw that the lights were from cinemas, night clubs, and all-night cafés. Kohn rubbed his hands. "Come," he said, taking a faster pace, then suddenly veering off onto a winding side street that seemed dark after the bright glow. Kohn put a hand on Gottleibsohn's arm and motioned for quiet.

In a moment Gottliebsohn heard it too: the sound of a

concertina, voices in song. It came from a cellar doorway. Kohn pointed. Blinking, Gottliebsohn made out the small sign: *Weinstube.*

"This is more like it," Kohn said. "Always go up the side streets. The bright lights are for tourists. Here's where you'll find a tougher crowd, those who live off tourists, but come here to relax."

While he was delivering himself of this, Kohn was leading the way down the narrow staircase. Gottliebsohn was reluctant to follow, but saw no way to avoid it. Kohn waited for him, then indicated that Gottliebsohn would have the honor of entering first. "Come on," he said when Gottliebsohn hung back, and gently pushed him through the doorway.

At his entrance, the singing faltered. Kohn came in and it stopped altogether. There were only a scattering of couples, some men together at a large table, and three heavily made-up girls at a table by themselves. Kohn was not in the least perturbed by their scrutiny. He headed for the long bar which ran across one side of the room, pulling Gottliebsohn with him. The singing picked up again, stronger than ever.

"A good sign, that silence," Kohn said happily. "They're worried about cops."

The bartender looked at them suspiciously.

"Schnapps," said Kohn, and could not help licking his lips.

"*Bier,*" Gottliebsohn said.

When they were served, Gottliebsohn paid; Kohn had not yet been issued any German money. When the bartender saw that the bills were new he looked more suspicious than ever.

"We're from out-of-town—" Kohn began casually, when Gottliebsohn broke in.

"From Israel," Gottliebsohn added.

Kohn's face darkened. He had not wanted to have their identity revealed. "Neither one of us look it, you fool," he said furiously, half under his breath. "Now you've ruined this place for us."

The bartender seemed momentarily startled. And then he became elaborately courteous. "Wouldn't you gentlemen prefer a table?"

"Perhaps," Kohn said, before Gottliebsohn could say no. "We'll see how we feel when we finish these."

The bartender nodded and left to serve the tables. From the way the men looked over at them, Gottliebsohn was sure they were being told what they were. He looked at them in turn. Most were his own age, Hitler's generation. Immediately Gottliebsohn felt the familiar surge of emotion—except this time, instead of a cold almost analytical hate, it burned so inside him he clutched his chest.

"You need another pill?" Kohn asked, suddenly concerned.

"No, no, I'll be all right in a moment," Gottliebsohn said.

The bartender was serving the table of girls.

"Look at those," Kohn said, elbowing him. "Maybe that will take your mind off your indigestion, send the blood to another part of the body, hey?"

"What do you mean?" Gottliebsohn asked. "They're children."

"Look at the paint on their faces," Kohn said. "They're prostitutes. No doubt about it."

The girls were looking in their direction. Gottliebsohn turned away, embarrassed, so he did not see one of them get up and walk toward them. The nudge in his rib brought him back around.

"Welcome to Germany," the girl said, and giggled rather nervously. She wore a purple leather tam and a black leather jacket buttoned up to her neck. She was pretty enough, in an earnest child sort of way.

"Thank you," Kohn said. "We appreciate that."

"Speak for yourself," Gottliebsohn muttered rudely.

"We, the other girls and I, we'd be pleased if you would join us at our table for a drink," the girl said, looking anxiously at Gottliebsohn. Kohn was right, Gottliebsohn thought. She was young, but she was also very battered. His heart wrenched at her spoiled youth, and he was furious with himself for the weak emotion. He was about to refuse her when Kohn pressed his elbow warningly.

"Of course," Kohn was saying. "We'd be honored."

The bartender brought chairs. A round of drinks was ordered. When it came, the girls insisted on paying. The others were equally young, equally used.

"I'm Ilse," the one who had come for them said. "That is

Ursula"—pointing to the girl whose smile revealed crooked teeth—"and Alexis," a waif whose large ears broke the symmetric helmet of her neck-length hairdo.

"Ernst," said Kohn, with a laconic thumb, "and Albert."

Gottliebsohn was startled. Somehow he had not thought of Kohn as having a first name.

"You speak German very well, Albert," Alexis said.

"I speak many languages well," Kohn said.

"And your friend doesn't speak at all?"

Kohn laughed.

"I speak perfect German when I want," Gottliebsohn growled. "I was born in this lousy country, after all."

"Oh."

He had embarrassed them. Gottliebsohn looked away. The others in the room were taking elaborate precautions not to seem to be watching. Gottliebsohn became even more uncomfortable.

"And you came back?" Ursula said, smiling doubtfully.

"Only for a visit, I'm afraid," Kohn broke in, before Gottliebsohn could answer.

"Is this your hometown?" asked Ilse.

"No," Gottliebsohn said, and he named the village, Warsfeld, where he was born.

"Oh, I know that place," said Alexis. "It's up near Bad Wildungen, isn't it?"

"Yes, near the woods," Gottliebsohn said.

"You don't have the accent of someone born in those parts," Ilse said. "In fact, it's more like mine, somehow."

"I've been away a long time," Gottliebsohn said, shrugging.

"You think Jews will ever live in Germany again?" Alexis asked them shyly.

Gottliebsohn choked on a foul word.

The girls drew back, offended.

"You mustn't mind my friend," Kohn said. "He's under rather a strain. This is his native land, after all."

Ilse put her hand on Gottliebsohn's arm. "I can guess how you must feel," she said. "But you mustn't blame us for what happened. We're not like our parents."

Gottliebsohn felt his flesh crawl. His arm tensed as though he would fling her hand off, but he did not move.

"If you stayed here for a while, you'd see how different we are," she continued earnestly.

"You'd like that, wouldn't you?" Gottliebsohn said. "It would be almost as if nothing had ever gone wrong between German and Jew—or at least that you'd been forgiven. You could point to your few Jews as proof of that."

"Ernst," Kohn said warningly.

"Please don't hate us so much," Ilse said. "Not us. Our parents, yes. We despise them as much as you do."

Kohn said, "Hate is an emotion for children." He didn't like the turn the conversation had taken—such seriousness was hardly conducive to talk about sex, and sex was what was uppermost in Kohn's mind.

"Your psychology is a little weak, is it not?" Gottliebsohn said angrily to Kohn. "After all, who teaches hate? The Germans taught me. Adult Germans!"

"Please," Ilse said. "I did not mean to upset you. If you would rather we did not sit together—"

"Now, now," Kohn said soothingly. "We're quite delighted with your hospitality. Ernst, you're giving these young girls the wrong impression of us—and, I might add, of our mission here."

Gottliebsohn flushed that Kohn, who was not even an official member, had found it necessary to remind him.

"The next round is on us," Kohn said heartily when he saw that Gottliebsohn intended to settle down. "Bartender!"

Gottliebsohn noticed that the singing had stopped. "We've interrupted these people's pleasure," he said. "Don't you think we should go so they can have music again?"

Ilse overheard him. "*Spiel'!*" she cried to the man with the concertina. "Our friends would like music." And picking up a coin, she took it over to the musician and said something very rapidly to him. He began playing. Before sitting back down with them, Ilse shuffled her feet in time to the music, and did a little twirl.

"Ah, I knew it," Kohn said. "You girls are in a theatrical profession!"

The girls giggled. "We would like to be, all right," Ursula said. "But while we're waiting for our chance, we earn our living however we can."

"I thought so," Kohn said, pleased with himself. He elbowed Gottliebsohn. "You hear that, Ernst?"

"I hear," Gottliebsohn said.

"Don't think we invited you over here to proposition you," Ilse said fiercely.

"No, no," the other girls protested.

"Oh?" said Kohn, pretending to be downcast. "I'm quite disappointed."

Alexis giggled again. Ilse looked at Kohn thoughtfully. Then she looked at Gottliebsohn. "If you are truly interested," she said to no one in particular, "I'll spend the night with you."

"And the cost?" asked Kohn softly.

"No charge," she said angrily.

This was too much for Gottliebsohn. "Have you no shame?" he burst out. "To offer yourself like that, whether for money or not does not matter, like some cheap little whore—what if your mother could see you, have you thought of that? Do you think to shame your parents? Forget your parents then, think of your friends, think of your brother, what this would do to him if he knew—"

Gottliebsohn became aware that Kohn was gripping him, painfully, just below the elbow.

"You know this girl?" Kohn asked, incredulous.

Gottliebsohn faltered, stopped. Finally he shook his head.

"Then what's all this about a brother?"

"Everyone has a sister or brother," Gottliebsohn mumbled.

"Even you?"

"I'm sorry," Gottliebsohn said to the girl. "I've talked to you as I would have to my own sister."

"He hasn't been feeling well," Kohn said to the girls, who had edged away, frightened, from the table. "I'm afraid the homecoming is a bit too much for him."

The place had become very quiet. The bartender muttered something and kept his hands out of sight below the bar.

"Perhaps you'd better go," Ilse said.

Kohn's face darkened. "You think I'm afraid of a few knackwursts like those?" he said contemptuously.

"The bartender is an incorrigible," the girl murmured. "He rah-rahs the old ideas as if they hadn't been proved

bad. We tolerate him—he's a curiosity, a freak, but it's possible he's very dangerous."

"I would like to leave anyway," Gottliebsohn said, getting to his feet.

Kohn sat undecided; then, reluctantly, he got to his feet.
His job was to stay with the other man. "Listen," he said,
leaning close to the girl, "we're staying at the Dressen. If
you're still free later on, I could look for you in the lobby.
Or here if you prefer."

"I'll see how the evening goes," she said indifferently.

"You see what you've done?" Kohn said bitterly, as they
walked rapidly back to the hotel. "Loused up a perfectly
good thing for me—and for yourself, too, for that matter.
What got into you, anyway? What do you care about a
German slut? There's something very strange about you,
mister. If you're not leveling with me, I suggest you come
clean now. Because I'm going to get to the bottom of this,
you can bet your last pfennig on that."

Gottliebsohn did not answer. He was frightened by the
intensity of his reaction to that girl. Anyone would have
thought she meant something to him, the way he had lashed
out at her. He did not understand his behavior himself. All
he knew was that something about her stirred conflicting
emotions in him, desire and revulsion, tenderness and loath-
ing, and the next thing he knew, he had been shouting. But
when he tried to think about what had disturbed him—her
face, her clothes, her manner of speech, her resemblance to
someone he knew or had once known?—his mind went absolutely blank.

"You don't find it ridiculous," he said finally, "to discuss
shame and guilt with a whore?"

Kohn came to an abrupt stop. He attempted a laugh, but
it came out badly. "You're all right, Ernst," he said at last,
clapping the other on the back. "You've got a real sense of
humor."

"I didn't mean it to be funny," Gottliebsohn said.

"Well, think about it for a moment," Kohn said. "The
conscience of a country kept by its whores."

When they got back to their room, Gottliebsohn went to
the bathroom, where he fought down the urge to vomit. He
changed into pajamas in private; not out of modesty, but to

be away from the other for as long as possible. Coming back finally into the bedroom, he poured himself water from the bedside pitcher and swallowed two pills.

"What are those?" Kohn asked. "They're not the same as the others, are they?"

"Sleeping tablets," Gottliebsohn said.

"You troubled with insomnia too?" Kohn asked. "You're really a mess, aren't you? Why don't you use that stuff?" —pointing to the Scotch. "It's always worked well for me." And he poured himself a nightcap.

"Where are you from originally?" Gottliebsohn asked.

"Berlin," Kohn replied, as if he were amused.

Gottliebsohn made no comment. Then he watched, startled, as Kohn, undoing his shirt, revealed a holstered gun.

"I've always had to smuggle my baby in before," Kohn explained, putting the gun under his pillow. "I'm not used to all this diplomatic-immunity business."

Gottliebsohn crawled into bed and turned his back on the frightening little man. He closed his eyes and waited for the drug to take effect. It was not lack of sleep, but too light a sleep, that afflicted him. Whenever he was wrought up, he tossed in that gray, blurred twilight. It was then that the nightmare would come.

He could hardly bear that terrible dream. It had gotten to the point where he was afraid to sleep at all, not sure that his own screams would continue to bring him, cold-sweated and trembling, back from the dreadful regions where his memory had gone. One day he would sleep too long, he thought, and then the meaning would be all too clearly revealed.

5

THE MEETING SEEMED TO DRAG ON IN-terminably. Each side had brought a series of position papers; the Germans stressed the amount already paid out for specific loss in properties; the Israelis were more concerned with the intangibles—cost of resettlement of refugees, interrupted earnings ability because of death of head of family and, where a family had no survivors, an indemnity for the "general welfare."

But these were old issues, and everyone at that long polished table knew they were being brought up only to reestablish the boundaries of disagreement, and there was a consequent lack of interest in the droning proceedings.

Gottliebsohn had already broken three pencil points. One more and he would have to signal for another to the buxom little blonde whose job it was, in patrolling the Israeli side, to perform such tasks. As her blue eyes fell upon him, he put down his last pencil, then attempted to conceal his nervousness by clasping his hands and letting his fingers secretly fight each other.

Von Haupt, seated opposite him at the long conference table, was not attempting to conceal his boredom. He and Gottliebsohn, as corresponding economists, had already authenticated the figures that were termed, on the German side, magnanimous, and on the Israeli, barely adequate, and their presence now might have been thought to be superfluous had not both known that at some point in this tedious morning they would be asked on the one hand to question, on the other to defend, whatever new proposal the Israelis had brought.

As the voices muttered on, Von Haupt thought longingly of his family's mountain retreat near Garmisch above Munich; there had been a late spring snowfall, and he was anxious to invite a few friends for several days of skiing before this last of the season powder should melt. But if this first meeting was any indication, he would not get his leave before the end of the week, if then.

Yet Von Haupt knew better than to reveal any of his real discomfort, indeed his disdain, for these lengthy proceedings. Not many of his class had been so fortunate after the war; some were in prison; most were living anonymous existences in areas far from their places of origin. It was a failure of leadership, Von Haupt thought. And bad luck. But one made his own luck, after a fashion, he reflected. If he had not been one of the aides to Speer when that brilliant Minister of Production had decided to countermand Hitler's orders to destroy all of Germany's industrial plant in those last terrible days of the war—well, he supposed one could call that luck, but he preferred to think of it as a fortunate coincidence, managed in a very real sense by himself, since he had requested the position with Speer in the first place.

He had become one of Speer's secret emissaries, traveling at night, by car, bicycle, and sometimes on foot, going from city to ruined city, persuading, with the help of an authoritative letter and an occasional phone call from Speer himself (only possible in certain instances, since most of the lines were down), those fearful plant managers to disregard that Austrian maniac's explicit orders. The most persuasive argument, of course, particularly to those in the path of the Russians, was that the advancing enemy armies would be more likely to treat leniently those managers who kept their factories intact. Those whose labor forces consisted of inferior peoples were a separate problem, of course. While he would have preferred to avoid them entirely, he thought it his duty to use his not inconsiderable influence to suggest that the better course would be to let them go free, hoping that the poor wretches would take off of their own accord, and be thankfully out of sight when the armies came. As it turned out, most stayed, out of feebleness, no doubt, and were damning evidence against the unlucky managers.

But as for Speer and himself, since they had been so remarkably successful in that secret revolt (beneficial not only to the enemy but eventually, as Speer had known— men's memories being short—to Germany itself), when taken before the Allied Tribunal, Speer had gotten off with a twenty-year sentence and he, having had no direct responsibility, had been cleared.

Von Haupt might have retired from government service had not most of his family's estates lain in what became East Germany. Almost penniless by his standards, he had been in no position to turn down that Bavarian politician's offer to serve as his appointee in the coalition government. The Bavarian, tainted by accusations of neo-fascist behavior, needed people without Nazi backgrounds, and with Von Haupt, who was also of the nobility, he got what he considered a bonus situation. Von Haupt knew that he could find no better sanctuary against the uncertain future than a somewhat anonymous position in government. And if his new colleagues were too middle-class for his taste, Von Haupt was a realist and he recognized that his own class would eventually find little place for itself in the new Germany; this government position would enable him to live out his days in something approximating the old style.

And then had come the Israeli mission, and the Bavarian, sensing a possible political advantage, had insisted that Von Haupt become part of the negotiating group, an involvement that the Baron did not care for; since his mentor's attitudes were well known, his presence could only be looked on with suspicion. It was ironic, Von Haupt thought, for he had always liked the Jews. As had most of his friends. The Jews were so splendidly amusing. Not the assimilated—bankers and business types, those more German than Germans—but the artists, musicians and philosophers, dancers and singers, whose eccentricities of taste and behavior were exceedingly diverting. Every family that he knew had been involved somehow with a Jew, either through some special interest, as in those amateur societies dealing with the sciences, or, and this was more likely, sexually. A family that had not been blooded by a Jew could not be said to have a very ancient lineage. Hitler had recognized this, and in the beginning had been practical about it, "forgiving" some four hundred their Jewishness (which included, some said, the hangman, Heydrich), but finally, the contempt with which he treated the aristocracy revealed what he really thought of their mongrelization.

Von Haupt had been against ridding Germany of its Jews. It was like bread without yeast. Without leavening, the bread did not rise, and one was left with something as flat and tasteless as that dreadful Jewish cracker, the matzo. What had given Germany its particular vitality, what had enabled Bismarck to mold a nation out of diverse populations, was that within his artificial borders lived a cohesive alien race and an equally cohesive, equally alien, leadership.

And now the one was gone, the other ineffectual. Von Haupt sighed quietly. He had argued (languidly, for such was his style, and then only to intimates), that the aristocratic General Staff's acceptance of Hitler, expedient as it was and contemptuous as was their attitude, was a mistake. An army cannot function independent of its nation, as if its rules and regulations protected it from civilian corruption. Events had proved him right. Eventually the army had sworn allegiance to the man instead of the office, and had conformed, however reluctant, to the Nazi code, even participating finally in racial murder.

Von Haupt sighed again. To find himself participating in these negotiations, for a politician whose motives were not all that clear and who was perfectly capable of wrecking any agreement that might be reached, should it suit his own purposes, was distasteful, and even somewhat nerve-racking. He had come to believe in the underlying, never-spoken German purpose in agreeing to the Israeli mission— expunge the past, pretend that the guilts and the prejudices never existed.

What about these Jews? he wondered. Could they go so far as that to reach an agreement? Von Haupt stared across the table at his Israeli counterpart—a German Jew, by his name. He was a quiet fellow; difficult to imagine what he was thinking. No doubt, though, that he had been one of those who had assumed he was assimilated—by his appearance alone he was typically German, with that complexion, short nose, and blue eye, and he carried himself with that stiff dignity the educated middle-class German so frequently assumed.

Gottliebsohn became aware that he was being stared at. He reddened, and partially shading his face with his hand, pretended to an intense interest in the speakers.

Bettmann and Hortsky had alternated readings of the prepared documents and were now acknowledging the other's statement. They paused, and a more strident voice entered the proceedings—Auerbach's—and Gottliebsohn straightened in his chair. It was coming, the Israeli proposal, the one on which Auerbach had focused the entire point of the mission.

"Gentlemen," he was saying, "I, for one, would like to see something more tangible come out of our discussions than credits, moneyflow, weaponry, and so on, which, after all, remain vague in the public mind. I would like to see something *physical,* something our people can look at and know is permanent, a German presence in our country that can become a monument, if you like, an actual representation that indeed our two nations have come to an accommodation."

"You obviously have something already in mind," Bettmann said after a slight silence.

"That is so," Auerbach admitted. "A factory is what I have in mind."

"Are you generalizing?" Bettmann asked. "Or are you speaking of a specific kind of factory?"

"That would depend on our mutual needs, wouldn't it?" Auerbach said. "But offhand, I know of two areas in which we are sorely deficient: pipeline—water, as you know, is our blood—and vehicles, all sorts of vehicles, from cars to trucks and tractors. Even an assembly plant would be valuable. Think of it; German vehicles—but made in Israel!"

Again there was a silence. On the surface it did not seem too outrageous a proposal, but everyone there knew how audacious it really was. Not too many years before, when German reparations had first been announced, there had been riots in Israel. And that had been over such intangibles as indemnities and credit. Had they really come so far so fast? Gottliebsohn wondered. But he trusted Auerbach's judgment.

"If we decide it is to be vehicles," Bettmann said finally, "would you permit the manufacturer's mark to appear?"

Auerbach winced, though he knew the German was merely probing to see how far they would go. "That we obviously could not do," he said. "Not at first, not for many years. Eventually perhaps."

"Then how is this plant a German *presence*?" Bettmann wanted to know.

"It would be generally known that the plant is German," Auerbach said. "The word would spread very rapidly, believe me; ours is a small country, the news would be border to border within days. But we could not offend our people with the German mark. The presence they could, they would, tolerate, as long as a mark is not thrown in their faces."

"They can pretend it does not exist, you mean," Bettmann said sardonically.

"But they will know it does," Auerbach insisted. "Eventually they may tolerate the mark, too."

Bettmann became thoughtful. "Our factory," he said then. "But run by Israelis?"

"Why, yes," Auerbach said, frowning slightly. The German was up to something. "What are you thinking?"

"I am thinking," Bettmann said, "that the purpose of this conference is to arrive at means of a closer accommodation. I am thinking that a German presence should not merely be symbolic. I am thinking that at the very least, a German factory should have German management."

There were silent intakes of breath all around the table. Germans in Israel? Working, living, mingling with Jews? It was unthinkable. Wasn't it? Gottliebsohn looked at Von Haupt. His opposite was regarding him coolly, a look of amusement on that aristocratic face.

"Now, my friend," Von Haupt said, whispering across the table, "we will see who has the most sincerity."

Gottliebsohn ignored the other, turned his attention to Auerbach. He was being strangely silent. Was it possible that shrewd politician had not anticipated this counter-proposal? For the moment even his own anguished worry was displaced by an overriding curiosity as to how the co-director would respond.

Auerbach *had* been taken by surprise. He had expected

the Germans to be so startled by his request that they would hesitate, retreat, call for a recess. Instead, their chief of delegation had calmly taken his proposal and extended it to a logical extreme. Did he have that kind of authority? Being German, he must have. Auerbach looked down the table at the German side—whatever immediate reactions they might have had were now replaced by expressions of impassivity. They were waiting for his reply.

Auerbach looked to Hortsky. That old man was regarding him with a kind of hopefulness; perhaps the younger men like Auerbach were capable of actual wisdom. So far, he was unconvinced.

Auerbach turned away, trying to sort out those matters of immediate practicality from all the factors that tumbled chaotically through his mind. Suggesting a German presence in human terms on Israeli soil would bring acrid debate in the Knesset, a call for a vote of confidence, probably inconclusive; the matter then referred to the people in a new election. With the coming of age of vast numbers of the new generation, their vote might just counteract those whose memories would never permit them to accept *any* accommodation, symbolic or real. But he was not sure. Dared he risk it? There were other factors. By establishing a German presence, they might give pause to the Arabs' constantly threatening fantasy of a push to the sea. Philosophically, if such hate as was between German and Jew could be overcome, then why not the differences between two Semitic peoples? More important, since Arab ties with the Germans were so complex, it would make another act of war more difficult. He could use this latter argument to good effect in the political campaign. A people would surely not jeopardize their security for the sake of an unworthy emotion. He himself had learned to swallow his hate when he first became aware that an accommodation was not only necessary, but inevitable. And as he had worked toward making this mission a reality he had even come close to forgetting that he had ever had reason for hatred, recognizing that personal emotions are a burden in the political world.

Auerbach studied his own delegation for a moment, then looked to Bettmann again. "You can appreciate, I am sure," he began slowly, "that your proposal is not something that can be accepted on the spur of the moment. We will need

time to consult our membership, time to consider any ramifications that may not be immediately apparent."

"Of course," Bettmann said, with a glance at Hortsky.
"But may I remind you that this conference is receiving a
great deal of attention, not only in our two countries, but in
many parts of the world? Too long a delay might give rise to
rumors of dissension which would do neither side much
good."

Bettmann watched Auerbach closely. He was not certain
but that he had made his counterproposal too soon, and he
became a bit anxious. He had not made the proposal off the
cuff; he had anticipated that the Israelis would make some
far-reaching demand, and he had prepared his own response
carefully.

The Germans too needed some sort of dramatic accommodation. It was important that they resolve their guilt.
Unfortunately, Bettmann thought, most of his countrymen
were not as aware as he was of the necessity for atonement.
For the most part they denied guilt, felt no shame, and
were, in fact, becoming increasingly irritable about this
whole Jewish business. The Jews were gone? Good riddance.
Pay them off, and let's get on with our own affairs. Not for
them such subtleties as he must contend with.

The rest of the world was not so quick to forget. At last
count, in the English language alone, there were five novels
dealing with the Nazi terror. A brutally realistic drama was
playing simultaneously in London and New York, and had
been shown twice on an American television network. Two
motion pictures, one French, one Italian, dealing with the
holocaust, were now in production. This deluge of material
was bound to have its effect, because of a domestic reaction,
even on the foreign services of the western powers, who
could otherwise be more realistic. The nations of Eastern
Europe, of course, had more immediate reasons for remembering.

But if the Jews were to accept Germans in their own
nation, much would change; the future would be weightier
than the past; then and only then could they look to their
relationships with other nations on a slate-clean basis, freed
from the suspicion and the poorly hidden contempt with
which they were always met.

It was worth the political risk to himself, he thought, if

he could accomplish this for his country. He had known, when asked to head the German delegation, that it was meant as a trap, a dead end for his career. As a former Socialist he was against more than a token rearmament of Germany; he wanted no part of any nuclear "trigger." Because he had spent the Hitler decade in exile, he was considered by many to be not much better than a traitor; he could not take any stand without suspicion. But if he could pull this off, if he could accelerate a settlement, he would be catapulted into a new prominence. Where his opponents saw a trap, he saw a great opportunity. If he could make his nation this gift of an unencumbered future, they would have to show their gratitude by voting his party into a dominant position. It would not matter then that he had been absent from Germany during her worst time; it would, with the young, be an advantage. For it was the young who would be most decisive in the next elections. As for his own age, he was ten years younger than Hortsky, and that old man had remained politically vigorous. Yes, Bettmann thought, he would have his chance yet to be Chancellor—and avoiding the inquiring, supercilious glance of the man who had been placed inside his delegation as an informer for his political enemies, he looked hopefully to Auerbach for a reply.

"Why don't we refer the matter to our economists for a feasibility study?" Auerbach said at last. "Our Gottliebsohn and your Von Haupt will certainly have many details to work out. We can always point to their sessions as representative of the good intentions of both sides. At the same time we can, without public notice, consider all the political ramifications of your proposal."

"An excellent suggestion," Bettmann said, nodding. "Baron von Haupt, I would urge you to make all possible speed."

"That will depend on Herr Gottliebsohn," Von Haupt said, aware that Bettmann hoped to put a kind of moral pressure on him. Not that he minded particularly; he only wanted to remind his delegation leader that there were others who could be held responsible. "If he is prepared to make some specific suggestions—how many trucks, how many tractors, and so on—then I am certain we can arrive at some plan rather quickly. For my part, I am prepared to work any and all hours, whatever may be necessary."

Gottliebsohn felt his spirits sink. He had hoped that his own role in these proceedings would be minor. And now he was, once again, being pushed into the foreground. He glanced up at Auerbach, saw that the other would have no patience with his doubts, and looked sorrowfully down at his hands again. At that moment he became aware that someone else was trying to get his attention.

Kohn had arrived at the meeting late, had slipped into his seat so unobtrusively that his arrival had gone largely unnoticed—except by Professor Schenke, who had been a bit put out over his opposite's absence, but who now visibly relaxed. Kohn looked significantly at Gottliebsohn, then at his watch. Gottliebsohn understood that Kohn wanted to see him before he began his meeting, and though he was nervous about Auerbach's reaction, he was more concerned about doing whatever that investigator asked.

"I will need the rest of the day to get my figures in order," Gottliebsohn said apologetically. "I was not prepared to have things move quite so fast . . ." Auerbach looked annoyed but said nothing.

"Yes, of course," Von Haupt said, shrugging in the direction of Bettmann. "What about this evening then?"

Gottliebsohn nodded. The meeting broke up. Kohn intercepted Auerbach. "There's a visitor due in from Israel in half an hour," he said meaningfully, "who may prove of some value to us."

"Who is it?" Auerbach demanded impatiently. Ever since their understanding, Kohn had adopted this annoying conspiratorial air.

"His name is Glass," Kohn said. "Norman Glass. He's an American psychiatrist."

"When did you hear he was coming?" Auerbach asked, lowering his voice and leading Kohn away from the others.

"I was just on my way here when I got the cable," Kohn said. "From an attorney named Levin, who is consulting for the Interior Minister."

"Levin?" Auerbach said. "Are you sure of the name?"

"Positive," Kohn said. He looked curiously at the mission co-director, who seemed very upset by this news. "Do you know him?"

"He is a prosecutor," Auerbach said, worried. "The Interior Minister must be very sure of himself. Have they turned something up—do you know?"

"Nothing they've told me about," Kohn said. "But this headknocker's bringing along a dossier on everything they've got so far. It would be in that."

"Would it?" Auerbach asked.

Kohn shrugged. "Why would they keep anything from me?" he asked, but the doubts rose in him. "Shall I pick him up?" he asked. "I can feel him out to see what they may have told him. Besides, if we're going to work together, I should know what kind of a man he is."

Auerbach shook his head. With all the problems that had arisen at the meeting, to have to involve himself with side issues was extremely annoying. But the matter of Gott-liebsohn was too important to let pass by default. He wanted a firsthand look at this American psychiatrist.

"I'll see to him," Auerbach said. "You stick with Gottlieb-sohn, make sure he understands that this doctor intends to help him, that he's someone we asked for, not them. I'll see that you have time with him later." And, making his good-byes, Auerbach directed the limousine driver to take him to the airport.

The flight in had not been a very pleasant one for the American. While he could not deny that the case fascinated him, he did not like to participate in matters that he felt were beyond the scope of his own limited emotional experi-ence. The man was accused of being a collaborator. What did he know about such things? How could he determine guilt or innocence in the complex behavior patterns that had been prevalent in the Europe of the years preceding the war?

But then, according to Dean Wolfe, that had been pre-cisely the reason they had chosen him.

Wouldn't his wife, Estelle, have found that amusing? She would not. It had been his objectivity that she blamed for their estrangement, his detachment from the passions of ordinary men. It meant nothing to her that his profession dictated a certain attitude which, through habit, he brought into his home. The Microphone, she called him, and The Great Recorder, and it was no wonder that a great many strangers, overhearing her acrid comments to him at special gatherings, thought his first name was Mike.

What she wanted from him he could not provide. The fact that she ran with the minority types in college should have given him the first clue: her attempts to get close to and understand Oriental and Negro and Jew were laudable, a demonstrable sympathy for the outs from one of the ins (her family socially prominent Californians), but who knew she would carry it to inordinate lengths? How deeply even superficial attitudes can penetrate a personality, if they are held long enough! And when she announced that she wanted their child, a handsome boy of four, brought up as a Jew, they had what turned out to be their final argument.

Why not Unitarian? he asked. He agreed that a child was entitled to an idea of God, one that was reasonable, simple and just, and since she herself was Episcopalian and he had no religion worthy of the name, he thought it a perfect solution.

What a scene that had been. He blanched again just thinking about it. She called him shameful and a coward, accused him of denying his heritage, and when he pointed out that he was a Jew only for convenience of label, having grown up in a tradition that was mostly Protestant, and that had it not been for the European holocaust he would not call himself Jew at all, she had called him a hypocrite and he had suggested, politely, that she was mentally disturbed to even consider adopting a minority religion. At that, she had left his bed, though not his board, but made his life so subsequently miserable that he moved out of the house.

But he carried her accusations right along with him. Packed in with his reference books and his sinus tablets, his shaving mug and straight razor, his favorite neckties and four suits, three pair of shoes (one black, one brown, and sneakers), was the feeling that she may have been right. Perhaps, as she had said—*shouted*—it was not that *she* had married *him* as an act of rebellion against *her* parents, but that *he* had married *her* to obscure even further his origins.

He tried to dismiss the thought but it stayed with him, and like fat on a man who has always been lean, it began to slow him down. He became uncertain enough about himself to be unable to guide those uncertain others.

Did he not associate with Jews, as she claimed, because of an acting-out of self-hate, or was it simply as he always believed, that their ways were foreign, therefore abrasive? The company of those who were kosher, who spoke a jargon composed of Yiddish slang and ate highly seasoned foods, and those who, through some misguided search for a primitive need, turned to a forbidding orthodoxy, was uncomfortable for him.

Yet he had Jewish friends, and when he pointed this out, she rebutted him easily by stating that nobody *knew* they were Jewish: as infuriatingly stupid as this seemed, the doubts became increasingly heavy.

How fortuitous that the man who could help him was in the land of the Jews! But before they had a chance to begin the investigation of his own discontent, he found himself on a plane bound for Germany, where it would be up to him to piece together a past for a Jew who had been accused of a crime against the very people he himself, so his wife charged, falsely denied.

No matter what his personal attitudes, it looked to be a difficult case. The dossier interviews were contradictory, showing a man more comfortable in the company of children than adults, who preferred the transitory relationships of prostitutes (and Arab prostitutes, at that) to more legitimate women (was he afraid of the future as well as the past?), who had fought courageously against the Germans, yet was accused of collaboration. Not only that, the political factors involved might complicate their getting at the truth.

By the time the plane landed, Glass was more certain than ever that he had let himself in for something that he might not be equipped to handle. He hoped that neither he—nor his patient—would have occasion to regret it.

While he was in the passenger-document line, a customs official searched him out. "Dr. Norman Glass?" the man asked, subserviently polite. Glass nodded. "You are being anxiously awaited," the official said. "This way, please." He was escorted to a lounge where a swarthy balding man in an ash-flecked black suit was waiting.

"I am Auerbach," the other said, grasping his hand. "Co-director of the mission. We're glad to get someone so quickly."

Glass was surprised to be met by a person of so much importance.

"It's been rather a shattering experience for all of us," Auerbach said, "as I'm sure you can imagine."

"Particularly for the accused, I'd guess," Glass agreed.

Auerbach looked sharply at the tall, lean, well-dressed American, wondering if any sarcasm had been intended. "Yes, particularly for him," Auerbach said, deciding not. "Now, what about your luggage?"

The customs official, who had been hovering close by, stepped forward. "I took the liberty of having it passed through," he said, touching his cap. "It's been placed in the official car."

"That's very good of you," Auerbach said, and taking Glass by the arm, attempted to lead him around the other.

"Is there anything else . . . ?" the official asked.

"Nothing, thank you," Auerbach answered impatiently, and the other stepped aside. "That fellow," Auerbach muttered as he led Glass to the waiting limousine, "seems to have taken it upon himself to watch over us."

Glass made no comment, though he wondered what it was about the helpful German that caused so much antagonism—perhaps it was only the man's ugliness and the uniform, which, though it seemed a caricature of an earlier time, was still a reminder.

They rode in silence for a time. Glass took little interest in the passing scene, wondering how long it would take this obviously tense individual to tell him what was on his mind.

Auerbach, for his part, was considering the best way to approach this laconic American. It would probably not do, he thought, to be too blunt—bluntness was effective only when both parties in an encounter had something tangible to gain, like a promotion or a profit. In a case like this, where the American was unreachable by such ordinary terms, it would be necessary to find out what motivated him. As a practicing politician, Auerbach knew there were many ways to manipulate individuals—the trick was to find the proper leverage.

"It's a sticky business, this," he began. "How much do you know about what is going on?"

"Very little," Glass said. "I've been thoroughly briefed on my patient, if that's what you mean."

"And nothing else?" Auerbach asked skeptically.

"I *was* told there were some politics involved," Glass said, feeling that he was being pushed somewhat, though he couldn't say how.

"*Some* politics," Auerbach murmured. "And what were you told about me? That I am inordinately ambitious? That I would stop at nothing to further my career?"

"Something like that," Glass admitted.

"We are caught up so much by circumstance," Auerbach said then, reflectively. "I never intended to become a politician: I wanted private practice, but I became so involved in government projects that I couldn't find the way out—a rat in a maze, if you like. Then, because of some successful negotiations on indemnity with the occupying powers in Germany, I achieved a certain favorable public reputation, and I was tapped by the Prime Minister himself to run for election with his party. How could I lose? I am competent, I admit it, near brilliant, I admit to that also, but as to ambition: I deny responsibility for my career, though I accept it as the thrust of fate. And for that they call me ambitious." He paused. "I will tell you one thing—I would stop at nothing to further a cause of my country. I would have to believe the cause was right, of course. In my position, wouldn't you feel the same?"

"There are limits," Glass said hesitantly, reluctant to be drawn into a discussion, sensing that Auerbach, for all his seeming irrelevance, had a definite purpose. "How do you determine when you are more right?"

"Than others, you mean?" Auerbach said. "You are aware then of the opposition to this mission. But surely you, as a psychiatrist, must see the rightness of our position? You, more than most people, must know that hate corrodes the soul! It is one thing to cleanse oneself with hate, like using acid on an accumulation of crud, but leave it too long, and it begins to eat at the container, *nicht*? Yet there are those in my country, those who claim the moral position, who want to continue hating. They would stop at nothing to bring about our mission's failure. Now which side is right? Those who wish to cling to a corroding emotion, or those who must take more practical matters into consideration? What good comes to us if we continue to hate the German? We may remain wary of him, with sufficient reason, but hate? That is unreasonable, is it not?" Auerbach's face was working, and he took a moment to compose himself. "I have not accomplished this reasonable attitude so easily as you might imagine," he went on finally. "After all, my own family were destroyed, in Rumania. Out of fifty-eight, three are left."

Glass felt embarrassed and repelled by the other's vehemence. How little he knew about the complex motivations of those Jews who had survived the holocaust and were struggling to find a way in which to accept the world that had emerged from the ashes. He could sense the intensity of the feeling that had been suppressed, but only guess at the fear of those who never wanted to forget the horror, lest it somehow, like a nightmare when one is asleep, come upon them again. Because he had been born in America, and thus escaped the final humiliation, he did not feel he had any right to participate—let alone judge.

"It's not for me to say," Glass said. "Is it?"

"Perhaps it will be, finally," Auerbach said enigmatically, taking out a handkerchief and wiping his moist face and hands. He was momentarily uncertain and contemptuous of himself. He did not know whether that last personal revelation had been to ingratiate himself into the confidence of the American, or whether he might not have been asking the other, as a psychiatrist, to agree that it was not so easy to put fifty-five dead relatives to permanent rest. "Did you know that it was I who requested your assignment?" he continued. "Not you personally, of course, but someone very like you. A man without bitterness, a man who could be objective." He paused to allow the point to be made. "I thought Gottliebsohn—who has sworn to me his innocence —was entitled by his past service to me and his country to a complete refutation of the charges against him, something a prosecution-oriented Israeli psychiatrist might be unlikely to do. Now I find that the opposition is determined to find him guilty. Can you blame me for wanting to put you straight on what's going on?"

"I'm not sure I understand you," Glass said.

"Were you not briefed on this case by a man named Levin?" Auerbach asked. Glass nodded. "Did you know he is a prosecutor?" Glass shook his head mutely. "He is a member of the opposition party," Auerbach continued, satisfied by the expression on the American's face that he was making headway. "He is not above using Gottliebsohn to bring everything we have built so carefully toward crashing down about our ears."

"Levin may be opposed to you," Glass said slowly, "and I can't say I care for the man's methods, but he certainly seemed objective enough."

"Did he?" Auerbach asked sarcastically. "How do you explain that I was not notified of your arrival here?"

"Yet it was you who came to meet me," Glass said.

"Do you think a man in my position can afford not to have other, unofficial means of getting information?" Auerbach said.

Glass was not sure what kind of response, if any, was expected of him.

Auerbach tapped the brief case that Glass carried. "That would be the Gottliebsohn dossier, I take it?" Glass nodded. "And everything that is known about Gottliebsohn, so far, is there?"

"So far as I know," Glass said, struggling against becoming resentful.

"Levin told you nothing more?" Auerbach persisted. "Some new piece of evidence incriminating Gottliebsohn, for example?"

"No," Glass said shortly.

"And you would tell me if there were, wouldn't you?" Auerbach said, looking shrewdly at the other and guessing that he had reached the point where he could be pushed only a little further.

"I would tell you anything that you are entitled to know," Glass said.

"And just what does that mean?" Auerbach asked.

"You must know that anything my patient tells me— anything we may turn up in his past—" Glass said, "he is entitled to have kept confidential."

Auerbach said, "The sanctity of the doctor-patient relationship, *nein*? I would like to suggest to you that if you value your patient's well-being, you will keep me informed of your progress. Particularly if you discover that your patient is guilty—which I doubt, mind you—you will come to me with it at once!"

"It isn't my place to do that," Glass said, paling at the prospect of that kind of involvement.

"Let me put it this way, Doctor," Auerbach said impatiently. "If you find out, or if Gottliebsohn confesses to you that he is guilty—rest assured that it won't remain secret long. These things have a way of coming out. Understand the seriousness of the situation in which you find yourself. There is more than politics involved here, or my personal career. He could be sentenced to death."

Glass had only been vaguely aware of what could be in store for the accused man, and to hear the punishment, the revenge they would take if he was guilty, put him almost into a state of shock.

"And if I came to you first with that kind of information," he said finally, reluctantly, "how would that help? What could you do for him?"

"A great deal," Auerbach said. "I have promised Co-Director Hortsky—you know the name, of course—that if charges are brought against Gottliebsohn, I would act as attorney. Knowing in advance that these charges might be true would be of immeasurable help. I would not be able to suppress them, but I could probably challenge their validity enough to save the man's life, at any rate." Auerbach paused to let his words have their proper effect. "Look," he said, adopting a reasonable, almost ingratiating, tone, "all I'm asking is for you to give me a chance to cope with whatever you discover." He hesitated briefly. "I would think you would jump at what I am suggesting. I am giving you the opportunity to find your way out of what might become a very touchy situation—if you should find yourself making judgments as to your patient's welfare that are outside your area of responsibility, for example."

Anger and a kind of fear struggled for dominance in Glass. He was being coerced. Yet it was no simple, obvious coercion; it was as if Auerbach sensed something in the very facelessness of his soul, some disquietude that caused him to shrink from overinvolvement—and was offering him a freedom from responsibility that was more than attractive. But still he kept himself from agreeing, perhaps out of pride, or in the unrealistic hope that the situation Auerbach described would never come to pass.

"I assume we have an understanding?" Auerbach asked.

"I don't know," Glass said slowly, disturbed because of the weakness that equivocation revealed. "I won't know until the time for that kind of a decision is actually here."

"Of course," Auerbach said, as if he had to be satisfied with that, but secretly pleased with how this whole thing had turned out, far better than he had any right to expect. He leaned back in his seat, then immediately sat forward again and lit another cigarette, understanding that it would not do, in front of this now disturbed American, to appear complacent. "You will meet Captain Kohn, the man officially in charge of this investigation, in a very few minutes. I would suggest that you not be misled as to where his sympathies lie. He is prosecution-oriented, and nothing will ever change that."

Then Auerbach settled back, finally content to let his companion brood over the ramifications of everything he had told him.

6

KOHN AND GOTTLIEBSOHN WAITED FOR the psychiatric summoning in their hotel room. Kohn had ordered lunch sent up—a thick potato soup and liverwurst sandwiches on black pumpernickel, and beer in tall, narrow-necked green bottles—but Gottliebsohn had left his untouched.

"You're not kosher, are you?" Kohn asked, wolfing his food down, greedily eying the other's portion. Gottliebsohn shook his head. "You'd better eat. The headknocker will have eaten, you can be sure of that—they never like to work on an empty belly."

Gottliebsohn got up and went to the bathroom again. He was extremely nervous. It was the same throat-choking, bowel-seething dread that he used to experience before battle—or before reluctantly settling into a sleep that he knew held terrors for him. But those were experiences of short duration. This time he might face a truth that he would have to live with forever. As bare as his life was, like living in a room without furniture, might he not be better off than to be told what he was, if what he was was not palatable to him? But he denied to himself that he could have been a collaborator. Whatever he may have done that continued to disturb his sleep so many years after, he knew in his bones that he would have been incapable of so despicable a crime.

Gottliebsohn came out of the bathroom.

"Constipated?" Kohn asked.

"The other," Gottliebsohn said shortly.

"Fear does that," Kohn said benignly. "Now if the knocker can give that blocked memory of yours the same kind of laxative . . . here, have a little beer at least. It'll settle you down."

"You have it," Gottliebsohn said, and went over and sat stiffly in the chair again.

Kohn shrugged, and opening the second bottle, poured it into his own glass. "I can't say I blame you for being nervous," he said. "I don't like the headknockers myself. They're always finding excuses for the lousy things people do. Either that, or they give you a lousy reason for the good things."

Kohn tasted Gottliebsohn's soup; it was cold. Almost idly he took up the other's sandwich. For some reason he was very hungry, as if it were he and not Gottliebsohn who was soon to be subjected to an unsettling experience.

A knock at the door and Auerbach entered. He was nervous and irritable. His nose wrinkled. "Who's been drinking?" he demanded.

"Me," Kohn said. "It's only beer. But he wouldn't have any."

"A good thing," Auerbach said. "Can you imagine the psychiatrist's impression if he smelled alcohol on his patient's breath?"

"Let's hope he doesn't get so close to him," Kohn said. He looked curiously at Auerbach. "What's he like?"

Auerbach shrugged. "An American. Pumped full of ethics and ideals, like all Americans. But you'll meet him. You judge for yourself."

"You tried to talk to him, hm?" Kohn asked significantly. Gottliebsohn did not seem to be listening; nevertheless Auerbach made an angry quieting gesture to Kohn. Then he went over to where Gottliebsohn sat staring morosely into space.

"This is an awkward time for all of us, Ernst," Auerbach said. "But you should know that I've talked the whole matter over with Hortsky, and we've agreed that it's too important to make do with a superficial answer to your accusers; we must establish your innocence once and for all. I believe in your integrity, Gottliebsohn; in fact, I've staked my own reputation on it. Now don't let me down."

Gottliebsohn looked up. What was the other saying?

"I don't mean to let you down, Director Auerbach," Gottliebsohn said. "But what if I am guilty of . . . some other crime?"

"Other crime?" Auerbach asked. "What sort of other crime?"

"I don't know," Gottliebsohn said. "But it's possible, isn't it? I was a young man then, the times were difficult . . ."

Auerbach looked at Kohn, then back to the seated man. "If you are," he said slowly, "and if you remember what it was, you must come to Captain Kohn and myself with it first. I am certain that whatever it was can be worked out between the three of us."

"And what about the psychiatrist?" Gottliebsohn asked.

"He is not your judge, after all," Auerbach said. "His job is only to put back your memory."

Only? thought Gottliebsohn hopelessly, but he said nothing.

"Are you ready then?" Auerbach asked. He looked critically at the other. Gottliebsohn was close-shaven; his hair had been wet-combed; he obviously intended, should neatness count, to make a favorable impression. Auerbach was reassured. A man who cared about his appearance would not too readily surrender to despair, he thought.

"You take him up," Auerbach said to Kohn, and he gave him the room number. Kohn nodded; Gottliebsohn stood up. "I wouldn't let him see how chummy you are," Auerbach murmured, as a final precautionary observation.

"Chummy?" Kohn said indignantly, standing stock-still. "You really think that? Don't let appearances deceive you. I'm supposed to keep an eye on him, and that's exactly what I'm doing. But what's the harm in being pleasant, so long as we have to room together?" Kohn was really disturbed; the fact was he had stopped thinking of the other as a criminal.

"None, of course," Auerbach said, "as long as you keep it private," and walking the two men to the elevators, had nothing more to say to either of them. He watched them out of sight, sighed, and returned to his own quarters, where he settled down to the hours of work necessary to revising the position paper for the mission, hopeful that whatever took place in the room upstairs would not make that work come to naught.

The small sitting-room alcove that was part of what the hotel called a suite was not Glass's idea of the proper environmental setting. He preferred a more clinical atmosphere (let the patient face up to the fact, first, that he was sick, and second, that the treatment might be neither comfortable nor falsely reassuring).

But he had prepared the place as best he could, removing those incredible pictures and taking out all the overstuffed furniture, replacing it with a table and straightbacked chair for himself, a similar chair for his patient. Glass believed, as do some stage designers, that a dialogue can set up more meaningful reverberations against a background which brings in no extraneous associations. Now he waited impatiently for his patient to arrive.

The expected knock finally came; Glass opened the door and let the two men come in. He did not permit himself even to guess which was to be his patient; such speculation was fruitless, and might, by some inadvertent gesture or glance on his part, get the session off to a bad start. The large man halted uncertainly just inside the room; the smaller, balding, freckle-faced one walked on past Glass to the alcove and studied the setup with some curiosity.

"I'm Captain Kohn," he said in English, walking back to them, not offering to shake hands. "That's your man there." Kohn's eyes glittered; he was never comfortable in the presence of priests, rabbis, or doctors who specialized in the mind, and he covered this up by adopting a spuriously efficient and cheerfully self-confident attitude. "Since we're to work together, I think we ought to have it out which of us is to call the shots. It'll make it a lot easier in the long run."

Glass blinked in astonishment at this pleasant assault, then turned and spoke quietly to Gottliebsohn. "I'm Dr. Glass. Would you like to sit down in the other room? I'll only be a few moments."

"You speak German?" Kohn asked, feigning surprise.

"German was my doctoral language," Glass said.

"Is it good enough for this sort of . . . interview?" Kohn asked.

"It's formal," Glass said. "But quite complete."

"I had planned to act as translator for you," Kohn said, pretending disappointment. "I speak many languages well, one reason I'm so good at my work."

Glass had been watching Gottliebsohn's halting progress to the alcove, noting the reluctant manner in which he entered the small room. Now he returned his glance to the captain. He didn't know whether to be angry or amused, but as he studied the smaller man he began to realize that there was little about the other that was amusing.

"I'm afraid that wouldn't do, Captain," he said quietly. "It's customary in my work for the doctor to be alone with the patient. I take it you haven't had any experience in psychoanalysis?"

"Not me," Kohn said, eyes narrowing as he wondered if this headknocker meant anything personal. "I don't believe in it. A crack-up is a crack-up and all the talk in the world doesn't have enough glue in it to put a man back together once he's broken down."

"But the idea is to get to a man before he reaches that stage," Glass said, protesting in spite of himself.

"You can't stop the inevitable," Kohn said, shaking his head. "Once a man gets it set in his mind that he's going haywire, there's no power on earth can stop him. I know. I've seen it too many times."

"I take it then you don't agree with my being in on this," Glass said.

"Don't get me wrong," Kohn said. "It's part of the system nowadays and if you don't go along you can get chewed up. All I'm saying is any man trained in asking questions should be able to get the truth out of Ernst . . . Gottliebsohn."

"You think he's shamming then?"

"It's like I said," Kohn said patiently. "What a man thinks he is, he is. Gottliebsohn thinks he's a blank. But here and there, with the right questions, he's bound to let loose bits of information—without even knowing he's letting it out, mind—and with enough of those we should be able to get at the truth."

Glass studied the other. "Obviously you *are* unaware of how we work," he said finally. "We're listeners, for the most part. We try and make it easy for the patient to talk, about anything he wants to talk about—particularly, of course, those things which are *verboten*. We'll try and *guide* a pa-

tient's talk, but we don't question in the way you mean.
When you question a man, he mentally runs for cover. As
for him not even knowing he's letting out information—
well, that just won't do. We'll stop right there and look at it
from every possible point of view. We look for the whys, not
the whats. You're after evidence. I'm trying to help a man
find himself. And if we, my patient and I, can find out *why*
he's blanked out the past, we just might be able to put it all
back together for him right at that very moment."

"And you just might dry him up forever," Kohn said,
unbelieving.

"Well, what do you suggest, Captain?" Glass asked impatiently, though he knew it would not do to become
angry.

"I suggest we don't have the time to wait until you *guide*
our man to a revelation," Kohn snapped. "We have to find
out damn quick what he was up to in '38 and '9. But we
won't be able to do it unless we put the pressure on."

"You have something in mind?" Glass said coldly.

"Nothing out of the ordinary," Kohn said. "It's standard
in my game to take the accused back to the scene of the
crime. It's amazing what that can do to loosen a tongue. No
matter what the crime, or the punishment, a look at where it
happened, reenacting how it happened, and the next thing
you know there's a detailed confession."

"You're talking about a guilty man," Glass said.

"I have to make that assumption," the captain said.

"But I don't," Glass said.

"It doesn't matter," Kohn said, shrugging. "I'm not asking you to change your style. If you don't question, you
don't question. I can take care of that end of it, anyway. But
it would help if you fed me things to question him *about*. So
far we don't have a hell of a lot to go on, you know."

Glass stared at the other.

"For my part," Kohn went on, "I could feed you things
he needs guidance on. A fair exchange." Kohn paused. "You
weren't sent here to obstruct this investigation, I take it?
You were sent here to help?"

Glass felt a nerve jump in his face and wondered if the
other had seen it. Kohn had, and was pleased.

"Look," he said. "Unless we work together, we don't
have a prayer."

"I won't get in your way, Captain," Glass said slowly. "But I'm not sure just what, if anything, I'd be able to pass on. Certainly nothing that isn't pertinent to your end of this."

"That's all I ask," Kohn said, satisfied that he had made his point.

"Then I'd best get started, hadn't I?" Glass said, looking at his watch.

"Don't let me keep you," Kohn said.

"You weren't intending to wait here?" Glass said.

"I'm to stay near him at all times," Kohn said. He smiled blandly. "Didn't you bring along a packet of material for me? I could be looking at that while I'm waiting."

Glass hesitated for a long moment, then went to the bedroom and got the dossier. "Why don't you read it in here, Captain?" he said. "That way my patient can have the privacy he needs."

"Of course," Kohn said. He took the material and seated himself complacently in one of the overstuffed chairs.

Glass had to make some effort to keep from slamming the door. Taking a moment then to compose himself, he went in to face his patient.

Gottliebsohn was secretly sweating in those parts of the body which are fortunately hidden from view. He had heard the two men talking in the other room, and while he could not make out the words, the knowledge that they were discussing him in those antagonistic tones made him even more uncomfortable than he had been.

He was not at all prepared for the way this doctor looked. Those with whom he had dealings before had all seemed to be untidy men, so involved with the problem before them that their own appearance, and even the condition of their body, did not interest them. This man was not only young, with the good teeth and lean body of an athlete, but he was dressed exceedingly well, in a gray-striped suit that seemed English. He had known he was to be probed by an American—Kohn had told him this disdainfully—but he had not expected him to be so different.

How could they possibly expect this dapper kind of person to understand any of the things that had happened to him?

Gottliebsohn was afraid, and he rationalized his uncertainty by telling himself that this tense young man could hardly expect to have any sympathy for someone like himself, a grotesque, an awkward and drab civil servant, a melancholy man whose guilt, whatever it was, could hardly be expected to be even interesting, however violent. Gottliebsohn slouched hopelessly in his chair. He told himself that he would listen to what the other had to say, much as any other patient with a more traceable ailment, and if he didn't like the proposed treatment, he would simply refuse to have it.

Glass sensed the other's fear and took it to be a normal reaction under the circumstances. "Sorry about the delay," he murmured. "But there were a few things I had to get straight with your . . . the captain." He seated himself behind the table, and taking out his pen, made a few casual notes on his tablet. Later on in the interview, as the note-taking continued, his patient would not be startled or think what he was saying was unduly important. "Do you know why I'm here?" he asked then, looking up.

"To find out if I'm lying, I suppose," Gottliebsohn muttered.

"And are you?" Glass asked quietly.

"No," Gottliebsohn said shortly.

But everyone lies, Glass thought, at least to themselves, about one thing or another, right up until the moment of death, some even denying that reality. This man's lie, of course, was on a much greater scale earlier on in the game, and what they had to do was look for the reasons. But how was he to explain that to him?

"Then why should you think that's why I'm here?" Glass asked.

"I wasn't sure I was believed," Gottliebsohn said.

Glass held up his copy of the dossier. "This was given to me in Jerusalem," he said. "It contains all your background that is officially known, including your army service. Your medical history makes it quite believable." He hesitated. "But amnesia itself is a form of lying, isn't it?" he said. "The mind is making a statement that the past does not exist. I'm here to try and prove to you that it does, to help you prove it to yourself. It won't be easy. In fact it will be impossible unless you truly want me to help you. But then you know that. You've been through it before. Your record shows you were given Sodium Pentothal—for truth—and you were unable to tell them anything."

Gottliebsohn stirred uneasily. "They said the trauma was very deep."

"They tried hypnosis too," Glass continued, "again without success?"

"I never went under," Gottliebsohn said. "My resistance was too strong, they said."

"Why is that, do you suppose?" Glass asked.

Gottliebsohn shrugged. "I don't know."

"Can you hazard a guess?"

"No," Gottliebsohn said finally.

"Well, we're going to try a different approach," Glass said patiently, as if he had all the time in the world to gain the other's confidence instead of only the next few hours. "We're going to try and put your memory back together, piece by piece. Those pieces don't have to be in order—think of it as a jumbled-up jigsaw puzzle, where we begin by trying to make some kind of sense out of the scatter. But we'll need as many pieces as we can get. I'll want you to tell me anything you remember—people, places, smells, sounds, tastes, feelings. I already have here"—Glass indicated the dossier—"some evaluations of your character from people who know you now. We will look for people who knew you then, use *their* memories to stimulate and reconstruct your own. Here is a start already made in that direction." Glass handed Gottliebsohn the newspaper article he had been given by Dean Wolfe.

"It won't do any good," Gottliebsohn said, when he had finished reading the story.

"Why do you say that?" Glass asked.

"I looked everywhere for my relatives, and so did the governmental agencies," Gottliebsohn said. "We discovered no one."

"This story is being published in this country too," Glass said.

Gottliebsohn was surprised. It had not occurred to him that they would look for information in Germany.

"None of my relatives would still be alive in Germany," Gottliebsohn pointed out bitterly.

"But others who knew you might," Glass said.

Gottliebsohn breathed heavily through his nose and

thought about those who might know him. "What do I give a damn for them?" he said finally.

Glass observed his patient in silence. Gottliebsohn shifted uneasily in his chair, amazed at his own rudeness, wanting to justify it to himself—and to this silent other. "Don't you think what the Germans have done is enough to make a man despise them?" he asked. And then, before Glass could answer, he clenched his fists and cried, "But of course, how could you know, you grew up in America!"

Glass felt the heat in his face, and his lips tightened. Why should he be concerned because a statement of fact sounded like an accusation? He should not feel shame over chance and circumstance. Yet shame was clearly the emotion he felt.

"What I think is of no consequence," Glass said, as quietly as he was able. "We're here to find out what you think."

"About the Germans?" Gottliebsohn demanded.

"That might be a good place to start," Glass said. "But not what you think about them now, at least not for the moment. Keep in mind that we're interested in reconstructing your past. Can you remember how you felt about Germans . . . before?"

Now it was Gottliebsohn's turn to fall silent. And though he honestly wanted to cooperate, as much to make up for his unmannerly behavior as for anything else, he found himself becoming even more upset. "You are not even a Jew!" he burst out, at last. "How can I describe to you anything I feel or think when there is nothing in your own life that even comes close to it?"

Glass, who had been hoping that the other's distress would be only momentary, was suddenly reminded of his own doubts. How could he explain what he was? That it depended upon your definition of Jew? That by birth he was, but that by upbringing and attitude he was not? That by common feeling he was not, but that by force of circumstance he was? Could Gottliebsohn understand? And even if he could, did he have any right to imply that a search for the other's guilts would parallel his own? But if he were to get the man's cooperation he had to give him an answer.

"All men have certain things in common," Glass began slowly, hoping to avoid any final statement. "We all have the capacity for love and hate. Perhaps not many have experienced these emotions so deeply as yourself, but they are not for that reason less understanding. In my case I have been trained to understand, to recognize emotions and look for the causes. There are more similarities between us than you imagine. I have had friends and enemies and wants and desires, just as you have. You were in an army, I was in an army too—are not all armies much the same? You grew up in a village, I grew up in a small town. Can we really be so very different?"

Gottliebsohn looked warily at the American. "You grew up in a small town?" he asked.

Glass nodded. "Small towns must be much the same the world over," he said.

"I wouldn't know," Gottliebsohn said.

"There are usually farms around small towns," Glass said. "Around your village too. Have you ever visited a farm?"

"I don't remember."

"If you ever stood in a barnyard you'd remember," Glass said. "Can you try, right now, to visualize a barnyard?"

"I couldn't even begin."

"Try," Glass said. "Surely you at least have an idea about the smell of a barnyard? Think of manure—the word only —what does it convey to you?"

"Nothing," Gottliebsohn said stubbornly.

Glass touched his palms together and became aware that he was perspiring. He wanted to succeed with this man for more reasons than he was immediately aware of, or cared to think about just now. "Will it take a Jew to help you then?" he asked, at last.

"I'm not sure I understand," Gottliebsohn said, honestly puzzled.

"Will only a Jew do?" Glass asked harshly. "Do you really think a Jew would have more insight into what is blocking your memory than a gentile?"

"Yes," Gottliebsohn said. "Of course."

"I am a Jew," Glass said.

Gottliebsohn stared. Glass wondered at his own coolness; because he had found it necessary, for the first time in his professional life, to identify himself in order to make progress with a patient, what had he expected—a peal of thunder and a lightning bolt, earthquake and a great wind, the stillness of a final peace?

"It is true," Glass said, more easily now that he had made the admission. "What must I do to prove it to you?"

"You don't look it," Gottliebsohn said doubtfully, trying to reconcile what he had believed this other to be with what he was being told.

"Neither do you," Glass said gently, suppressing a sudden wild urge for laughter. He knew it would be hollow and mocking. "Shall we continue then?"

Gottliebsohn nodded reluctantly. He was sensitive enough to know that the other's revelation had not come easily, and the fact that the psychiatrist was going to so much trouble to win his confidence somehow bothered him.

"Look here," Glass said, "there's no use going into this unless you're certain you want to go on."

"How can I be certain about anything?" Gottliebsohn asked miserably.

"Perhaps you should think again about what you may be letting yourself in for," Glass said, remembering his encounters with Auerbach and the captain.

"I have thought about it, night and day, for over twenty-six years," Gottliebsohn said in a sudden rush of emotion, for the first time feeling that this sympathetic man could, and should, be confided in. "Do you have any idea what it's like to have no past? To look into the mirror every morning and to be confronted by the face of a stranger? Most people remember how they looked when they were young; they notice every little change: a new wrinkle, a liver spot, an enlarging mole, a receding hairline, a double chin—but all that happened to me at once. I was born middle-aged. I exist only in the present. I live in a void. I have certain mannerisms, certain habits, but none of them is familiar to me! If I tug my ear I don't know if I tug my ear because my ear itches, or because when I was young I watched my father or my teacher or an older friend tug at *his* ear, and I thought it a mark of thoughtfulness, of intelligence, of savoir-faire, to tug at the ear like that. I only know that I tug, a meaningless gesture. I have a temper, though few people know it—but where do I get it? If I come from a family of tempers I could understand it, even be comfortable with it, not suppress it as I do, but not to have any reference point makes me cringe from myself whenever I want to blow my top. I have no memories. Nothing I can recall makes me sad or wistful or angry or glad—I only know that I am, I exist, but my existence is meaningless, robot-like. I am run from within by a switchboard; no reasoning motivates me. If I hate—and I do hate, Doctor, I hate very well indeed—I cannot discover why this particular emotion shakes me so. I cannot love—don't ask me why—I am afraid to love for fear that my reasons may be dreadful, may be wrong. I tell you, Doctor, I would rather have my past back and suffer whatever punishment that past deserves than to live any longer like this!"

Gottliebsohn was trembling, his face was flushed, he found himself leaning far forward in his chair, practically shouting in the psychiatrist's face. Catching himself up, he sat back, struggling to regain his composure.

Ordinarily Glass would feel little response to a patient's emotional catalogings. Now, however, he was not only sympathetic to Gottliebsohn's plaints, he had actually been moved by them. "Tell me your first memory," he said at last.

"My first?" Gottliebsohn said doubtfully, his voice still shaking.

"What you *do* remember," Glass said, "from as far back as you can."

"It was in Cologne, in 1939, the summer," Gottliebsohn began, once again reexperiencing the familiar ordeal. He then described slowly his emotional state, the run through the damp night stalked by he knew not whom, the imaginary struggle, the dank and gloomy apartment building, the dodging along back alleys to the railroad station. He described the cattle cars with their human cargo, his begging to be let in, and finally his hiding on top one of the cars, being slung off through the dark rain, and his long, painful journey to the Belgian border. At last he stopped.

"And you believe some of that is hallucination?"

Gottliebsohn hesitated. "It was like a nightmare," he said, "everything so confused, with the rain, and the stink of wool—why would I be so conscious of that particular smell?

—as though it leaked from my own pores—"

"When did you first become aware of it?" Glass asked as the other's voice trailed off.

"When I came to myself in the alley," Gottliebsohn said, "I remembered nothing. Not my name, where I was, nothing. I was a blank. I was winded, as if I had run a great distance, and terror-stricken, but whether it was because of something that had just happened or because I found myself without memory, I did not know . . . my nose was stuffed with the wool stink and I looked myself over to see if what I was wearing caused that nauseating reek, but no, I was wearing a cheap cotton suit, nothing there to account for the smell . . ."

"Go on."

"Later, thinking back," Gottliebsohn said, "I thought if there *had* been a struggle, that might account for it. The Nazi soldier, if there was a Nazi soldier, might have been wearing a wool uniform." He stared at Glass. "Doesn't that sound logical?"

"How does it sound to you?" Glass asked.

Gottliebsohn looked suddenly frightened. "I don't think there was any struggle," he said, abruptly reversing himself. "In fact I am certain I imagined it."

Glass said nothing.

Gottliebsohn's face worked. "I've gone over it and over it in my mind," he said, "and I sometimes have difficulty in believing that any of it is real, the whole thing is so like a nightmare!" And shuddering, Gottliebsohn dropped his face in his hands.

Finally when Glass still said nothing, he looked up. "If there *was* a struggle, why should I think I imagined it?"

"You're the only one who can answer that," Glass said.

"Well, I can't answer it," Gottliebsohn said truculently, and clamped his mouth shut.

Glass looked at his notes, and to fill in the hostile silence, circled those words which Gottliebsohn had used more than once. He was not surprised to see how often the word nightmare appeared.

"Would you prefer to talk about your dreams?" Glass asked then, quietly.

Gottliebsohn remained silent. He was afraid to tell this

man about his nighttime terror. Why? This man was trained
in the understanding of dreams, he should welcome the opportunity to have that dreadful enigma explained, and yet
he shrank from explanations, as if somewhere in that half
world lay a terrible secret which he must at all costs keep
hidden.

"I don't dream," Gottliebsohn said.

Glass said nothing.

"Don't you believe me?" Gottliebsohn demanded.

Glass did not respond.

"How is it that you always know when I'm lying?" Gottliebsohn asked then, hopelessly.

Glass looked at him for a moment, debating whether to
adopt the role of omnipotence; he then thumbed open the
dossier to the appropriate section. "According to your
former medical officer," he said, and then quoted: " 'The
insomnia of which patient complained, while certainly ag-
gravated by battle action and the continuous duty-tour
without leave since joining British forces, has, without
doubt, prior (that is, civilian) antecedent.' " He looked up.
"He prescribed chlorpromazine hydrochloride for you. Is
that what you took at the airline terminal when you were
informed of the accusation against you?" Gottliebsohn
nodded. "But you are taking twice the recommended
dosage—that means only one thing, Herr Gottliebsohn, you
have built up a tolerance for this particular drug, a tran-
quilizing drug, as I assume you know. A few pills were
found in the night table at your apartment. Why not the
bathroom, Herr Gottliebsohn? Because your sleep is disturbed, isn't that so? And when you want those pills you
want them fast. What could it be but bad dreams?"

Glass gave the other a few moments to absorb this. And
then he said softly, "It was such a gross, transparent, stupid
lie. And you are none of those things. You wanted me to
know you were lying, isn't that true? Why?"

Gottliebsohn became quite upset—partly because of
how much could be deduced from so seemingly innocuous a
circumstance as pills kept on a night table, but mostly because he was suddenly aware of the conflicting desires
within himself, to know, and not to know. He could no
longer trust himself. He had no sooner vowed to do one
thing than he found himself doing another. And still this

other patiently waited, waited for him to open his mouth, ready to subject him to an experience that was exceedingly painful, and would, he knew, grow frighteningly worse, like a dentist probing without anesthetic ever nearer the root nerve.

"Ordinarily," Glass said, when he saw that Gottliebsohn was going to remain shakenly silent, "I would call our session to a halt, give you time to think things through. But we don't have time! I would think the least we can do, you and I, is to mark off the bounds of your memory. After that you can decide whether you want to continue."

"I exist only in that document," Gottliebsohn said, pointing a trembling finger to the dossier. "There are the boundaries, there in those pages."

"Your dreams are not in this document," Glass said.

Gottliebsohn shivered. How could he explain about that nightmare struggle? He could still smell the rancid sweat of fear pouring off his victim, feel the slippery tendoned neck under his own bleeding hands, clawed by the doomed man, see so clearly the image of himself in the dilated pupils of those bulging eyes—and was sickened by the most awful emotion of all in the sudden fear of his own death. The misshapen face of the man he was strangling became that of his own—his mirror image in those sightless staring eyes became that of someone he did not recognize!

"What is it, Herr Gottliebsohn?" Glass asked, alarmed at the sudden distortion of his patient's face.

Gottliebsohn heard him, and slowly his expression and his breathing returned to normal. "I kill someone in my dream," he said at last. "Three and four times a week I am a murderer!"

"Do you want to tell me about it?" Glass asked.

As Gottliebsohn sat in the thickening silence he saw that it would not do to leave it; besides, he wanted to continue, this listening other had not blanched in the slightest. The only thing was he had to be cautious, lest he reveal something beyond reason or reality. If he went too far . . . he could not decide and made a helpless gesture.

The other came to his assistance. "Perhaps if you described the atmosphere of the dream?" Glass suggested.

"The atmosphere?"

"What is your mood in the dream?" Glass asked. "Most

dream-nightmares are pervaded with gloom and great anxiety. What is the weather? The sun never shines in nightmares. Are you hot or cold, is it windy or still—"

"There is no atmosphere in my dream at first," Gottliebsohn said. "It is like being in limbo."

"And how do you feel about that?" Glass asked. Gottliebsohn did not answer. "No feelings?" Glass asked.

"I am frightened," Gottliebsohn said. "Terribly frightened. And I begin to run. At first I don't know why I'm running, and then it all gets terribly confused. For a while I am being chased and I am frightened, and then it is I who am chasing someone else and I am excited and angry. It changes from moment to moment; I am chasing and suddenly—and I cannot tell you how it comes about—it is I who am fleeing for my very life."

"Where do you run?" Glass asked in a murmur so as not to disturb the beginning flow, but to encourage him so quietly he would not even be aware of him.

"In a kind of tunnel," Gottliebsohn said. "The walls are made of mirrors, black mirrors, wet mirrors, so black and so wet that your reflection in them is always wavering—as if on the verge of disappearing, you know?—but it never does. And that tunnel is endless, so that no matter how hard or how far I run I can never escape him."

"Your reflection?" Glass murmured.

"*Him*," Gottliebsohn said. "Because it isn't a reflection at all, you see?"

The psychiatrist of course did not see, but he kept absolutely still.

"It's someone else, outside the tunnel," Gottliebsohn said. "All this time he's been keeping pace with me. You would think out there in the rain he might slip and fall, but no, he's sure-footed as a goat, and he's right in step. Finally I can stand it no longer and I stop. Out of breath, panting as though my lungs will burst, and I hear an echo of my own breathing, only *his* panting is short and sure, like a train engine in the station which can't wait to get started. I can't tell you how infuriating all this is, to be mocked by your own reflection, and so I turn and reach *into* the reflection, and my arms go straight through, you understand? Out into the rain, where they become immediately drenched up to the elbows, and I grasp him, *me*, securely by the throat, and

I yank him inside with me, where it's dry and I may strangle him at my leisure. I look forward to strangling him, let me tell you. Never in my life have I hated anyone like I hate that black reflection! I reach out and through and yank that reflection inside with me, but while I am doing this *he* is reaching out and through and yanking me out in the rain with *him!* We have each other by the throat; I have him inside, where it's nice and dry, except for my sleeves up to the elbows, and he has *me* outside, where it is pouring cats and dogs, and I immediately become drenched, while he can strangle me in relative comfort—except for his wet sleeves, wet wool sleeves, which scratch my face and fill my nostrils with their sheepskin stink. There is an enormous struggle and I am both places at once, both strangling and being strangled, and in the one instance I am mad with fury and in the other mad with terror, as I feel his life and my life slipping away, and we look into each other's eyes, see each other reflected in the other's eyes, like lovers, like mad lovers! And then, in his eyes, where I am admiring my reflection in an excess of vanity, it is suddenly no longer my reflection I see but that of a stranger. And in that instant, before I can recognize him—for he is somehow familiar—he whom I am strangling dies, and the eyes go blank. I have never known such terror! And in the same instant, he who is strangling me does his job equally well, and I stare terrified into his eyes, where I see myself being strangled by someone I know very well. Just as I am on the verge of identifying him, I am dead!"

Gottliebsohn made a sound like a dry sob. "When I wake up," he said, "I know that I am dead. For without memory I am not much better than a dead man, am I?"

Glass was enormously moved. He shoved the objects on the little table about, opened the dossier, closed it, made some notes—all done to gain time so he might once more adopt the impassive, noncommittal role most suitable to him.

"And you know what I do when I awake?" Gottliebsohn said almost conversationally, as though he wanted to deaden the other's interest, negate the importance of what he had told, "I feel over my face like a blind man, and nothing about my own features is familiar." And then suddenly he was pleading with the psychiatrist. "Why do I do that, do you suppose? What does the dream mean?"

"What do you think it means?" Glass asked.

"Nothing," Gottliebsohn said, caught up short, disappointed and resentful.

"Surely after all these years with that nightmare," Glass said, "you must have some ideas about it."

"I try not to think about it at all," Gottliebsohn said stubbornly.

"Why not?" Glass probed him gently.

Gottliebsohn stared fearfully at the man who had become his inquisitor. "Isn't it obvious?" he asked finally, his voice trembling.

"Nothing is obvious, Herr Gottliebsohn," Glass said.

"I probably did kill someone!" Gottliebsohn cried, and then ducked his head, like a child who expects to be struck for some obscene audacity. "Don't you see?" Gottliebsohn went on when Glass made no comment, his face as impassive as if he had only been told about some minor prank. "It all hangs together. I have these vague memories of a struggle, and then this dream, this nightmare, which is always the same, in which I strangle another person . . ." His voice began quavering but he looked covertly at the psychiatrist to see if he was reacting at all.

"What was your motive?" Glass asked casually.

"Motive?" Gottliebsohn stammered, bewildered and angry.

"But of course, motive," Glass said evenly. "Every killing, even the most seemingly senseless, has a motive. Even when the victim is unknown to the killer and 'happened' to get in his way, we find, if we're lucky enough to get the murderer, that what he has done makes sense to him. The same has to be true in your case."

Gottliebsohn felt a growing numbness. Somewhere in his mind a reason for what he had done began to take shape, but as he cringed from whatever it was his memory stopped.

"Herr Gottliebsohn?" Glass asked, puzzled by the sudden immobility.

Gottliebsohn started, blinked, looked at the doctor, surprised to see him still there. "I am sorry," he said, massaging his forehead, "I seem to have lost track."

Glass was intensely curious about what had just happened to his patient, realizing it had been a crisis of some sort.

"We were discussing what the motive for your dream-killing could be," he said.

"My *dream*-killing?" Gottliebsohn said, bewildered. He had made what amounted to a confession of crime and the other was not accepting it.

"The struggle is only supposition," Glass pointed out. "The only thing tangible we have is your dream. It is there we must look."

Gottliebsohn licked his lips, which were suddenly dry. Was it to lead the other *away* from his dream that he had made such a point about what could have happened? And now they were back where for some unknown but deeply felt reason he dreaded being more than anything.

"I remember no motives," Gottliebsohn said finally.

"But you had feelings," Glass said. He glanced at his notes. "You were frightened, excited, angry, you say. What about?"

Gottliebsohn made an unknowing gesture.

"You were upset enough to kill," Glass mused. "The . . . other . . . must have done something extraordinarily awful to make you as angry as all that. Let's explore that for a moment. What would make you angry enough to kill?"

Again Gottliebsohn massaged his brow, trying to make his mind work, but his head ached and nothing would come.

"Then tell me this," Glass continued, when he saw that Gottliebsohn was either unable or unwilling to answer, "what is the feeling you have toward your . . . victim . . . now?"

Gottliebsohn stared at this clairvoyant other. How had Glass known about an emotion so deep that even he who possessed it had been unaware of its existence until this very moment when that question, like some dreadful incantation, had brought it to life? He wondered whether he would ever dare voice it. Then he heard himself, unbelievingly, stating the awful fact aloud.

"Hate," Gottliebsohn said. His voice was shaking. "It is hatred I feel." And he shrank back, expecting a look or a gesture or a word of condemnation.

But Glass was not even surprised. "And you don't know who he is?" he asked. Gottliebsohn shook his head hopelessly.

Glass hesitated. He could guess at the fear that lurked in the clouded mind of his patient. The man believed he was guilty—of something. Before he chanced defining it for him, however, he should first eliminate alternate possibilities. "You have been decorated for heroism," Glass began slowly. "During your army service did you ever personally kill anyone?"

Gottliebsohn nodded.

"And how did you feel about it?" Glass asked.

"They were the enemy," Gottliebsohn said, shrugging.

"You feel no remorse?" Glass pressed.

"They were Germans and Arabs," Gottliebsohn said.

"What about the rebellion?" Glass asked. "Didn't you fight the British? Didn't you participate in terrorist activities?"

"No, never," Gottliebsohn said. "I saw action only with the official resistance units. I could never have killed a Tommy deliberately."

His dismay seemed real, Glass thought. And there then went Attorney Levin's contention that there had been something odd about Gottliebsohn's desertion from British forces, as if a pattern was to have been revealed, or something spiteful, a turnabout on his benefactors.

"Isn't it possible," Glass wondered, "that you feel subconsciously guilty about killing the English? And that those you have killed come back in your nightmare to haunt you, which would explain your great anxiety and your anger, which cause you to kill them all over again?"

Gottliebsohn did not even have to think about it. "No," he said. "It's nothing like that."

"I didn't think that it was," Glass said. And then, at Gottliebsohn's look of surprise, "but I had to make sure."

While Gottliebsohn was trying to puzzle out the behavior of this strange doctor who went first one direction and then another, Glass was worrying about how best to approach his patient with a preliminary diagnosis. He was aware that the position he had been taking was uncomfortably close to that of an interrogator—which, while it might bring them more quickly to a dramatic breakthrough, could also have unsettling consequences.

"Let us stay with your dream," he said carefully, and was not surprised to see his patient blanch. "In your dream you kill someone. Someone for whom you still, even in your waking hours, feel hate. Is that accurate?"

Gottliebsohn nodded reluctantly.

"And how was it you described your . . . antagonist?"

Gottliebsohn frowned. What was the other getting at? He had given no description—the other was faceless . . .

"Where do you first see him?" Glass asked, aware of his patient's bewilderment.

"In the tunnel," Gottliebsohn said. "In the mirror tiles. When I first saw him, I thought he was"—Glass nodded encouragingly, and Gottliebsohn finished in a rush—"a reflection of myself!"

"Is it possible," Glass said, "that it is indeed yourself whom you are strangling, that it is yourself whom you hate so violently, that what gives you this murderous impulse to strangle yourself is some wrong you have committed, some wrong which seems so awful to your conscience that you have killed your memory to atone for it?"

Both men's breathing could be heard in the sudden quiet. They stared at each other, doctor and patient, while the full portent of what had been said became even more clear to both.

"Shall I continue?" Glass asked.

Gottliebsohn nodded, dumbly.

"You have confused dream and reality in your mind," Glass went on, "not at all unusual, except that in your case it has reached a point where it is drastically inhibiting your mental processes. Because you believe that you *are* guilty of some act that society, or yourself, or both consider reprehensible, you have mistakenly assumed that the dream-killing is a real one." He paused to give Gottliebsohn an opportunity for dissent, but the other only continued to stare. "By your own admission," Glass went on, "you have killed men in the past, and those killings do not disturb you. Because, as you say, they were Germans, and Germans deserved to be killed. By your own admission you feel no remorse for the killing to which you confessed. You still feel hatred for your victim. My friend, do you truly believe that is the guilt for which we are searching?" Glass paused again, momentarily uncertain of just how far he might safely go with the other. And then, remembering how little time they actually had, he pushed caution aside. "Tell me, Ernst," he said. "Was that confession not designed to throw us *both* off the track?"

Gottliebsohn could not deny it, as much as he wanted to. Again, the fear of some awful secret the dream held inundated him, leaving him weak and trembling inside. It was possible, he thought. But when he tried to nod his agreement he found that he could not do that either.

"If you're upset about leading me—us—astray, don't be," Glass said, guessing at the conflicting feelings which left his patient understandably immobile. "We've accomplished a good deal. We now know that you have a conscience larger and more vulnerable than most men's. And yet, at the same time, it is a typical conscience. Some kinds of killing hardly affect it at all. I do not fault you for that. War is the great excuse in which it is not only permissible but praiseworthy to indulge every hostility. I think we can eliminate killing as your ... problem."

Gottliebsohn was listening raptly, not sure whether that surge of feeling within himself was relief or a new fear.

"What we must look for now," Glass continued, "are those things which *would* bother your conscience. What troubles you more than anything else?"

"The accusation," Gottliebsohn said finally, morose and reluctant.

"Is it possible," Glass asked, now equally hesitant, "that you have been a collaborator? And that such a ... a ... an *offense* against morality was, is, so repugnant to you that you have killed all remembrance of it in your mind?"

Gottliebsohn paled. He felt suddenly faint, and he touched his trembling fingers to the sweat that suddenly edged his hairline. He shook his head weakly. "Do you think I have not gone over the possibility in my mind a hundred times since the accusation?" he said. "And I tell you that no matter what the provocation or the reward, to save my family or myself and to become wealthy into the bargain would not be enough to bring me to do so despicable an act!"

"How do you know?" Glass wondered, hiding his uneasiness at the vehemence of the reaction.

"Because I hate them too much!" Gottliebsohn cried.

"Then the same as now?" Glass asked.

Gottliebsohn slumped in his chair. How could he answer? He had no memory. "I am not the kind of a man who could collaborate," he said finally.

"What kind of a man are you?" Glass asked.

Gottliebsohn became extraordinarily depressed. "I don't know," he said.

"But you're not absolutely blank, you know," Glass said. "There are certain clues in the way you live, what you do that you're proud of, and those things of which you are ashamed . . ." His voice trailed off as he became aware that his patient had stiffened, was now alert and worried, staring at the dossier which the doctor was inadvertently handling.

"What do you know about how I live?" Gottliebsohn asked.

"Well, for one thing," Glass said, "I visited your flat." He watched the other closely, but saw no signs of any resentment; indeed, Gottliebsohn felt none; he was worried about what might be in the dossier. "You are an excellent photographer," Glass went on. "Why did you give it up?"

"After the protest in the office," he said finally, "I saw for the first time what I was doing. And I knew that I had no right to catch people like that. Its almost . . . indecent."

"Oh?" Glass said.

"People have a right to privacy," Gottliebsohn went on more strongly, wanting the other to understand. "If they act a part in public that is different from what they really are, what business is it of mine?"

"And so you put your cameras away?" Glass said. "Couldn't you have changed your style . . . ?"

"I tried," Gottliebsohn said, "but it was no use. It seemed I always pressed the shutter when the subject was off guard. I didn't realize it until the film was developed—and there it would be, the mask down, the inside man peeping out."

Not unlike the patient himself, Glass thought, making a note. He was enough afraid of *his* inner man that he had mentally killed him off. It seemed another proof of the analysis.

"What else did you find?" Gottliebsohn asked, eying the dossier again.

"It wasn't so much what we found," Glass said, remembering Levin's observation, "as what we didn't find." He hesitated, then decided it would not hurt to ask. "There seems to be an absence of mirrors in your place?"

Gottliebsohn made do with a half truth. "The one in the medicine cabinet broke," he said. "I never bothered to get it replaced."

It seemed an obvious enough answer, Glass thought—perhaps too much so—but he didn't want to chance their hard-won relationship by showing doubt.

"What is in there?" Gottliebsohn asked then, pointing to the dossier, unable finally to restrain his curiosity.

"How you look to others," Glass said. "You remember, I said we had interviewed those who knew you . . ."

"And what did they tell you?" Gottliebsohn asked, desperately anxious.

"That you keep to yourself," Glass said. "That you are neat, orderly and well mannered, seem uninterested in any meaningful relationships with women, and except for your weekends away from your apartment, you live an exemplary, if solitary life."

Gottliebsohn paled. "You know about the weekends?"

"There has been an investigation," Glass reminded him.

Gottliebsohn stared, trying to gather from that impassive face how much the other knew. But the doctor regarded him steadily, and he saw that the only way he could find out was to ask.

"Do you know where I go on those weekends?" Gottliebsohn asked, trying to be casual and failing.

Glass nodded.

"But how could you?" Gottliebsohn demanded. "I told no one—no one—where I go. And I never gave my name . . ." He paused, remembering what he had once suspected. "I was followed, wasn't I?" he said then. The doctor nodded. "Miss Gronski," Gottliebsohn said. He had thought that might have been she inside the café on the afternoon she had brought him the supper, though he had not even considered that she would follow him, and therefore had taken no precautions. But the following Monday in the office, her attitude had been much stronger than was called for by his refusal of her company. That poor woman, he thought, shrinking inwardly as he pictured her distress. He could not blame her for telling what she knew; to have cooked such an elaborate meal, the hours she must have spent on the casserole and those delicate pastries, only to have him refuse her company *and* the food. How could he have explained to her that he wanted no attachments? No question but that he was clumsy about dealing with people. If she had only let him know she meant to come. But he was so startled by her sudden appearance he had been unable even to do the gracious thing . . .

Gottliebsohn sighed and began fumbling in his coat pockets.

"What is it?" Glass asked, puzzled by the other's behavior. He had expected some kind of outburst, perhaps a denunciation of the informer, and instead his patient looked as if he might in a moment weep.

"My pills," Gottliebsohn said faintly.

"Try and hold off a bit longer," Glass said. "We've been through a lot together already. Surely we can go this last little distance . . ."

Gottliebsohn stopped his search.

"Tell me about your Arab women," Glass said.

Gottliebsohn could not bring himself to look at the psychiatrist. "I am too ashamed," he said finally.

"Ashamed?" Glass asked. "Of what? Of going or of being found out?"

Gottliebsohn could not, or would not, answer.

"Why do you go to Arab women?" Glass asked.

"A man must have some release, mustn't he?" Gottliebsohn murmured. "And better them, where there is no possibility . . ."

"Finish your thought," Glass said, as Gottliebsohn fell silent. The other did not reply. "Possibility of what?" Glass asked, gentle but urgent.

"I don't know," Gottliebsohn said then, bewildered and upset. "Just as I was about to say—whatever it was—my tongue seemed swollen and numb!"

Gottliebsohn was terribly shaken. The thought which had come out of the blankness in which he had been groping had been so intolerably blinding, like lightning at dark, that his mind had closed against it, and a moment later, when he had wanted to think what it was, he could not remember. It had to do with some act, or prior thought, of so forbidden a nature that it was, quite literally, unthinkable.

Gottliebsohn fumbled in his pockets again, found what he was after, and looked imploring at the doctor.

"Take your pills," Glass said. He watched, no longer trying to hide his concern, as Gottliebsohn swallowed the pills dry. The case, which had seemed on the verge of becoming clear, had suddenly become complex. He was not sure where it had taken its sudden turn—he would have to go back over his notes for that—but he was sure that somewhere he had missed the point. As he observed the downcast figure opposite him, Glass wondered if his patient was not on the verge of a breakdown. How severe it would be if it came was a matter of conjecture, of course, and though he cautioned himself against overdramatizing the situation, Glass could not help believing that it might be of psychotic intensity.

Did he have any right to take this man any further? He was not a citizen of Israel, not enough of a Jew to be able to judge a crime against other Jews—or even enough of a man to judge a crime against humanity. He thought briefly of Auerbach and his offer to take the responsibility, then pushed that tempting proposal out of his mind.

"Let me be quite frank with you," he said. "It might be best all around if we put a stop to this right now."

"I don't understand," Gottliebsohn said.

"Amnesia is not a condition one picks up gradually," Glass said slowly. "The amnesia victim suffers from a violent shock of some kind, either emotional, or physical, or a combination of both. Now none of your records indicates that you suffered from shell shock or battle fatigue." He waited for confirmation and Gottliebsohn finally murmured an agreement. "We must assume, therefore," Glass continued, "that your amnesia has only emotional cause, some incident or series of incidents so mind-shocking that the memory circuits closed down. All communications between the past and the present, the subconscious and the conscious, between the kind of person you were then and the kind you are now, have been shut off. Your reluctance to reopen communications may be well founded. Finding out what you are hiding from yourself—what you are lying to yourself about—may have equally mind-shocking consequences for you now."

Gottliebsohn pushed himself up in his chair. "Are you warning me about something, Doctor?" he asked.

"If we break through too suddenly, too dramatically," Glass said, "before you are conditioned to handle the information, it could lead to the kind of complications that would leave you unfit for society, incapable of performing normally."

Gottliebsohn tried to absorb what he was being told. "You think the accusation against me is true," he said finally, "and you are trying to protect me, is that it?"

Glass wondered how it was that the other could so readily assume a conspiracy between them. Were his forebodings so obvious? "I am speaking only as a medical man, nothing more. What happens to you outside this room cannot concern me." For a moment he believed himself, and then he knew that he lied. He kept silent nevertheless.

"Co-Director Auerbach is convinced that I am innocent," Gottliebsohn said. "And he has explained how important it is for me to be cleared."

"For the sake of the mission?" Glass wondered noncommittally.

Gottliebsohn stared. What was the man implying? That his attitude was a fiction? But why *had* he agreed to come here to Germany? Why *had* he permitted himself to be used for purposes for which he had nothing but disgust? He tried to shake away the unspoken argument. He could not manipulate his figures. The figures were unimpeachable, were the only verity in a world full of confusion and mistrust. And yet, how neatly the cold unassailable figures could be used to prove the political point, how easily the economics could be made to seem inevitable. And when would the Germans decide to slaughter again? Was there anything he could do to stop them?

"None of this is my doing," he said. He hesitated, frowning. "You don't think because I am working with them now it proves anything about the past?"

"I make no comparisons," Glass said. "Only you can do that."

Gottliebsohn struck his fists together so hard the pain traveled to his shoulders. "I was never a collaborator," he said. "I will prove it to you, Doctor. Let us continue!"

"I can't answer for the consequences," Glass said slowly.

"I have trust in you," Gottliebsohn said—and he did.

Glass believed him. But he was not flattered, recognizing the statement for what it was: subtle transference of responsibility. Perhaps it was time, he thought, to remind the other that they were not alone in this.

"Are you aware of what sort of procedures you are going to be involved with now?" he asked. "Captain Kohn wants to try more physical means of jogging your memory. He is planning a visit with you to the scene of your . . . wanderings . . . in Cologne."

After a long moment Gottliebsohn nodded understandingly, though his stomach twisted in disbelief. Why should he be so afraid of what was upon due reflection a necessary step?

"When you return," Glass continued, "we will have another session. I'll want you to tell me your reaction to everything you find there—leaving nothing out, mind—whether it's in the present, or a past memory. Don't worry about where it all fits, that will come later. Just remember I can't see into your head . . ."

"But surely you're coming too?" Gottliebsohn asked in a sudden panic.

Now it was Glass who was startled. He had assumed that he would conduct his end of the investigation in the usual manner, getting Gottliebsohn's evaluation of the events after they took place, then comparing his reactions to what Kohn had to say.

"I'm afraid of him," Gottliebsohn murmured then. "I know it's stupid of me, but there's something about him—if you came along I'd do better, I know."

Gottliebsohn was pleading, though he kept his dignity. Glass tried to steel himself against the other's silent importuning. What could he do? It was Kohn's area; he would not be pleased to have someone along liable to second-guess him. Glass saw how genuine was the other's fear.

"I'll bring it up to the captain, see what he says," Glass said at last.

Gottliebsohn's relief was instantaneous. Again it seemed that his patient assumed he had taken on his burden. He would accept it, Glass thought, but only momentarily—at the appropriate time he would, as he must, shift it back. He stood, as a signal that the interview was over.

Gottliebsohn stood too, feeling muscles that, from his grimaces, must be cramped and stiff from tension. The pills, however, would soon do their job—and Glass wondered whether giving them to him had been a good idea. It might be better to let that tension build.

Thinking over the alternatives of procedure, Glass went through the anteroom to the bedroom door. He knocked; there was no answer. Opening the door he was momentarily surprised. Kohn was not where he had left him. And then he saw him, on the bed, apparently asleep.

"Captain Kohn!" Glass said sharply, and the slight figure immediately responded, drawing his legs up, twisting to face the doorway as if he expected to be attacked.

"Oh, sorry," Kohn said, grinning when he saw who it was, glad that he had not drawn the gun he had automatically reached for. He elaborately stifled a yawn. "In my line we try to get a few winks whenever we can. Never know when there might be days on end without it."

After he had finished reading the dossier, he had tried to listen through the door, but heard only vague mumblings. Finally the combination of the heavy lunch, the many beers and the long wait got to him, and he had succumbed to the temptation of the bed. He looked at his watch; swore to himself. "We'll have to hustle now." He bent down to put on his shoes and asked, almost too casually, "Make any progress?"

"I believe so," Glass said, wondering how best to bring up the subject of the trip.

"You going to tell me about it?" Kohn asked. "Well?" he said belligerently when Glass did not answer.

"That depends," Glass said carefully. "I've been thinking about your plans for Cologne, and that it might be a good idea if I came along too."

Kohn nodded thoughtfully. But he was not ready to answer. "Is he guilty or not?" he demanded.

"Of what?" Glass countered. "The collaboration? He says not; and somehow I believe him—but that's him *now*, not him *then*. He has done *something* of which he is terribly ashamed." He hesitated. "You're looking for what he may have done. I'm looking for what he was as a person. Maybe, by putting the two looks together, we can come up with answers for each of us."

"Well now, that's what I suggested in the first place," Kohn said, grinning broadly, though he was worried that this headknocker may have gotten Gottliebsohn to tell him about that "crime," and after he had promised to keep it just between them.

"I know," Glass said, as if it were an admission of a mistake.

Kohn licked his fingers and smoothed his hair on each side of the part. He thought it might not hurt to have the psychiatrist along; in fact, the pressure on the suspect might be redoubled.

"I had always planned for you to go, Doctor," Kohn lied, elaborately casual. "Can you be ready by seven tomorrow morning?" And without waiting for an answer, he went on into the other room.

Kohn looked at Gottliebsohn curiously; except for a kind of paleness, a tinge of green about the gills, he looked as if he had weathered his ordeal well enough. Kohn wondered briefly how he himself might behave with an arrogant outsider probing his secret motives, thumping at his head like a clairvoyant phrenologist. Then, irritably, he dismissed such thoughts as diminishing the kind of toughness he must keep if he was to stay on top in this rapidly changing world.

"You look like you could use a drink," he said.

"No . . . no," Gottliebsohn said. "I must get to my work. But you're welcome to whatever's left."

Kohn became suddenly angry that one of his habits may have thus casually come to the attention of the listening psychiatrist—habits, as a precautionary measure of his occupation, should always be hidden. However, he let neither of them see that he was disturbed.

"That's quite generous of you, old man," he said. "But I've satisfied my thirst. Besides, by the time you're through being bounced around between this fellow and myself, you may need it yourself." And with a falsely cheery wave to Glass to push home the point to the watchful Gottliebsohn that they were working together, and taking a policeman's grip on his arm to remind everyone that he never forgot his first duty, he escorted his captive out the door.

7

"IT BOTHERS ME THAT THEY SHOULD have brought such a person as Captain Kohn along as part of their mission; yes, I know what they said—he is here as an observer, he is being groomed for diplomatic tasks—somehow that answer is not an answer, it smacks of evasiveness; yet how can I even suggest to Hortsky that I do not believe him?" Bettmann was obviously not expecting comment, and neither Professor Schenke nor Baron von Haupt made any.

The two men sat uneasily in Bettmann's office, not understanding why they had been chosen to attend so intimate a meeting about so touchy a subject; Schenke, it was true, had raised the original question about Kohn's presence, but after subsequently reporting Kohn's answer, he had thought his part would remain on that much lower level. Von Haupt, aware of his own dubious credentials so far as Bettmann was concerned, thought almost anyone on the German delegation should have been preferred to himself. But they remained silent, knowing that Bettmann would in his own good time make it all clear to them—or as much of it as he thought they should know, he being a notoriously close-mouthed man.

Bettmann, for his part, was not at all certain that what he had in mind was such a good idea. But he did not see that he had any choice. He was committed to the success of the negotiation, had indeed been optimistic about reaching a dramatic final accommodation—until Schenke's disquieting report on the possible purposes of the presence of that assassin. Yes, assassin, Bettmann repeated to himself. No matter what the moral justifications, his hunting down of war criminals was outside the rule of law, and Bettmann had an acknowledged-master-of-bureaucratic-techniques respect for law. Even Hitler, that lunatic Austrian, had understood how necessary it was for Germans, and had been careful to work within a legal framework. But these Jews were not so respectful of rules.

Other pressures were working against him, too. His wife had pointed out an article in the paper this morning, quoting a speech by a high-placed politician arguing that Germans and Jews should keep their distance—let time, and not action, heal the wounds. It was a persuasive argument and Bettmann could see why many Jews as well as his own people might be quick to accept it. But they were not so sensitive as he to the disturbing trends in the nation. The recent elections in Bavaria and Hesse in which the right-wing party got an amazing near ten per cent of the vote were an indication of how close to the surface a certain fanaticism remained. Partly, of course, that vote indicated a continuing resentment against a divided Germany, against the United States for abandoning what Germans had believed would be a permanent alliance against the Russians—in short, a refusal to accept a situation whereby West Germany remained a small, relatively powerless country. He could understand the longing, even be sympathetic to it, but it was not realistic; only by Germany's demonstrating to itself, and to the world, that it had given up any dreams of power, could the nation become whole again, psychologically as well as geographically. But other politicians were not interested in such long-term and subtle outlooks—they were playing to the fanatics; if they succeeded, the right wing would be brought into the federal government itself—and there would go Germany's last chance to come to terms with its past. If he were unsuccessful here the field might well be left to his, and Germany's enemies.

Bettmann looked distastefully at the man he had been forced to take as a delegation member, and who was perhaps responsible for the presence of Kohn. The long wavy hair, the hauteur of the pale-eyed glance, even the ribbon that ran from his lapel to the monocle in his breast pocket, were all affirmations of an attitude that the other disdained to hide, even knowing, as he must, how offensive this was to the head of delegation. One would expect a dueling scar, Bettmann thought, that other arrogant mark of class, but for some reason Von Haupt, though he came from a military family, had not gone to Heidelberg, preferring more leisurely academics. It was said that he was brilliant, far more intellectual than many of the Ministers under whom he had served, but that a distaste for the rough and tumble of politics kept him from the position which might have been his. Bettmann had realized that it would not be easy to force him into a corner, which was why he had asked Schenke to be present.

Not that he could expect any overt help. Professor Doktor Schenke was a civil servant, not a politician, and though his goals met with Bettmann's wholehearted favor, Bettmann had been given no reason to believe the feeling was reciprocated. It was true that Schenke, while assigned to the German negotiating team, was theoretically under Bettmann's jurisdiction, but it did not follow that he would do anything that was asked of him—particularly since what Bettmann would have liked to ask fell under the heading of confidential material, material that might, if revealed, be of some practical, if scandalous, use to a politician like himself. What he was counting on, therefore, was the hope that Schenke's presence, given the nature of his occupation, would be sufficient to threaten the peace of mind of the Baron von Haupt.

Lighting an enormous cigar, his political trademark, as if that cloud of smoke might also cloud his intentions, Bettmann plunged ahead on the only course that seemed open to him.

"It could be that my concerns are groundless," he said. "Their captain might be here legitimately; he might be here on an assignment outside the mission, using it as a convenience. But I think we had better operate on the contrary assumption. I have brought you gentlemen here to help me evaluate the various possibilities; Doktor Schenke, for obvious reason; Herr von Haupt—"

"*Baron*," Von Haupt corrected mildly.

"For reasons that will become plain in a moment," Bettmann went on, ignoring the interruption. "Doktor Schenke, would you be good enough to give us your thinking?"

Schenke nodded, reluctantly. He was not too pleased about the situation in which he found himself. He had not missed the little exchange—he was aware of the political antagonisms behind Von Haupt's appointment; he had no place in such quarrels. He must keep his bureau outside politics. Whatever party was in power, the bureau must survive, and it was important that he survive too. Only a man like himself could fully protect Germany's honor. A less discreet individual could literally bring chaos to the nation, permanently damage its moral nature.

"It seems to me," Schenke began very cautiously, trying to make out Bettmann's features through the haze of smoke, "that they would hardly bring him along on so important a mission if he were merely after someone in Germany."

"Go on," Bettmann said, as Schenke paused.

Schenke glanced at Von Haupt, somewhat intimidated by the other's presence. But when the other merely raised his eyebrows, he shrugged and went on. "It is likely that whoever Captain Kohn is after—if he is after anyone—is on the delegation."

There was a little silence.

"But surely our delegation has been thoroughly checked?" Von Haupt asked finally.

Bettmann puffed at his cigar, then turned an inquiring look on Schenke. "And has our delegation been checked?" he asked.

"Not specifically," Schenke said after a moment, "but then, no one asked that this be done . . ."

"Precisely," Bettmann said. "There was no need, or at least so I thought. I know the backgrounds of most of our members personally. In those few instances where I do not —such as yours, Baron von Haupt—I had assumed that the other . . . sponsors . . . would have satisfied themselves as to the . . . purity . . . of their appointees."

Von Haupt stared at him. He was beginning to understand why Bettmann had included him at this meeting. "Surely you are aware that I was one of the first to be cleared after the war?" he murmured.

"Of course," Bettmann said. "But you were a rather prominent member of the hierarchy, were you not?"

"I never belonged to the party," Von Haupt said contemptuously.

"But you had something to do with factory labor allotments?" Bettmann asked.

Again Von Haupt paused. "Such things were in my department," he admitted finally. "It was a bureaucratic matter," he went on, though ordinarily he would have disdained to explain himself. "We processed requests, then made labor available by quota—many of those who were chosen to work survived," he concluded rather lamely.

"I would appreciate it if you would tell Baron von Haupt what you told me about Captain Kohn," Bettmann said, turning to Schenke.

Schenke moistened his lips. "His specialty," he said reluctantly, "is going after men who have somehow avoided being brought to judgment. He has gone after those with clearances before. If in his opinion the court has been too lenient, or if they have ignored what *he* considers crimes, he may take them as legitimate quarry."

"And you think that he is after me, is that it?" Von Haupt asked, after a moment, of Bettmann.

Bettmann shrugged. "I don't know who he is after," he said.

"You think they would risk the mission . . . ?" Von Haupt began incredulously.

"Who is the *they* you speak of?" Bettmann interrupted impatiently. "Not all Jews want this mission to succeed. We know that Kohn's superiors are almost pathologically opposed. We can assume that Kohn shares those sentiments."

"But how could he possibly be assigned to their mission then?" Von Haupt protested.

"Surely we know how easy that can be," Bettmann said pointedly.

Von Haupt became silent.

"Please do not misunderstand me, Baron," Bettmann said. "I am not accusing you of war crimes, no, nothing so grand. In the first place, I have no right to question you; in the second, I have no specific information—nothing but that . . . investigator's presence. But as the one responsible for the German position, I can afford to overlook nothing. Including the possibility that this mission is a diversionary tactic. The Israeli government may prefer hard cash to this 'accommodation' with us—there are, after all, many previous demands that were turned down by us; perhaps they mean to embarrass us into giving them—"

"The mission diversionary?" Von Haupt said. "Come, you can't believe that!"

"Can't I?" Bettmann said sourly. "Politics can be as insanely childish as the people who are involved in them."

Von Haupt said nothing, but the expression on his face revealed his doubt.

"I don't think it unlikely that some Jews," Bettmann said, "upset with our new Chancellor and his former membership in the party, no matter that he was an underling, may wish to symbolize their displeasure by attacking someone else, someone reasonably high up, unbeknownst to the others, perhaps."

"But wouldn't the others be suspicious of the captain?" Von Haupt asked finally.

"It depends on what they have been told," Bettmann said. "That is what I need to know before I can approach Hortsky about it. Even then . . ." He hesitated; the time had come. "Baron," he said formally, "you are the only one now with any contact with the Israeli mission. Your meeting with Herr Gottliebsohn this evening is the only one scheduled. Do you think you might feel your opposite out; see how sincere they are about their mission; see if he has any unofficial knowledge about the real purpose behind the captain's presence?"

Von Haupt was not a little surprised, though he kept his imperturbable attitude. He could appreciate the irony of the situation in which he found himself. What better man for this task than one whose self-interest gave a singular urgency to the quest? The implication that it might be himself they were after was the only thing that made it possible for Bettmann to even make the request, knowing that he was an ally of a political enemy. Whatever he found would be kept quite confidential.

Von Haupt permitted himself a brief smile. "I will try," he said finally.

Bettmann sighed, lay his cigar down, fanned the smoke from his face. "What kind of a man is this Herr Gottliebsohn?" he asked then, his pleasure at having accomplished what he had set out to do replaced by a new anxiety. "Can he be drawn out, do you think?"

Von Haupt shrugged. "He's not overly chatty, speaks only when spoken to, that sort of thing. He's a German, you know. I get the feeling that he doesn't care much about being here. A melancholy type, taken all in all."

Bettmann nodded glumly. "You were never investigated by our own War Crimes Bureau?" he asked.

"Not to my knowledge," Von Haupt said, pretending to be amused. He looked to Schenke.

"Nor to mine," Schenke said hastily.

"Why would you not know about it?" Bettmann asked.

"There is always a huge lot of unevaluated information in our files," Schenke said.

"I would personally appreciate your looking for any evidence," Von Haupt said, anticipating Bettmann's request.

Taking out his monocle, a sign of his disdain for whatever jeopardy these two assumed he might be in, Von Haupt took his time screwing it into his eye.

"Good luck to you," Bettmann said.

"I appreciate your confidence," Von Haupt said dryly, and giving each of them a little bow, he left.

When Kohn got back to his room that evening after leaving Gottliebsohn in the conference room with Von Haupt, and after a quick trip to the ornate, restfully dark hotel bar, he found a letter from Attorney Levin:

Captain Kohn:
The Interior Minister has asked me to convey to you his official regards, and his continuing personal interest in the case of Gottliebsohn. He has asked me to establish the proviso that he be kept absolutely current on whatever progress, or lack of it, is being made. Do I make myself clear as to the Minister's concern?

For my part, I have always made it a practice to operate in an open, above-board manner—the search for truth and justice can only be hampered when men conduct themselves like adversaries—but I am aware that in this case some of the personal motives involved may have clouded the situation, and given its importance, I caution you to conduct yourself with your usual circumspection. When, for example, you proceed in the direction I shall outline for you now, I would suggest that at this early date it need not concern Mission Co-Director Auerbach, who already must be heavily burdened with the thousand and one details of the negotiation. As for the American psychiatrist Glass, with whom you have been instructed to work very closely, while it is true that he has been given the privilege of pursuing an independent course, in my opinion the nature of his inquiry bears little relationship to our own. Therefore, exercise restraint as to how closely you take him into your confidence.

When you have looked at the dossier you will note that much of it is concerned with what may have taken place in Cologne in 1939. We are confronted here, from a legal standpoint, with testimony that any court in the world would rule out as untrustworthy—*as it now stands*. However, were we to come up with corroborating evidence, hard, specific evidence, we may be able to confront our man with the kind of factual material that will serve to loose his tongue (or his memory, if he has actually lost it). In any case, we should be able to at least remove him from a position of responsibility.

What we must do, therefore, is to get hold of German records for that period. With their known reputation as archivists, it is quite likely that a great deal of data may have been stored by them. At Ludwigsburg, as you know, is the West German Center for the Investigation of Nazi Crimes. Professor Schenke could make the pertinent records at that Center available. He is not likely to do so, however, unless you can assure him that it is not a German we are after. (It would be best if you never had to reveal who our man is, but we leave that to your discretion, and the continuing circumstances.) You must find out how devoted Schenke is to his stated duty, and what he may consider his responsibility to his own people. We can sympathize with such conflicts, for we find ourselves with similar problems; but our problems, of course, come first. How can it be otherwise?

Good luck. I look forward to hearing from you at your earliest convenience.

Levin

cc: Chief Interior Ministry

Kohn cursed aloud. He reread the letter, slapped his lank thighs in exasperation, paced up and down, then picked up the bottle on the bedstand and took a healthy swallow. He had not meant to touch Gottliebsohn's bottle—that was why he had stopped in the bar, still irked that the psychiatrist may have picked up Gottliebsohn's reference to his drinking habits—but he needed the drink.

The whiskey soothed him, and he sat on the bed again to reread Levin's letter. The message had alarmed him. He had thought they were aware, somehow, of his "arrangement" with Auerbach. But it became obvious on rereading that the warnings were precautionary only. Now that he looked at it more calmly, coolly, he saw an advantage here for him. Should matters not work out as Auerbach wished, he, Kohn, would still be on excellent terms with the people in his own department. Now that he thought about it, being here on the spot, being able to take advantage of the situation which-ever way it turned, was a stroke of the best kind of luck. On the one hand, with Auerbach, he had as much as been prom-ised a very top-ranking job. On the other hand, through Levin and the Interior Minister, should things go their way with an appropriate assist from him at the right moment, when the scales were tipping in their direction, his reward might, in the new government that would have to be formed after the failure of the mission, be of equal importance.

Kohn smiled to himself, his good humor restored. He looked at the almost empty bottle. Not a bad sort, Gottlieb-sohn, he thought. He would have to buy the fellow another bottle on his next trip out.

Reaching for the phone, he asked the operator to locate Professor Schenke, probably at his chancellory office. It took a little while, but his luck held.

"Schenke here," the dry voice on the other end of the line announced.

Kohn took a silent breath and began his part in that undertaking which might prove the most hazardous of his notorious career—certainly it was the most treacherous: one slip, and he could lose everything he had worked all his life for. "Captain Kohn on this end, Professor," he said. "I was wondering whether we might not have a drink together." There was a brief silence, Schenke no doubt startled by the sudden request. "With everyone else involved in meetings and what not," Kohn went on, "I find myself rather at loose ends. I thought it time to get better acquainted, maybe compare notes. Who knows, we may be able to pick up a thing or two from each other on how we run our separate operations."

"But certainly, Captain," the guttural voice came then. "Where would you like to meet?"

"At Ria's," Kohn said, naming a bar where diplomats gathered. "It's a pleasant place and with us getting together, convivial-like, in plain sight, there's no reason for anyone to think we might be up to something."

"Why should anyone think that?" Schenke asked after a moment's pause.

"Twenty minutes?" Kohn asked. And when the other agreed, he hung up. Let the fat heine stew for a bit, he thought. Let his mind simmer with the dozens of possibilities as to why he might have asked for a meeting; when he finally made his request known it would seem, by comparison with the no doubt boiling Germanic imaginings, so innocuous that he might be granted the records without undue delay or hesitation.

Twenty minutes later, Kohn strolled casually into the bar; Professor Schenke stood up and motioned to him from a table near the back. It was a good location: secluded, yet not so hidden anyone coming upon them accidentally would think them surreptitious.

"You have a knack for interrupting my social life, Captain," Schenke said, making do with a bow rather than a handshake. "First you got me out of the opera, and now you will no doubt make me late for a dinner engagement."

"But why didn't you tell me?" said Kohn. "We can get together another time as easily as now."

"Please," Schenke said, motioning him back. "They are friends of my wife—I prefer being with you, believe me. In fact, I've been hoping we could sit down like this for some time, only I've had the distinct feeling that you've been avoiding me."

Kohn looked hard at the other. The German was plump, ruddy, and unwrinkled as a stuffed sausage—but under that bland brow, peeping out from those pale eyes, was a shrewd intelligence. This was not going to be all that easy. He decided to ignore the implied question: better to not answer at all than to have any possible rapport dispelled by an obvious lie.

"Have you ordered a drink?" Kohn asked.

"I took the liberty," Schenke nodded—and the waiter came with two clear schnapps in tiny glasses.

"Excellent," Kohn said, rubbing his hands. "Can you bring the bottle?" he asked the waiter, who nodded and did that, while Kohn sniffed the liquor, smiled, saluted the other and tossed the glassful off in a gulp. It burned beautifully all the way down. A good thing he held his liquor well, he thought, refilling his glass. By drinking he might further disarm the other, who would not imagine so casual a tippler being on a mission of any great import. "Nobody but the Germans know how to keep the bouquet in a liquor," he said.

"You are a connoisseur, I take it?" Schenke asked, casual as the other. Kohn had to admit it. "I am glad to see," Schenke went on, "that you are able to appreciate some of the Germanic virtues. That—outside the specifics of your occupation—you seem to bear us no real animosity, unlike one or two others on your mission."

Kohn shrugged, but showed his teeth slightly to indicate that his was a two-sided coin; he could be dangerous as well as pleasant. "I have a job to do," he said, "and I do it in the best way I know. Many people misinterpret me," he went on sorrowfully. "I can show you newspaper columns about me from all over the world—some of which impugn my motives dreadfully."

"I can sympathize with you," Schenke said. "My own job is thankless, to say the least. The government and a few, a very few, of the intelligentsia, want me to root out the evil that may still be among us. But the majority of our people are made uncomfortable by each new arrest and prosecution; they feel that we have done enough, they want to forget their guilt, and they are growing exceedingly restless. This in turn makes the government uncomfortable, and were it not for international pressures my department would no doubt be abolished. I sometimes wonder why I bother to stay on. Unspoken abuse can be as hurtful as any said aloud."

"Why do you stay then?" Kohn asked, genuinely interested.

"You think I don't ask myself that question a dozen times a day?" Schenke asked. "Unfortunately," he sighed, "because of my other prior profession, I am always able to answer myself."

"I don't understand," Kohn said.

"You knew I was a professor?" Schenke asked.

"Of what?" Kohn asked.

"Philosophy," Schenke said wistfully. "You can't imagine how pleasant it was, the life of the intellect, and the students who in those days would not have dreamed of challenging their professors—ah, how pleasant, how corrupting, that subservience. I began to believe in my own omnipotence! You know how dangerous that is, particularly for a man who lives by his brain? After the dreadful Hitlerian debacle, I emerged from the ruins—I had been, to all intents and purposes, living underground, a mental underground, which is far dingier than anything the earth knows —and looking about me, determined to do what I could in the rebuilding of my country. My philosophical bent trapped me! I saw that only by rooting out and destroying our guilt could we be rid of our chronic illness. If the study of philosophy was ever to have any validity for me again, it had to be practical, it had to be put to a worthwhile use. And so I, philosophically, took on this job. But don't think I don't understand my countrymen's feelings! I sometimes wish there were an opportunity to relieve them just for a little of this continuing guilt, perhaps by showing them that there are people other than Germans who are also culpable, also capable of—what is the colloquial expression?—lousy behavior! Of course I am perfectly aware that I wish this selfishly—to relieve the pressures that are on me, the contempt with which my own countrymen view me."

The two men sat in a mutually commiserating silence for a time, each all the while eying the other for some glimpse of the real purpose behind his professed attitude. It was not that Kohn did not believe Schenke; he had learned that it was always worthwhile to start by taking people at face value. There was no question in his mind, however, but that Schenke was hoping for a comparable revelation from him. Perhaps he could use the professed hope of the other to further his own cause?

"I would think," Kohn said carefully, "that in your files you would have many examples of wrongdoing by other than Germans."

Schenke became secretly alert. Ever since the meeting that morning he had been a troubled man. While it was possible that Von Haupt was guilty by some standards of war crimes, it was a guilt of omission, a guilt all Germans shared, of following orders, of not disturbing the chain of command, of looking the other way, and it was no good trying to bring a man to justice for something so vague; the people would simply not understand it. One reason his bureau had functioned as well as it had, Schenke thought, was that he had always been exceedingly careful. The men he went after were obvious brutes—crude, loathsome types: concentration camp commanders, torturers, medical experimenters, people whom any society would be happily rid of. But subtle guilts—that was another matter; if he attempted such prosecutions he would fail. Germans would look, once again, as if they were whitewashing the past. And with a person like Von Haupt, with his connections, the very existence of the bureau would be placed in jeopardy. Schenke had been sincere in the speech he made to Kohn . . . but he could not help being resentful of these Jews who in their search for revenge might wreck what he had built so carefully. By prosecuting the obvious criminals, Germans could feel they were doing their duty. It was the feeling that was important, Schenke thought. As a philosopher he had learned that. This other was talking as though he actually expected to get his cooperation! It was true that he seemed to be hinting at something that could throw an entirely different light on the whole situation, but that might be a diversionary tactic. Schenke decided that he must be extraordinarily wary.

"Our bureau is concerned only with Germans," Schenke said finally.

"But still," Kohn persisted, "in your work—your researches—you must have run across material that implicates others."

"Others?" Schenke asked.

"Polacks, frogs, bohunks, hunkies," Kohn said. He hesitated. "Jews," he concluded, because he had to.

He had Schenke's complete attention now. "Anything like that," Schenke said, "we send on to the appropriate governments."

"We have never received anything from you," Kohn said.

"But my dear captain," Schenke said, "why should you? Your nation is too recent to have jurisdiction."

"Then what do you do about cases involving wrongdoing by Jews?" Kohn asked.

"Jews of what nationality?" Schenke asked. "If they are German, we have them on file of course." He looked briefly sad. "Even Hitler," he said, "considered the German Jew to be—how shall I put it?—indigenous. Superior, if you like, to Jews from other parts. The German Jew, Captain, was the last on the list for . . . disposal."

Kohn felt his face flame and he dropped his eyes so the other should not see the hatred in them. He busied himself refilling the other's glass—half empty—and his own, bone dry save for the oily essence on the sides.

"Well then," he said when he had regained control, "you do have incriminating material on German Jews that you have never used?"

"How can we use it?" Schenke asked. "It would be considered another form of persecution. The public is not equipped to recognize these nice philosophical distinctions: we consider them German, and yet the outside public would consider them Jew. Either way, it is the German who is considered monstrous."

"Turn them over to us," Kohn said easily.

Schenke was silent. "Are you looking for anything in particular, Captain?" he asked at last.

"It's like a busman's holiday for me," Kohn said. "There's not a lot for me to do here as an observer and I get itchy. I thought it would be interesting and in the spirit of our mission—*nein*?—to take a look at your files." He tongued the inner sides of his glass, looking covertly at the other; when he saw that he was not believed he panicked just a little and then came up with his most telling ploy, a maneuver which in retrospect he recognized as workable because it was so very close to the truth. "Look here," Kohn said, "that's not quite accurate. It's a bit more than I've told you. You know how government work is; my old department is jealous about my transfer; they didn't want to let me go at all, but they'll make it smooth for me if I do this one last job for them."

"And what job is that?" Schenke asked, trying not to show his eagerness and failing.

"Why, as I told you," Kohn said blandly though his pulse quickened, "picking up any information you might have regarding German Jews."

"What *kind* of information?" Schenke asked. "Much of the material we have is uncorrelated—and will remain so until we have a specific category in which to place it." He waited.

"I wouldn't know about categories," Kohn said at last. "There have been a few random, unsubstantiated charges made—by some of our more unstable types, I might add—and whatever I get from you will be compared."

"Random charges?" Schenke asked, raising his eyebrows.

"Let a man achieve a measure of success in which he is publicly recognized," Kohn said, "and there is certain to be an accusation made, a charge leveled against him—"

"What sort of accusations?" Schenke persisted, interrupting.

"Of collaboration, for the most part," Kohn said, sliding quickly over the hated word.

It could be true, Schenke supposed, and yet he should assume it was something calculated to throw him off. In either case, he thought then, Germans were involved. He wanted to point this out. But Kohn was still talking.

". . . So whatever you have in that category would be appreciated," Kohn said.

"Come now, Captain," Schenke said, "you must not suppose me so naïve. Where was this collaboration alleged to have taken place? Why are you so reluctant to tell me?"

"I was against all this," Kohn said truthfully. "But we too have those who want to purify our country. Let sleeping dogs lie, I say."

"If they are your own dogs," Schenke muttered.

Kohn shrugged, not refuting it.

"Where was this collaboration?" Schenke repeated then.

"Cologne, the summer of '39," Kohn said. "I would like whatever you have on those who may have cooperated in an important way with the authorities."

"Nothing else?" Schenke asked, heavily ironic once he understood how much Kohn was asking.

"That depends on what you turn up, doesn't it?" Kohn said. He paused, wondering how far he dared go. "In case we need corroborating evidence," Kohn continued slowly, deciding against asking directly for the names of German officials, "could we get it?"

"I have not yet agreed to help you, Captain," Schenke said.

"But we are not after Germans," Kohn said. *This time,* he qualified silently, while he kept a reassuringly direct gaze on the other. "Besides," he pointed out, "you will have a chance to evaluate whatever it is you come up with before you discuss it with me. You will see that your cautions are unnecessary."

"I hope so," Schenke said, as a warning. He paused. "I will see what we have, Captain," he said then, standing up. "It may take a few days. In all probability, I will have to return to Ludwigsburg myself—I wouldn't want my people there to get the wrong idea. Luckily the conference has been recessed, so my trip back will cause little comment."

"I haven't had a vacation in years," Kohn said. "Maybe I ought to take advantage of the time off myself. How is Cologne for sightseeing?"

"Interesting," Schenke said, equally bland. "I would suggest you take a Rhine steamer. The river is particularly lovely this time of year."

"I may just do that," Kohn said. "Thanks for the tip."

He remained slouched in his seat as Schenke bowed and left. It wouldn't do to be too polite. It would be out of character, and make the other wonder if there wasn't indeed more to this than he was letting on. He watched Schenke stop on his way out and take care of the bill. One thing about the Germans, he thought, they were excellent hosts. So long as one didn't wear out his welcome, that is—or assume an intimacy that didn't exist, as the Jews, to their everlasting sorrow, had discovered.

The captain motioned the waiter over and asked that the bottle be sent up to his room. It would be a long and tiresome wait. He had to remain on call for Gottliebsohn.

That sly devil Gottliebsohn, he thought, amused. Turning down those *zoftic* young German hussies, pretending to be offended, and all the time he had a thing going about Arab women. There was no predicting a man's taste by how he looked, the way he acted, or what he said. Kohn wondered what other secrets Gottliebsohn might have that even a headknocker would have difficulty discovering, but that might be revealed to a comrade. He decided to be extraordinarily pleasant to Gottliebsohn on the way to Cologne, and faintly contemptuous with Glass (as Levin had implied he should be), and see if he couldn't get a hint from the one that might enable him to worm out a secret from the other.

It was past midnight when the call from Dean Wolfe, in Jerusalem, was put through to the room of Mission Co-Director Hortsky.

"You weren't sleeping?" Wolfe asked, though he knew his old friend's habits very well.

"Old men don't sleep," Hortsky retorted. "You know that. We merely doze, mostly during conferences and speeches. I've been reading. Minutes of the economic committee meeting that was held this afternoon. Boring stuff." But he did not mention the other disquieting report from Auerbach.

"And how goes it, this new love affair of yours with the German?" Wolfe asked, hoping that Hortsky's answer would somehow put off the necessity to involve himself any further in this matter, which was already complicated enough.

"I am too old for love," Hortsky said. "A little sex, maybe, now and then, to remind myself of how it used to be, when such things were important."

Wolfe had to laugh in spite of the seriousness of the information he had to relay. "You are an old bull," he said fondly.

They had been friends since their student days. Though Wolfe had refused to be recruited into the Zionist movement, and had been amazed and skeptical when Hortsky had actually gone to Palestine to live, they had kept in close touch, their letters lively and full of argument about homeland, and faith, and new flags and old customs, and it was Hortsky who arranged, finally, for Wolfe's appointment, when it seemed he might end his days an obscure professor at a minor American college.

Before then it had been Hortsky, too, on his last tocsin-sounding, doom-saying trip through Europe, just before the holocaust, looking like nothing so much as a harsh-tongued Old Testament prophet, who had warned Wolfe to get out, to leave his beloved cafés and music halls and lecture podiums and society salons, leave his charming city, with its wide streets and old castles and great parks. But Wolfe damned the other's vision as hallucinatory, refusing to believe that his beloved Viennese could ever be capable of fanatical behavior.

It was not that he could not see the dark undercurrents beneath the whipped-cream life. In his tastefully furnished office on Langegosse he listened to his patients, the high-born and the nouveaux riches and the brutally powerful and the sensitively artistic prattle on—about how overwhelmingly Momma-Poppa was, about dislike and envy all around them, about how they could think of nothing but the secretary-maid-footman-butler-chauffeur-gardener-young-friend-of-the-husband-wife, whose swelling buttock-bosom-crotch put into their minds the most awful thoughts, taking away high resolve and resistance to low behavior as if it were so much late snow under a spring sun. But their subterranean life, for all its gloomy sexuality, never seemed to interfere with their daily business, about which they proceeded with equanimity.

Wolfe had forgotten about the young. The callous, impersonal young, to whom an idea was an emotion (the more obscene the idea, the more powerful the emotion), and who had grown up in a mutative generation, in which the organ of compassion had been stunted at birth. As a teacher, he had been treated with a politeness that he had failed to recognize was merely a mannerism, a superficial attitude like a neat bandage over a festering sore.

Then he had witnessed a riot. His favorite student—an aristocratic boy he had been grooming in seminar with the excitement of an old teacher who has finally, after fruitless years, found the perfect clay for his crafting fingers—was leading a pack of hooligans (remarkably well dressed hooligans, with the soft skin and hard eyes of the upper classes) in the systematic, well-organized destruction of a syna-

gogue, at the same time supervising a disinterested, almost
by-the-way beating of an elderly Jew who had come out to
defend his temple.

Wolfe had confronted the boy, walked into the melee
shaking with rage, and the other had shrugged contemptuously, as if all that had passed between them was of no
consequence, though he stopped the riotous activity out of
some lingering deference to authority. The next day he received a note: *I am sorry, Herr Professor, but causes are
more important than individuals.* The day after that, Wolfe
left; left everything, left home, left art collection, left
classes, left mementoes of his dead wife and distant family,
left his practice, which included two incipient suicides, a
nymphomaniac and one potentially violent psychopath, left
his position as chairman of the most respected department
of psychiatry in all Europe, with its renowned innovating
(and short-sighted) faculty and its eager student body, containing so many superior (and one absolutely brilliant)
minds, left his belief in the perfectibility of man.

Though he had accepted his present position (a man
must live, though he disdained life as purposeless), he no
longer preached the sacredness of the individual, but rather
his sameness to all others. And yet his most enduring friend-
ship was with a man who prided himself on his independence, who treasured those aspects of himself that were most
unique. Wolfe could guess how the other had chafed in
retirement, how he must have leaped at the chance to lend
his presence to the controversial mission, secure in the belief
that his countrymen would never doubt his motives. Wolfe
had no such certainties about human loyalties, and he worried about the old man's suffering public vilification, or the
humiliation of being judged senile.

There was a very real chance that this could happen.
Though Hortsky had built his reputation as a dissenter,
arguing for unrestricted immigration during those days
when the other now equally old men were dreaming of a
select Zion, preaching revolt whilst the others went along
with the mandate, resigning, finally, at the height of the
scandals of the party he had helped found, articulately
heartsick that here, in the Promised Land, Jews could become corrupted by their own righteousness, his dissents
were always clearly understood. Even when he had argued

for clemency in the trial of that Nazi butcher whom they had captured and brought to Israel for justice, his appeal, though disregarded, made a strange kind of sense. The Jewish hierarchy felt they must prove their toughness (and in a strange sick way, the failure of assimilation, making a case against the failure in nerve of the European Jew). And all they had proven when they hanged the man, Hortsky said, was that the Jew was no different from other men. How much better to have kept the monster imprisoned among the very people he had tried to exterminate, a living symbol of how low it was possible for man to stoop, an example of their courage that they were unafraid to keep the Devil chained —and alive.

But now he was engaged in an enterprise that was thought by a great number of his people to have dubious value, and his arguments in its favor, so far private, told only to Wolfe, would be difficult to understand. The public could understand Auerbach—he spoke in practical terms. But how would they react to Hortsky's more mystical beliefs? What if they knew that the fierce old man had determined that he would, as probably his last knowing political act, make an effort to rehabilitate the German—and not incidentally, the Jew?

It was not that Hortsky believed in the "new" German, or the innocence of the younger generation, or the "non-participation" of those who were left of the old. What he believed in was the efficacy of example, however theatric. He was certain that if a people came to believe in their own goodness, they would inevitably become good. He loved to quote his version of the Aesopian fable, telling of the legendary wolf who came among the flock disguised as a lamb and who, when accepted as a lamb by others, found that his base heart had been transformed with love of kind. But to accomplish this, the Jew must remain lamb-like; otherwise the transformation might work in reverse. And with only wolves in the world, on whom then would they turn and feed? Someone must call a halt to hatred, that most base of human emotions, and who better than the two peoples between whom so much cannibalism had been practised?

The dean had listened cynically, unbelieving, and then pointed out that the original version was more nearly correct: when the flock had been put into shelter for the night, the wolf, discarding his lambskin cloak, had eaten his full of the trusting lambs.

But Hortsky had refused to listen. And when the dean saw that his friend was determined to go ahead with the mission, he had ceased his arguments as being futile. Now he found his own worst fears being realized. If the mission failed and the cause was a scandal, Hortsky would take the brunt of the blame.

"And are the negotiations going well then?" Wolfe asked.

"Almost better than we had a right to expect even," Hortsky responded, after only a moment.

But Wolfe had noted that brief hesitation. "Just two days ago, in Tel Aviv, they stoned the German ambassador again," he said.

"I read the papers," Hortsky said. "And the orthodox still stone those who drive on the Sabbath, with the blessing of their rabbis. It will pass. Everything passes, in time. Time was invented for that purpose, not?"

"There are rumors around the university," Wolfe continued, disliking the fact that it was he who must tell the old man these things, "that the mission is a fraud, that the real purpose is not, as stated, only a step beyond the usual reparations and grants-in-aid, but much, much more—where we in effect forgive the Germans their sins!"

"But that is a distortion," Hortsky said, growing perturbed. "We have never hidden the purposes of the mission."

"They were never made absolutely clear," Wolfe said. "And you know how easily a faintly outlined truth can be blurred to look like something else—particularly if there is a side issue which can be blown up."

"You mean Gottliebsohn," Hortsky said uneasily, for the first time aware that their conversation might have deeper significances.

"How is he?" Wolfe asked.

"Tired, I expect," Hortsky said. "He and his German opposite spent most of the evening working out the statistical logistics on a proposal that was made." He paused. "But you didn't call me in the middle of the night just to chat about negotiations . . ."

"It's Gottliebsohn I've called you about," Wolfe admitted. "A person who knew him intimately has been found, and I'm not sure how we ought to proceed."

"I don't see the problem," Hortsky said. "Who is this person?"

"His sister," Wolfe said.

Hortsky paused to take in this unexpected development. "How nice for Gottliebsohn, the poor fellow, all alone in the world," he said then. "But where has she been until now?"

"She teaches in a *kibbutz*," Wolfe said.

"And how does she happen to come forward now?" Hortsky asked.

"She hasn't," Wolfe said. "That's what worries me. Her husband wrote in response to the newspaper article."

"And that worries you?" Hortsky asked, as Wolfe hesitated.

"It is such a strange letter," Wolfe said. "The husband wrote that his wife is fragile, given to attacks of 'nerves'; that she is unaware that he has written us; that she has, until now, lived as though the past did not exist—seems to run in the family, doesn't it?" Wolfe observed parenthetically.

"You are a hard man, Isaac," Hortsky said.

"Don't confuse hardness with lack of sentimentality," Wolfe said sharply. "There's nothing more harmful than misplaced sympathy."

"We'll argue the point another time," Hortsky said. "I'm still not clear as to why you are worried."

"The husband wonders if it couldn't be arranged for Gottliebsohn to visit the *kibbutz*," Wolfe said. "Meanwhile, he says he will 'prepare' her for meeting her brother. Why that 'prepare'? She hasn't lost her memory, she's aware of her brother—I get the feeling that she wants nothing to do with Gottliebsohn. And that doesn't sound too good for us, does it?"

It did have an ominous ring; it could be because she knew about a collaboration. "Couldn't it be some family feud?" Hortsky asked at last.

"I think we should assume that it isn't," Wolfe said.

"What have you told the husband?" Hortsky said slowly, trying to absorb all the disturbing implications.

"Nothing yet," Wolfe said. "Nor anyone else, for that matter. If you're close to an agreement," he went on doubtfully, "perhaps we can just sit on this until you get back . . ."

"There are complications," Hortsky said. He had been reluctant to tell this good but cynical friend, but obviously he now had no other choice. "The Germans are uneasy about Kohn. They were asking Gottliebsohn—imagine, Gottliebsohn—what Kohn is doing here!"

"And how did he handle it?"

"Surprisingly well, according to Auerbach," Hortsky said. "He said that it hadn't occurred to him to question Kohn's presence, but he saw no reason to assume that it was anything except what it was stated to be; and then he refused to discuss it further, as being outside his area of competence."

"That was quick of him," Wolfe agreed. Somehow, from everything that had been learned about the man so far, he had not assumed him capable of thus operating under pressure: it indicated a surprising ability at deception. He wondered if Glass was aware of this hidden trait.

"You see how this complicates things," Hortsky said.

Indeed the dean did. "I think we'd better get brother and sister together as soon as possible," he said.

"Send Gottliebsohn home?" Hortsky said. "That would be awkward."

"Then we'll send her to Germany," the dean said. "That might work out best in any case—give our people first crack at her. I haven't informed the opposition about this development yet; you'll remember that the newspaper article gave the Institute's address as a cover; so far they haven't thought to guess that I am in collusion with you—though one of the Interior Minister's men, a lawyer named Levin, was questioning me just yesterday as to how it happened that an American psychiatrist was brought in. I'll notify them after I've shipped her off, and that should give us enough of a head start to cope with whatever it is she knows."

"And how would you go about sending her to Germany," Hortsky asked, "if even her husband is reluctant to discuss her brother with her?"

"I'll go to the *kibbutz* myself," Wolfe said. "I can be very persuasive, I know a great deal abut the nervous systems of women—and don't forget, with this beard, I cut quite an imposing patriarchal *figger*." He used the English accent for ironic effect, which was not lost upon Hortsky.

"Why do you go to so much trouble," Hortsky asked then, "when you do not agree with our purposes here?"

"Do you need to ask?" Wolfe said.

"I appreciate this, old friend," Hortsky said. "Believe me, I too will be glad when all this is over. I want to *potz* around with my flowers, swing in my hammock, be nagged by my wife, eat some desert fruit with my new teeth. This climate does not agree with me—and the food! What the Germans do to fish is unbelievable!"

"And of course there are no Jewish delicatessens there?" Wolfe said.

Hortsky did not answer.

"I will notify you of the woman's arrival time," Wolfe said then. "I think it will be best if you meet her, reassure her, before you introduce her to the American."

"He seems a well-meaning young man," Hortsky said.

"It's more important that he be competent," Wolfe said sharply.

"And isn't he?" Hortsky asked.

"For the most part," Wolfe said. "He has a penetrating mind, brilliant in some situations—but he's erratic. He takes chances, intuitive chances, and they don't always work out. Like all of us, he's got problems of his own. Keep an eye on him. If it ever looks like he's up against it, talk to him. And if he doesn't seem to respond well, have him call me."

"That 'patriarchal' effect?" Hortsky asked.

"Perhaps," Wolfe said, his mind on other things. "Look here," he said then. "I don't think it's wise to tell this sister about the charges against Gottliebsohn. If they're not proved out, it will just disturb her unnecessarily. All we should be concerned about is what help she can give us in restoring her brother's memory. If the . . . other comes out of it, so be it. But we don't have to look for it. Your captain will get on to that soon enough."

"Very well," Hortsky said, though reluctant to participate in any evasion. But the other's concern had reached him, and when their conversation concluded, his worry kept him awake for most of the night.

8

THEY TOOK THE EARLY MORNING STEAMER out of Bonn. The three men were an odd group in more ways than one, gawking at the waterfront sights like ordinary tourists, and yet so different one from another in stance, attitude, and dress.

Gottliebsohn was outwardly morose, and his appearance, as he stood with his hands jammed into the pockets of his ill-fitting suit, broad shoulders hunched, large feet spread against the roll of the deck, made him seem shaggy and phlegmatic as an old bear. Inwardly, however, he was terribly excited, his heart alternately leaping and shrinking with anticipation and dread of what they might find up river. That unnerving session with Von Haupt and his subsequent talk with Auerbach had made it apparent how necessary it was to find out the truth about himself and have done with the whole business. Von Haupt had been extraordinarily persistent. At first, Gottliebsohn had not understood what the other was getting at, but when it became clear that it was Kohn he was being questioned about, he had thought he might faint from shock and dismay. Somehow he had managed to fend the other off. The meeting with Auerbach was not much better. The normally cool mission co-director seemed flustered by his report. Instead of the sympathetic manner that he usually adopted when speaking of Gottliebsohn's affliction, he was curt and unfeeling. Gottliebsohn could understand his distress. The negotiations were approaching that delicate stage when both sides must finally demonstrate good faith, and this question mark of a key man was throwing the entire proceedings in doubt.

Kohn had a headache—probably from tension, he thought. Although that schnapps might have had something to do with it—he wouldn't put it past that kraut bartender to have added a private stock to the labeled brand—yesterday's directive from Levin and the conference with Auerbach late last night had left him feeling that he was suspected by both sides. Then, too, though he had expected Schenke to put a tail on him, the actual sight of the heavyset fellow in the dark suit and slouch-brimmed hat on the dock made him doubly irritable. They were not even taking ordinary precautions to hide their surveillance. Since they were not followed aboard, he could assume that some other *Wienerschnitzel* would pick up the job when they arrived in Cologne, and this deliberate show of mistrust could only mean a warning by Schenke to keep his inquiry within bounds. It was only a matter of time too before they put together those newspaper stories about Gottliebsohn's amnesia and the presence of the American psychiatrist, and they would likely make a final and most accurate conjecture when word got back that these particular three were making a sightseeing trip together. Kohn swore to himself. He could not think which was worse: the Germans believing he was hunting a German, or wondering what a Jew might have done to put a man like himself on his trail.

Glass, the reluctant passenger, was feeling pleasantly sad, and he diagnosed the symptoms as homesickness. Part of it, certainly, was his wanting out—although the uncertainties of the previous day and the premonition of disaster he now put down to fatigue and emotional strain, his tensions seeming to have evaporated as easily as the morning mist along the banks of the river. How could anyone have foreboding thoughts on a day so nearly perfect? He had even come to terms with himself about the role he would play on this trip back into Gottliebsohn's past: he would be a silent observer, intruding himself into Gottliebsohn's relationships with Kohn only when his patient seemed to be getting into emotional trouble. Though he would have preferred the psychiatric end of this investigation to proceed along more normal lines, in the sanctuary of an "office," he could see where this field trip, so-called, might even have certain advantages. He would be able to observe his patient's reactions firsthand, without having to depend on his admittedly uncertain memory. In fact, Gottliebsohn's observed reactions with what he said about them later might prove very revealing.

But Glass found it difficult to keep his mind on the business at hand. He had to remind himself continually that he was in an alien land. This broad river, those grassy banks, these green rolling hills, with stands of grazing cattle, reminded him of nothing so much as his native Midwest. If it were not for the occasional castle that loomed so imposingly historic from a promontory above, he might imagine himself home, at the place of his best times, when he was young, joyous at being alive, not caring a damn about personal relationships, content with exploring the limits of senses that were purely physical, running as hard and long as possible through meadows like these, falling headlong, exhausted, face buried in the damp sweet-smelling clover, his own sweat mingling with the earth's dew. It seemed impossible, as he inhaled the morning's fragrance, that people from a land so abundant, people like these who crowded the rails, pleasant-eyed, rosy-cheeked, chubbily dimpled good-humored people, could have been capable of such monstrosities as had so recently shaken man's belief that he had a reason for being, or even, or particularly even, his belief in the existence of God.

The day became almost imperceptibly tinged, as with a sun that is metallic and gaseous, fouling the morning air.

"Feeling queasy?" Kohn asked.

"Not at all," Glass said.

"Enjoying the trip then?" Kohn persisted.

"It is interesting," Glass said. "I've not been to Germany before."

"You haven't missed a thing," Kohn muttered, looking over the other passengers, the thought having suddenly occurred to him that the cop on the dock may have been a plant to distract him from their real tail.

"Apparently not," Glass said, trying hard to ignore the other's harshness. "It's a lot like my home state. I guess that's why so many Germans settled there—a familiar environment."

"And what are they like, your Germans?" Kohn asked, pale eyes contemptuously on him at last. "Like these sausages? Full of pork?"

"Maybe the grandparents," Glass said patiently. "But the young, they are completely American."

"And what does that mean?" Kohn persisted. "No prejudices, is that what you're trying to tell me?"

"Not deep, not like these over here," Glass said, denying it, wanting to forget, for the sake of what was left of his optimism, those examples of hate that he had been blissfully unaware of when young. He had been awfully shocked when he had first been exposed, in life and in literature, to the complex antipathies of which the human was capable— not merely for those of another religion or color, but in fact, in one way or another, for everyone outside the self—even those one presumably loved.

"I do not think I would like America," Gottliebsohn said, surprising the other two. They had not known he was listening.

"Why not?" Glass asked. "You can have whatever environment you want in my country. If you don't care for this sort of thing"—and he made a sweeping gesture to include all the spectacular scenery rolling by as they steamed rapidly upstream—"you can find what you *do* like. You can even choose a desert, if that is to your liking."

"I did not choose the desert," Gottliebsohn said, resentful of the interpretation. "I chose to be with my people." He hesitated. "America would be too confusing."

Glass considered this. It made sense for Gottliebsohn to surround himself with those whose religion, appetite and manner would give him a sense of kind. But he seemed almost deliberately lonely, he resisted assimilation, he fended off those who tried to form a meaningful relationship. Could it be that the diverse population confused him, searching as he was for a simple identification, or was there another, more deeply emotional reason that caused him to bristle like a cactus whenever anyone tried to touch him?

"I wonder where the bar is?" Kohn suddenly muttered. His face lit up as he spotted the small sign over the entryway to the main cabin. "I have a blasting headache," he said then, remembering that Glass had once before noted his liking for liquor. "There's nothing like Rhine beer for what ails you. Ernst, you look like you could use one yourself."

Gottliebsohn shook his head. It was apparent he wanted to stay near his doctor. Kohn's face darkened. It was also apparent to Glass that Kohn must be feeling particularly lousy—that was twice he had projected his own bad humor onto others.

After Kohn left, without another word, doctor and patient stood at the rail, gazing at the river traffic, increasing now as the morning lengthened. There were many barges, carrying everything from lumber and steel to oil, many flying foreign flags, Swiss and Dutch predominating, along with an occasional passenger steamer like their own. They passed a village; a steamer was loading from the small dock, poultry and produce bound, no doubt, for the city marketplace.

"Is any of this familiar?" Glass asked finally.

"None of it," Gottliebsohn answered after a moment.

"And yet your village, according to the map, is only two hours from the river," Glass said.

"You can live and die that close and never see it," Gottliebsohn said.

"How do you know that?" Glass asked.

"In my bones," Gottliebsohn said, suddenly filled with melancholy. "But that's not memory, is it? I probably heard it somewhere."

"What is it, Ernst?" Glass asked. "What's bothering you?"

"Isn't it obvious?" Gottliebsohn asked.

"Nothing is obvious," Glass said gently.

"I'm afraid of what we might find," Gottliebsohn said in a rush.

Glass made no comment.

"Of course, with you along," Gottliebsohn went on after a moment, "it's not as bad as it might be. It'll keep *him*"— he nodded in the direction where Kohn had gone—"from pressing me too hard."

His patient was making an obvious plea for support. Glass hated to deny him, and yet it was perhaps better that he make the coming procedure clear, than to have him confused and apprehensive.

"Ernst," he began, "this trip is Captain Kohn's responsibility. I can't possibly interfere, no matter how hard he presses you. As long as I'm here, of course, I will look for those things that may be of help later. Remember how I said Kohn was going to approach this retracking, this walking backward in your footsteps? We'll visit every place that we knew you were, we'll go looking for landmarks. You can't have been in Cologne and not seen the cathedral, or so I've been told. Well, I wouldn't expect you to be able at this moment to draw it from memory, not even a rough sketch. But when you see it, that's another story. There'll be a kind of recognition, a fitting of the real outline into the shadowy outline that exists, that *has* to exist, in your brain. When that happens something should spill over, some feeling, some remembrance of a smell or a sight or a sound . . . you must tell me at once, or if you don't want to mention it in front of Kohn, give me a sign of some sort, so I may note the time and the circumstance, and we can go over it again later." He looked to see if the other understood. "But for the time being, Ernst, you'll be on your own."

After what seemed an interminable silence, Gottliebsohn went to an empty bench and sat down, discouraging, by the manner in which he sprawled along it, anyone else from joining him.

Perhaps, he thought wildly, he ought to welcome a finding of guilt and have done with it, with all of them, with Auerbach and Hortsky and Glass and Kohn and yes, that German, too, that supercilious bastard who showed his prejudice against Jews with every disdainful word he uttered . . . but the moment passed. Was it possible that because he had been accused of a past impossible collaboration, he could think of ruining the present one, that out of an accumulation of resentment of all those who were pressuring him, he might go so far as to incriminate himself? He swore to himself that he would never admit to a false guilt, no matter that it would free him from the conspiracy to ignore, if not forget, the German atrocity. But new fear crept into his mind, like a mouse into a cage after cheese, and he felt sick with doubt.

Glass observed his patient with some concern. Gottliebsohn's turning from him was not totally unexpected; it was part of the process for patients to feel hostility toward the psychiatrist at some point, but the intensity of the reaction, the manner in which he sat, brooding, his shoulders moving fitfully like a sleeper in nightmare, indicated a new conflict was working, like yeast, in his mind.

None of the three men bothered with one another for the rest of the fifty-five-minute trip. Kohn, after two beers, settled himself into an easy chair in the lounge, where he promptly fell asleep. Gottliebsohn alternately sat and paced the deck, too nervous to remain inactive for long, afraid to dwell on the disorder in his own mind. Glass went up to the observation deck, where he stood by the rail, outwardly tranquil as any tourist, but inwardly worried whether, like his patient, he was not keeping something from himself, something it would just not do to forget.

Kohn had everything perfectly organized. It pleased him to let others think he operated haphazardly; that was part of his effectiveness; with Gottliebsohn unaware of how carefully worked out the whole thing was, he would less likely be on guard against the kind of revelations Kohn was after. He had taken the three letters which had been forwarded from the German newspaper in response to the article on Gottliebsohn, put two of the addresses together with that of Gottliebsohn's former apartment in Cologne (gotten from his old German identity card), kept the third on a hunch, and poring over a map of the city, had planned their schedule, taking into account not only the proximity of one address to another, but also the sequence of Gottliebsohn's movements on that last night he remembered, which had been provided him by the psychiatrist.

Then his plans suddenly changed. He had intended to walk his man through in a straightforward reenactment, but the appearance of the German cop dockside when the boat arrived decided him to go at it a bit differently. Not that that upset him. On the contrary; the fact that he had spotted him first crack out of the box, a shabbily dressed, thick-glassed older man (Schenke's bureau was obviously hard up for personnel) put him in a remarkably good humor. His headache was gone, he was well rested. Kohn decided to lead the other astray; he would enjoy losing him; it would not make that much difference to his procedures; and then he could concentrate on the job at hand.

"We're going to walk," he informed the other two, as

they hesitated outside the exit of the docking terminal. "It's not that big a city—anyway, not the parts we're going to prowl—and in any case, Ernst is a great walker, right, Ernst?"

Gottliebsohn nodded doubtfully; as they moved into the stream of foot traffic, he tried to stay between Kohn and Glass, edgy about getting too close to these hurrying Germans, but the sidewalks were narrow and in a moment some sudden strange jostle on Kohn's part put him a half step in front and Gottliebsohn found himself brushing shoulders with the people he so much despised and feared. He hunched his shoulders and hurried to keep up with the fast-stepping Kohn, dodging, as well as he could, these pedestrians who seemed so intent on their own business that they were unaware of the intruders.

They were walking along the river front. They passed a small stone church, and then Kohn led them along a narrow iron-gated street away from the river, pausing in front of a building marked *Rathaus*.

"City hall," Kohn said. "Recognize it, Ernst? Here's where you would have come had you any business with city officials."

Gottliebsohn stared at the tall structure, ending in a kind of medieval tower. "I would have no business here," he stammered.

"Right you are," Kohn agreed cheerfully, glancing back, and then led them north along a wider street. They passed along the rear of the cathedral, and in a few minutes they saw where he was headed: the railway terminal.

Gottliebsohn would have liked to stop, think it over, approach this remembered area with some kind of prepared attitude, but the pull of Kohn's progress allowed no time for hesitations. His thoughts, in spite of the brisk pace, were slow and gloomy; he distrusted Kohn's cheerful attitude, he was still sore about his analyst's defection, and he was unhappy about having agreed to return to this city, site of the beginning of his grief and self-doubt. Now that he was here, he wondered why they were not doing this walk-through in the dead of night, since his last memory took place then.

Then the station shook him out of his torpor. They walked into the terminal building, its arched ceiling towering above them, and with a daytime gloom, the sounds echoing through that immense aluminum chamber, railroad cars being coupled, a departing train, the sobbing of an overworked engine—it all did remind him of that earlier time, setting off answering reverberations in his memory. He began to reexperience the familiar emotion: the anguish and the panic about arriving always too late. Even now, pressed on either side by companions in a time far removed from that terror, he felt a constriction in his chest, as if he might be deprived of the ability to breathe.

Then Kohn took him by the elbow, led them through a crowd coming in from an arriving train, and suddenly darted down a stairway leading to an underground passageway. Halfway through the tunnel, Gottliebsohn hung back, staring incredulously into the light reflecting darkly off the polished tiles. They were white, not black as in his nightmare.

"What is it, out of breath already?" Kohn asked urgently, then took them up a stairway leading to track number three. Near the top he halted them, and looked curiously at the panting Gottliebsohn.

"I have a thing about underground places," Gottliebsohn muttered between breaths. Was his dream like a photo negative—the opposite, as his doctor said, of reality?

"Too many bunkers and bomb shelters?" Kohn asked.

"That's probably it," Gottliebsohn agreed, and avoided his doctor's stare.

They waited for Kohn to continue, just under the level of the platform, but he made no move until a crowd came through the tunnel and up their particular stairs. Quite a few streamed by before he led them up, mingling with the group boarding a train, but working his way continually down the platform until they reached a stairway leading back to the main terminal. Gottliebsohn had a few bad moments again going back, but they were soon out of it, and out of the building, too.

"Lost him," Kohn chuckled, elated, looking back. "The Germans had a man following us," he explained, "but he'll still be back there, seeing if we didn't board that train." He hesitated only a moment then, looking thoughtfully at the pale Gottliebsohn. "This is about where your memory stops, isn't it?" he asked. "As I recall it, you said you remembered coming to this terminal to look for your family. How did

you get here? Can you backtrack it?" And then, as Gottliebsohn hesitated: "Don't stop to think—just go where your
feet take you. Now let's get out of here before that *'schnitzel*
comes out and spots us."

Gottliebsohn immediately began walking in a direction
that seemed somewhat familiar; the daylight made a difference, of course, but he thought he recognized a side street,
and then an alley partway down, but when they ran into a
dead end he stopped, unsure of his ground.

"It was night when I was here before," he said apologetically.

Glass, who had been hanging back, assuming that Kohn,
as he had suggested, intended going into Gottliebsohn's past
gently, unwinding his memory from his point of departure,
grew irritated that he had been mistaken. He wondered why
it had been necessary to "lose" the German. He stared at
his patient, puzzled about that evident desire to please. Apparently he was forgetting his earlier doubts as he involved
himself in the search, and Glass began to worry about his
widening swings of emotion. But he said nothing.

They came out on a narrow street, working their way
around the dead end. They saw then that the street had
been blocked because of rubble, still left from the war.

Kohn, who had memorized the city's map, was disgruntled about the blocked street. Gottliebsohn had been heading in the right general direction. Now he seemed confused.
Without comment, however, Kohn led the way. A few
blocks further on he stopped in front of a vacant lot.

Gottliebsohn looked at him wonderingly.

Kohn shrugged, disappointed. "This is where it was," he
said. "The apartment building your folks were in," he went
on, impatiently, as Gottliebsohn looked blank.

Gottliebsohn stared at the vacancy, picturing the building that had once been, and the awful, frantic search. But
with the building gone so was the emotion. He looked
dumbly at his doctor.

Glass, looking for a reaction, understood when there was
none. Kohn did not, but kept his own counsel. He had better
things in store for Gottliebsohn.

"This way," he said, leading them to an address a few
blocks away. "We've turned up your old landlady."

Frau Gonser was indeed old, and if it had not been for

her querulous nasal whine, they might have missed the harelip in that wrinkled face. They sat in her gloomy parlor, shades drawn against the light, shut windows keeping in the smell of cooking cabbage, sour as age.

"I lost everything in the bombing," she said. "Except my records; I kept those with me at all times, you can bet, though a fat lot of good it has done me. The Nazis confiscated the building . . . my husband had unfortunately bought it from a Jew, without prior authorization, trying to help out, good-hearted soul he was, paying more than it was worth; the lawyers got my property back, but it wasn't till this year that the rubble was cleared off. And where am I going to get the money to rebuild? I'm entitled to the rents that the Nazis collected, but the lawyers say it is very complicated and it takes cash to keep them interested."

"Tell us about the Gottliebsohns," Kohn said.

"I remember them very well," she said, beginning to rock in her chair. "Poor souls, country people, unfamiliar with city ways, worried about their daughter, about what was going to happen to them . . ."

"What did happen?" Kohn asked, interrupting.

"I never heard," she said, looking at him suspiciously, eyes like a sick hen's. "They left in the middle of the night. I was away, against my will, visiting friends of my husband, knowing you should never leave property unattended, and sure enough when we got back they were gone, bag and baggage, the place cleaned out, slick as a whistle, not an item I could hold for the rent. He'd"—elbow jutted out from her black shawl toward the shallow-breathed Gottliebsohn—"come and gone already too, but no envelope under my door, not a note, nothing, and we never heard from him again. A month's rent you owe me," she said directly to Gottliebsohn, her rocking coming to a halt on the front edge of her runners, leaning forward so far it seemed she might tip right over. "You'll remember I asked for it in advance, and my husband said you were short of ready cash but that you had ways of making money and were good for it, that you had connections, and besides, we couldn't turn people out into the streets, could we? My husband was a kind man, God keep him. Who else could we rent to in any case, with our whole building already filled with Jews? You'll want proof, I suppose, with your memory gone; it's all in my account books, nothing in the paid column opposite the Gottliebsohn name, I'll show you."

"Sit down, please," Kohn said.

"How much is it?" Gottliebsohn asked, his face flushed, reaching for his wallet.

"Just hold on, Ernst," Kohn said. "When the lady has told us what she knows you can decide whether you want to pay her."

Glass felt his own face growing hot, sympathetic with Gottliebsohn's, cringing at this assault on his patient's sensibilities.

"It's a just debt," Gottliebsohn mumbled. He pulled out his money.

"At least figure the difference in the mark's value then and now," Kohn said, but saw that it was hopeless and subsided. "You'll remember to mark your account books paid?" he said, when the transaction was completed. She nodded, pleased with herself. "Now tell us what you know about Herr Gottliebsohn."

"I know nothing about Herr Gottliebsohn except what my husband told me," she said, putting the money in the folds of her shapeless garment.

They stared at her, momentarily unbelieving.

"I tried to find out more about him, you can bet," she went on. "But his family was no help; they would barely talk about him—you'd think I was snooping for the police."

"Why the police?" Kohn asked. She looked bewildered. "Why do you mention police?" he repeated, suddenly harsh.

"No reason," she whined. "Except he was so mysterious, never showing up at the building except that one time I was gone . . ."

Again they stared. It was Gottliebsohn who asked the question. "What do you mean, Frau Gonser, 'never showing up'?"

"Just what I said," she shrugged.

"My identity card carried that address," he protested, thoroughly confused.

"I wouldn't know about that," she said. "You must have worked that out with my husband."

"I had to have lived in your building," Gottliebsohn went on, becoming frantic. "Where else . . . the identity card . . . ?"

"I knew who my tenants were," she said angrily. "Even those who tried to put more people in than the rent called for . . ."

"You told us you asked Herr Gottliebsohn for the money in advance," Kohn said. "Now you say you never met him."

"I talked with him only by telephone," she said.

"And your husband told you nothing more about him?" Kohn said, incredulous.

"Nothing more than I've told you," she said, and then her face began working. "A good thing too, or they may have taken me along with him."

"Why did they take him?" Kohn asked.

"I never knew," she said. Suddenly she began to weep, dry-eyed, a barren old woman whose juices had long ago evaporated, but whose past fears still produced reactions that seemed a mockery of former emotions. "I never asked. I didn't want to know. I didn't want to go with him."

They were happy when they got out on the street again. "Well, Ernst," Kohn said, after they breathed deeply enough to expel that stale air from their lungs, "it seems you got around this town under false pretenses. Why? To what purpose? Where *did* you sleep? And what were those connections of yours?"

Gottliebsohn shook his head helplessly. The discovery that his identity card carried a misleading address came as a shock. That card had been the beginning of what little memory he had, and to find out now that one of the primary assumptions he had made about himself was not true gave him profound misgivings. What else had he assumed about himself that might be untrue? He began retreating into his comforting blankness. "I remember nothing," he said.

Glass knew better; he had seen the brief illumination on Gottliebsohn's clouded face, and then the familiar flinching away from the truth—but he kept silent.

"I would have thought her voice would be enough to recall at least that nastiness to you—but, no matter," Kohn said. "We have others to see. There's a young man who turned up documents with your name in them."

"Documents?" Gottliebsohn asked apprehensively. "My name—what kind of documents?"

"We'll know soon enough," Kohn said, indicating the direction they should walk. "He insists on a personal interview. He's a poet, writing a book about his family; wants to put you in it, maybe. I checked him out—he's relatively well known. Dieter Krieg, real name Krieger, but he likes the shorter version since it means war or battle—what do you make of that, Doctor?"

Glass preferred to make nothing of it.

The poet lived in a partially demolished building. Inside a dark room, bricks and boards had been arranged into makeshift furniture; after seating them, Krieger leaned back in a sailor's hammock which apparently also served as a bed. He was young and slight, his blond hair shaggy, a blue turtleneck sweater turned up to his chin.

"Sorry about the dark," he said. The windows were painted black, a canvas tarpaulin covered the doorway. A hanging ship's lantern gave the only illumination. "But I find the dark gets me started whenever I have difficulty getting the images to flow. It's like sleep in a way; by concentrating you get the subconscious to let go of some really fascinating ideas. You might try it yourself, Herr Gottliebsohn," he said politely.

Gottliebsohn shrank inwardly from even the idea. All he needed, given the state of his nerves, was to coax his nightmare out into a false night. He looked covertly at the psychiatrist, almost fearful that there might be something to the outlandish idea.

But Glass seemed merely amused. "And are you a seaman, too, Herr Krieg?"

"My uncle was," the other said, "and I'm writing this book from his point of view—that is, what it *should* have been, coming home after ten years' absence to find his country gone mad, and his wife—my aunt—involved in a conspiracy against the government. At first in my book he is terribly confused, but then as he becomes involved in the life ashore, he too gets carried away, and he begins to believe it is his wife who is mad and eventually he has her committed. He eventually discovers that the asylums—you know the meaning of the word, of course—have been turned into extermination camps, and that he has sent his wife to her death. That only gives you the barest skeleton of the plot; it's allegorical; what I really intend is to show Germany as it really was, one great lunatic asylum. The tragedy of Germany is that the people believe it all the fault of low-born scoundrels and gangsters taking over the government, when in fact the civil servants, the bookkeepers, those whom the rest depend upon to keep the record straight, they went mad first and the rest followed. But all that is on one level. I want my book to be very real, and so I am putting myself in my uncle's shoes and am reading everything I can find about my aunt—"

"All this truly happened then?" Glass interjected.

"Certainly," the poet said. He grimaced. "I am more fortunate than most. There was at least one sane member in my family. Can you realize how tragic it must be to have only fools, madmen and monsters among your antecedents?"

"Your aunt was in a conspiracy?" Kohn asked.

"Of a sort," the poet said. "At first she and the others merely ignored the new laws. Later on they began to scheme on ways to circumvent them."

"The others?" Kohn said.

"Her tenants," the poet said. "She owned a house in what was a very fashionable section in those days, which she turned into apartments rented only to those persons she considered worthwhile. Outcasts, artists, radicals, one pimp I know about, and probably a prostitute or two—not ordinary streetwalkers, mind, but girls who slept around on the highest levels. She held a weekly salon, to which she invited others of like persuasion—"

"And were they successful?" Kohn asked.

"They were exposed too soon," the poet said.

"Your uncle exposed them?" Kohn asked.

The poet shook his head. "I'm afraid not," he said sadly. "I'm having him do so in my book, for dramatic reasons—in reality when he saw what was going on he cut short his leave and took another ship out. He was no different from any other German; he tried to ignore what was under his nose."

"Who, then?" Gottliebsohn asked, for some reason suddenly concerned about this young man's relative.

"One of the tenants, I'm sure," the poet said. "It all

points to one of them. The others, those who visited her salon, were too personally involved."

"And how does Herr Gottliebsohn fit into all this?" Kohn asked, at last getting to the important question.

"Why," Krieger said, "he was one of the tenants. I know he's without memory—but I had hoped that by showing him my aunt's ledger, her picture, and so on, he might recall something . . . that would help him and me also."

All during this recital Gottliebsohn had been trying to guess at what possible connection there could be between this young man and himself. Now to be told that he had actually lived in that house where they conspired against the Nazis seemed more nightmarish than anything he had ever dreamed. How could he ever have been able to forget such people? It seemed impossible—but suddenly he knew that there had been a connection. But how, in God's name, had he ever come to be with this young man's aunt? He could not remember.

Getting out of his hammock, Krieger picked a stiff-backed journal from a pile of papers.

Gottliebsohn looked blankly at the list, neatly printed in a narrow column. The names blurred with his reluctance, and with an effort he focused his vision. But whatever he had been afraid to see was not there. None of the names meant anything to him.

He looked up, relieved and yet puzzled. "Why is my name starred?"

"I was hoping you could tell me that," Krieger said.

"Because I was a Jew, probably," Gottliebsohn murmured.

"You have a photograph, you said?" Kohn said to Krieger.

Krieger rummaged through the papers. The photograph he found was of the murky brown so prevalent in the Europe of that time, showing the aunt posed in an ornate, high-backed chair. She was wearing a wide-brimmed hat, and Gottliebsohn thought her very regal, though he also thought, by the roguish tilt of her head, perhaps, that he detected in her a mad look. But she was not at all familiar.

Kohn pointed out the large jeweled cross, somewhat out of place over that modest black dress. "Was she Catholic?"

he asked. Krieger nodded. "Let me see her guest book," Kohn said, and then, turning to Gottliebsohn, "it's interesting you could live in her house and not remember her!"

Ignoring the now flustered Gottliebsohn and working backward from the page the blotted name was on, Kohn examined every entry until, as he had hoped he might, he found one that was familiar.

"What was Father Stieffel to your aunt?" he asked, mentally congratulating himself for having kept that third letter.

"He was her confessor," Krieger said.

"Do you remember *him*?" Kohn demanded, turning on Gottliebsohn, pointing.

Gottliebsohn stared at the scrawl, with the tiny *fr.* that indicated a priest. He did not recognize the name, but somehow the picture of a priest, a man in black with indeterminate features, stuck in his mind.

Glass, watching carefully for reaction, saw his sudden immobility and knew that something had happened. He decided to act before his patient's retreat—for he was certain it was that—had gone too far.

"Remembering something?" he asked pleasantly, leaning over the other's stiffened shoulder, surreptitiously pressing his arm.

Gottliebsohn started. "Nothing . . . I mean, I don't remember . . . how would *I* have had anything to do with priests?" he answered, stammering.

Kohn said nothing, thinking about the letter he had received from Father Stieffel: he had read about the memoryless Gottliebsohn, and wanted to express his sympathy; he himself had occasional moments of forgetfulness, and he knew what it was like to want to forget those dreadful days; he too had spent months in a concentration camp; it ended with a prayer for Gottliebsohn's soul. Kohn's first inclination had been to toss it away, and then, on a whim, he had kept it. And now it turned out that his hunch was right—while it might have been only coincidental that a cathedral priest should have shown interest in an amnesiac Jew, it now seemed there was more to it than that: they had both been intimates of this poet's aunt, and both, furthermore, had had their names blotted by what seemed a careless drop of ink (and what Gottliebsohn, curiously, saw as the Jewish star

. . . Kohn must remember to ask the psychiatrist what that might signify). For the moment, however, he had other surprises for Gottliebsohn.

"You said you would take us to your aunt's house?" he asked, reminding Krieger of the offer in his letter.

The house was some distance away. But they walked, at Kohn's insistence; he thought to wear Gottliebsohn down physically as well as mentally. The poet, who now wore dark glasses, dropped back with Glass.

"You don't say much," he observed. "The other's a policeman, I'd wager, but I haven't been able to guess you. A bureaucrat of some sort—a lawyer?"

Glass told him.

"It's the glasses," the other said apologetically. "People don't come through as well as they ought. It's what I want, of course; by keeping the present dim, the past becomes so much more real."

"And is the book going well?" Glass asked politely.

"Not a bit well!" the other cried. "I'm having trouble with my characters; they absolutely refuse to behave as I want; no matter how much I despise them, some remain most dreadfully sympathetic. I thought meeting Herr Gottliebsohn would give me a firsthand look at what the reality was—but he doesn't seem himself, there's nothing there I could grab hold of, it's as if he were an automaton; you know the story, without a heart, but desperately seeking one."

Glass looked curiously at the other. "You're not far off," he said. "The man is empty—mechanical, if you like. And it's not a heart he's seeking, but a personality. He literally doesn't know how to act. All these years with a cut-off memory is like a tree cut off from its root system: the tree withers and dies; in his case it has been the personality."

"My countrymen wish to forget," the poet said. "You think that is bad?"

"I think it is impossible," Glass said flatly.

"And what if they do not forget," the other persisted, "but what they remember is inaccurate?"

"Then they will live falsely," Glass retorted. "They will be like mutants, grotesque in the first generation, eventually perhaps the 'normal'—but at what cost to mankind?"

"And what if they choose to ignore the past," the other

said. "What if, like your friends on the negotiating committee, they ignore the hate and contempt they must feel?"

"If we lived our daily lives in response to our deepest
emotions," Glass said slowly, "we wouldn't last ten days. We
respond one way to the world around us, and another, usually in bed, to the one inside."

"You are a Freudian?" the poet asked, looking at him
shrewdly.

"All psychiatrists are, in a sense," Glass responded. "But
I am not a disciple, no."

"Well, what about my characters?" the poet asked. "How
can I make them work the way they ought?"

"Think of them with separate realities," Glass said. "An
inner and an outer. If they mesh, as sometimes they do, it is
called madness."

The poet laughed aloud. "That is what my own trouble
is then," he said. "I am all of a piece—all poets are, or
should be, to act as you describe we call hypocrisy. But I
see you are right; that is reality, that hypocrisy, and it is the
rest of us who are mad, for madness is being different from
the norm, *hein*? Well, it is the theme of my book, I will try
again. But how I despise those poems and novels which are
all to the point, so artificial, somehow . . . but here we
are."

The house was set back from the street, fenced in, a
large lawn leading up to the entrance. They gathered uncertainly at the gate.

"There are still tenants," Krieger said. "But your old
room," he said to Gottliebsohn, "is vacant. It is the attic, too
hot for most people, only one little window."

Gottliebsohn had no doubt he had been here before—
the shortness of his breath and the turbulence of his emotions, no matter that they were unidentifiable, were proof
enough. Like a blind man whose other senses become enormously acute, he could *feel* how much whatever had happened here must have meant to him.

Glass observed his agitation. "What is it, Ernst?" he
murmured.

"I don't know," Gottliebsohn said, looking in some won-
derment at his suddenly trembling hands.

"You lead the way," Kohn said.

Gottliebsohn did not move.

"What's the matter?" Kohn asked, falsely solicitous. "Remembering something?"

Gottliebsohn took a breath and stumbled forward. Inside the spacious front hallway, which smelled of wax and furniture oil, yet was somehow unclean, as if they breathed the dust of memory, he hesitated again, looking at the doors on either side.

"*Now* what is it?" Kohn asked, as if he were having difficulty keeping his temper.

"I'm not sure how one gets to the attic," Gottliebsohn said, looking beseechingly at Krieger, then his doctor.

"Of course you know," Kohn said sharply. "Move!"

Gottliebsohn, seeing that no one was going to help, and wanting to get away from his tormentor, chose the door on the right-hand side. It opened to reveal a staircase.

Kohn looked triumphantly at Glass, and then followed Gottliebsohn, who had begun climbing. Gottliebsohn hesitated on the second landing, then went to a narrow doorway and opened it to reveal a narrow, steep stair. The only illumination was from a dirt-flecked skylight. Again they climbed, and again Gottliebsohn hesitated, this time before the only door.

Kohn reached past him, turned the knob, and flung the door open. Then, with his policeman's hand, he urged Gottliebsohn forward.

His heart pounding, Gottliebsohn stepped inside. When he ducked his head out of some prior habit, before he saw that the ceiling was low, he knew that he had indeed been in these shabby quarters before.

There was very little furniture: a sofa and an easy chair slip-covered against dust, a dust which already lay thick on the small round table in what served as a dining area.

"Phew!" Krieger said. "But there's no way to air these rooms—perhaps that's why so many flowers." Looking where he pointed, they saw groups of what once had been flowers, brittle and dry, in makeshift vases, cups, bottles and bowls.

Gottliebsohn drew his trembling forefinger absent-mindedly along the tabletop, wondering whether it was, in fact, the same dust he had breathed so many years before. He looked at the tiny kitchen, picturing himself heating water for tea on the small stove, then wandered into the bedroom and stood transfixed: the bed, which he stared at with some strange reluctance yet stared nevertheless, the bed was very large, too big for the room, big enough, that bed, for two.

"Well?" came Kohn's harsh voice from behind him.

"I'm not sure," he said hesitantly; then, coming back into the front room, he let his eyes slowly go back over each item of furniture which began to seem vaguely familiar, though he couldn't have said how—and then he became aware that something was missing.

"Where is the piano?" he asked before he could stop himself.

Krieger smiled broadly. "You *are* remembering then!" he cried. "It was here until a year ago—a small upright, badly out of tune—I loaned it to a friend."

"I wasn't aware you played," Kohn said, interrupting.

"But I don't," Gottliebsohn said.

"Why would you have had a piano then?" Kohn asked, frowning.

"It must have been here when I moved in," Gottliebsohn said, thinking it was a mistake to have even mentioned it. "I would have had no furnishings of my own. Look here," he went on, showing him his clumsy hands, strong but short-fingered, knotted now with his tension. "You can see that I couldn't have, with these . . ."

"The piano belonged to a previous tenant then?" Kohn asked of Krieger.

"It must have," Gottliebsohn answered instead, then shrugged to cover his fear. He wanted to put his hands over his ears, to stop the sudden sound of that out-of-tune piano in his mind. How did it happen that he suddenly remembered this music and that it moved him so strongly he wanted to weep, when the only music he cared for, that he played over and over on the nickelodeon in the cheap little café across from his flat, was the Hebrew and Arabic folk songs? Why, if he did not play himself, did he hear an elaborately romantic Strauss waltz, notes tumbling one over another, seductive three-quarter time, the melody so beautifully clear that unmusical as he was, if he had been asked, or if he dared, he could have whistled it on the spot?

"Are you all right, Ernst?" Glass murmured, concerned.

"It's nothing," he lied, shaking his head, trying to shake the sound of that waltz away. "I'm trying to remember—and it won't come," and hoping that would explain his sudden emotion, he walked away from them over by the table again —only to stand, perplexed, as he stared at the tabletop. Initials were scrawled where nothing had been before. Before he might assume that supernatural forces were at work he looked at his smudged finger, and realized that it had been himself who had tested that dust—but what in God's name did those initials mean? *K.B.* He heard someone moving close to him, and before he could stop himself he had wiped the table clean.

Glass stared at his patient, now industriously scrubbing his hand with his pocket handkerchief.

"What had you written there?" Glass asked, after a moment.

Gottliebsohn, folding his handkerchief so the dirt should not show, put it nonchalantly back in his breast pocket, wondering how much, if anything, the psychiatrist had seen.

"Whose initials were they?" Glass continued quietly.

"I don't know," Gottliebsohn said, frightened. And then he had an inspiration. "Perhaps the one who informed on that fellow's aunt!"

Kohn was with them now. "What's going on?" he asked suspiciously.

Gottliebsohn was momentarily relieved to see that the psychiatrist was not going to answer. And then he realized that as far as the psychiatrist was concerned, it was his decision, not the doctor's or Kohn's. And if he lied to this persistent investigator or withheld information, he was only postponing an inevitable reckoning.

"I wrote some initials in the dust," he said awkwardly at last. "It was unconscious on my part; I hadn't realized I was doing it . . ."

"Initials?" Kohn said sharply.

"K.B.," Gottliebsohn answered. And before Kohn could ask, he continued: "I don't know what, or whose . . ."

The poet had drawn near. Kohn turned to him. "Anyone in your aunt's house with the initials K.B.?"

"None of her tenants," Krieger replied, after taking a moment to remember the list. "But there were others in that house, too: servants, her personal maid, a secretary."

"Maybe the initials are those of the informer!" Gottliebsohn burst out, unable to restrain himself.

Kohn stared at him for a long, too long, a moment. Then he turned to the poet again. "What finally happened to your aunt?"

"She was sent to a home for mental deficients," Krieger said.

Gottliebsohn was afraid of what he was about to hear.

"She died there," Krieger went on. "Euthanasia. It was step one for the Nazis. The Germans accepted 'mercy' killing for defectives, and then, later . . .'"

No one responded for a moment. Then Kohn went on. "And how did Father Stieffel manage to survive?"

"Someone at the Vatican interceded," Krieger said. "His mind went in the camp, and I suppose the Nazis figured he was harmless. Anyway, Father Stieffel was sent to the camp not so much for political activity as for shielding Jews. He eventually got into trouble with his own Church for that, since he was accused of forging documents—baptismal certificates, that sort of thing. His defense was interesting, in that he claimed to have made genuine conversions. It put the Church in an awkward position, of course. How could they refuse their protection to converts? However, it came out that he had officiated at marriage rites for nonbelievers. Jews married to non-Jews were left alone for a long while, you know."

"And have you talked to him?" Kohn asked.

Krieger shrugged. "I tried. It's difficult to make sense of anything he says. He has no real responsibility at the cathedral; he's an embarrassment to them really, but a martyr, you see, a hero to the young; and so they keep him on, always fearful, of course, that he may make a statement or give an interview condemning the former Pope. At which time they will point out that he is deranged."

Kohn nodded. "Would you let me borrow that guest book? I'd like to go over those names."

Krieger said, "It's those initials you're after, isn't it? I'll look for them for you."

Kohn, though he was irritated, gave the other the name of the hotel in Bonn.

"This way," the poet said as he parted from them at the front gate, "I'll be able to find out what *you* find out. I need it for my book."

"Where to now?" Glass asked, once Krieger was out of

sight, curious as to Kohn's sudden haste.

"Church," Kohn replied, and neither Glass nor Gottlieb-sohn asked him anything more.

When they arrived at the cathedral, Kohn left them before the massive double doors while he went along the outside corridor, looking for the chancery office.

The two men stood in silence for some time. The doctor wanted his patient to absorb it all, in mass and in detail, this medieval concept that had remained a powerful modern symbol. The twin spires of the cathedral arrogantly speared the heavens, and Glass wondered why the double effort. It was more than an architectural concept; there had to have been a religious motive—showing the essential dichotomy of man, perhaps: flesh and the spirit, the religious and the secular, love and hate. But however two-faced man might be, he was in fact only one idea. And by the record, the doctor mused, not a very good idea at that.

Gottliebsohn found it difficult at first to even look at the structure. He knew that he had seen it before, it fit so neatly into a faded outline in his mind—but he thought he remembered it only superficially, as meaningless to him as a picture on a tourist postcard. Gradually, however, as his eyes kept lifting to the doors, he began to realize that this place had a deeper significance, and before he quite knew what he was up to, he found himself approaching the entrance. It was all so dreamlike, so slow-motion! He imagined himself approaching the entrance: thought it once, thought it twice, and the third time began actually walking through the vaulted doors. When he found himself inside the gloomy cavernous interior Gottliebsohn halted, certain he had made some terrible mistake. He experienced the same throat-choking dread that signaled the onset of a dangerous enterprise. The great echoes, the drifting incense, the muffled mutterings of priests and penitents from the scattered confessionals, the yellow light from the stained-glass windows, the flickering candles in the semidark, throwing shadows that gave frightening expression to the painted figures of plaster saints and terra-cotta Magdalenes (were those terrible grimaces real or imagined?), a creaking door, the scuff of shoes on the dusty cement flooring—all, sound and image alike, set up answering reverberations in his mind, and he thought he might take leave of his disordered senses.

"What is it, Ernst?" Glass whispered, halting beside him. He had been surprised when Gottliebsohn had suddenly, without a word, left his side to go into the cathedral; he had followed a moment later, equally silent, watching carefully, and if it had not seemed that the other might stand there forever, his head cocked, eyes fixed in an unblinking stare, he would not have spoken at all. Now, at his words, Gottliebsohn shook himself and continued on into the echoing gloom.

Gottliebsohn was frightened, as if he walked toward some dreadful confrontation, but he had not the slightest premonition that he was going to act as he did then. He had no memory of any knowledge, even superficial, however rudimentary, of the Catholic religion; he did not remember ever having been inside a church before, and yet he obviously knew enough to parody a basic ritual. As they came in front of that altar, where a cheerfully corpulent German Mary reached out to mother the afflicted from an alcove jammed with crutches, canes, tattered bandages and prosthetic devices, he stopped to stare at the painted eyes of the chipped plaster effigy—then dropped to one knee, genuflecting!

The doctor was startled, of course. But though he was conscious of a certain awkwardness on Gottliebsohn's part, he had no idea that his clumsiness had any significance other than unfamiliarity. In fact, he was touched, thinking that Gottliebsohn had been moved to pray, even to an alien goddess, for relief of his affliction.

Neither of them noticed the two priests who had paused before this altar. The younger man, somewhat bored with having to keep the other company, had his mind on more temporal matters, and he now looked with some amazement on the kneeling Gottliebsohn.

"That's just backward, my son," the priest said, leaning over and tapping him on the shoulder. Gottliebsohn, lost in the mysteries of his own thought, shrugged the hand away. The priest flushed and tugged at Gottliebsohn to stand up. "What?" he demanded. "Do you mock the Madonna then?"

Gottliebsohn became very pale. Getting to his feet, he stepped back from the infuriated priest. "I don't mock," he protested.

The older priest looked up from his beads, frowning at

the commotion. "What is it, Father?" he asked.

"This man profaned the altar," the younger priest whispered. "He genuflected with his left knee, used his left hand to make the sign of the cross!"

Glass took in his breath. He had always been careful not to intrude on the beliefs held by others, sensitive about his own lack of faith. How were they to explain? To identify themselves as non-Catholic was not enough, and he shrank from the accusation of un- and even anti-Christian behavior that might result from the knowledge that they were Jews. Before he could think of what to say, however, the older priest had come between his angry colleague and the frightened Gottliebsohn.

"Who are you?" he asked, peering closely into Gottliebsohn's whitened face.

"It was accidental, I swear, I meant no disrespect," Gottliebsohn stammered.

"Of course you didn't," the old man said. "What is it you want, my son? Why have you come back? You must know it is dangerous."

"What are you talking about, Father?" the younger priest asked, puzzled as to how an obvious infidel could seem natural to the older man.

"He gave the proper sign," the old man said.

"You mean that backward genuflect was deliberate?" the young priest said, astonished.

"He is one of the converts," the old man said impatiently.

"I am not Catholic," Gottliebsohn protested.

"But you gave the sign?" the old man said, frowning worriedly. "How would you know that sign?"

Glass thought it time to intercede. "You had to have been here before, Ernst," he said.

"I don't remember," Gottliebsohn insisted desperately. "I meant no disrespect . . . there was something about the altar," he admitted finally.

At that moment, Kohn arrived. He had found the office, only to be told that Father Stieffel was somewhere in the cathedral. He had hoped that the interview could be conducted in more businesslike surroundings; he had an almost superstitious dread of the symbols and artifacts of this mysterious religion—and then to return to find Gottliebsohn and the psychiatrist gone, and he forced to enter the cathedral alone, took as much courage as he possessed. He hurried through the cathedral, shrinking from those sights, sounds and smells which seemed to him sure manifestations of the supernatural. When he spotted the others, however, the sight of his companions with two priests drove everything else from his mind.

"What's all this?" he demanded of Glass.

Glass hesitated only a moment. He had no right to withhold information of this nature from Kohn; he would find out soon enough in any case. He told the other what had happened.

"Father Stieffel?" Kohn said. All stiffened at the threatening authority of that harsh voice. Neither Glass nor the young priest had ever heard that kind of voice before, but somehow they recognized it as hinting at special cruelties. "You know this man?" he asked then, pointing at Gottliebsohn.

"I don't quite place him," Father Stieffel said. "But then, there were so many."

"So many?" Kohn demanded.

"Converts," Father Stieffel said.

"Ah, converts," Kohn said. "Special kind of converts, weren't they?"

"Mother Church does not discriminate," Father Stieffel said.

"But they were special, weren't they?" Kohn demanded.

"Yes," the old man admitted finally. "They were Jews. But they were genuine conversions," he insisted in turn.

"Is that right?" Kohn said innocently. "But I thought the charges against you included forging baptismal papers, that sort of thing."

The old man became visibly upset. "I never broke God's law," he said, his voice quavering.

"Please," the young priest broke in, "you can see Father Stieffel is not well."

"It's all right, Father," the old man said. "They have come to me for help. He gave the sign."

"Tell us about that," Kohn said, suddenly ingratiating.

"Those who were to escape the secular laws were told to genuflect at this altar at certain hours," Father Stieffel said. "I kept an eye out for those poor communicants, and saw to it that they were given religious instruction."

"And you don't remember giving *him* instruction?" Kohn asked, indicating the shaken Gottliebsohn.

"There were so many," the old priest said sorrowfully.

"Who denounced you?" Kohn asked, as if his curiosity were inadvertent. But it caught the old man's wandering attention.

"They said one of my communicants," he said. He hesitated, and then looked hard at Gottliebsohn, as if with a little more effort it would be possible to remember. The others looked, too, and under their questioning stares, Gottliebsohn grew dizzy with shame.

"It wasn't me," Gottliebsohn whispered, his voice cracking with the effort to make himself heard. But they were all listening now to the old priest.

"Later, at the camp," the old man said, "I heard the true story. A soldier had followed one of my special communicants to this altar—like you," he said, to the younger priest, "a boy with quick eyes. We thought that no one would see that the sign was simply backward. But he spotted it."

"A soldier?" Gottliebsohn asked, incredulous. He looked at the psychiatrist, and knew that both were thinking about the same confirming incident—his hallucination was real, he *had* been followed . . . but why had he forgotten the cathedral? Could it be that he had been somehow responsible for the capture of this priest?

"I am so terribly sorry," Gottliebsohn mumbled awkwardly, stunned by the seeming revelation.

"You're sorry?" Kohn said. "Why are you sorry?"

"It was me the soldier followed," Gottliebsohn said. "It's my fault the priest was captured."

"How is it your fault?" Kohn demanded. He turned his ire on Glass. "Why is it his fault?"

"I must have done something to have had the soldier follow me, mustn't I?" Gottliebsohn said, in an agony of remorse. "And if I was careless, the priest suffered."

"You couldn't have known," the old man said, but his face worked at the memory.

"Do you remember the priest?" Kohn demanded. Gottliebsohn shook his head. "He is a former tenant of Margaretha Krieger," Kohn said then, to the old man. "Ernst

Gottliebsohn, do you remember the name?"

"Margaretha?" the priest said. "But she is dead."

"Ernst Gottliebsohn is not," Kohn said, pushing the other forward.

"There were so many," the old man said, sorrowing, and Kohn finally saw that it was no use. The priest had little sense of time, his own memory confused, the past like the present, and the future nonexistent, as it must have been then.

Kohn turned at last to the younger man. "If he should happen to remember anything . . . specific," he said, "I'd appreciate it if you got in touch with us." He scribbled his name and hotel in his notebook, then ripped out the page and handed it to the reluctant man.

"You are the first to have returned," Father Stieffel was saying to Gottliebsohn. "I hope there were others so fortunate."

Gottliebsohn nodded dumbly, and was grateful to Kohn for getting them away. But they stood uncertainly on the cathedral steps, each of them, for separate reasons, too disturbed to make any suggestions as to what they should do next.

"Let's get some coffee," Kohn said finally, pointing to an outdoor café across the square.

They took a table in silence and sat glumly until the waiter brought their order; three coffees, and a brandy for Kohn, which he poured into his cup.

"Why was that soldier following you, Ernst?" he asked, the liquor seeming to revive him.

Gottliebsohn shook his head. He was still numb from the scene in the cathedral, the picture of it frozen in his mind like a slide projector which has stuck and the image telescoped, wrong-end-to, so that he seemed to be looking at it from an enormous distance, himself a faceless bulk, kneeling before that altar, and in the background, filled in by the priest's words, a lurking soldier whose features, try as he might, he was unable to make out. The feeling that he might recognize the other if he would only step out of the shadow left him in a state very like shock.

"Did you deliberately lead him to the cathedral?" Kohn demanded.

"No!" Gottliebsohn burst out. "Not deliberately. I couldn't have!" Then he shrank from the curious stares of those at the surrounding tables.

"Couldn't have?" Kohn asked, raising his eyebrows.

"I wasn't that kind of person," Gottliebsohn whispered.

"On that again, are you?" Kohn asked sardonically. "Well, tell us then—what kind of person *were* you?"

Gottliebsohn did not answer.

"What were you doing in Cologne, anyway?" Kohn went on. "That old witch says you had ways of making money—how did a Jew make money in 1939?"

"I may have done illegal things," Gottliebsohn responded weakly, "but it was only to get enough money to get out of Germany—and I would never have collaborated, never. I hated them too much!"

"Did you?" Kohn asked, falsely pleasant. "And how would you know that, you having such a bad memory, and all?"

Gottliebsohn stared at his pitiless interrogator, terribly afraid of what was coming next.

"What was your business with that priest, do you suppose?" Kohn asked then, still pretending affability.

"To get my family out of Germany, maybe," Gottliebsohn managed finally. "If he forged documents, like they say . . ."

"You've missed the whole point about our good priest," Kohn said, suddenly savage. "He wasn't just rambling on about those conversions of his—as far as he was concerned, they were genuine. He didn't mind breaking manmade laws, but he's never broken one of God's. He'd do anything for those special communicants, forge baptismal papers, backdate conversions—so long as there was a conversion first! If you did have business with this priest, my friend, it wasn't to get your family *out* of Germany, but to fix it so you could stay *in!*"

"What do you mean?" Gottliebsohn managed to say.

"Father Stieffel arranged it so his specials could disappear into the population," Kohn said. "You were planning to stay in Germany, Ernst. You were going to fade into the background!"

"But I tried to join my people!" Gottliebsohn said, protesting violently.

"After you were found out!" Kohn said. "Why *was* that soldier following you? If it wasn't deliberate, as you say, then it's more than likely that someone was suspicious of you. Why would anyone be suspicious of you, a nondescript Jew, undercover, on the run . . . maybe you'd had enough, Ernst, maybe you were going to disappear, become a real German, a Christian . . ."

"No!" Gottliebsohn cried, but this time his protest was feeble. "I wasn't that kind!" He looked beseechingly at the psychiatrist.

"You're taking a lot for granted." Glass said at last. "He lived in the home of a woman who knew this priest very well; why couldn't he have been a member of their group, perhaps even a courier . . ."

"I'm giving him the benefit of the doubt as it is," Kohn said harshly. "Two people with whom he was in contact were denounced to the Gestapo . . . by whom? The soldier? Okay, let's say it was the soldier. But what reason would he have to be suspicious of our man here if he weren't involved in some business with the Nazis? Listen, I want to get Ernst off the hook just as much as you do—only I can't go in to the people I'm responsible to with nothing more than some vague statement that Ernst Gottliebsohn is not the type to have collaborated!"

Glass could think of nothing to say. How could he come up with an effective defense when he couldn't help wondering himself what would have been strong enough to keep Gottliebsohn in Germany at a time when he would have been confronted on all sides by a discrimination that was growing increasingly violent. He tried to imagine himself in a similar situation, and though he understood how enormously difficult it would be to leave the country of your birth, he did not think he could even consider fading into the background of a people who, if they did not actively hate you, still looked upon your fate with a massive indifference. It would take a complicated personality to accept that kind of a situation, and he just did not know enough about Gottliebsohn to make a judgment on whether he would have been capable of it or not. Or for that matter enough about himself to know what *he* might be capable of. Then Glass became somewhat uneasy. Was he losing his detachment? He was here, after all, to investigate this man's character, not his own. He shook those troubling thoughts away and tried to concentrate on what Kohn was saying to his patient.

"Look here, Ernst," Kohn was saying, as if he felt genuinely sorry for Gottliebsohn, now slumped despondently in his chair, "I don't think you're the type to have collaborated either. But you've got to give me something to go on. You've got to start remembering! What were you up to in Cologne? Why was the soldier following you?" He paused. "If you leave it this way, it just doesn't look good," he said.

Glass watched Gottliebsohn carefully, not at all liking the drawn face, worried whether he might not be going to have an attack similar to the one in the Israeli air terminal Kohn had told him about. But after a long silence Gottliebsohn stirred and looked vaguely about the café. "Where is the bathroom, do you suppose?" he asked finally.

"Inside, probably," Glass said, pointing to the building from which the waiters served. "Would you like me to go with you?" he asked, as Gottliebsohn got somewhat unsteadily to his feet. Gottliebsohn shook his head.

They watched him disappear inside. "He's afraid," Kohn said. "His guts are growling with it." Kohn motioned to the waiter and ordered three brandies. Glass did not protest. They sat in silence. After the drinks came and still no Gottliebsohn, Kohn drank his, then began frowning. "He's taking a damn long time," he said.

"Perhaps one of us ought to see him," Glass said, getting to his feet.

But Kohn was on his feet too, and moving quite rapidly into the building. By the time Glass got there, he was met by a suddenly flushed Kohn coming out.

"He's run for it," Kohn said, trembling with fury. "He didn't have to go to the toilet at all—came in here and went right out that side door. What does he think he's doing? Where does he think he can go? He must be out of his mind!"

For the moment, Glass had no answer.

9

GOTTLIEBSOHN KNEW EXACTLY WHERE he must go, though in the first excitement of the running away he had no idea how he would proceed once he got there. Certainly there was no premonition that he would find himself resorting to not one, but two impersonations. Once out of sight of those two incongenial companions, he could think only of how little time he might have before they guessed his destination. He headed directly for the railroad station, walking swiftly, but having to restrain himself from breaking into an outright run.

As he approached the terminal, however, he hesitated, his heart pounding, remembering that pedestrian tunnel, not at all sure he would have the courage, should his train be on a far track, to descend into those frightening depths again. Of course he had no other choice. While Kohn had been questioning him that darkness in his mind had lifted long enough for him to remember an earlier flight—but from what? He had come to Cologne on the run, he was certain of it; but he had no idea why. And he had realized that the only solution, short of going mad, or admitting to the inadmissible, was to return to his beginnings.

He purchased a ticket for Hagen; from there he could take another train to the village of Warsfeld, where he had grown up, where he must search for the truth about himself.

"Which track?" he asked the man in the cage, shielding his face, not wanting the other to get too close a look in case he would be questioned when Kohn came tracking him.

"*Fünf*," the man said nasally, without even looking up. Gottliebsohn thought that lucky, but when he found the directional arrow for track five, he saw that his worst fears had been realized.

He prowled the entrance to the tunnel like a wary wild thing until, hearing the loud-speakered announcement that his train was leaving, he held his breath and plunged down the stairs.

It was a bad few minutes. He emerged from the exit sweating and out of breath and disoriented, for one terrible moment unsure of who he was or what he was doing beside this waiting train. Then his memory refocused and he experienced a moment's blinding pain, as if he had stared into an exploding flashbulb. Though his vision was restored, he was left with an aura of light at the peripheries of his sight, and a pounding headache. He looked for his pills and then remembered he had none—his doctor had taken them.

He boarded a first-class coach just as the train was pulling out. He had purchased the most expensive accommodations, hoping for privacy. At least that was working for him: he found an empty compartment and sat by the window. The train rattled over the bridge as they crossed the river and he settled down to getting control of himself for this unlooked-for, unwanted homecoming. And then, inevitably, the doubts rose. How would he be able to walk among, let alone question, those who had surely acquiesced, if not actually participated, in the murder of his family? And what about them? How would he feel if he were German, trying to forget the past, and were suddenly face to face with the personification of his guilt? He flinched from his window reflection.

But it was the only way he could resolve, once and for all, the question of what kind of person he really was: whether he had been in fact, a collaborator.

He was well aware that for all these years he had been only a shell of a man; he knew that the reason behind his restricted, tentative, careful behavior was the fear that in a moment's unguarded attention some secret ugliness inside him might slip out. Why else that nightmare? Only during those drunken evenings in the Arab quarter did he feel safe. The rest of the time he lived in a constant fear that who he was was not worth keeping alive. He had once, in a very bad lonely time, considered suicide, but he had felt an obligation, somehow, to live and to conduct himself with as much dignity as possible, and though he could not for the life of him discover why or to whom he owed such an enormous debt, not believing in God however much he tried, however often he had (though no longer) visited the synagogue, he never again thought about self-destruction.

Then, gradually, the signs that he might be something other than he believed had multiplied: a sudden raucous laugh, so startling, coming from himself who never laughed and seldom smiled—what inner hysteria did that brief hilarity signify? And that flaring rage which no one had ever seen or even guessed at, tempered perhaps by those long walks, and the soccer, and those weekend debauches, revealed once when after a nightmare he had surprised himself in the mirror, and suddenly had slammed his fist into the glass. Then, disconcerted by his own violence, he had burst into tears—for whom or for what? It was shameful that a grown man should break down and he wondered at his own weakness. The trouble was, he thought, he lived an honorable, upright life (he excused those visits to the Arab quarter as something apart from himself, a demand of the flesh), and yet he was haunted by a dream which gave the lie to his public behavior. His psychiatrist said that dream was only a symbol of guilt—and yet there *had* been a soldier following him!

Gottliebsohn pressed his face to the window. Little by little those racketing wheels calmed him. That clatter was soothing to his tangled nerves. After a time he realized that he had taken a seat facing backward. Had it been an unconscious effort to emulate the procedures of his psychiatrist and Kohn? He did not know. But as he watched the scenery flowing by, not unlike an unwinding film reel, he began to wonder if time could ever in his mind be made to run backward as well.

On either side were meadows and orchards, cultivated fields and a scattering of trees—black pine by their look— perhaps seedlings brought by bird, wind or stream from the distant forests. The feeling of isolation that he carried always was suddenly intensified. He felt that they had indeed crossed an invisible line separating present from past. He tried to imagine what it would have been like for him here as a boy and a young man. Had he tramped through that forest, pilfered fruit from that orchard, lain in that cool meadow under the noonday sun? He could not remember. Had he been energetic or lazy, mean or pleasant, close to his father, or a momma's boy? He could not remember. Was he athletic or bookish, ambitious or dull, a good scholar or a poor one? He could not remember. Did he make friends easily, was he aggressive or shy, popular or shunned? He could not remember . . . he could not remember!

When the train stopped at Hagen, Gottliebsohn decided to take a bus the remaining distance. While it was true that if Kohn tracked him this far he would guess his final destination, the fact that he had not gone on by train might momentarily throw him off.

There were not many passengers: a couple dressed in funereal black, a farm girl returning from a holiday, a scattering of elderly men. Gottliebsohn walked to the back of the green-painted vehicle. The bus lurched off. Its springs were stiff and the narrow road had enough dips and bumps to make it a rough ride. Gottliebsohn was told it was a half hour's trip, time enough to think about just how he would approach the problem of getting information, but when a roadside sign indicated the village was only four kilometers off, he began to panic. With no memory he didn't know where to even begin: Who had known his parents best, who would be most likely to know why he had run away, friends or enemies? And how could he even bring himself to ask?

The bus halted on the village outskirts to let the girl off. Gottliebsohn called to the driver, and stumbling down the aisle, got off himself. The girl looked back at him: something in his face made her quicken her step, but Gottliebsohn studiously faced the opposite way and tried to get his bearings.

The village was half hidden by trees. As Gottliebsohn watched the bus turn a corner and disappear, he cursed himself for not having ridden it to the regular stop. Though to a tourist the remote stillness of the small place might seem charming, to Gottliebsohn the quiet was ominous, and he was reluctant to show himself. The town hall, he thought then, the place of records, that was where to start. But he was strangely unwilling to go directly to an official place.

Just across the street was a building with an unmarked gas pump. In the driveway in various stages of disrepair a tractor and a cultivator were standing. But no one seemed to be about, and the entrance door was shut. Gottliebsohn began walking toward it anyway. He had some vague notion of starting his personal investigation right here. He felt an urgent need to talk to someone, anyone, who was not official or important. Then, he told himself, he would get himself used to the way the people here spoke; he might lose some of the awful tension under which he labored. Secretly he hoped to find someone who would have known him—after all, it *was* an exceedingly small place—so he might get all the information he wanted without proceeding any further. Gottliebsohn feared that if he went into the village he might not come out the same person as when he went in. And he was desperately afraid of what he might discover that could change him.

On the other side of the building was a small door. Finding it unlocked, Gottliebsohn walked on in. A large van, which looked as if it might have once been an army vehicle, took up most of the space. From its interior came the sound of hammering. Gottliebsohn approached it warily; he peered inside. Three men were busily at work—one holding a light, the other two fitting in some sort of sheet-metal framing. There was the sharp smell of bruised metal.

"Is one of you the proprietor?" Gottliebsohn asked, coughing politely.

The man using the hammer, squat and muscular, stopped what he was doing immediately. The other two looked around, startled, but at a murmured word went back to their work. The short man came toward Gottliebsohn, and squatting before him, wiped his hands on a greasy apron. Gottliebsohn couldn't know it was deliberate, but the man had certainly obscured his view.

"What is it you want?" the other asked. He gave off an odor of sweat and kerosene.

"I was looking for the town hall," Gottliebsohn said, which was at least partly true. He squinted at the other's sullen face. Was it possible that he could know him? They were the same age—perhaps they had been schoolmates! But he found himself unable to ask.

"Go east five blocks, then a block to your left; you can't miss it," the other said.

"Thank you," Gottliebsohn said, but he made no move to go. "What are you making?" he asked, to keep the other's attention.

"A camper," he answered finally, his manner indicating it was none of Gottliebsohn's business.

"Your own, or for a customer?" Gottliebsohn wondered, working hard now to get the other to be at ease with him.

"You interested in buying one?" the other growled. All three were staring blankly at him. Why were they acting so peculiar? Gottliebsohn wondered. Were they always so suspicious of a stranger? At least he had their attention now —but when he went to tell them who he was, he found that he just could not do it.

"Not really," Gottliebsohn admitted. "I was only curious." And he turned to go, defeated. Then he hesitated. It had come to him how he might question them without revealing his identity!

"Are any of you native to this village?" he asked nervously.

All three continued to stare. "We all are," the squat man said at last—a reluctant admission.

"Did you know Ernst Gottliebsohn?" he asked then.

There was the briefest of pauses. "The name is not familiar," said the squat man.

"Gottliebsohn was—is—from this village," Gottliebsohn said. "There was a sister, too," he continued, when there was no response. "Ruth. The family had a store. Yardage and notions."

One of the men in the back of the van cleared his throat. "No store like that here."

"Not now," Gottliebsohn agreed. "Before 1939." He wondered if he imagined a sly grin, or whether it was a trick of the uncertain light.

The man with the apron had turned to stare down the other. "We were farm boys," he said. Then to Gottliebsohn, "We didn't know those in the village."

"You didn't go to the school here?" Gottliebsohn asked.

"Only for seven forms," the other said. "You don't expect we would remember a village boy from that long ago?"

"I suppose not," Gottliebsohn said doubtfully. He turned away, seeing that it was useless. What upset him as much as anything as he walked slowly outside was that they were not even curious about who he was or why he was asking questions about someone they must have known—it was not possible to have been a Jew in a village this size and not be known!

Did he have the right place? Warsfeld was listed by the Jewish agency as his home; could they have made a mistake? Gottliebsohn, in a panic, began hurrying up the street, but when he saw what must be the building he wanted, above the trees, his pace grew slower. He was still not clear how he should proceed.

The town hall was marked by a plaque set into the cornerstone. There was no one in the little square. Inside, the corridors were also deserted, and all doors leading off them were shut. Gottliebsohn began to wonder whether he had not arrived on some holiday. But walking the length of the building, he found the door he wanted—and it was unlocked.

The room was crowded with files, floor to ceiling and wall to wall. In a space which seemed to have been cleared just for her, a graying older woman worked over a tiny desk.

"Grüss Gott," she said, and got up to see what he wanted. She was intimidating, angular and stern, braided hair coarse as rope, her fingers, holding the stub of a pencil, strong as a workman's, and Gottliebsohn inwardly quailed. How could he get this implacable guardian of the past to open her files to him without an official order? He knew the German mentality—inflexible, unyielding, unamenable to any importuning.

"Grüss Gott," he muttered, the familiar Christian greeting falling like stones from his tongue, and wondered if it would not be best for all concerned to ask an innocuous question and then return to the custody of Kohn. But then that first inspiration (in the garage? or had he known all along how he would evade them?) gave way to another greater one. He immediately recoiled, trembling at the audacity of what had come to his mind. How did it happen that someone like himself, so usually unimaginative, could have harbored the thought, let alone act on it? But even as he debated with himself about attempting a performance so outrageous, he found himself pulling out his diplomatic passport. Slapping it on the counter, he opened it to his photo (careful to keep his hand over the name), and after allowing her ample time to absorb its significance, returned it casually—though his heart was pounding—to his pocket.

"My name is Kohn," he said. "I am a member of the Israeli delegation to Bonn; perhaps you have read something of our negotiations in the newspaper? *Nicht?* No matter. I am in your village—unofficially, for the moment at least—seeking information about a former resident, one Herr Ernst Gottliebsohn. You keep the village records in this room, correct?"

He could see that he had startled, perhaps even impressed her; it was nothing to what he felt himself. He could hardly believe that it had been himself talking, especially in that peremptory tone. Now he waited, unable to breathe, for her to recognize his imposture.

"What sort of information?" she asked.

"Everything you have," he said, and suddenly went into a fit of coughing to hide his relief, taking in great gulpings of air. "Herr Gottliebsohn *did* live here?" he went on anxiously when he had recovered himself, facing up to her frown.

"Is he the one alive then?" she asked.

He was astonished by the question.

"Twenty years ago," she said, "just after the war, there was an inquiry made by a survivors' association on behalf of some member of the family—"

"Yes, yes," he said, impatient and disappointed, "that was for him. The son. Herr Gottliebsohn. But your response was inadequate, that is why I am here now."

"After twenty years?" she said, faintly incredulous.

Gottliebsohn hesitated, aware that a miscalculation now would send him away empty-handed. "Something has come up," he began rather lamely, and then the knowledge of how Kohn would proceed quickened his tongue. "Herr Gottliebsohn, knowing I was to be in Germany, asked me to come here for him," he lied.

"Could he not come himself?" she asked.

"He is very ill," Gottliebsohn said truthfully.

"What is his trouble?" she asked.

"He has no memory," Gottliebsohn said, and fought back a sudden rush of emotion. He cursed the weakness in himself. Kohn would be unfeeling, he thought; Kohn, furthermore, would hardly be intimidated—he would work at this tough old woman until he got what he wanted. "He is under a doctor's care," Gottliebsohn went on. "He has a constant melancholy; nothing seems to encourage him; lately he has begun thinking a good deal about his family, whom he cannot remember, and about the place where he was brought up, which he does not remember either." As he talked, Gottliebsohn felt better: he began to feel more like Kohn and less like himself. "My visit here is his doctor's idea, really; it is felt that whatever I can bring back to fill in those memory gaps will help restore him." He could not be sure but he thought he might have stirred compassion there.

"What has caused this . . . illness?" she asked doubtfully.

"Shock," Gottliebsohn said, remembering the psychiatrist's words. "An emotional upset, like an earthquake. Shame, probably."

"Shame?" she said.

"It's like this room," he burst out. "Can't you imagine shame so great about what's inside those filing cabinets that you would want to lock the door and swallow the key? That's what has happened to Herr Gottliebsohn!"

"I have heard that some villages burned their files," she said calmly enough. "That is stupid, the work of unbalanced minds." She smiled, and he felt a chill. "But you needn't worry, everything is here." She opened a gate and led him to the back part of the room. "I was afraid you were here to make a claim on the property. That must be done in Bonn." They were surrounded by files. "I have worked here since 1925," she said. "Most of what is in these cabinets I have placed there myself." She did seem as dusty and unused as the room itself. "Where would you like to start?"

"Let's work backward," he said, no longer aware that he was using Kohn's technique; it had become his own. "What is the last thing you have on the family?"

She knew exactly which stack. Pulling out a drawer, she found the file she wanted. The top paper was a memorandum from the regional police office in Cologne authorizing travel permits for three members of the Gottliebsohn family: Jakob, Hannah, and Ruth.

"What about the permit for Ernst?" he asked, trying to hide his anxiety.

"There was none," she said, without looking. "Ernst had been gone long since."

It was true then, Gottliebsohn thought. He had hoped the statement of Frau Gonser would be proved false, that the memory of a solitary flight was untrue, that these files would show that the young Ernst had come to the city together with his family.

"How did he go without a permit?" he asked finally, terribly disappointed.

"He would have managed," she said.

"*Why* did he go?" he asked.

She shrugged. "No one seemed to know. He just dropped out of sight. Even before his father sold the store."

She stared at him as if doubtful whether to proceed, then searched another cabinet and pulled out a folder. "The file on the Gottliebsohn store," she said.

Neatly clipped to the folder was a sheaf of memoranda, all directives from the Interior Ministry. After the one "requesting" that all retail shops owned by Jews be so identified was some official correspondence excluding war veterans from the edict. It had been noted that Herr Gottliebsohn, though he was a holder of the Iron Cross, had refused to sign the appropriate document. Eventually, regional headquarters had directed that he be treated as he wished —like an ordinary Jew.

"I don't understand?" Gottliebsohn said, puzzled.

"Perhaps the son didn't either," the woman said dryly. "Jakob was a stubborn man. He said he would not hide behind any cross, even one made of iron."

"You knew him?" Gottliebsohn asked.

"I had gone to work here the year they moved into Warsfeld," she said. "I filled out the first business license."

"Go on, please," Gottliebsohn said sharply.

"They brought the boy in," she said, "too poor for a nanny to leave him with, or maybe for luck—they were so *close* somehow, not afraid to show their affection in public, not like we Germans—"

"Weren't they German?" Gottliebsohn asked, offended.

"Is a Jew ever anything else?" she asked. Gottliebsohn could not answer. "Jakob had a chance to be German," she continued sternly, "and he would not take it. He married a Jewess, too—each to his own kind, *hein?* Hannah was from Poland, besides; not that she wasn't a lovely woman—dark eyes and skin the color of calf—you could see where a man would be taken with her. She it was who usually came in afterward to pay the tax or to register as an alien. She kept saying she would have me over for tea. They lived back of their store, you know, and she could have. But somehow it was never convenient. Hannah did most of the waiting on trade. Jakob kept the shelves stocked, swept the floor, and so on. He was always polite, but he was not much for talking. It would be better had he done. Hannah never learned to speak our language well, and the Polish accent was offensive to us Germans, you understand."

Gottliebsohn did understand.

"And the child?" he asked at last.

"A handsome boy," she said. "Dreadfully spoiled. Pulled drawers out, climbed to the tops of cabinets, ran up and down the aisles. When I spoke to him, he laughed. And when I cuffed him to make him mind, he laughed then too, and tried to kiss my hand. Hannah was upset. She didn't understand that the boy and I got on together. Jakob understood. He brought the boy with him to register the sister's birth—Ruth, her name was. I suggested at least a German middle name. But Jakob was a stubborn man. And the boy never came back."

"You never saw him again?" Gottliebsohn asked.

"Only from a distance," she said. "Wheeling his baby sister around the square, later taking her for walks. There was no reason to come here. And since Hannah never saw fit to invite me into the back . . ." She closed her mouth tight.

Gottliebsohn thumbed through the document file. He stopped at a formal request for police action, signed by Jakob Gottliebsohn, dated November, 1938. Vandalism, the statement read.

"That was Crystal Night," she said.

"So?" he wondered.

"All over Germany the windows of Jews were broken,"

she said. "Why should our village be any different? Jakob had gone out of his way to flaunt his Jewishness, even putting the Hebrew star on his window. Some of our young men were offended."

"Why was there no police report?" Gottliebsohn demanded, angered.

She shrugged. "The police could not arrest people for doing what was popular."

"Gottliebsohn was reluctant to ask the next question. "And where was . . . the son . . . during all this?" Those young men, he thought, anguished, must have been schoolmates.

"He was already gone," she said.

Gottliebsohn grieved for those four: the lovely immigrant woman, the silent and proud man who stocked while his wife clerked, the sister only sixteen, the brother twenty-two when he had found it necessary to leave. He imagined how close that family was, and if they had been too poor to hire a German nanny, the children must have been left to themselves in the back rooms; with him six years older he would have been given the responsibility of caring for her, distracting her with toys, taking her out for sunning, and even in later years participating with her in the mock-solemn games of girlhood . . . How could he have left them?

Blindly he turned the papers in the file. Eventually he stopped at a bill of sale dated March 1939. "But this is robbery," he said.

"Jews were not permitted to own property," she said.

"At least no one in the village took advantage," he said. The buyer was listed as from Düsseldorf; then he saw a shading of expression in her face. "What is it?" he demanded.

"The Düsseldorfer was a cousin of a local man," she said. "But someone had to buy. Jakob was lucky to get a hundred marks. There was little merchandise left, you see. Jakob had a closing-out sale."

"And the villagers flocked to buy?" Gottliebsohn said bitterly. He had seen the tax forms—since 1936 the trade of the store had steadily declined.

"There were bargains," she said without expression.

"I should like to visit friends of the family," he said. "They did have friends?"

"They kept to themselves," she said. "Except for a farm family, with whom I believe they were close. Jakob tided them over a bad time."

"What are their names?" Gottliebsohn asked.

"The two sons were killed in the war," she said. "The parents are dead, too. A nephew owns the farm—but he is not local."

"Well, who then is left who knew them?" Gottliebsohn asked, frantic lest this visit made at such risk would turn out to be fruitless. "Surely there is someone," he said, "who can tell me about Ernst Gottliebsohn?"

She did not respond immediately. He waited quietly, somehow knowing with the insight of the mentally desperate that it would not do to press her.

"The schoolmaster might be able to help," she said finally, though obviously reluctant.

"The schoolmaster!" he said, delighted. "But of course! He would be just the one! He would know about Ernst's character, his ability in studies, how he got on with his fellows . . ."

"You misunderstand," she said. "The one of whom you speak never returned from the war. The present master would have been a schoolmate of Ernst's." She hesitated, still doubtful. "Hans Eichler could tell you a great deal—if you caught him in the proper mood."

"Where will I find him?" Gottliebsohn asked eagerly, ignoring her strange reluctance.

She looked at the tiny clock pinned to her smock. "He would still be at the schoolhouse," she said. "There are ten minutes before class lets out." He nodded his thanks and turned to go. "Herr Kohn," she called, catching him at the door. "You must not take what Schoolmaster Eichler says too much to heart." He understood that she was warning him. "Give my best to Ernst," she said then. "Tell him I am sorry about his family." He shook away this sudden unwanted concern.

The schoolhouse was a short walk. He met only two persons: both ample-figured *Hausfraus* of middle age, both dressed alike in suspendered skirt and a tightly laced blouse out of which the bosoms swelled, each sweeping the side-walk in front of her house, eyes downcast, as the stranger walked by. Try as he might, he recognized neither, though he gave each a once-over as he stepped out of the way of the busy brooms. It was an inhospitable town, he thought bitterly. This false modesty concealed an aversion to outsiders. And what if he told them who he really was? Would they pretend, like those kerosene-odored garage men, not to remember?

Classes were letting out. Gottliebsohn stood across the street, watching the children march out, as alike as regulation could make them, the boys in haltered shorts and bowl haircuts and clumsily knotted ties, the girls in plain smocks, all silent until they were three steps into the street, and then with a shout or a high-pitched laugh, a skip, a jump, a jostle, they became as disorderly as *kinder* everywhere.

Gottliebsohn looked for a boy who might be like the boy for whose memory he searched. Was there not one squint-eyed, brown-haired, olive-skinned exotic among all these sun-flowers? Surely the Hitlerian weeding-out had not rid this soil completely of its extraneous elements? He saw then that they were not so much alike, that the noses ranged from button snubs to beaks of imposing dimension, that beneath the bangs there were low brows and high, that the eyes were round, narrow, lidded, dull or shiny as the intelligence behind them. There was one boy too who walked by himself, though whether out of pride or shyness it was difficult to tell. Gottliebsohn's heart went out to that isolate—and then he steadied himself. Kohn would not behave so. Kohn would not be sentimental.

The schoolmaster was at his desk, packing books and papers into a satchel. He looked up, startled at this unexpected visitor. He was thin and may have been handsome once, though now his face was pinched, lines of bitterness or pain grooved into either side of his mouth.

"You are Herr Eichler?" Gottliebsohn asked. The other nodded. "I have come about Ernst Gottliebsohn."

The other stared. Gottliebsohn grew nervous during the prolonged scrutiny—he felt as he imagined those who are brought into a police line-up must feel: guilty or not, there is a fear of identification—and he labored to make a plausible story for one whose glittering eyes indicated a skeptical intelligence. That old woman, a recordkeeper, was one thing; this schoolmaster, who had been his schoolmate, quite another.

"You remember him, surely?" Gottliebsohn asked.

"I have reason to remember Ernst," the other said, obscurely significant. But Gottliebsohn's attention was distracted by his voice: harsh, almost metallic. Then he noticed the scar on the other's throat, and guessed that he had a damaged larynx. "What about him?" Eichler grated.

"He is ill," Gottliebsohn said. The other made no response. "It is a mental illness," Gottliebsohn went on. "That does not surprise you? You saw signs of it then, even as a boy?"

"You have reason to ask me that, I assume," the other said, not taking his eyes from him.

"Herr Gottliebsohn has lost his memory," Gottliebsohn said. "His doctors feel that whatever information can be gotten from those who knew him would be helpful."

"His doctors?" Eichler asked. "And who are you then?"

"I am his psychiatrist," Gottliebsohn said, hesitating only a moment.

Eichler laughed. Gottliebsohn wasn't offended. Neither was he surprised by this second impersonation. Kohn would not have worked on this one, and he had given up being startled by the adaptability of his own mind. "We are both plagued by doctors," Eichler said, "Ernst and I. But I refuse their comforts." Reaching below him, Eichler pulled up a pair of crutches, and kicking away the chair, was suddenly standing.

Gottliebsohn sucked in his breath. The man was a cripple. His right pants leg was tucked up under his belt, empty. "My advice to Ernst is to dismiss his doctors and make do with what he has."

What was the man saying? Gottliebsohn became disturbed. "He is a cripple, like you!" he burst out. "The Germans amputated a part of his mind! Because his wounds do not show does not make him any less pitiful!"

Eichler seemed amused. "Ernst Gottliebsohn pitiful?" he said. "I cannot imagine it."

Gottliebsohn bit his lip. He did not know whether that

description was how he felt about himself, or how he imagined his psychiatrist, Glass, felt about him. But he would not waste time trying to separate the confusion of identities in his mind. That bloodhound Kohn would be on him soon enough.

"You must take my word for it," Gottliebsohn said more calmly. "He greatly needs help."

"And you think *I* can help him?" Eichler asked.

"If you could tell me whatever you remember about Ernst," Gottliebsohn said. "What he was like."

Eichler sighed. Taking his crutches in one hand, he hooked back his chair, and with a hop and squat was seated. "You have come to the right place. Sometimes I think I am the only truthful man left in the world. But it is difficult, you know. Very few people want to know it. Are you certain you . . . Ernst . . . wants the truth from me?"

"Why not from you?" Gottliebsohn asked.

"Because I am married to Fritzi," Eichler muttered, and then looked slyly at Gottliebsohn. "Your patient did not mention this woman to you? He has forgotten her too then? Fritzi would not care to hear that. But if it is the truth, she should hear it. I will think about telling her. Fritzi and Ernst were once very close. But then, so were Fritzi and a number of others. She was the only one who would have me. Or was it the other way around? Is what your patient has contagious, Doctor? I seem to have forgotten which way it was myself. But we are a charming couple, the town cripple and the town . . . but what would you call a girl who had so much love in her that she gave it out, almost for the asking, to at least a dozen boys in the village, including the village Jew? Surely you can put a name to it—there is a scientific term for it, is there not, Doctor?"

Gottliebsohn remained very still. He remembered no girl named Fritzi, but then he was not trying at this moment to remember, but rather in his role as doctor to gather information that he might use later, when alone, at his leisure.

"You do not wish to comment, *hein?*" Eichler said. "I am not your patient, of course. You want the truth, you say? Well I will tell you the truth. Ernst Gottliebsohn was an opportunistic bastard. And he was too charming for his own good."

Gottliebsohn became puzzled and wary: was the statement a teacher's trick, a paradox meant to dazzle and stun
the mind? He wanted to believe this German lied to get back
at the man who had allegedly shared his wife, but he
somehow knew it was the truth.

"Not that I blamed him," Eichler continued. "He didn't
have much choice. With old pig-snouted Heinlein—he told
you about him, surely, with that oink-oink voice? the
schoolmaster? left to die in Russia, shot in the back by a
soldier in his company—filling our heads with that crap
about racial inferiority, it was inevitable that Ernst had
to fight some of us to prove our schoolmaster false. A good
thing he was strong. Those of us Ernst licked left him alone.
But how he ever won Heinlein over, I never did quite figure
out. Perhaps it was the soccer. The schoolmaster was a
nut about the game. And Ernst was the best goalie in
memory . . ."

"Goalie?" Gottliebsohn said, interrupting. "I thought he
played forward."

"He was much too slow," Eichler said. "His reflexes were
quick, but he just could not run very fast."

Maybe, Gottliebsohn thought, he had learned how to
run faster during those frightening years.

"Anyway," Eichler was saying, "it couldn't have been
just the soccer. Ernst was careful not to be too smart, he was
always respectful; even when that pig was abusing him in
front of the class, somehow Ernst convinced him that he
thought him nothing less than a great man. I couldn't have
done it. To hide your innermost feelings in that way, to pretend to be something you are not, simply to get along in the
world . . ."

"How could you know his innermost feelings?" Gottliebsohn demanded, unable to hold back in the face of so many
outrageous declarations.

"I have better sources than you, apparently," Eichler
said. "He told his sister, Ruth told Fritzi, Fritzi told me. You
needn't look shocked. Fritzi told me only because I ran
Ernst down to her. None of it made any difference to me,
however. I didn't like Ernst for other reasons. How could I?
He was—is—older than I; he got along, I didn't; he was
strong, I was weak; he was clever, I was only sincere . . ."

Eichler stopped while his mouth moved into what was apparently a grin. "His being a Jew had something to do with it, of course. I even resented him that little privilege. It made him different—it was what, in my opinion, made him outstanding."

Gottliebsohn felt his face redden. The twisted compliment embarrassed him terribly, as if the other had touched a sore point, a secret that had, up until now, been so well hidden that he had been unaware of it himself—he *enjoyed* being a Jew, with that awful kind of pleasure that certain beggars and sick persons have; an affliction demonstrated the punishment of God . . .

"You are shocked by the truth, I see," Eichler said. "Because I was not his friend, you do not wish to believe me."

"I would like other viewpoints," Gottliebsohn admitted. "And something a bit more specific. Why he left Warsfeld, for example."

"You want details, you must ask Fritzi," Eichler said.

"No one else?" Gottliebsohn asked, reluctant to confront a woman with whom he had allegedly been intimate. "Friends, neighbors? I would like to visit the place where Ernst lived—environmental factors are quite important."

Eichler stared. Then—"But of course!" he croaked, reaching for his crutches. "Where are my manners? The truth is never one-sided. You should have a chance to hear what others say." It was probably as near as he could ever come to pleasantness. As he stood up, looking curiously at the silent, lip-biting Gottliebsohn, his crutches skidded. Gottliebsohn, somehow sensing the cripple's sudden uncoordination, moved and caught him under the shoulder, horrified by how weightless this maimed schoolmaster seemed.

"You're very quick," Eichler observed, after he had gotten his crutches under him. He picked up his book satchel, and his clumsiness suddenly gone, took the three steps to the street in one move; when Gottliebsohn looked about for a car he shook his head. "I like the villagers to watch me gimp about," he said, winking. "It keeps their memories fresh."

They walked on the roadway to give Eichler room for his splayed crutches.

"Where do the people keep themselves?" Gottliebsohn

wondered, staring at the shuttered windows.

"They come out on the Sabbath," Eichler said. "Otherwise they mind their business."

"And the children?" Gottliebsohn asked.

"They are in the kitchens, stuffing themselves," Eichler said. "Later they may go to the park."

They turned the corner and were suddenly on a narrow street with a number of shops: a grocery, a dairy, a hardware store. Eichler stopped in front of a gloomy store front. Gottliebsohn looked up at the sign: *Muhler's*, in gold leaf over a painted black background. Had the sign been there in Jakob's time? Would he find the Gottliebsohn name under those painted layers? He tried to look in the window, but the interior seemed dark, and all he saw was his own reflection—and he became dismayed at the sight of himself, hands cupped around his eyes, peering anxiously, hoping for some earlier vision, and seeing only this nondescript worried figure, like an omen of failure.

Inside, the store had a musty smell, as if the stacks of materials on the counters had been there too long. A tinny bell rang as they passed through the door, and after a listening moment, they heard someone stirring. A light was switched on, and under it stood a lean man in a storekeeper's smock. Inside glass cases a few items—spools of faded yarn, packages of thread, needles and scissors—were scattered over the shelves.

"So it's you, Schoolmaster," the proprietor said. "What will you buy?"

"A chocolate bar," Eichler said, "if you have one that has not seen too many summers. And in exchange for this business, which I can see you clearly need, we'd like a tour of your living quarters."

There was no question but that Eichler was enjoying the other's sudden consternation. "This gentleman is on a sort of pilgrimage to the past on behalf of . . . one of his patients. He is a doctor. A psychiatrist, you understand? A Gottliebsohn is his patient. And he has promised this Gottliebsohn to report on any changes. You have no objections, surely?"

The other finally, reluctantly, opened a gate between two of the counters.

The rooms at the back were low-ceilinged and small, cluttered with too much furniture. A woman, lean as the

man, appeared in the kitchen door. Her husband waved her
back.

Gottliebsohn examined the room section by section. The
walls were filled with photographs in oval frames, but of
course those were Muhlers, not Gottliebsohns. But he wondered whether that slantwise crack in the ceiling plaster had
been there before, and if so, why did that recall nothing to
him?

"Where is the piano?" he asked finally.

"The piano?" Eichler asked.

"The place was bare," Muhler said. "My cousin had
shipped everything to Düsseldorf—he took the furniture in
payment for the damage."

"What damage?" Gottliebsohn asked.

"The broken windows," Muhler said.

"I don't recall a piano," Eichler said.

"Ruth played the piano," Gottliebsohn said.

Eichler looked at him curiously. "She couldn't even read
music. I remember Fritzi used to kid her about it—she had
a lovely voice, but she needed another voice to keep her on
pitch. Perhaps because she was so terribly near-sighted. She
just couldn't make out the notes."

Gottliebsohn frowned. He heard again the waltz, halting
now in the stumbling manner of a child, and he closed his
eyes, trying to remember how it had been in these crowded,
low-ceilinged rooms: the stern Jakob and the lovely Hannah, the near-sighted Ruth with the sweet voice. But what
was the atmosphere—lax or strict, silent or filled with
music? Opening his eyes he looked at his hands. Those awkward fingers could never have been at ease on a keyboard. It
must have been his sister who played; they must have had a
piano. Yet he could not quite remember!

"Were you ever here?" Gottliebsohn asked finally.

"Once," Eichler said. "With Fritzi. At Ruth's invitation.
On a Sunday. I don't know where Ernst was—probably
chasing some farmer's daughter—but the folks were swell.
Jakob was deep in a chair, behind a cigar—Dutch, I believe,
a wonderful aroma!—reading some crime magazine full of
murder and passion. Frau Gottliebsohn brought out milk
and strudel. But you want environmental detail, *nicht?* I
was surprised by all the colors. I had imagined, I can't think
why, that it would be drab. I stood on a Persian rug; the

colors were hypnotic and Frau Gottliebsohn told the story of its design—from the court of Xerxes, she said—and Herr Gottliebsohn came out from that smoke cloud to describe haggling with an Armenian peddler—he had bought it in Berlin, as a wedding gift—and I spilled milk on it! They were very kind and even invited me back, but I never returned!"

Gottliebsohn pictured it all, the sleepy Sunday afternoon, a hospitable family, rooms crowded with love, and no matter how valued the possessions, cigars were permitted in the parlor, and there was no fuss made over a little spilled milk . . . and where was he? He could not imagine himself trifling with some farm girl—but then why should Eichler lie?

He looked suspiciously at the other hunched over his crutches, eyes moist with remembrance. "You are certain there was no piano?"

Eichler seemed startled. "Of course I am certain," he said.

"Ernst insisted there was a piano," Gottliebsohn said.

"But he has lost his memory, *nicht?*" Eichler said. "Perhaps he remembers a piano from another place, and it is confused in his mind, poor fellow."

There *had* been a piano in that rooming house in Cologne, Gottliebsohn thought, but who there then had played it? Played in such a way that it was still sounding in his mind after twenty-six years?

Gottliebsohn looked about him once more, trying to picture how these rooms must have looked with a fabled Persian rug, and different walls, and the smell of baking strudel, and an aromatic cigar—but it was finally impossible.

Eichler stopped at the counter to pick up a chocolate bar. "Fritzi dearly loves chocolate," he said, once on the street again. "I shouldn't cater to her weaknesses, but then I never could resist her. Were the rooms any help?" he asked abruptly.

"Very little," Gottliebsohn said morosely.

"You must come to my home and see Fritzi," Eichler said. Gottliebsohn shook his head. "Fritzi would never forgive me if I let you leave without seeing her." Gottliebsohn stared, wondering why Eichler was so persistent. "You *are*

Ernst Gottliebsohn, aren't you?" Eichler finally said.

Gottliebsohn was as horrified as if he were caught in some crime.

"You needn't be embarrassed," Eichler said. "I can understand your reluctance to let me know who you really were . . . but I insist." He lifted a crutch and nudged Gottliebsohn into a walk. "I suspected you a long while before," he said cheerfully, as he swung himself along. "Not that you didn't play the part well, but you reacted too strongly, more than a psychiatrist would . . . and you have changed, of course; suffering did that, *nein*? But now that I look close— look deep, as the poets say—I can see the boy I knew inside you: the arrogance is still there, *nicht*? Even though you try to hide it with a sullen exterior. Do you feel like gloating, Ernst? I would not blame you. Gloat over me then. You see before you the ruin that is Germany."

Eichler's house was small, on a street without sidewalks. There was a tiny, well-kept yard, bordered by flowers, blues and pinks. "It turned out that Fritzi had a passion for gardening," Eichler said. "That no one would have guessed, eh, Ernst, considering her other hobbies?"

Gottliebsohn wanted to be a mute, deaf, dumb, and blind to what the other was implying, yet every sense was quivering in dread anticipation. He was ashamed, yet not ashamed enough; embarrassed, but not so embarrassed he did not look forward to seeing the woman with whom it was claimed he had been intimate. Gottliebsohn wished fervently to be somewhere, anywhere else, even in the custody of Kohn, and yet knew that this despised, lip-licking curiosity was stronger in him than all other feelings.

"Fritzi," Eichler called. "We have a guest! Pretty yourself, *liebchen*—he is an old friend!" The parlor was neat and cheerful. Eichler indicated a chair. Before they might sit, however, a stout woman, who Gottliebsohn could see had once been rather pretty, came into the room. By her flushed cheeks and the fine perspiration on her brow he guessed she had been in the kitchen.

"Don't you remember him?" Eichler said. "Look closer, Frau Eichler, he can't have changed so much as all that."

She had been staring at him with an almost greedy curiosity, and then, coming closer, touching his chin with flour-whitened fingers, she lifted his head. "How shy he is," she said, "and a grown man, too! Is this one of your jokes, Hans? Who is he then?"

"Think," Eichler said. "Who, of all the boys in the village, was your very favorite?"

"You were, Hans," she said, without hesitation.

He laughed, harshly, causing Gottliebsohn that inadvertent shiver—and yet he saw the affection there, all the more moving because reluctant.

"Which boy made you giggle most?" Eichler went on. "Which, of all of them, brought you little presents? Which—"

"Ernst Gottliebsohn!" Frau Eichler cried. "Is it possible?" She took Gottliebsohn into a cushiony hug. "But why did you stand like a stone? Couldn't you have given me a hint?"

Gottliebsohn stood helpless, aware of her warmth, inhaling her rich kitcheny smell, like fresh-baked bread, wanting to return her embrace, but afraid for her in front of the watching husband, afraid for himself if he should let go, fighting back the sudden rush of feeling. How dared she be so affectionate, especially after the hints had been dropped . . . but the woman chattered on, as if oblivious to the old jealousies.

"Go easy on him, Fritzi," Eichler said. "Can't you see he's embarrassed?"

She let him go. "Why should you be embarrassed?" she asked, but she was blushing.

"He doesn't remember you, is why," Eichler rasped. His wife looked at him, suddenly frightened by what she did not know. "It seems Ernst has lost his mind," he continued. "Part of it, at any rate."

She stepped back. "You do not remember me?" she asked slowly, her face stiffening with shock.

Gottliebsohn shook his head, distressed for her.

"He wishes us to fill in the gaps for him," Eichler said. "To tell him what *we* remember. All the little details."

"What kind of details?" she asked, looking doubtfully at her husband.

"Now is it you who are embarrassed?" Eichler demanded harshly. "Not in front of him, surely? I have already told him that you two were lovers." He grinned cheerlessly. "There, it is said. Now there need be no embarrassments. I will get the schnapps. That always helps the tongue to wag freely."

Frau Eichler smiled painfully, but her eyes remained steady. "You mustn't mind Hans," she said softly, after he had gone into the other room. "He is very bitter since the war. Not just about being crippled—I think he would have been able to bear that—but because he believes his countrymen are despicable. They feel no shame, he says. They deny their history, or say they had no knowledge of it. So Hans became obsessed by what he calls truth. He won't accept an artificial leg because he says that would be deceptive, a cover-up, a camouflage of reality. And the leg would help him—you must remember how active Hans was, he loved the outdoors . . . he tried once to go hiking with those crutches, and he got entangled in some undergrowth . . . the leg would permit him walks at least. He taught German history in Solingen, but they insisted he wear one of the government legs. The only reason he is permitted to teach here is they can get no one else—though they claim an exception was made because it is his own village . . ."

Though Gottliebsohn was anxious to get on with his own purposes, a sense of propriety overcame his inner urgencies. It would be unseemly, he felt, to interrupt this kindly woman's irrelevant reminiscing, no matter what his reasons for haste.

Eichler returned with a bottle. His wife went to a cabinet for glasses.

"Get to anything important yet?" Eichler asked.

"We were waiting for you," she said. "Besides, I don't quite understand what he wants to know . . ."

"Tell him what he was like in those days," Eichler said. "I've told him myself, but he's like everyone else, he doesn't know the truth when he hears it . . ."

"You were a devil," she said to Gottliebsohn, smiling at the remembrance. "Too handsome for your own good, sassy as sin, a laugh like a hoot owl, always in the thick of mischief . . ."

"He didn't believe me," Eichler said, pouring the liquor.

"But so much fun we forgave you everything," she said.

Gottliebsohn listened, trying to fit what she said to his own person. Was it possible for him to have changed so much? The psychiatrist said so, but all the same he found it difficult to believe. Where then had that laughter gone?

"Why don't you dig into that overflowing chest of yours and bring out some old keepsakes?" Eichler said. "They bore me," he said to Gottliebsohn, "but you may find them interesting."

"I know just the thing," Frau Eichler said, clapping her hands, and hastened out of the room. She returned carrying a large album. She placed it on his lap, and leaning over him, turned the pages. It was a sentimental girl's scrapbook, filled with every kind of memento, from a baby spoon to a garter ("French," she said, and blushed), a lace handkerchief to a pressed flower ("My first corsage"), a confirmation crucifix to a tracing of her first high heels, dance programs to movie posters. And, of course, photographs. "Our school picnic," she said. "All of us are in it."

He was almost reluctant to look, somehow afraid of what he would find in that yellowing picture. He picked out Fritzi immediately—she was *zoftic* even then, dressed in a fluffy dress like a patterned cheesecloth, with a huge ribbon in her hair and a truly enormous smile. Eichler was more difficult, though he found him finally in the back row, standing on a bench with the smaller boys, a solemn youth, looking off in Fritzi's direction.

"What's the matter?" Fritzi asked softly. "Can't you recognize yourself?"

She placed his finger then on a young man with tousled hair who grinned straight into the camera. He was sitting in the first row on the grass, bare knees akimbo, hands on his thighs; a cocky boy, no doubt about that, and as he studied the young man a feeling of sorrow rose in his breast, almost choking him with its intensity. Was it grief over a wasted life that moved him? The other—he thought of that youngster as someone outside himself—looked so full of promise, and when he thought of how empty his life had been he felt as if he had failed the boy, broken some sacred oath made to him long ago.

"It's a terrible photograph," Fritzi said. "The way your face blurred I'm not surprised you weren't able to pick yourself out, especially since your memory is bad, like you say."

He was reluctant to ask but he had examined every

youthful face and could not remember any. "And which is my sister then?"

"Oh," Fritzi said, "she's not in the picture, silly, she was home sick that day, or it was some sort of Jewish holiday . . ."

"But I was there," Gottliebsohn said, deeply ashamed.

"Your father never kept you from school," Eichler said.

"But if he was so proud of being a Jew?" Gottliebsohn protested.

"He was not religious, all the same," Eichler said.

"Everyone seems so happy," Fritzi said wistfully, "except you, Hansie."

"That's because you had rejected me for Ernst," Eichler said.

"I never rejected you," she said quietly. "And I was not with Ernst that day, either. He was with Hulga."

"I'd forgotten that," Eichler said. "No wonder he looks so pleased with himself. And how does she look?" He studied the photograph. "Do you know she's actually licking her lips?"

"Let me see that," Fritzi said, taking the picture. "Just as I thought, no such thing. Where's your code of truth now?"

"The truth is, she could have been licking her lips," Eichler said. "Ernst was a favorite of all the girls. Isn't that true, Fritzi?"

She nodded slowly. "He could always make us laugh. Girls like to laugh—you never knew that, or understood that, Hansie."

"Oh, there was more to it than that," Eichler said. "He was exotic, *nicht*? He was a Jew. Not only the only Jew in the school, but the only one for miles around. The village of Hagen claimed they had *two* Jews, but I never believed it. And didn't our girls here, like girls everywhere, dream, when they were old enough to realize why they itched between their chubby thighs, of exotic men, yellow men, black men, Jews? And our own Jew was not too different in appearance from German boys, even handsome, in his way, as the devil is said to be. And when the boys whispered to the girls stories about strange rituals by candlelight in the rooms back of Gottliebsohn's store, the drinking of blood, and God knows what all, trying to frighten them, didn't that only make them more eager than ever to have the Jew perform a few rituals with them? Didn't it, Fritzi? Of course it was not necessary for him to take advantage . . ."

She had her hand to her dimpled mouth. "Was it you who made up those stories, Hans?" she asked, suddenly distressed.

Eichler did not answer. He was watching Gottliebsohn. "You did take advantage, didn't you?" he said.

"If you say so," Gottliebsohn managed finally, though he was appalled. Again he felt as if he were listening to stories about somebody else, as if he were following in another's footsteps. Certainly the man he was now had no relationship to the boy they had described, and if they were one and the same, incredible as it seemed, he would have to make a major adjustment in the way in which he did his thinking if he were ever to be able to accept it. And accept it he must— he knew that—if he were ever to become whole again.

"If *I* say so?" Eichler said. "Only you can tell us what the truth was."

"Perhaps the girls took advantage of him," Fritzi said. "Did you ever consider that, Hans? That he might have been too kind to refuse us?"

"Ah, no, Fritzi," Eichler said. "That's your gambit, not his."

Her face reddened. "Enough, Hans," she said sternly. "Where are your manners?"

Eichler sighed. "You see how it is?" he said to Gottliebsohn. "Even in one's own house one cannot push the truth too far."

Gottliebsohn saw how it was. His heart went out to this lovely affectionate woman who, if the world had been different or if he had been, he might conceivably have married. He wanted to defend her now, but he reminded himself that he had no right—and then he became aware that Eichler was raising his glass. "Shall we drink to the prodigal's return?"

"Why do you say that?" Gottliebsohn asked. He was suddenly trembling and both Eichler and Fritzi were looking at him, surprised. But he no longer cared. He had sat quietly while the two of them had their private quarrel, a curious kind of lovemaking, while jokes were made about occult Jews, while improbable stories were told about his youthful personality, and it seemed meanwhile the most important question would never be asked—until the toast brought it all into focus. "What do you know that you are not telling?"

"I?" Eichler said, shrugging. "I know nothing. It is Fritzi you must ask."

"Why did I leave the village?" he asked of her.

She looked at him pityingly. "Answer the man," her husband said.

"You quarreled with your father," she said finally.

"Ah," Gottliebsohn breathed, and looked longingly at the glassful of schnapps. But he vowed that he would not drink until he heard it all.

"Your father had received a letter from the Jewish Community Council, a Rabbi Nachman, requesting certain information—names of dependents, property ownership, and so on. You were furious. You didn't want your name mentioned, you said, nor your sister's either; in fact you didn't want him to answer at all. Those lists were for the Nazis, you said. And when he answered anyway, out of pride in being a Jew, you said you were not going to wait for them to pick you like an overripe berry, you were going to leave, and they should not expect to hear from you again."

Gottliebsohn flushed, ashamed for that young man who had denied his identity, and yet understanding his need for survival. He had had an instinct for it, he thought, remembering what had been found out in Cologne; he had even been extraordinarily skilled in methods of disappearance—though something along the way had obviously gone wrong. What had caused him to reassert his Jewishness? That soldier, who had never let him rest?

"I didn't abandon them," he said finally. "I arranged an apartment for them in Cologne."

Fritzi looked at him wonderingly. "Was that you then? Ruth said it must be you. The Jews in nearby villages were told to gather in Düsseldorf. Yet your family went to Cologne. They received a letter of instruction from the commissioner of police himself, telling them exactly what they must do. One small suitcase each, absolutely not one bundle more. They were to emigrate, the letter said."

Gottliebsohn gaped at her. He raised his hand to his

head, which was hot, and then realized it was the hand with the glass in it.

"You always were kind of a slick character," Eichler said, as if it were a compliment. "But the commissioner of police —how *did* you manage that, Ernst?"

Gottliebsohn wanted desperately to drink the schnapps, but found he was unable to move. If he could break the shock that held him in a vise and drink, he might then be able to talk, and in talking, deny what was being implied about him.

"Stop it, Hans," Fritzi said. "How can you be so cruel?"

"He came here for the truth," her husband muttered.

"Ernst?" Fritzi said, as he sat with the glass held as if glued to his forehead.

Gottliebsohn started. He put the glass down, untasted. "I must go," he said, and making an enormous effort, got to his feet.

"Don't you want your drink?" Eichler rasped.

Unthinking, Gottliebsohn drank the glassful at a gulp, then fought to keep it down. "I was apparently not slick enough," he said finally, his voice hoarse as the other's. "They put my family on a cattle train—I never heard from them again."

Fritzi burst into tears. Eichler and Gottliebsohn stared at her, and then it was Gottliebsohn who reached out and patted her awkwardly on the shoulder. She stopped as suddenly as she had begun, looked once sorrowfully at her old friend, and left the room. A moment later she was back, holding a snapshot.

Two young girls with arms about each other: Fritzi and another, her hair to her waist, beautifully exotic, though she dressed like a German, whom he guessed must be his sister.

"You can keep it," she said.

"Is it your only one?" he said.

"You keep it," she insisted, putting it in his coat pocket, and then kissed him good-bye, a long, lingering, tear-sodden kiss.

Eichler insisted on walking back to the main square with him. "It's a nightly ritual," he said. "I'm meeting some fellow members of our little veterans' club."

When they reached the bus stop it was almost dark. The

sign indicated a bus within fifteen minutes. Eichler stood with him, hunched over his crutches, looking morosely into nothing, or himself.

Gottliebsohn wished he would go. He wanted to be alone with his own dark thought. He had to decide what to do with this new information. Tell Glass? Tell Kohn? He shivered. Never. But to keep it to himself seemed impossible. Yet how could he give them added evidence that pointed to his having been a collaborator? It was not possible, he kept telling himself . . . and yet it had been he who had arranged for the apartment in Cologne, and they said it was he who had arranged for the travel permits. Unless that letter from the commissioner was a forgery! He grasped at that thought as his salvation.

They heard booted footsteps on the cobblestones. Three men approached through the gathering dusk.

"Are you joining us then, Eichler?" one called, and Gottliebsohn recognized the squat man from the garage.

"In a minute," Eichler said.

The three walked on.

"Were they in school with us?" Gottliebsohn asked, unable to still that first curiosity. Eichler nodded. "They did not remember me," Gottliebsohn said resentfully.

Eichler looked at him sharply. "You talked to them?" Gottliebsohn nodded. "Where?"

"In the garage," Gottliebsohn said, wondering at the strangeness that had come over Eichler. "They were rude. You'd think they'd be pleased to be complimented on their work."

"You asked them about the van?" Eichler said, incredulous.

"What about the van?" Gottliebsohn asked. The other did not answer. "Hans?" Gottliebsohn said.

"It was a mobile gas van," Eichler said at last. "Those men ran it—they would have been shot, you understand, had they refused—and when the orders came to retreat, they brought it back, somehow managing to keep it hidden until after the war."

"A gas van?" Gottliebsohn said, not wanting to understand.

Eichler gave him his twisted smile, the one probably used on uncomprehending students. "For Jews, gypsies, polacks, and Russian commissars. I wanted them to keep it as it was, make it a touring museum. A fabulous idea, there's a fortune in it. But they wouldn't hear of it. They're making it into a camper, you know, a dry-land yacht, so they can vacation every summer in style." He laughed harshly, that croaking, frog-like sound that made Gottliebsohn shiver in disgust. "Don't look so horrified," he said. "There are worse things hidden in German hearts." And he left him, swinging away after the three ex-soldiers, his crutches throwing up little spurts of dust as they dug into the street.

10

AUERBACH AND HORTSKY ARRIVED AT the conference room to find the Germans, Von Haupt, Bettmann and Schenke, there before them. The Israelis silently took their seats across the table. They had not been told the purpose of this hastily scheduled meeting, but neither had the slightest doubt what the subject would be. They were ill at ease not only because they were not prepared for this confrontation, but because that cryptic message form Kohn, stating that he and his charge would be unavoidably delayed, hinted at bad news. Why else had he not been more explicit? And since neither he nor the American had seen fit to tell them where they were spending the night, there was no way of getting in touch.

"Where are the other two?" Bettmann asked, looking at his watch.

"I did not know it when you called," Hortsky said nervously, "but they apparently decided to spend the night in Cologne."

"Apparently?" Bettmann said sardonically.

"Gottliebsohn had finished his conference with Von Haupt," Auerbach interjected. "I saw no reason for him to stick close. This is not a full meeting in any case; why is it necessary for him—"

"It is Herr Kohn's presence we most wanted," Bettmann interrupted. They could see now he was quite angry, and was containing himself with the greatest difficulty. "Please!" he said, as Hortsky stirred himself to speak. "We are perfectly aware that Herr Kohn is not in Bonn. He told Schenke that he was merely going on a sightseeing trip—yet he went to a great deal of trouble to lose the men Herr Schenke assigned to follow him—why?"

"You had him followed?" Hortsky asked, shaken.

"Would you do less?" Bettmann demanded. "A man of his reputation, loose in Germany . . ." His own words seemed to anger him more. "We would like to know where he has gone . . . and to what purpose?"

Auerbach and Hortsky avoided looking at each other. The German had to be answered, but to give him an answer that would satisfy him without revealing their own predicament seemed impossible. However, Auerbach elected to try.

"I assure you," he said, "that Captain Kohn's purposes are for the benefit of us all. There is nothing about his activity that is directed against Germans . . ."

"Why then is he being so secretive?" Bettmann demanded.

"Perhaps it is habit," Auerbach said. "Perhaps the idea of surveillance annoyed him, as it would me; or perhaps he did it for sport. Our captain might not show it, Herr Bettmann, but he has a sense of humor."

Bettmann glanced at Schenke, who looked doubtful. Then he returned to Auerbach. "It may be as you say, habit or annoyance. But in his talk with Doktor Schenke he took great pains to keep from us his specific quarry. And then when I asked Baron von Haupt to inquire in a gentlemanly manner, off the record, of your Herr Gottliebsohn whether we need be concerned, his attitude was most evasive."

Hortsky cleared his throat. "I can see why you are disturbed," he said. "But let me add my assurances to Herr Auerbach's. There is nothing about Captain Kohn's presence here that need concern you."

Bettmann smiled bitterly. "Gentlemen," he said, "let us not be naïve. We are aware that your captain is responsible to a Cabinet Minister who is opposed to your mission. Your assurances are meaningless."

Auerbach flushed, but what could he say? It was the truth, so far as the Germans knew it, and however galling to have to listen to a German evaluation of their major weakness, the alternative was worse: how could he explain to them that Kohn was perhaps disloyal to his superiors?

Schenke murmured to Bettmann, who nodded, though not enthusiastically.

"Doktor Schenke thinks you should know that he agreed to search his files for some information that Captain Kohn had requested. But since the captain was so vague, he has been unable to be selective. If he had the name of the man you are suspicious of, he could, of course, be much more helpful."

"Of course," Auerbach said noncommittally.

"If you feel you cannot give us the name," Bettmann said, "then you can at least arrange for the captain to return now to Israel?"

Auerbach slowly shook his head. That was impossible. The mission had been allowed to proceed in the first place only by his agreeing to Kohn's presence. But again, how could he explain without giving the whole business away?

"I thought not," Bettmann said sourly. "And we, of course, cannot make him persona non grata without repercussions from your government, correct?" Auerbach nodded reluctantly. "Then I submit to you, gentlemen, that we are at an impasse—unless you are willing to tell us who or what Captain Kohn is after, we will be forced to suspend negotiations!"

In the sudden quiet they heard a flicking sound, and saw that it came from something that Von Haupt was doing with his fingernails. He must have been conscious of their stares, but he did not leave off the contemplation of his manicure.

"You must be equally aware," Bettmann continued, in a more persuasive tone, as if his seemingly bored associate had reminded him, "of our own internal problems. Our government, too, is not unanimously in favor of what we are after here; there are those who would like nothing better than to have these negotiations broken off."

"That does not apply to me personally," Von Haupt said calmly, without looking up.

"No," Bettmann agreed. "But the Baron is responsible, as your captain is, to the dissidents in our government. I asked him to attend this meeting for that reason—he can testify that we are not willing to compromise our honor no matter how much we may desire an accommodation with you."

Not willing? Auerbach thought. Or not able? They were vulnerable, he suddenly thought, even on their own negotiating team—he remembered studying the dossier on Von Haupt; he might be just the sort of person that Kohn and others would think worth the chase. A rush of feeling almost overwhelmed Auerbach then; those others included himself! At that moment he was tempted to chuck away all of it; he was sick of what he must swallow in dealing with Germans, wearied by the seemingly endless obstacles to a successful conclusion, and he longed for the luxuries of private citizenship, where he might give vent to personal spleen. The moment passed, leaving him shaken and dismayed by the intensity of feelings he had thought long ago buried.

"Well?" Bettmann said, and then again he seemed disturbed by his own harshness. "Gentlemen, I urge you to tell us. If it is nothing that we need be concerned about, as you say, then what harm? If it is our confidence you seek, I can assure you in turn that whatever you tell us here will never leave this room."

"I give you my personal word," Von Haupt said.

Auerbach stared at the German—who was now engaged in polishing his monocle—then looked to Hortsky. That old Zionist was frowning thoughtfully. But then he could be objective, Auerbach thought; no gassed relatives were lined up behind him at this conference table. But that was unfair, Auerbach immediately thought—what was the matter with him, anyway? Fatigue, perhaps, he was not sleeping well— and making an effort he said, "Will you give us an hour? It is necessary that Co-Director Hortsky and I discuss this in private."

By the time they got to Hortsky's room, the old man was very agitated. "Why did you not tell them no immediately?" he asked.

"Because we cannot refuse them!" Auerbach said, making no attempt to hide his annoyance.

Hortsky stared. "What are you saying?" he asked. "You know the Interior Minister made that one of his conditions—"

"I know," Auerbach interrupted harshly, "that if the negotiations are suspended the I.M. will use that as an excuse to press for our recall."

"But if we tell them," Hortsky protested, "Kohn will report back, and we will be recalled in any case."

"Kohn is with us," Auerbach said.

Again Hortsky stared, "How do you mean, 'with us'?" he asked finally.

Auerbach shrugged. "I had a talk with him early on," he said. "He agreed that the success of the mission is something he wants to work for also." He avoided Hortsky's shocked look. He had not planned to tell the other. "It is not that he is being disloyal," Auerbach said. "Technically, he is under mine—our—supervision. We are entitled to a first hearing of anything his investigation uncovers."

"And you think he will actually do this?" Hortsky asked.

"I know he will," Auerbach said, thinking of certain arrangements he had made to bind Kohn more closely to him.

"*I* would think," Hortsky said, "that Kohn would be very angry to have the Germans know about Gottliebsohn."

"But he will understand that it was necessary," Auerbach said. "It will make his job easier, in any case; this way, as you heard, the Germans can be of much greater help—then, too, he will have the sister to interview—there will be no trouble about Kohn; he will have more than enough to occupy him . . ."

Hortsky looked at him thoughtfully. "You seem to have it all rather well worked out," he said at last. "Why do you delay telling the Germans?"

Auerbach lit a new cigarette from an old, and then brushed the ashes from his lapel. It bothered him to see this evidence of his nervousness. The fact was, matters were not so carefully arranged as he had made them out. Though he had from the first anticipated some sort of German reaction to the presence of Kohn, he had had no idea it would be so strong when it came, certainly not to the extent of this ultimatum. And while his mind had begun immediately casting about for alternatives, he had soon realized there were none. His sources in Israel had warned him that the opposition was gaining strength; he recognized there were other risks

in agreeing to the German demands—he was not all that
sure of Kohn, nor of the German reaction; it was to lessen
those risks that he had asked for time to talk with Hortsky.
He needed his collaboration. Now he wondered how apparent it was that he was after more than advice from the
knowledgeable old man. He had to be extremely cautious.
Other men, equally clever, had tried to bind Hortsky to
their enterprises, and all, so far, had failed. Hortsky reserved the right always to dissent, taking pride in his reputation for independence. He did not want power, only respect—and to Auerbach it had been a good bargain. But
now he needed far more from Hortsky than lip service to a
larger cause.

"Two reasons," Auerbach said finally. "The first is fun-
damental—you must never let anyone win a victory too
cheaply. It is not sufficiently appreciated."

"And the second?" Hortsky asked doubtfully.

"I could never make a decision of this importance alone,"
Auerbach said. "It is not that I am trying to burden you
with my responsibilities," he hastened to add. "I only want
to know that what I am doing is right. And that means I
need your private concurrence. Publicly, I will shoulder the
blame, if there is any."

Hortsky looked at him suspiciously. "You think I am
afraid of responsibility?"

"That is not the point," Auerbach said. "We had agreed
to a certain procedure, hadn't we? I am willing to stick by
our bargain, without recrimination, that when it came to the
specifics of our accommodation with the Germans, you
would not be involved. But it is the specifics that complicate
the matter now. I think we *can* get an agreement, in principle, now. If Gottliebsohn is cleared, we can continue our
talks . . . if he is guilty, we can postpone discussions about
how the agreement will be implemented until a later time.
It permits us to salvage something . . ."

"But what about Knesset ratification?" Hortsky asked.

"They can ratify a *principle* with a clear conscience,"
Auerbach said. "We in the executive branch will be responsible for the subsequent details."

"It's an evasion," Hortsky said. "I don't like it." Auerbach
had not thought he would. "Our people are entitled to the
facts. How else can they judge intelligently? Believe me," he

continued when Auerbach looked doubtful, "I know the heartache when a people will not listen—even Moses had his troubles—but sooner or later they come around. Have a little faith!"

"I have faith," Auerbach burst out, "in facts, and in judgments based on facts. But if the guilt or innocence of Gottliebsohn is the key to the success or failure of our mission here, what good are your facts then?"

"I admit it is beside the point," Hortsky said, shaken, "but it is your own fault. You were the one who exaggerated his importance!"

"Not him," Auerbach protested. "His statistics."

Hortsky looked at him sourly. "You don't really think you can separate the two?"

"No, of course not," Auerbach admitted. "Perhaps we should look for the miracle," he went on sarcastically. "It may turn out that Gottliebsohn is innocent, after all. The sister is certainly an important find; she may be of enormous help."

"I would not count too much on the sister," Hortsky said.

"Oh," said Auerbach. He had guessed as much ever since Hortsky had picked the woman up.

"I did not question her," Hortsky said hastily. "Dean Wolfe suggested I leave that to the American. Wolfe was not too hopeful." He hesitated. "Look here. I am more interested than you imagine in the success of the mission. And I will do everything in my power to get an agreement ratified . . . I will attend meetings, I will make speeches, I will talk to certain members of the Knesset who are obligated to me . . ."

Auerbach forced a smile. "I did not expect less from you," he said.

Hortsky looked at him incredulously. "That does not satisfy you?" he said. "What more would you have me do?"

"Help me defend Gottliebsohn," Auerbach said quietly. "If it comes to that."

Hortsky turned very red. Auerbach looked away; though it was so important to his own future, as well as that of the mission, he felt sorry for the other, and was tempted to somehow unsay the request. Like all single-minded men, he thought, Hortsky had permitted a virtue to become a vice. His pride, so splendid in public life, he wanted against all reason to be equally splendid in his personal life, and so he would in a moment commit himself to an undertaking that would risk a lifetime's reputation, that would never, because it could never, be made public—all to prove his courage to one other man in the privacy of a hotel room. How explain to Israelis that they had sought the cooperation of Germans in determining the guilt or innocence of an accused Jew?

"Look here," Auerbach said. "I will only call on you if the opposition drags Gottliebsohn into the debate. If we can keep this quiet until *after* ratification, but if it then turns out that Gottliebsohn *is* guilty, I will defend him alone, as agreed."

"I would help defend him even then," Hortsky said, glaring at him. "I have never refused a Jew in need."

Auerbach shrugged. "Then you agree we must get the Germans to a first-step agreement?" he said.

"I seem to have no other choice, do I?" Hortsky said.

"No," Auerbach said. "I'm afraid you don't," and getting to his feet, he went to tell the Germans the name of their accused.

The three men arrived back at the hotel an hour before dawn. Kohn had done all of the driving; Glass sat with Gottliebsohn in the rear seat of the car they had rented. They had found him on the narrow, graveled road between Warsfeld and Hagen. When the headlights illuminated that disheveled figure bent over the side of the road, they had almost passed him by, thinking him drunk; then Kohn, through some hunter's instinct, had stopped, and they saw that it was indeed Gottliebsohn, vomiting into the ditch.

He had been almost pathetically grateful to see them, surprising Kohn but not Glass (who had been the one to deduce where his patient would go), and though he was at first incoherent, they had eventually managed to make out that the trip to his former village had been, literally, a sickening experience. Glass gave him two of his pills, but Gottliebsohn, simultaneously offered a drink from Kohn's flask, took the drink and felt immediately so much better that he dropped the tablets into his pocket unused.

Kohn, once his charge was safely in tow, lost his earlier

surliness and became quite concerned (Glass noticed that Kohn seemed increasingly fond of the other, a not infrequent occurrence between prisoner and keeper); it was to Kohn that Gottliebsohn finally confided what disturbed him most: he had evidently arranged, through someone in the Cologne police, for the almost-impossible-to-get travel permits for his family. While Kohn brooded over the dark implications of that, Glass was able finally to get the rest of it—those flashes of what his patient had been like as a boy, so unlike what he had become, and what he considered himself to be. He felt like a patchwork now, he told Glass; he felt as if his personality had been stitched together out of bits and pieces that had strayed somehow to hand, and if he were to describe himself, he said, it would be as a sketchily contrived scarecrow of a man, all of whose parts were different and out of whom peeked disconcertingly a stuffing of straw. The only time he had felt at ease with himself, he told Glass (as if it were an afterthought, though the psychiatrist recognized it as a confession), was when he had adopted the mannerisms and attitudes of Kohn and himself. Glass reassured him, pointing out that it was a typical enough reaction for someone in his situation: he was not only being chased and therefore in need of an alias, but he was afraid to identify himself to those whom he had come to hate. "I was afraid to be a Jew!" Gottliebsohn cried, and thereafter subsided, staring out the window of the little car into the chilling darkness. What he did not tell this sympathetic doctor was that while admittedly superficial and brief, those two impostures had given him a kind of satisfaction that went beyond anything normal.

Auerbach had left an urgent message for them at the desk; no matter what the hour, he wanted to be wakened immediately upon their arrival. Glass suggested, and Kohn agreed, that they get Gottliebsohn to bed first; Auerbach had not mentioned him specifically, and Glass was afraid that if his patient went much longer without rest he might pass into a psychotic state. He was semi-hysterical as it was; that excessive if brief garrulity had been followed by a deep melancholy, out of which he could barely be stirred—symptoms of a potential psychosis. Kohn apparently had his own reasons for wanting Gottliebsohn out of the way.

In the meeting with Auerbach where they learned of the

sister, and more surprisingly of her presence in Bonn, Kohn did not mention that Gottliebsohn had run away. He was frank enough about everything else: his report was gloomy. Auerbach did not seem surprised; seated on a sofa in his bed-sitting room, he smoked with a distracted air.

"And what is your prognosis, Doctor?" he asked finally. "Do you too think your patient is guilty?"

Glass pursed his lips, hesitating, aware that his answer would make him seem foolish. "No," he said firmly, at last. "I don't. I trust in his feelings, you see. He insists he could not have collaborated. I believe him."

"In spite of what the captain has found out?" Auerbach asked.

"It's all circumstantial," Glass said. "And hardly compelling, even so. There are hints as to his behavior and character then, but no more; we still don't have a definite idea of what he was like!"

"Captain?" Auerbach asked.

Kohn shrugged. "Circumstantial or not, it is clear that he *was* involved with Nazis, as the accusation says. It's true he may also have been involved with an underground group, but even there, he's suspect—there was an informer, and he *thinks* he may have been the one, though he claims he would have led the Nazis to their organization unknowingly. Now I'm not saying there weren't extenuating circumstances, that he may not have been playing the Nazis for fools, but where else did he get travel permits for his family?"

"He was involved with forged documents, wasn't he?" Glass said. "The permits could have been forged as well."

"I suppose," Kohn said, unbelievingly. "If we only knew *why* he intended to stay in Germany . . ."

"He says he did not," Glass said.

"That's just the point," Kohn said hotly. "He says one thing, and whatever we turn up points just to the opposite!"

"It's apparent," Auerbach said, interrupting, "that we need a corroborating witness. Someone who was actually there with Gottliebsohn in Cologne at the time."

"I'm trying to find one," Kohn said bitterly. "Schenke said he would check his files, but he didn't say he would tell me what he finds."

"He will now," Auerbach told him, lighting another

cigarette. Kohn and Glass stared, aware of a difference in his tone. "They know what we're after," he said. "Schenke will now be cooperative."

"They know?" Kohn demanded, unbelieving.

"We had no choice," Auerbach said wearily. "They threatened to suspend the negotiations. They were not too happy, I might add, about the nature of the charge; they can see it getting sticky for some of their people too."

"Schenke wouldn't be unhappy," Kohn muttered. "That krauthead has been praying for something like this."

"What about the sister?" Glass demanded, incredulous that in all this talk of a corroborating witness they were not even concerned with her. "She will know what her brother was up to. They were exceptionally close."

"Were they?" Auerbach said. "And how do you know that?"

Glass started to answer, hesitated, then said, weakly, "Gottliebsohn says so."

"He remembers that?" Auerbach asked.

"Not exactly," Glass said, avoiding Kohn's warning glance. "It was what people told him."

"Then why is she so reluctant to see him?" Auerbach asked.

Glass tried not to show his dismay. Every way they turned, the omens were bad. "There would be many reasons," he said finally.

"You still have faith," Auerbach said. "Very commendable, I'm sure. Unfortunately, my dear young American doctor, it will sound no better from the witness stand than it does here, now, in this room. Let me be brutally frank. You must want what is best for your patient, you say, and devil take the rest of us . . . well and good; that is your professional stance and you are probably uncomfortable outside it. But I'm damned if I can see how this coddling is doing your patient the slightest good! We need a breakthrough, and we need it soon. What profit your kindness if Gottliebsohn is sent to prison . . . or worse? I say your kindness is a disservice, and what is more, a weakness on your part!"

Glass could feel the heat in his face. Kohn avoided his look, and that was worrisome, too, for Kohn should have been delighted at his discomfiture—apparently matters were too serious for childish feuds.

"As for you, Captain," Auerbach said, "let me suggest that you delay any communication with Jerusalem. I would remind you that your responsibility, for the moment at least, lies here with us."

Now it was Kohn's turn to redden. But he kept his temper and quietly said, with a violence the more frightening because subdued, "I *never* forget where my duty lies!"

Those two men, Glass thought, when Auerbach dismissed them, had prior understandings. But he turned his mind away from what they might be as not his concern, and began planning how best to approach the sister.

Glass eventually went to see the sister alone. Before each man went to his room for a much needed sleep, he and Kohn worked out a rather complicated procedure—Kohn would appear casually at the psychiatrist's suite to see how things were going for his "friend"; invite them all downstairs for a drink; Glass, on some pretext, would keep Gottliebsohn with him while Kohn took the woman to the bar; the doctor and his patient would join them later. Kohn, surprisingly enough, made no objection when Glass pointed out that it would look strange for him to be present when brother and sister met. It might be, Glass thought, that Kohn really meant to be cooperative now; then, too, Auerbach had cautioned them that the sister knew nothing of the charges, and both men had agreed that if she was as "nervous" as Dean Wolfe and Hortsky had indicated, such knowledge might only frighten her into silence about whatever she remembered.

Glass also thought it best to have a precautionary interview, though he did not mention this to Kohn. Before finally getting to bed, he asked the desk to deliver a message that he wished to see her about one, that afternoon, in her room.

She did not answer his first knock, though he was exactly on time. He rapped again, more loudly, and was about to knock again when the door opened—only enough that she might identify her caller. Reluctantly then she allowed him to come in.

She was a small woman, rather frail, who would be attractive, he thought, were it not for thick-lensed glasses which distorted her eyes in a manner that was at once wistful and unappealing. Her hair was long and had the richness of color, a reddish-brown, of a younger woman, though she wore it severely done up in a bun. She was obviously ill at ease, and it was he finally who suggested that they sit down.

"I thought it would be best for everyone concerned," he began, "if you and I go over a few things before you see your brother. A reunion like this, after so much time, so much . . . heartache (he did not like the word, but he had seen the tattoo on her fragile wrist, not quite hidden by that clumsy watch, and it was the first word that came to mind) . . . is not easy at the best of times, and given your brother's condition, it may prove difficult for him. And for you too, I imagine." He paused and she gave a little shrug which he found difficult to interpret. Was it indifference? He could not believe so. "He's been under a rather enormous amount of pressure," he continued quietly, so as not to alarm her unduly, "and frankly, I'm concerned about his emotional stability, particularly if he were to receive too sudden or too great a shock. As his doctor, I'll want to prepare him for that eventuality, but in order to do that, of course, there are certain things I need to know."

She had been listening intently, if reluctantly, and now that he paused she spoke, shrinking into herself at the same time as if she expected to be criticized for the interruption. "Certain things?"

"Perhaps unpleasant things," he said. "Amnesia is a block set up by the mind against memory because that memory is too disturbing to live with. If the memory comes back too abruptly, before the patient has been properly conditioned to receive it, he may not be able to handle it any better now, in the present, than he was at the time he forgot. Am I making myself clear? What I would like to know is, is there anything *you* know about that your brother would not want to remember? That he would be afraid to remember?"

She looked at him for what seemed an inordinately long time, and because of those distortioning glasses, he could not tell whether that was a look of mockery on her face, or grief, or both. Before he might decide, however, the expression was gone.

"I don't think I knew my brother well enough to answer that," she said.

"I was under the impression that you were very close," he said.

"Close?" she said. "Did Ernst tell you that?"

"He couldn't be certain, of course," Glass said, "since his memory is rather patchy, but it seemed to him and to me from what people said that you must have been close."

"Well, I suppose we were, in a way," she said, when it became apparent that he was insisting on an answer. "Because my—our—father was a great believer in family ties. He didn't believe in anything else, not God, certainly. Family. The family came first no matter what, and Ernst was forced to take care of me when he would rather have been doing something else—playing kickball, maybe." She gave the little shrug. "If he wants to think of that as close, I have no objection."

"I'm not as worried at the moment about how Ernst thinks of your relationship," Glass said, "as I am how you think of it." He could feel her withdrawal. "I understand that you were reluctant to even see your brother. May I ask why?"

"Does it matter?" she asked finally. "I am here."

"I am afraid it does," he said. "If your brother senses a . . . disapproval . . . on your part, it could harden his subconscious resolve—already very strong, mind you—not to remember; it could frighten him back into that cave he's been crouching in for so long. Now if your reasons are petty—that is, a typical childhood disagreement—then I'd like you to speak freely of it to your brother, reassure him that such animosities are not worth bothering about. If your reasons are not petty, then I'd like to know about it now."

He had been unable to hold her gaze. Somewhere along the way she had dropped her eyes and now seemed very interested in a wrinkle she had found in her khaki skirt.

"Well?" he said.

"I have no reasons whatsoever," she said, not looking at him, but with a note of irritation creeping into her voice. "You asked if we were close, and I tried to answer that."

"But you were reluctant to come here," he pointed out patiently.

"I didn't see the point," she said finally. "As far as I knew, everyone was dead. And in fact I began to prefer it that way. We all have things we would like to forget, Doctor. The dead do not come to life so easily."

"Your brother is not dead," he said.

"In my mind he is," she said. "He died with my parents."

He stared at her, almost reluctant to ask the question. "Why do you link their deaths with your brother?"

"Because he was not with them, and should have been!" she cried, and suddenly burst into tears.

He did not go to her, remaining seated, waiting her out. He judged that her tears had been a long time coming, that she had withheld them from her husband, and then from Dean Wolfe, and that she had been stoic during the lonely flight and stoic in her silent hotel room, and it was not until he had touched a secret nerve that she broke down and wept. But those were still superficial tears, he reasoned, tears of frustration and anger, and would not last long. No stranger could touch her innermost feelings, he guessed. Only a relative could do that.

She took off her glasses to wipe her eyes. And as he had supposed, without them she was quite pretty. But she put them back on and looked at him defiantly.

"Not with them where?" Glass asked quietly. "In a concentration camp?"

"They did not go to a camp," she said, lifting her head proudly. "When the police came, my father shot my mother, and then himself."

"But not you," Glass said, shaken, but determined not to relax the pressure now that he had her talking.

"I did not want to die; not then, not there," she said. Her face twisted. "As it turned out, I survived. So I was right, wasn't I?"

"Your brother survived, too," Glass said. "Are you blaming him for something you did yourself?"

"Maybe if he had been with us when we left Cologne, everything would have been different!" she cried.

"Ernst wanted to be with you," he said. She looked at him then, finally surprised. "His last conscious memory," he continued, "is that of himself going to your apartment and finding you all gone. He believes that something happened to him on the night you left that prevented him from being with you."

"Does he?" she said. "Did he tell you what that something was?"

"He doesn't remember," Glass said. "We were hoping you could tell us."

"Ernst never planned to go with us," she said. "He's lying if he told you that."

"Are you certain?" he asked. "He seemed so positive—he was so shocked to find you gone—he even begged the guards on that cattle . . . concentration camp train to put him in with the others."

"What concentration camp train?" she asked. "We left Cologne on the Bruxelle express."

Glass was silent. Had there not even been a freight train with a human cargo? Was that part of the hallucination? It fit in, all right, with his theory that Gottliebsohn had murdered himself—his frantic search could also have been an acting-out of guilt that he had not been with his family. But he became uneasy. It all began to seem somehow too pat.

"That will relieve your brother's mind enormously," he said at last. "He believes you were all on a camp train."

"It didn't matter in the end," she said. "When we got to France we were aliens, enemy aliens, do you understand? The French put us all in a camp—oh, one much nicer than anything the Germans had—but then the French surrendered and we were turned over to the Germans because we were German citizens, *verstehen Sie*? So all my brother's efforts were wasted."

"What efforts?" Glass asked.

"Oh, didn't he tell you?" she said. "It was he who arranged our exit permits. But not one for himself."

"Do you know that for a fact?" Glass asked; he saw the doubt come into her face.

"Father would have told us," she said finally, "if Ernst were going to leave Germany with us. He was not one for surprises." But she seemed shaken, at least momentarily—and then the moment passed. He saw it pass and he guessed that a convincing thought had come into her mind. "Ernst would never have gone with us," she said. "My brother was not one to change his mind."

"Then you knew his mind was made up to stay?" Glass asked. "He told you that himself?"

She stared at him, and something in her magnified, distorted eyes chilled him. "I never saw my brother after he left Warsfeld."

"Not once while you were in Cologne?" he asked. She shook her head. "Then he could have changed his mind, couldn't he, without your knowing it?"

She said nothing, though her mouth tightened stubbornly.

"Ruth," he said, "what is it that your brother doesn't want to remember?"

"How would I know that?" she asked. "Do we ever know what anyone else is really thinking inside? Maybe you think you do, Doctor, because that's your job, but how can you ever really be sure?"

"We're guessing a lot of the time," he admitted. "The trick is—and it's a trick, only we call it intuition, or insight, but in the best sense of those words because they are acquired only after half a lifetime of practice—the trick is to know when and what to guess." He hesitated. "My guess, Ruth, is that you know what your brother's blacking out." She made no answer. "Won't you tell me, Ruth," he pleaded. "It's important to him, believe me."

"I told you I don't know," she said.

She was lying; he was sure of it, but he could see no way of getting the truth out of her, short of keeping at her as Kohn would, or Levin, using interrogation as the medievalists used the rack, a verbal twisting that stretched the mind. And he could not bring himself to cause any more pain to a woman who had already suffered more than her share—particularly when he could not know if what she told him then would be of benefit to his patient.

He got slowly to his feet. All he could do was try to see that the meeting with her brother brought it out—hopefully because of compassion. But if it came out of hurt or bitterness, he had to be alert enough to prevent lasting damage to his patient, or to her.

"I'll go see to your brother," he said. "He had a pretty rough day yesterday. I wanted him to sleep this morning. But I expect we'll be ready for you within the hour."

She made no comment, though she seemed to shrink into herself again.

"You should keep in mind," he said, "that your brother is a sick man. If his behavior seems odd or disconcerting, try and bear with him, please."

She fumbled with the watch. "I just want to get it over with," she said.

"I'll ring you up when we're ready," he said, and left her to her forebodings.

Ernst Gottliebsohn sat by an open window, still in rumpled pajamas, letting the midmorning breeze cool his feverish skin, staring unseeingly at the hotel gardens below. The tray of sweet rolls and coffee that Kohn had thoughtfully arranged was only half eaten, forgotten on his lap, when Doctor Glass arrived. Gottliebsohn did not turn to acknowledge his visitor, being in a kind of stupor that was, after the night he had spent, almost pleasurable. He was resentful, finally, when Glass insisted on getting his attention.

Glass was shocked by his patient's appearance. Gottliebsohn was haggard and sallow, and Glass wondered whether he had been mistaken to have denied him an additional sedative. It was part of the increasing pressure he wanted put on the other, a heightening of sensitivity, a breaking down of barriers between the two consciousnesses. But this hollow-eyed lethargic who stared at him so morosely now could hardly be said to have experienced an increase of awareness. If anything it was just the opposite.

"Did you have a bad night, Ernst?" he asked guiltily.

"Why don't you ask *me* that?" Kohn asked sardonically from the table where he was laboriously going over his notes. "I was up with the bugger half a dozen times, and it wasn't till I got the idea of leaving the lights on and getting most of what was left in the bottle down him that he finally fell off."

"Did you dream?" the doctor continued, ignoring the other.

"Not exactly," Gottliebsohn finally managed. "It is impossible to dream," he wanted to say, "when you cannot sleep." And it was not until that unlikely samaritan, Kohn, had forcefully suggested the whiskey, and the lights, that he had been able to keep his eyes closed without fearing the images that would come swirling out of his mind's darkness. The visions he had then, perhaps because of the stunning effect of the liquor, were totally different from the hallucinatory nightmare he feared—and yet somehow had an equally frightening intensity. For in that all too familiar limbo between sleep and wakefulness, all he had experienced in the past few hours crowded his mind and his senses: he smelled that cathedral incense and heard again the chant of priests; the piano waltz started off very strongly, played by sure hands; that doll-like Madonna stared at him unblinkingly; he watched a boy looking tenderly after his baby sister; inhaled the aroma of an expensive cigar; walked into a gloomy shed and looked into a bluish light and coughed at the acrid, sulphurous smell— and suddenly all became incredibly confused, with himself standing before priests whose incense gave forth the odor of sweat and trying to cleanse himself in baptismal fonts whose water turned grimy and thick as blood; and riding the front seat of a motor van, he listened to radio news of atrocity against the background of a waltz played by stumbling, childish hands, while behind him, curtained by silence, Jakob and Hannah and Ruth were trying desperately to get his diverted attention, his father waving a cross, an Iron Cross, at him, and worst of all, beside him on the seat, a crowned, featureless Madonna shushed those piteous ones with a finger long as a claw and stained blood-red.

A dream? Not exactly. The fault of this damned doctor who would not use his medical knowledge to prescribe mind-deadening pills, and who must have known, after he had been found so terribly sick, vomiting into the ditch all he had learned about himself and all he had learned about Germans, that his need for the drug was greater than it had ever been.

"Hallucinations?" Glass asked, looking closely at the other.

"Everything's all mixed up," Gottliebsohn said helplessly, glaring at the one responsible for this immense weariness and upset he now felt.

"You're very angry with me, aren't you?" Glass said sympathetically. "I don't blame you; I'd probably feel the same way myself; maybe I can make it up to you with the news I've brought you this morning."

Gottliebsohn stared dully at his doctor.

"Your sister has been found," Glass said.

Gottliebsohn became convinced that he was out of his mind. He had heard and yet not heard, and he could not tell, looking at the listening attitude of the other, whether he had been asked a question, or told something, or indeed, whether there had been anything spoken at all. It was so quiet. He thought, finally, that it was possible he had heard nothing but his own thoughts, and he even forgot what it was he believed the doctor had said.

"Did you hear me, Ernst?" Glass asked, becoming concerned about the strange placidity of the other. "We've found your sister! She's here, right now, in this hotel, waiting to meet with you."

His sister found? His sister, here, in Germany, in this hotel? It was impossible—and then suddenly Gottliebsohn's heart, which he had believed on the verge of stopping altogether, its beat as intermittent and hollow as a funeral drum, began to pound away at a great rate, and his sluggish body regained some of its strength, and his mind began flipping over images with the awkward rapidity of an amateur magician looking for a particular card—and not finding it.

"Who?" he said. "Which?"—without quite knowing what he was saying—and then he grasped the hand of the other, grateful for the deliverance of his beloved sister, and yet afraid, somehow, to meet her, and hoping that his doctor would understand the shame he felt. Because he did not: whether it was for something he had done, or for something about his own unprepossessing appearance. What would she think when she saw him?

"It's all right, Ernst," Glass said. "You get yourself dressed now. A shower and a shave will do wonders for you."

Gottliebsohn nodded, speechless with a dread he did not understand, and went to do as the other suggested.

The reunion took place in the doctor's suite. Glass went to get the sister first; then Kohn brought Gottliebsohn by, leaving him at the door.

Gottliebsohn came hesitantly inside, staring incredulously across the room at the small woman seated in the alcove. The doctor had warned him that she would, at first, seem unfamiliar, but to finally look at his own flesh and blood and see a stranger became immensely disconcerting.

It was as if he were confronted by an imposter.

He came forward a little way, and stopped. "Is it really you?" he said.

Glass urged him forward, wondering at so much doubt.

Gottliebsohn resisted. "The glasses," he said. "I don't remember the glasses."

"Ruth?" the doctor said, and after a moment she took them off.

Gottliebsohn walked all the way to the alcove then. She shrank from him, eyes blinking near-sightedly. He looked her over carefully, trying to see in this frightened woman the lovely girl so dim in his memory, who in spite of every effort he had made, in spite of all the descriptions he had been given, persisted in remaining a stranger.

"Is it really you?" he repeated.

"It's what's left of me," she said finally.

He became terribly embarrassed. "Oh, I didn't mean anything like that," he said. "In fact, you're still pretty. Prettier even than you were as a girl."

"You remember her then?" Glass said, pleased.

"Yes," Gottliebsohn lied, finally. He fumbled in his pocket and brought out the photograph. A corner was bent, and he swore at his own carelessness: how could he be so clumsy with the one thing that proved anyone had cared for him? Before handing it to her, he smoothed the corner, then took one last look—it was Ruth, all right; he could see the similarity now.

"Where did you ever get this?" she asked, her eyes suddenly brimming.

"Fritzi gave it to me," he said.

"Fritzi?" she said incredulously. "But when have you seen her?"

"Yesterday," he said. "We took a trip to Warsfeld. She's married to Hans Eichler. You remember Hans? He's terribly crippled now, a mess."

"Hansie crippled?" she said.

"They both spoke of you," he said. "Perhaps you might visit them."

"I could never go back there," she said, and now her eyes were dry.

"They loved you, Ruth," he said. "Fritzi was your friend."

"I suppose she was," she said.

There was an awkward pause, and he realized that he was trembling. He sat down in the facing chair, but tentatively, on the edge of the seat, looking to her for approval. She handed the photo back.

"You keep it," he said.

"I don't want it," she said. He put it reluctantly back in his pocket.

"How is it for you now?" he asked finally. She shrugged. "Any children?" he asked hopefully.

"None," she said.

His face fell. "Then we are the last," he said.

"If you feel so strongly as that," she said, "why don't *you* have children? I would think plenty of women would jump at the chance to marry a man so important."

"I am not so important," he said, wondering if she were being sarcastic.

"My husband thinks so," she said, "and all his relatives, among whom are some unmarried women who are not half bad. When you visit our *kibbutz* you must take your pick."

"Visit you?" he said slowly, beginning to smile. He was so wound up in his immediate troubles that he had not thought what his future might be like. Not that he would expect it to be any easier. One never got used to loneliness. But now this fragile woman, his long-lost sister, was inviting him for a visit, and the idea was very appealing.

"Georgi can hardly wait," she said. "He looks forward to many long talks with you. About politics. And economics. Georgi is a farmer but he reads all the newspapers and he thinks that if things had gone just a little differently he might have gone into politics. Like you."

"I am not in politics," he said.

"It is all the same to Georgi," she said.

"And what about you?" he said.

"It makes no difference to me," she said, refusing to look at him.

He stopped smiling. "I spent years looking for you," he said. "I listed with all the agencies, and your name never turned up."

"Georgi looked out for me in the camp," she said. "I married him there, took his name there."

"But didn't it occur to you I might be alive?" he asked.

"Why should that occur to me?" she said, suddenly excited and angry. "As far as I knew, you were better off dead!"

"I know I have a lot to answer for," he said.

She subsided as abruptly as she had flared up.

"I must have hurt you terribly," he went on slowly, full of some unknown sorrow for her. "I ask your pardon."

"You don't have to answer to me, Ernst," she said, interrupting. "Look to your own conscience."

"I never wanted anything but the best for you," he said.

She stared at him. "What are you talking about?"

"Don't *you* know?" he asked finally. He was not sure himself what he had meant; the last had come from him as though someone else were sitting here, on the edge of a hard-backed chair in the gloomy alcove of a psychiatric sitting room, someone else confronting someone else's sister, both talking as if both were other than themselves—else why these strange words, words which each in his turn failed to understand?

"You chose to go your own way once," she said bitterly. "Why so contrite now? It's too late for such feelings; they do no one any good . . . least of all, I would think, yourself."

"You will not forgive me then," he said hopelessly, speaking for the other. "What was it I did wrong?"

She would not look at him, obviously very upset.

Glass thought it was time to interrupt. "We know Ernst lived in Cologne, probably under an alias," he said. "But we don't know why."

"I know nothing of his activities in Cologne," she said.

"He may never recover his memory unless he finds out what he was doing there," Glass said.

She gave the little shrug.

"Ruth," Gottliebsohn pleaded, "whatever it was, tell me. We were close once, don't push me away now!"

"We were never close," she said, her face working.

"I watched out for you, always," he said, shocked by her denial.

"You watched out for me?" she said, incredulous. "How, watch? By Poppa's command? By Momma's orders?"

"I took care of you of my own will," he insisted.

"You hated taking care of me," she said. "Why don't you

admit it? I cramped your style—you would rather have been off rowdying with the other boys, or in the woods with some girl!"

"I loved you, little doll," he said, disturbed by the injustice. He paused, breathing heavily, becoming angry with this woman who denied the love he had felt for his lovely young sister. "It's you who has the bad memory!" he suddenly cried. "It's you who resented my watching out for you! But without me, you would have had a bad time with the boys . . . what did you know about boys, anyway? Even the shy ones have been known to get under the blankets with a girl, particularly a lively girl, and will you deny now that you were lively . . . ? But I saw the boys eying you, and you eying them back, and if I hadn't always been handy to knock a few heads together . . . but I couldn't watch over you always, could I? You couldn't wait to get off by yourself, once I was gone; the first glib-tongued lizard in flannel pants that came along—how could you shack up with a creep like that? How could Father let you go off to Cologne by yourself? If I'd been home it would never have happened . . ."

She crouched back in her chair, wide-eyed and apprehensive. He looked at her in amazement. He blinked once, slowly and heavily, and his mind, like some ponderous slide projector, changed view for him. Who was she? And what was that he had been shouting? The words had spilled from him without thought, as if he were drunk—and indeed he had been giddy with anger—and something, some other spirit, as during the time he had been under treatment with those special drugs, had possessed him, and he found himself speaking words that came from something fugitive and strange inside himself.

"What are you talking about?" she whispered at last.

"I don't know," Gottliebsohn said, terribly frightened.

"I was never in Cologne before you sent for us," she said.

"I know," he stammered. "Fritzi told me that." He became extraordinarily confused. During that awful harangue he had acted as if everything should have been clear and specific when in fact it was blurred and obscure. He glanced quickly at the silent, listening Glass, that feeling of fright and shame even stronger in him now.

"And you dare to accuse me of something like . . . like *that*," she said, her voice shaking.

"I don't know what got into me," he said.

"When it's *you* who . . ." She fell silent, trembling, and both men saw the gooseflesh on her bare, painfully thin arms.

"Tell him, Ruth," Glass said.

"He's the one who had the affair," she said tightly. "He lived in Cologne with a German girl!" And then she began weeping desperately.

Gottliebsohn felt as if he might go out of his mind. He sat stunned, unable to fully comprehend what he had just heard, looking from this hysterical woman to the watchful psychiatrist, the silent witness to this incredible lie. And then he was almost immediately overwhelmed by a contrary feeling that it was all true. In the recesses of his mind memory stirred and he waited, both fearful and anticipatory, for the crying to stop.

"May I get you something, Ruth?" Glass asked finally. "A drink, a glass of water?"

She shook her head, and after wiping her eyes, took her glasses from her lap and sat back. "When Ernst brought us to Cologne," she began, slowly, "we never saw him. He talked to us only by telephone, and that mostly to Poppa— Poppa said that Ernst did not want to be seen by anyone in our building. Because, Poppa thought, Ernst was engaged in underground work, and did not want anyone to know who he really was. But I found out the real reason, didn't I, Ernst?"

Gottliebsohn leaned away from her. "What was that?" he asked hoarsely, though he was afraid to hear.

She looked to Glass, who nodded to her encouragingly, beginning to see how everything fit.

"You shouldn't have been so tender-hearted with me, Ernst," she said, her mouth twisting with the memory, "when I complained about being cooped up in that dinky flat. And I begged you—remember?—to come take me for a walk through the city, a city I'd never seen, could only see from a curtained window, and I offered to meet you somewhere else if you were so frightened you'd be seen. But you wouldn't even do that; you sent Lena instead. That was a mistake, Ernst. She told me everything. Oh, not right away, I had to win her confidence, first; but that was easy, she was really quite nice—for a German!"

"Lena?" Gottliebsohn said, and somehow the way the name felt on his tongue he knew it was familiar, and a feeling stronger than anything he had ever felt, though he could not quite identify it, seized him by the heart as if he were about to have an attack.

"Yes, Lena!" she said, furiously. "Stop pretending you don't remember!" She looked to Glass. "No one could forget a girl as beautiful as she was, hair so black and glossy, and pale, pale skin, with enormous blue eyes . . ."

"Lake-blue eyes," Gottliebsohn murmured.

"And a body so supple as . . . as . . ."

"A willow," Gottliebsohn said.

"She was so stunning, Doctor, how could he forget?" She looked accusingly at Gottliebsohn. "How could you? Oh, I could see how you would fall in love with her, how any man would, and she was such a lovely person, too, inside, sweet . . ."

Like an angel, Gottliebsohn thought.

"And how is it that a family could be so Nazi as hers, and she live with a Jew? At first I thought maybe she did it because she wanted to spite them, but then I realized that she loved you; yes, truly, yes she loved you, Ernst, with all her heart. And you have forgotten her?"

"Lena," Gottliebsohn said, staring at the floor. He was terribly distressed. His heart ached for the beautiful Lena, the angelic Lena, who had loved a Jew and lived with him in a time when to love anyone was difficult, let alone a sneaky mongrel Jew who had strange business with priests and the Catholic nobility and German cops, and whose youth had been spent in defiling German girls and who had left Lena, finally, to shift for herself, left her at the mercy of a corrupting city, abandoned her to make what she could of herself, and she with nothing but beauty and an angelic soul, and he knew how useless in a tumultuous, monstrous time such attributes were, and he shuddered to think what may have become of her, and the guilt and the anger racked him so that he broke out in a cold sweat.

"Do you remember her, Ernst?" Glass asked, watching him with some concern.

Gottliebsohn nodded, wretchedly. "But it's all so damn vague," he protested, wondering why he was only able to remember those things that other people told him, that however strong his emotions his memory was so frustratingly incomplete. He looked beseechingly at the strange frail woman with the strong temper who had provided him with such an agonizing memory. "I loved her," he said.

She peered at him myopically, and her anger left her as suddenly as it had come. "I know you did, Ernst," she said. "Lena told me how much. She wanted you to get out, to leave Germany while you could, and she would try to join you later. But you would not, she said, you insisted on staying; it was your country, you said, you were more German than Jew, and besides, she said, you had it all worked out. You would take a different name and the two of you would be married as Catholics, and all would be well. What you were forgetting, she said, was the fact that her family would still be in Germany, and that her brother would never let the two of you be in peace, although you argued that as a soldier he would be sent away, and while he was gone the two of you would disappear. But it didn't matter, did it, Ernst? As it turned out, you left her."

Her pitying tone was too much for Gottliebsohn. His eyes spilled with sudden tears, and he despised himself for his weakness. "Please, little doll," he said, "no more."

She peered at him through the thick lenses. "What is that you say?" she asked, frowning. "You called me that earlier too."

"Little doll," he mumbled, wiping his eyes with his awkward thumbs. "What I used to call you when we were kids. You looked just like a doll; remember how we used to play you really were, and you made the sound like those dolls that were so popular then, more like a calf than a baby ... *maaaa, maaaa*. How the other kids laughed."

She stared at him for a long time. Finally she glanced at the watching psychiatrist. She seemed very upset.

"What is it, Ruth?" Glass asked sharply.

"Nothing, nothing," she said evasively. "But isn't this enough now? There's nothing else to tell."

"Is there anything more you want to ask your sister?" Glass asked the distraught Gottliebsohn.

He made an effort to get himself under control. "You

meant it about the *kibbutz?*" he asked. "Visiting you and your husband? All the relatives?"

She stared at him, then nodded, then looked at Glass as if anxious to get done with it, to get out of the room.

"All right," Glass said, standing up in response to her unspoken request. She got up, too, and when Gottliebsohn put out his hand she seemed reluctant to take it, though with another glance at the watching psychiatrist, she did so—giving it a hasty up-and-down shake and letting go.

In the sitting room Glass delayed her with a question, knowing Kohn would come soon.

"Will you stay in Germany until Ernst is better?"

"What about my husband?" she asked. "I have obligations to him, too. I hadn't planned on being here more than a day . . ."

"A day?" Glass said, startled. "But we had hoped you could spend a little more time with your brother." She was shaking her head discouragingly, as if frightened by the idea, and he hastened to add, "Well, let's all have a drink together, at least, and talk it over then. You don't have to decide right now . . ."

Before she could answer, there was a knock at the door and Kohn came in.

11

THE INVESTIGATOR WAS TOO DISTRACTED to notice the strained atmosphere. He had just received a telephone call from Herr Professor Doktor Schenke that had left him tense and pale with suppressed excitement, and he had neither the heart nor the mind to pursue these peripheral matters when major revelations seemed in the offing. The director of the War Crimes Bureau had apparently turned up an important witness—which meant they could work damned skillfully and fast if the incentive was strong enough. It was not certain, however, that he would get to confront the witness himself—any interrogations might have to be conducted in writing, a time-consuming and frequently ineffectual affair, and Kohn, knowing he had only forty minutes in which to plan an appeal to the German for personal contact, could not help being impatient with this family business he had let himself in for. Then, too, that dark Jew, Auerbach's, implication that he was now irrevocably his man infuriated him—he was no one's man; he would prove that, if necessary, when the time came.

But as always, Kohn was able to keep his true feelings to himself. "How did everything go?" he asked, falsely cheerful. "Did the little reunion pan out as everyone hoped?" His glittering eye fell approvingly upon the woman. "You're the long-lost sister, are you?" he said, reaching down for her limp hand. He made a kissing sound in the German manner without quite touching her skin, but close enough to smell soap and nothing else: these *kibbutzniks* were all much alike—no perfumes or lotions or scented oils for them. "I'm Albert Kohn," he continued, "your brother's friend, perhaps his best, though I'm sure not his only. What say we all go down to the bar and have a drink to celebrate? I'll buy—my expense account needs some boosting, otherwise the clerks back home won't believe I'm working."

Glass forced a smile, thinking the other was overdoing it. "Why don't you and Ruth go on?" he said. "Ernst and I have some things to talk about. We'll join you in a few minutes."

Kohn wondered briefly at how distressed Gottliebsohn seemed. But the momentum of this little game they were playing had him now, and he offered his arm, then took hers and tucked it into his, then walked her, using a gentle but inexorable force, to the door.

"Give us time to get acquainted," he said in mock protest to Glass. He allowed her to precede him to the hall, then stuck his head briefly back inside. "About thirty minutes, you say?" he said. "I have an appointment I must get to."

Though his mind was still on his coming meeting, Kohn forced himself to make small talk. He was chatty about the weather, the dullness of Bonn, and the accommodations of the hotel. She barely responded, and as they rode down in the elevator to the bar, Kohn glanced at her covertly. Not much resemblance to the stolid Ernst, he thought, which was lucky for her; he could see where with a little make-up, some eye shadow, a redder lipstick and a touch of rouge she might be damned good-looking. Of course she was impossibly nervous, a trait in women which put him off. He had felt her tremble when he had taken her arm, and it would not surprise him if her pants were wet. Was this a permanent condition, or had the reunion with her brother shaken her up so much?

"What would you like?" he asked, after they were seated.

"Maybe some tea," she said.

"Come on, now," he wheedled, "I know Jewish girls aren't much for the booze, but maybe a little kirsch, it's nice and cherry-sweet, it's comforting, you will relax. I suppose that headknocker really put you through the wringer? Poor Ernst." He ordered the drinks—a double whiskey for himself, the dessert liqueur for her. "How *did* it go up there?" he asked, elaborately casual.

She gave a peculiar little shrug. "Well enough, I suppose."

"Were you able to shake his memory loose?" Kohn asked. She nodded warily. "Did he remember you?"

"He said so," she mumbled, looking away.

Kohn frowned, puzzled by her attitude. But he had to be careful not to have her guess that his role here was an official one. "Well, I suppose you've both changed a good deal," he said.

The waiter brought the drinks. He noticed that she shrank back when the fellow placed her liqueur before her, and he glanced at him: only a typical heine, he thought, but he could see where that beefy face might frighten someone who had been in the camps.

"Your first trip back?" he asked. She nodded. "Upsetting?" he asked. She nodded again, reluctantly, obviously suspicious of his affability. "I can understand that," he said ingratiatingly, "but you soon learn in diplomatic work to get along as best you can. It's a job like any other. Some things are distasteful, but when it's for the good of the country—"

"I would not have thought *you* would be part of anything like this," she suddenly cried.

"Why not me?" Kohn asked, pretending innocence, when he had gotten over his surprise that she knew, after all, who he was.

"Your job is killing Germans, not sweet-talking them," she said.

"Well," he said modestly, "not all Germans, just those who were criminal—"

"Is it true then that you've had a change of heart?" she asked, interrupting again.

"Who said so?" he growled, suddenly alert to an unknown danger.

"A magazine," she said. "You were assigned to the mission as a political afterthought, they said, and they said you are lending your hero's name to the government's purposes in return for unspecified favors!"

"A magazine said all that?" he asked, when he had somehow mastered his shock. "Which magazine?"

She named *Haolam-Hazeh*, a radical protest journal edited by young people, which someone had included in the bundle of reading matter given her at the airport. Dean Wolfe perhaps.

He fell silent, puzzling over the implications of the reports. That it had appeared in such a disreputable sheet made it less meaningful, of course, but the captain was astute enough to realize that the originating place of rumors had little to do with their eventual public acceptance, or the speed with which they traveled. Who had leaked it, his own superiors, or Auerbach? He opted for Auerbach. That shrewd individual had not climbed so high so fast without anticipating contingencies, and he certainly must have guessed that he, Kohn, had not been about to burn any of his bridges until he had made it safely to the other side. And it was like him too to get an additional use from the captain's presence, to make it seem like an endorsement of the mission. How the Interior Minister must be burning—his own man, his own insisted-upon assignee, made to seem like another German enthusiast! Kohn became angry and frustrated: angry about this besmirchment of his reputation, frustrated because no matter which way he turned, he could not seem to get this matter of his own future resolved until they were quits with the past of Gottliebsohn.

"I've had no change of heart," he muttered, uncomfortable under her magnified stare. "And I make no deals with my reputation; a man like me, sister, has nothing *except* a reputation—nothing else, no money put away, no security except for a lousy pension. But why should I look forward to a restful old age? I expect to die young in any case, if I don't get killed on duty, someone with a grudge is likely to look me up in some old people's villa, but still, I don't complain, except when some filthy rag prints lies about me." He finished his drink at a gulp, then glanced at his watch. Not much time left.

"You're not drinking your kirsch," he said.

She picked up her glass and sipped from it.

"Look, madame," he said, "there's no reason we shouldn't conduct ourselves in as pleasant a manner as possible, life's sour enough, God knows, *you* know, but that's still no cause for you to go around with your lips puckered as though you had just tasted vinegar. It's lonely enough here without us Jews giving each other a hard time. In fact, I was hoping you'd keep me company tonight. Ernst will probably want to get to bed early, and you and I could go dancing."

"I am leaving for Israel on the five o'clock plane," she said.

He looked at her unbelievingly. "So soon?" he managed. "But you've barely had a chance to talk to your brother."

Her face did strange things. "He'll visit us at our *kibbutz*. Maybe you can come too? My husband would never get over having *two* such important people as our guests."

"You really ought to stick around," he said, wheedlingly, while his mind raced ahead, trying to think what to do. It did not help that she spoke so mockingly—like a lot of women, she seemed to imply she knew something that he never would. "You've been married for twenty-four years, in that hammer-and-hoe *kibbutz* for twenty-two—I'd think a little night life would be welcome to break the monotony."

She stared at him. "I prefer the monotony, Captain," she said at last, "to anything you might have in mind."

"You misinterpret me," he said, secretly so furious he had difficulty preserving an air of suavity before this sanctimonious bitch; not that he was absolutely sure he hadn't a double motive. "I won't deny I find you attractive," he continued, "but believe me, that sort of thing couldn't have been further from my mind. I don't mind telling you my feelings are hurt."

"It's not often you are rejected, I suppose," she said.

He glared at her, then dropped his eyes so she should not see the suspicion in them. Something was definitely wrong here. She was in an incredible hurry to get back to Israel, she was not even anxious about when her brother would arrive downstairs to join them—and to top it all off, she was acting very peculiarly toward a man who was supposedly her brother's friend. He hated to let her go; not only might she be withholding information, but her mocking attitude rankled. But he saw no way to detain her without exceeding his authority—revealing his function and the accusation against her brother. Still, he wouldn't mind seeing her put through it a bit—and then he thought of a way.

"I'm sorry you feel as you do," he said then, looking

ostentatiously at his watch. "It means we'll have to say good-bye now—I can't wait for the others, I have another appointment. Would you care to wait for them here?"

She shrank from the thought of being alone in this German place. "I will go up to my room," she said. "I have packing to do . . ."

He signed for the bill and escorted her out of the bar to the front lobby elevators, wondering if the remark about packing was true. Had she been planning a longer stay, and had something about that meeting with her brother changed her mind?

Well, they would find all that out soon enough, he thought, and without depending on the soft-hearted approach of these diplomats and their wishy-washy psychiatrists.

As soon as the elevator doors closed behind her, Kohn hurried to the front desk, where he asked for the packet of mail he had left for posting to Jerusalem. Luckily, it was still there. Taking it into the card room, Kohn tore up the first letter, and then, very quickly (the note already having taken shape, from first word to last, in his mind at the bar) wrote another to replace it:

My Dear Attorney Levin,

You will find everything that is pertinent to date in the material to which this is attached. It is my opinion that the evidence so far proves neither one thing nor the other: neither our man's guilt, but certainly not his innocence. I am hopeful, however, that this frustrating situation is about to change. At this very moment, I am on my way to a meeting with Herr Professor Doktor Schenke that is likely to produce the hoped-for results. While I cannot of course be sure what the German has up his sleeve, I think that he has found an important witness, someone perhaps familiar with the activities of the *Nazi Polizei.*

I assume that you have by now been notified that the sister of Gottliebsohn has come forward, and was flown here to Bonn to expedite our investigation. Their reunion has just taken place. A report on that situation is *not* included, as by the terms of your agreement with the other side, the psychiatrist is permitted an independent procedure, and I was not allowed to be present. It is my guess, however, that she was not very much help. Unfortunately, in an interview *I* just concluded with her, she was most uncooperative with me as well. I am certain she is holding something back. If I had more time or a freer hand I would detain and question her further. However, she insists on leaving for Jerusalem on the five o'clock flight (Bonn time). I would suggest that you interrogate her immediately upon her arrival. I have no doubts but that you will be able to convince her to tell you whatever she is keeping from us—and from her brother, as well.

> Kindest regards,
> Kohn

P.S. I assume that a copy of this note will automatically be sent to the Interior Minister?

Kohn marked the cover envelope DIPLOMATIC/URGENT; added a *Call Addressee Upon Arrival,* then took the packet in to the clerk at the lobby desk. "I would like this sent out to the airport at once," Kohn said.

He was not, he told himself, walking out of the hotel, pursuing the matter merely out of irritation, though the woman had made him briefly quite angry. It was his duty to communicate even his hunches to his superiors. After all, he thought, as he beckoned to the waiting limousine, his hunches were based on a great many experiences down through the years, and he had become extraordinarily sensitive to those who had secret fears.

Herr Professor Doktor Schenke was not at all affable when Kohn arrived at his office in the chancellory building. "You are somewhat tardy," he observed, seating himself again behind his desk after a perfunctory bow.

"I was having an apéritif with a lady," Kohn said, knowing that Schenke would have had a report from plain-clothes men stationed at the hotel. He had been told about Schenke's reaction when informed his men had been given the slip—the other would not be disposed to allow him another such opportunity. "The time passed so quickly," Kohn continued. "You know how it is."

Schenke seemed doubtful. "I was under the impression you were anxious for our cooperation," he said.

"But I am," Kohn said languidly. One thing he would

not do, he thought, was pretend to any enthusiasm about working with Germans. And in any case, he would be more likely to turn this interview his way if he did not show eagerness. It had been his experience that those in authority would go to extraordinary lengths to impress any audience, however small, even to the extent of revealing what was better kept back. But he soon saw that he must not underestimate this man.

"Captain," Schenke said, "let us drop our charade. I am well aware that *you* would probably not have agreed to tell us who you are after. And I can understand that. One never likes to admit that one of his own people is criminal. For my part, I confess I was not displeased to find someone other than a German accused of a gross misdeed. It made up, a little, for not seeing what was under our noses. When you chose Herr Gottliebsohn as a traveling companion I should have known immediately that *he* was the one . . . but when you gave that incompetent the slip, it confused me, made me think, still, that you were after Germans . . . Well, interestingly enough, I find there *are* Germans involved here, and in such a way that if my orders were not so explicit I would not be all that eager to proceed."

"Will I be allowed to question your witnesses?" Kohn asked carefully.

"Not so fast," Schenke said. "I am prepared to cooperate fully with you . . . *if* you and I arrive at a private understanding."

Kohn became uneasy. "Didn't you say your orders were explicit?"

"Perhaps," Schenke said, "I should have said instructions, as being a bit more accurate. I can follow them or not, as I choose. It all depends on you."

Kohn remained silent. He did not see any way he could quarrel with the other without jeopardizing his position.

"You see, Captain," Schenke said, "if what we have turned up is not properly—how shall I say it?—*used*, then it can become very sticky for us. Do you understand?"

"I am afraid I do not," Kohn said.

"It will all become clear," Schenke said, "*after* I have your word of honor that you will keep whatever is told you here in absolute confidence."

Kohn shifted uncomfortably. Was the man out of his

mind? He must know he could not, would not, give any such assurances; they were blood enemies.

"You may use whatever is given you here for investigative purposes only," Schenke continued. "Under no circumstances can you take it into a courtroom as evidence; there must be absolutely no publicity."

"How can I give you my word," Kohn demanded, "when I don't know what it is you want suppressed?"

"I give you *my* word," Schenke said blandly, "that I am only trying to protect one of my own countrymen. Captain, I guarantee I will tell you nothing unless I have your word."

"You give me no choice," Kohn muttered reluctantly, feeling cornered.

The other waited. Finally, inwardly squirming, Kohn saw that he would have to make the statement explicitly. "I give you my word," he said.

Schenke smiled. "I thank you for that, Captain," he said, settling back in his chair. "Perhaps we will learn to live together, after all."

Kohn worried. Why had the other gone to so much trouble to secure his word? He must know in his profession such promises were meaningless.

"Now let me explain my problem," Schenke said. "We *have* turned up a witness to the time and the circumstances you are concerned about. He is not unknown to us, we have always been quite aware of his existence. But he has lived incognito for the past two decades, and we are reluctant to bring him any notoriety now." Kohn became alert. "You see, our man has been in his past doubly accused: on the one hand, of being a Nazi war criminal, and on the other, of being a traitor to Germany."

"I thought the two were synonymous," Kohn murmured, unable to resist the dig. But he had dropped any pretense of disinterest.

"Officially," Schenke continued, ignoring the comment, "he has been cleared of the one charge, and never tried, for lack of adequate evidence, or more properly, adequate definition, of the other. He changed his name, and his occupation, and has managed since to make a life of sorts for himself. We do not wish this man disturbed."

"But I thought it was your job—" Kohn began.

"Even if he were once more exposed to public view we

could not get a conviction," Schenke interrupted. "All that would happen would be an outcry in the sensational press, a rumbling from those fanatics in Bavaria and Hesse, a pointing of the finger from the East Germans . . . but he would probably lose his job. Our government, Captain, is a coalition of parties, held together only so long as they have a common outlook. It is a delicate union, not dissimilar from your own government. And this man's case could shake our coalition apart, believe me."

"Was he so important?" Kohn asked, frowning.

Schenke was silent for a moment. "It is very complicated," he said then. "And exceedingly subtle. There are philosophical nuances here . . . perhaps you will understand when I tell you his name. Swartzwald, Dr. Willy Swartzwald, former commissioner of the Cologne police, later head of the intelligence branch of the military police. Ah, I see you remember the case."

Kohn stared at the other, fighting to conceal his shock, wondering whether the other knew what had gone on behind the scenes in Israel. Swartzwald, when brought before an Allied Tribunal, accused of participating in the destruction of Jews and other subject peoples, was cleared through the testimony of a highly placed Jewish Agency official. Nothing more might ever have been made of it had not the official, later an important functionary in an Israeli government, been denounced as a collaborator. He was accused of having participated in the selection of those few Jews who were to be saved. There had been an enormous public scandal. By withholding information about the ultimate destination of those who were sent off to camps, he effectively sealed the majority's doom; trusting their leaders, the Jews had not rebelled.

"But I wonder if you understand our predicament?" Schenke was asking. "I understand your population being disturbed—to have a German saved by a Jew, a German whose involvement in the killing of thousands was never disputed, yet absolved because he saved a few hundred, well—but let me tell you about the German side. This man made immense sums through clandestine activities during the war; he saved Jews, it is true, but not philanthropically, mind you, but for personal gain. That we might stomach—a life saved is still valuable, whatever the man's motive—but what is unpalatable to us Germans is his being philosophically corrupt. You know, of course, that Germans have never emotionally accepted the Nuremberg principle that there is a higher law, an appeal to conscience, and so on, that supersedes a superior's orders. Orders must be obeyed, Germans feel, and they are greatly sympathetic to those whose defense was based on that premise. Germans *do* respect those who went all the way *against* Hitler. But they have nothing but contempt for those who followed *some* orders and disobeyed *others*. Himmler is despised today—at the very end, he tried to save Jews, as 'insurance' for his future; Eichmann, on the other hand, never deviated, and Swartzwald, though he took the oath to the *Führer,* was always in every circumstance his own conscience; he was not, understand, against Hitler. To have him cleared by a non-German court, because of the testimony of non-Germans, is intolerable! But how do *we* charge him? That he disobeyed Hitler is hardly a crime today; in any case, we no longer have jurisdiction over what may have been his past subversion of the bureaucracy . . ."

Kohn was hardly listening. He was remembering how he had reacted during the outcry over the freeing of Swartzwald, who had long since disappeared from public view. He had assumed that he would be sent out after the man, as he had after so many others, and had been told that he was to do nothing. It was explained that the government, who was defending the accused Jewish functionary, could hardly be expected to assume that the ex-Nazi was anything but innocent. He was crushed by the discovery that his own government could act out of expediency. As for the Jew, he could hardly bear to think about him . . . later, when the Jew was assassinated and the rumors got about that he had been killed not by revengeful survivors but by government agents, he was absolutely sickened—doubly so, since he was the one given credit (credit! not blame!) for the murder. He never bothered to deny it, knowing he would have been unable to refuse the assignment had it been offered him, even though the target of that vengeance was a Jew.

"You can see that it is complicated, can you not?" Schenke was asking.

Kohn could see that it was. To gain time he pulled out

his small cigars, took one, and tossed the tin on the desk to Schenke. He was careful about lighting it, so the other should not see the trembling of his hands.

"When may I talk to him?" Kohn asked finally. His mind had finally begun working again. He had forgotten, if he had ever known, that Swartzwald had once been commissioner of the Cologne police. The highest-ranking policeman in a city, particularly if he was corrupt, would have a literal wealth of information. He would have been aware of everything that went on, would have had extra-legal sources of information, would have had informers from the under- and other-worlds. In short he was likely, if the accusation against Gottliebsohn was true, to have some knowledge of, if not Gottliebsohn himself, at least those under his jurisdiction who would have dealt with him.

"You will remember you gave your word, Captain?" Schenke said.

Kohn nodded glumly, and could not help wondering if the other had not been having a little heavy German sport with him. It was the sort of irony that fat philosopher might appreciate, him being forced to ask someone like Swartzwald for evidence against a Jew. What the other did not know, however, was that Kohn was more interested in seeing Gottliebsohn, that poor suffering bastard, get off; if he were to expect a diplomatic appointment he could hardly execute Swartzwald, no matter what his past. Kohn, savoring this secret, bittersweet irony, felt strangely better.

Schenke leaned to his intercom, and spoke briefly to someone in another room.

"You brought him here?" Kohn said, surprised.

"It is convenient," Schenke said. "He is an official of our customs service, stationed here at the airport. The complications are never-ending. His appointment was arranged by the government. Our coalition partner has already been forced to swallow one too many ex-Nazis. Not only that, but our revered former Chancellor was the mayor of Cologne, and knew Swartzwald personally."

The door opened and a bulky figure advanced into the room. He was carrying his cap, like a *Wehrmacht* officer, in the crook of his elbow, but his stance was simply not military. Kohn did not stir, studying the other through a puff of smoke. He suddenly frowned. Those cold eyes, colorless lashes, and parchment skin seemed oddly familiar. Finally it came to him. This was the man who had taken such a great interest in their welfare, as though these Jews were *his* guests . . . and then Kohn remembered something else that was more important.

"We have met before," Kohn said when Schenke started to introduce them.

"I had the honor of escorting the mission through customs," Swartzwald said.

The ingratiating manner was offensive, Kohn thought. Beneath that subservience was the old, familiar German arrogance. Then Swartzwald took the indicated seat diffidently, as if not sure how long he would be permitted to remain, and Kohn wondered if Schenke or himself was the one feared.

"Customs Officer Swartzwald only knows in general why he is here," Schenke said. "If you would care to be more specific with him now . . ."

"How was it in Cologne in those days, Commissioner?" Kohn asked. "A fascinating time for you, I would think; the Nazis finally in full swing, in absolute control, a hundred new laws for you to enforce, curfews, restriction of travel, evictions, et cetera . . ."

"It was a difficult time," Swartzwald agreed carefully.

"Tell us about it," Kohn said.

Swartzwald looked to Schenke. "I thought there were to be specific questions?"

"We'll get to those soon enough," Kohn said. "I'm a policeman myself, of a sort, and I'm interested in what it was like, being a cop in those days."

Schenke had raised his eyebrows over Kohn's behavior, but he nodded encouragingly to Swartzwald.

"As you say, new laws," Swartzwald murmured finally. "As many as a dozen a day, and it was necessary to know them all, minutely, the S.S. did not have any faith in us—as it turned out, being efficient did not matter, we were taken over by them anyway."

"And you became part of the S.S.?" Kohn asked.

"Not me," Swartzwald said. "I saw the way the wind was blowing, so I accepted an army commission. They needed policemen, too. And for legitimate purposes, not like the Nazis. Of course finally that made no difference either, I was sent to the Eastern front, and Himmler just reached into the army and appropriated me."

"Liked the way you worked, did they?" Kohn said, smiling slightly.

"Not a bit of it," Swartzwald said, responding to the smile. "Just the opposite. Many Jews got out of the country through my district, and they somehow blamed me."

"Ah, yes, that's right," Kohn said. "You were a friend to the Jews."

Swartzwald became wary. "I had nothing against them."

"As much as we can expect, I suppose," Kohn said. "How did you help them get out?"

"I did it all under the regulations," Swartzwald said. "At that time, any Jew who could prove he was not an enemy of the state could get an exit visa. My office provided a dossier on the local Jews, checked out the permits, and so on."

"And that was how you made all that money?" Kohn asked.

Swartzwald reddened. "I am a poor man," he said. "I live week to week on my paycheck, which is small."

Schenke frowned. "His accounts were impounded. Don't you think you ought to get to the point, Captain?"

"It is all part of the point, Herr Professor," Kohn said. "You see, Commissioner Swartzwald," he went on pleasantly, "one of our people is suffering from amnesia. We are trying to re-create his background in order to stimulate his memory."

Swartzwald clucked sympathetically. "Has the poor fellow forgotten everything?"

"He does remember a few things here and there," Kohn said. "But they are scattered, and he has trouble relating them to each other. Since much of what he remembers was illegal, we thought you might be able to help us."

"Of what is he accused?" Swartzwald asked.

Kohn stared. "Why do you imagine he is accused of anything?"

"Because of Doktor Schenke's position, and you say you are a policeman and *he* remembers illegalities," Swartzwald said.

"All right then," Kohn said. "I'll put my cards on the table. He is accused of having done business with the Nazis."

Swartzwald grimaced. "I was never a Nazi," he said, "And I was never in business."

"You never sold exit permits for Jews?" Kohn demanded.

"I arranged for certain Jews to get out, yes," Swartzwald said. "And I did even more, I saw to it that they would not have to enter a strange country penniless. But those were financial techniques, and financial techniques cost money. We charged a certain percentage, as any bank or bonding company would, in order to keep the operation functioning."

"Who is the we you talk of?" Kohn asked.

"There was an organization of sorts," Swartzwald said. "It was very loose, of course . . ."

"Who was in it?" Kohn asked.

Swartzwald looked appealingly to Schenke.

"Oh not by name damnit, man," Kohn exploded. "What kind of people were in it?"

"All kinds," Swartzwald began hesitantly, when he saw that Schenke would not help him.

"Priests?" Kohn asked.

"There were a few," Swartzwald admitted.

"And Jews?" Kohn asked.

"Well, there had to be go-betweens," Swartzwald said, "someone we could trust, and them too, one of their own people, someone competent enough to handle all the little details . . ."

"Was Ernst Gottliebsohn a go-between?" Kohn demanded then. He was watching for it, and so he saw the recognition come into the other's face, but Swartzwald seemed to sense he was giving something away, for he immediately said, "I would not be able to remember a name from so long ago."

"But you recognized him at the airport," Kohn said, savagely. Kohn had remembered the little incident when they arrived, this man and Gottliebsohn over Gottliebsohn's passport.

"Not him," Swartzwald said. "His name. I had read about him in the newspapers, you see."

His manner was convincing. Yet Kohn knew that he lied. "You didn't remember him from long before, as one of your go-betweens?" Kohn asked, almost as if he believed him. Swartzwald, encouraged by this seemingly reasonable attitude, shook his head. "I know that you're lying, Willy," Kohn said then, softly. "You lied once before, at the airport, when you said you had never known any Jews, and you're lying now. That story about Gottliebsohn hadn't appeared yet when we met you."

Something very like hatred appeared in Swartzwald's eyes, and he looked down for a moment. When he looked up again his gaze was soft and bewildered. "I could have sworn that was why I recognized the name . . . memory does play tricks, doesn't it? You don't suppose—but then I never was very good at names," he went on apologetically. "It may have rung a bell without my even being aware of it."

"You're not making any sense," Kohn said, though he was secretly awed by the other's slickness. "You recognized the name, but not the person, you say, and yet you claim you are not good at remembering names . . . well what about when you saw the name in the paper?"

"I remembered it from the passport, of course," Swartzwald said. "That's why I attached no great importance to it; why it has become switched about in my mind."

"I think you remembered it from further back," Kohn said.

"I don't really think so," Swartzwald said. "Now that I think about it, I recall that for everyone's protection we all used code names."

"What are you telling me now?" Kohn demanded, incredulous. "That you would not have known the real names of your go-betweens, when they were so important to you personally? Willy, Willy . . ."

Swartzwald flushed. "I would know them if I chose to know them. But there was no need. I did not deal with anyone directly. And I have never believed in cluttering my mind with useless information, Captain. It's possible I knew the name inadvertently; in fact, I must have; otherwise why would it make such an impression on me, as you say?"

"And it wasn't Gottliebsohn who made the impression?" Kohn asked, though he saw that it was useless—the man was extraordinarily evasive.

"No," Swartzwald said. "At least," he went on after a moment, shrugging, as if responding to Kohn's obvious doubt, "I don't think so. But you see what my memory is . . . perhaps if I were to see him again, that newspaper photo was rather indistinct . . ."

Kohn wasn't sure what was going on here, and it bothered him. He was certain the other was lying. But why should he deny his memory? Schenke would have guaranteed him immunity from further prosecution, and protection from the Jews. Could he be shielding Gottliebsohn? Kohn thought not. Swartzwald was not one to hold loyalty to any man, and especially not to a Jew.

"I think we can arrange that," Kohn said finally, and turning to Schenke, asked to use the phone.

While he waited for the hotel clerk to call Glass, Kohn became increasingly perturbed. He was beginning to see where no matter how this thing turned out he might not benefit. If Gottliebsohn was even slightly guilty, everything he had been promised by Auerbach would go down the drain. And if he had been associated with this particular porker, he, Kohn, did not stand to gain a great deal from his own superiors either, since the memory of their involvement with the Swartzwald case might prove too embarrassing for them to accept his statement wholeheartedly. Kohn was well aware that that those involved in embarrassing cases, far from being rewarded, are usually shunted aside so their presence shall not be a reminder.

By the time Glass came on the phone, Kohn was so frustrated by the uncertainty of his own and Gottliebsohn's future that he had difficulty containing his anger. The head-knocker's attitude did not help.

"What happened with Gottliebsohn's sister?" Glass demanded. "We weren't all that late, and now she's even refusing to have a farewell drink . . ."

"Never mind her now," Kohn snapped. "I'm at the chancellory, Doktor Schenke's office, with a man who may have known Gottliebsohn in Cologne. How soon can you get over here?"

"I'm not sure Ernst can handle another confrontation so soon," Glass said, after a moment. "He's been pretty well shaken up by the sister."

"I can imagine," Kohn said. "But this may be important. You'd better get him over here." And he hung up before the other could argue.

His cigar had gone out. He relit it, but the taste was bad, and he got himself a fresh one. He paced the office, not caring how he must look to the watching Germans, then stood before Swartzwald.

"What do you know about Father Stieffel?" he asked.

Schenke nodded at Swartzwald to answer. "It was his case that caused me to lose my post," he said finally.

"How was that?" Kohn asked.

"It's all a matter of record," Schenke said, when Swartzwald did not respond.

"It seems that we had a report on the priest's activities, but little action was taken," Swartzwald said, finally.

"What sort of a report?" Kohn asked.

"A soldier," Swartzwald said. "A young officer, who came in and denounced the priest."

Kohn remained impassive, but he was greatly relieved.

"What I didn't know," Swartzwald continued, "was that a similar report was also given the Gestapo."

"By whom?" Kohn asked, puzzled by some discrepancy he was unable to identify.

"The same soldier," Swartzwald said. "It seems he had no real trust in the civilian police."

Kohn thought how pleased Gottliebsohn would be to hear that. And yet, as he continued to stare at Swartzwald, his feeling that they were near a solution left him. He became convinced that the other was lying once again. Did it matter? he asked himself. If it was a lie, in whole or in part, it was in favor of Gottliebsohn. Perhaps he should let well enough alone.

But as they waited for the two men to arrive, Kohn began to scheme how he could get the whole truth out of Swartzwald. He could not bear to let a German get the best of him.

12

AFTER KOHN AND HIS SISTER LEFT HIM alone with Glass, Gottliebsohn felt himself to be on the very edge of hysteria. All the rhythms of his body were off: his heart pounded erratically, his breath came in fits and starts, and when he tried a gesture or to put his chaotic thoughts into speech, he failed miserably—the gesture was out of sync, and he found himself with his arm suddenly frozen in midair, or he stumbled over words which had been familiar to him all his life. Or at least that part of his life that he remembered.

There was the problem. What he remembered. Or more accurately, what he did not remember. He knew that everything that had been told him was true, and he could in a kind of out-of-focus, soundless film run it through his whirring, projector-like mind, but when it came to picturing himself in those described scenes, he simply could not do it. The feelings were there, the pity and the shame, the agony of a lost love, but they were separate, apart from the experience, and when he tried to put himself *inside* that memory, he could not make that final transition. No, the boy and the young man that they had told him about continued to remain faceless, and he was reduced finally to checking himself, rubbing his nose and stubbled chin as reassurance that those familiar features were still the same.

He had told the psychiatrist, in desperation, about his

second hallucination, that orgy of priests, his family in the rear of the gas van while he drove on, unhearing, with a whore-like Madonna by his side, her fingers twining in his writhing lap, and all the other had done had been to ask him what *he* made of the damned dream. What could he do but lie? He believed that he had let his family go to their deaths, he said, unhearing and even uncaring, while he cavorted with a virginal whore. And when the other agreed that that was the obvious, apparent interpretation, he had been unable to hold back and he had blasted that intolerable smugness by telling his doctor he *knew* that the driver was not he.

That had shaken his doctor, all right, but it had shaken him too, because before he had stated it aloud he had not realized quite what his problem was: he believed, and yet he did not believe, that he was the person they described, and because he was unable to accept their memories he was unable finally to come to terms with his own.

Glass could see how close to a breakdown his patient was. He could feel the other's excitement, his sense of panic because he was unable to make the final breakthrough. And as much as he tried to reassure him that he was experiencing a "normal" progression, he had not succeeded. In that brief outburst, when Gottliebsohn insisted he was not the person they said he was, he had paused to question himself. What if he, Glass, had been missing the point all along? What if he had so directed the course of this mental investigation, through misinterpretation and wrong diagnosis, that he had actually *prevented* them from arriving at the truth? Before he might pursue this immensely disturbing thought, however, the call from Kohn had come.

"What about it, Ernst?" he asked, finally deciding to leave the decision to his patient. "Feel up to another session? Your friend Kohn has someone who thinks he may have known you."

"Who is it?" Gottliebsohn demanded, his heart leaping. "Did he say? Oh, you said he . . . not a girl—woman, then." And he sank back disappointed.

"A man, yes," Glass said, feeling helpless at his inability to get the other calmed down. He still didn't want to sedate him, and he forced himself to put aside the pity he felt. "Who did you think . . . Lena?"

Gottliebsohn nodded, his chin touching his shirt front, once again retreating into the familiar and therefore strangely comforting melancholy.

"Do you feel up to it?" Glass repeated.

Gottliebsohn roused himself. "Yes, of course," he said, finally. "We've got to continue . . ."

"We'll walk," Glass said. "It's only a few blocks from here, Kohn said."

Kohn met them in the anteroom. Though he tried to maintain his recent casual, offhand, friendly air, Gottliebsohn sensed something different in the attitude of the dapper little man, and he shrank inwardly from him. He had never lost his original distrust, and now that deep, abiding, premonitory fear returned under the calculating stare of those pale, faintly pinked, chillingly moist blue eyes.

What Gottliebsohn felt was Kohn's unease in how to proceed. Typically, the captain, even where he believed the accused to be innocent, would proceed as if he believed him guilty, very often with surprising results. But here, though he was upset by Gottliebsohn's possible collaboration and how deeply he may have been involved with that swine in the other room, there were other equally important matters to consider, not the least of which was that fence he continued to straddle. And so Kohn compromised: he gave Gottliebsohn a choice as to how to feel.

"We've got good news for you, Ernst, about one thing," he said. "We've pretty much got you cleared of the informing situation." He hesitated. "But it doesn't look so hot for you on the original charge."

Gottliebsohn stared at him, bewildered. Cleared of having been an informer? How? And yet, on the original . . . charge . . . it still looked bad. He did not know whether to be relieved or terribly distressed, and his confusion caused him to stumble over his questions.

"Save it for the fellow inside," Kohn said, and turned to lead the way.

"I know this is your show," Glass said, trying to convey the concern he felt for his disturbed patient by a significant look. "But I'd like to come along."

"Of course," Kohn said. "This may be our only chance at this witness, and if he comes up with something now that he'll deny having said later, we'll have you to confirm it. You being the 'neutral' and all—or have you forgotten why you were brought in in the first place?" Kohn opened the door to Schenke's office and ushered Gottliebsohn inside. Glass, face burning, followed along after.

The two men inside got to their feet. Gottliebsohn recognized Schenke as Kohn's opposite from the German delegation, and the fact of his profession made him instantly uneasy. The heavily built man in uniform seemed totally unfamiliar—but then as he bowed and the slight smile twisted his gross features, it all began to seem reminiscent of an ugly time, and Gottliebsohn felt definitely ill.

"Do you remember this man?" Kohn asked; Gottliebsohn made a helpless gesture, then shook his head no. "Willy Swartzwald," Kohn continued, "former commissioner of the Cologne police." There was no further reaction from Gottliebsohn, and Kohn turned to Swartzwald. "Do you remember him?" He watched Swartzwald closely. Every instinct told him that these two knew each other.

Swartzwald was studying Gottliebsohn carefully. "I'm not sure," he said. "There is something—but I can't seem to put my tongue to it—and they say *you* have lost *your* memory."

Gottliebsohn was repelled by something indefinable in the other's attitude—was he trying to communicate something to him under cover of that obvious sympathy—knowledge of a special sort, a feeling of conspiracy?

"What something?" Kohn asked.

"I'm not sure," Swartzwald said, but not looking at his questioner, only at Gottliebsohn. "He may be the one . . ."

"What *one*?" Kohn demanded, irritated, seeing that the German was delaying any definite statement for what could only be private reasons.

"There was an incident involving a German soldier," Swartzwald said. "Now what was *his* name—it is so long ago that it is difficult to recall . . . Brunst, Brenninger . . . *Brunner,* . . . that is it, Kurt *Brunner,* a lieutenant—do you recall that name?"

"Brunner," Gottliebsohn muttered, and was suddenly giddied by the knowledge that he had known that name, known it, in fact, intimately—it was the family name of his beloved Lena! "Yes," he managed, "I remember that name.

Wasn't he the one informed on the priest?"

"The same one," Swartzwald said.

"And on the Baroness von Krieg?" Gottliebsohn continued.

"Her too," Swartzwald said. He studied the shaken Gottliebsohn. "And one other, of course."

"Myself," Gottliebsohn said. Swartzwald nodded, and all the men except Gottliebsohn wondered why he seemed amused. Gottliebsohn was too frightened to be aware of it. "Did I lead him to them?" he asked finally, both anxious for and yet somehow dreading the certain knowledge.

Now Swartzwald looked thoughtful, though obviously enjoying himself. "You don't really remember?" he asked.

"I suggest you stop horsing around, Commissioner," Kohn said, "and tell us what you know." His voice was deadly quiet, and there was a little silence.

Swartzwald glanced at Schenke, who would give him no satisfaction. "Very well," he said, as if he had been reluctant to tell them this. "Brunner came to me about a Catholic conspiracy. Now I had nothing against the Catholics, and I was not about to waste my men's time—already badly overworked, mind you—because some overwrought young man had concocted an improbable story about illegal marriages and what not. The laws at that time permitted Jews married to gentiles to retain certain citizenship rights, and I for one could not see the harm in it if some dates were juggled—in any case, it would have been difficult, if not impossible, to prove. Besides, I suspected Brunner's motives"—he stared again at Gottliebsohn—"of being highly personal. He was an unappealing young man, very strident, unrealistic, not the type to whom one could explain why it was necessary for certain Jews to have privileges—particularly if that privileged Jew was living with one's sister."

Gottliebsohn let out a tortured breath. "That was why he was following me," he said bitterly, hating himself.

Glass opened his mouth to say something, then thought better of it. But he was uneasy about what was coming next. The fact that the soldier in Gottliebsohn's hallucination actually existed did not necessarily disprove his analysis of the dream. The threat he symbolized could have been internalized by his patient . . . and then Glass stopped that line of thought as a rationalization.

Kohn, for his part, was looking thoughtfully at Swartz-wald. Though this was the first he had heard about Gott-liebsohn having lived with a German girl, he was not par-ticularly surprised. It all fit very well with what had been uncovered thus far. He was disturbed about something else. Swartzwald had claimed to be bad about names, to be vague about past denunciations, and yet here he was, com-ing up with the name of an obscure soldier, rattling off the details of his involvement with Gottliebsohn, as if the whole thing had happened yesterday. Kohn granted him that the situation was interesting enough to remember, but still that contradicted his earlier inability (or was that reluctance?) to bring it to mind. Why had he waited until he had met Gott-liebsohn? Something, Kohn thought, did not ring true.

"Was Gottliebsohn working with you?" Kohn asked fi-nally, knowing that it was time, whatever his suspicions, to get to the important question.

"Yes," Swartzwald said, without hesitation.

The silence began to lengthen interminably.

"He's lying!"

As they all turned to look, Gottliebsohn became aware that it was he who had cried out, he who had his arms raised and was waving them about in a flamboyance of ges-ture totally unlike himself. He hung his head, ashamed of the outburst, but more ashamed, dreadfully ashamed to the point of nausea, of that young man who had been, according to this witness, a collaborator.

"Why so upset?" Swartzwald asked, with a slight smile. He turned to Kohn. "What are your laws? Collaboration is punishable if the beneficiary is solely oneself, *nicht*? But if many Jews are helped, that is another matter?" Kohn nodded reluctantly. "Then Gottliebsohn is not guilty," Swartzwald said. "After all, he made arrangements for many Jews to get out, for them to take a little more than the single valise they were entitled to—and if, at the same time, he earned enough to get his own family out, is that reprehensi-ble? Those Jews he helped were rich, he and his family poor. The rich helped the poor, as is only just."

Kohn studied the German. Even if he was telling the truth he was an unreliable witness, to say the least. He could imagine his superiors' incredulity over him, Kohn, ac-cepting it. As for Auerbach, he would not be satisfied either,

having wanted a definite position one way or the other . . .
Damn them all, Kohn suddenly thought. He turned to his
charge. "Well, Ernst," he began, trying to smile, "it's not as
clean as we wanted it, but—"

Gottliebsohn was not listening. He was looking at
Swartzwald, and the entreaty in his face was so naked that
Kohn did not want to look at him.

"What happened to Brunner?" Gottliebsohn asked.

"You don't really want me to tell *that*," Swartzwald said.

"Please," Gottliebsohn begged.

"Tell him, damn you," Kohn said harshly.

"He was found in an alley," Swartzwald said. "Apparently he had caught up to the Jew—pardon, *you*, Herr Gottliebsohn—" They wondered why he seemed to mock Gottliebsohn, who already seemed on the point of collapse.
"There'd obviously been a terrific struggle. He'd been choked
to death. Since you disappeared, it was assumed that you
had done it." He smiled benevolently. "I lost my job because
of you," he said.

Gottliebsohn felt increasingly faint. When Swartzwald
confirmed the fact of his hallucination, he had momentarily
reexperienced that nightmare struggle, and when he
reached the dreadful moment where he and his victim
stared for so long into each other's eyes, it seemed again that
his own essence, the very inner core of himself, was slipping
away, as happened in dreams or perhaps death, but just as
he began to worry that he was in fact dying, once more in a
limbo of non-identity, something went off in his mind, loud
as a gunshot, and he heard the echoing words *you, Herr
Gottliebsohn*, like a revelation spoken by a prophet, and an
ecstasy of the most profound sort flooded in on him: his skin
itched as the blood rushed to his extremities, his head ached
as that life-sustaining river roared in his ears, and he knew
a happiness so great he began to weep. His memory had
been given back to him. He no longer lived only in other
people's minds, but, at long last, in his own as well.

"And Lena?" Gottliebsohn managed, wiping his eyes.

"She identified the body," Swartzwald said, still secretly
amused. "There were the army identification tags, naturally,
but she was brought in as a matter of course. She dropped
out of sight soon afterward."

Kohn was staring at Gottliebsohn with awe and admiration. "You killed a heine officer?" he demanded. "And you lost your memory over *that?* But, *liebchen,* that's nothing to feel bad about—it's a praiseworthy act!" Kohn was almost beside himself with joy. "Think of it, man! We're home free! Wait'll Auerbach hears you killed a German! Why, he'll be able to make you a hero for that!"

"I am happy that you, at least, Herr Gottliebsohn," Schenke said, misinterpreting those tears, "are properly remorseful about the killing. Don't you agree, Doctor?"

Glass was in a state very like shock. He had been so convinced that the killing Gottliebsohn had dreamt had been hallucinatory, a symbolic acting-out of self-murder, that to hear it confirmed as an actuality now was almost too much for him to take. Even though he had begun to suspect that there was something amiss in the way he was looking at Gottliebsohn, the enormity of his mistake staggered him. But what could he do about it now? Look at him, his erstwhile patient, the absolved victim, weeping those tears of absolute joy! How could he possibly step in at this moment, in the presence of these criminal investigators, and explain that he had been wrong, and that therefore a lot of other things might be wrong as well? Besides, that hint of another truth that had entered his mind might be in its turn another, and equally monstrous, mistaken assumption.

He roused himself from his near stupor. His own symptoms were not too far from those which had worried him earlier in the day about Gottliebsohn.

"I think we'd better end this interview," he said. "Herr Gottliebsohn has been under an enormous strain, and I'd suggest we get him back to the hotel."

Kohn looked at him shrewdly. "You don't seem as happy about this as you might be," he murmured.

"You can see for yourself the state he's in," Glass said shortly. "And you're through anyway, aren't you? I assume you can get any depositions you need from Doktor Schenke?"

Schenke had risen to his feet, and Swartzwald followed suit, that suggestion of mockery still present as he studied the tearful Gottliebsohn. Was it possible, Glass wondered, that he too suspected that all was not as it seemed?

"I have had this meeting recorded," Schenke said, not quite meeting Kohn's eye. "It will be a simple matter to have it typed up and signed by all concerned. It will not leave this office, of course—though your superiors may come here to study it, if you wish."

Kohn stared at him. "When did the recording start?" he asked, quietly furious, understanding now why the other had pressed him earlier for his "word."

"I always record all conversations in this office," Schenke said. "It is so easy, in our business, to have misunderstandings."

Kohn forced a smile. "You won't have our earlier conversation typed up?"

"There's no need," Schenke said, smiling in turn.

Kohn motioned to Gottliebsohn, whose eyes were now dry and shining with his interior excitement, and left, followed by the two other men.

13

IT WAS KOHN WHO SUGGESTED THEY HAVE a celebration. By the time they arrived back at the hotel it was growing dark, and as he pointed out, no three men ever had a better excuse to drink steadily and well.

Gottliebsohn had refused the doctor's offer of his sedating pills. He did not want to deaden the tremendous feeling like shaken champagne that welled up inside him; on the contrary, he was willing to experiment to see just how euphoric it was possible to be.

He had been talking at a great rate. "It's all there, every little detail, I remember everything," he told them. "The smell of my mother's strudel, and of my father's cigar, is strong in *my own* nostrils, not just because others told me about it. And I was a crafty hellion when I was young, it is all true what Hans said of me, but I am sorry for nothing that happened in that village—only for what happened later in Cologne." He was sad, but even his sadness had a sense of buoyance about it. "I loved Lena so much. So very much. It was she who played the piano. She played for me in the late evenings, very softly so as not to disturb the neighbors, though occasionally I had to shut the windows for fear some passers-by might listen and be concerned over our happiness. And we were happy. She loved me, too, more than any man has a right to expect, particularly a man like me, who has had his way with so many girls. Do you think, Doctor, that is why I had only Arab prostitutes after I lost my memory, as penance for losing Lena?" But he did not wait for his gloomy doctor to answer. "After I got my family out I was going to the priest, Father Stieffel, to take the vows and marry Lena under another name, move to another city, even join the army—though that would have meant leaving Lena, and I wouldn't have been able to do that." Waiting for Kohn to order their drinks, he became lost in thought then for so long that Kohn had to punch him in the arm to rouse him. "The Baroness von Krieg was a friend of Lena's," he continued, coming out of his reverie. "Lena wrote poetry. I always told her she should put it to music, at least popular songs could bring in some money, but she only laughed at me, called me a materialist. But someone had to be practical." He was briefly puzzled, and that confusion he had lived with so long began to flatten his bubbling spirits, but he shook it off by remembering how much he had loved Lena. "I adored her," he said. "I would have done anything for her. And then her brother spoiled it."

"Well, you spoiled him," Kohn said, "permanently."

"He wouldn't leave us alone," Gottliebsohn said. "He believed all that bunk that Dr. Goebbels manufactured; he'd been in the Hitler Youth, he was too young and impressionable to understand how incredibly stupid the whole thing was, and when he found out his sister was living with a damned Jew, he practically went out of his mind. He wasn't very stable anyway—"

"How do you know that?" Glass couldn't resist asking.

"Lena told me," Gottliebsohn said, after a moment's hesitation.

"And how did you meet her?" Kohn asked.

Gottliebsohn muscled his brows, trying to bring the memory back. "When I first got to Cologne," he said slowly, afraid that if he went too fast he would lose it again, "I picked up odd jobs on the waterfront. I slept on whatever barges were untended. But it was getting bad down there; the watchmen, like everyone else in Germany, were getting meaner about everything, and I began to nose around for a place to stay. I overheard a seaman in the local café talking about smuggling emigrants out with forged papers, and I followed him home late one night—and it was the house that the Baroness von Krieg owned. I hung about all night and the minute I saw anyone stirring I rang the manager's doorbell. Lena answered, she was a friend of the Baroness. I asked to rent a flat and she said they were all taken. I asked if I could have the one the seaman had when he shipped out, and this panicked her. I could see she was worried about what I might know, and so I set out to calm her down—as you heard, I was always pretty good at handling women, and her nature was so trusting, after all. So I got myself invited inside for some morning tea. You know there are people who can't resist strays? Well, Lena was like that, and she got all my troubles out of me, and took them to heart. When she heard where I spent my nights she insisted I move right in with her, wouldn't hear anything different. We were to live like friends. Of course the inevitable happened. This time it was different. I loved this girl. You heard my sister?" he asked Glass, wanting him to confirm it for Kohn. "She told you how much I loved that girl."

"I believe you," Kohn said, amused by Gottliebsohn's stridency. The drinks had arrived, and he proposed a toast: "To Lena!"—then asked the waiter to bring a phone.

"And how much she loved me," Gottliebsohn continued, so suddenly downcast that he swallowed his drink, a whiskey, at a single gulp. "And I abandoned her."

"You had no choice," Kohn said. "You'd killed a German army officer, hadn't you? Her own brother? What makes you think she would have taken you back in?"

"You heard the police commissioner," Gottliebsohn said, defending his love. "She identified her brother, and said nothing else, not a word about me. And I left her alone with her grief! Who knows what she may have done?"

"Take it easy," Kohn said, "have another drink. It didn't happen yesterday." He ordered another round as he took the plug-in table phone from the waiter. "I think we ought to give our mission co-director the good news, don't you?" he said, and asked for Auerbach's room. While he was waiting for the call he asked, "And was Lena involved in the Catholic setup?"

Gottliebsohn nodded. "She introduced me to the Baroness. They were looking for someone to be a go-between. They had a higher-up in the police department, they said, but they had no Jews who were not already known to the

266

authorities. I was exactly what they were looking for."

Auerbach answered, and Kohn gave him a brief summary of what had occurred. Kohn invited that delighted gentleman to come down and have a drink with them, but Auerbach demurred, tactfully pointing out that the victory was primarily theirs. Not only would he not intrude for such sensitively personal reasons, but officially, he thought too much attention would be brought to the mission if the chief joined them at the bar. He spoke then to Glass, congratulating him, and then to Gottliebsohn, reminding him of his past belief, commiserating on the strain he particularly, though all of them to a certain extent, had been under, and then wished them a good party.

Kohn hung up, flushed with success. He drank his second drink, and over Glass's protest, ordered another round. He then put on a look of mock solemnity. "You all realize what's missing? Why this isn't really a party?" He looked at each in turn, giving them a chance to come up with the answer. He grinned as they gave him only blank stares. "Women," he said. "And what's a celebration without *Mädchen*?" He spoke now to Glass, forgetting his earlier antagonism, feeling that now he could afford to be benevolent since it had been he himself who had been mostly responsible for their success, and that this abject American, with his theories and his mental inquisitioning, had been in the final set-to unneeded. "Ernst and I just happened to know *three* girls in this miserable town," he continued. "How's that for luck? At a little *Weinstube*. Tell you what, Doctor, we'll even let you have first pick. Right, Ernst? I know your problem, Doctor, can spot the symptoms in a second—feeling all tense and wound up, aren't you? They are terrific little unwinders, women, go right to the main spring; it's an instinct with them. What do you say?"

Glass was momentarily tempted. Not just because he was worried about his patient, knowing that Gottliebsohn's excitement was unnatural, but because he himself had not been with a woman since he had left his wife, and he could almost (though not quite) delude himself that if he rid himself of the ache in his loins he might be equally rid of the one in his soul. But he decided that it could do no great harm to let Gottliebsohn shift for himself. Kohn would be there and could summon him in case of an emergency.

"I don't think so," Glass said. "I'm awfully tired; even if I wanted, I doubt that I would be worth much until I catch up on my sleep."

"You talk him into it, Ernst," Kohn said jovially. "Tell the doctor what's good for him."

But Gottliebsohn was secretly pleased that Glass was not coming. At the mention of those German whores he had immediately felt the same antipathies rising in his throat like vomit. He tried to swallow those doubts, to deny his feelings; with the restoration of his past he should be able to put aside his ridiculous fears and enjoy himself—but his revulsion was not dismissed so easily. And he knew that if his doctor was along, he would sense his ill-feeling, and begin to wonder why his patient should still behave as if nothing had changed. He would begin once again to question and probe, something he was sick to death of.

"Yes, by all means," Gottliebsohn said half-heartedly. "You must come with us."

Glass recognized the other's reluctance, and guessing the reason, was more than ever convinced that he should leave his patient alone for a time—perhaps, even, for all time. The moment he thought this, the psychiatrist thought too that the decision was too big for him to make alone, and that he would have to seek consultation.

"You two go ahead," he said, getting to his feet. "I'd just put a damper on all the fun."

"What'll we do with the third one?" Kohn asked, suddenly worried that the odd girl might complicate the evening.

"You'll think of something, I'm sure," Glass said, and left before there might be further protests.

Glass had intended to call Jerusalem the moment he got back to his room. Once inside the door, however, his resolution left him, and he wondered whether his tiredness was not, in fact, distorting his thinking, making him prey to strange imaginings. He looked longingly at his bed, made up for the night, thought how pleasant it would be between those starched sheets, under that down comforter, escaping into sleep, and then knew it would be impossible for him. Instead he went to the bathroom, took three aspirin, and sat down at his desk, depressed about doing what he must.

For the next hour and a half, Glass went over all his

material, starting with the dossier given him by Dean Wolfe, continuing with the notes Kohn had provided from his in-flight interrogation, and finally through his own jot-downs of what had struck him moment to moment with his patient. And as he finished his backward look, he was more puzzled and concerned than ever. The discrepancies, instead of being resolved by the confrontation with the German Swartzwald, seemed instead to have multiplied.

Gottliebsohn remembered a cattle train carrying his family to a concentration camp. And yet it turned out that he himself had arranged for seats on the passenger train to Brussels. Gottliebsohn remembered being followed, remembered the echoing cathedral and the soldier lurking in the shadows, was told that the soldier had been the informer—and yet *he* felt himself to be somehow guilty and apologized for *leading* the soldier to the church and to the house that belonged to the Baroness von Krieg. Gottliebsohn remembered his sister's living with a German, when in fact it was turned just about, and he was the one living with the "other side." And what about the remembered piano? Gottliebsohn even insisted, after Hans Eichler told him differently, that there had been a piano in his house. There *had* been a piano in the apartment of Lena Brunner, and perhaps she was the one who played. Why then did he believe it to have been his sister?

There was a discrepancy in Gottliebsohn's character, too. He had been variously described, by the acquaintances of his youth, as opportunistic, slick, corrupting, mischievous, and possessing an ability to "make all the girls laugh." Granted that one's character, in traumatic situation, could drastically change, does one ever lose a sense of humor? Gottliebsohn was essentially humorless. The fact is they were still, at the end, searching for Gottliebsohn's "character," and remembering the documents that coincided too neatly with the bounds of his memory, or vice versa, he had watched unbelieving as, when each bit of past personality was discovered, Gottliebsohn adopted it as his own, and became in effect the patchwork of his own descriptions.

In the beginning Gottliebsohn had claimed that he was emotionally incapable of dealing even on the smallest scale with one of his people's persecutors, that he could only be responsible for a single guilt. But at the end, after the meeting with Swartzwald, it seemed that he remembered *both* a killing *and* a collaboration. How could he be guilty of both?

Was he lying? Had he been lying from the start? Somehow, Glass could not believe so. Then others were lying. Swartzwald, perhaps? But what could be *his* motive? And then it occurred to Glass that perhaps his patient *was* lying —but only to himself.

Glass began pacing the floor. The truth was somewhere just out of reach, in those scattered papers on his worktable, and in his own fatigued mind. For some reason he was blocking it. Why? After the mistake about the dream, was he afraid to be caught in another gross error? Was it his patient about whom he was concerned, or was it himself?

Glass thought briefly of bringing all this to the attention of Auerbach. After all, the other had urged him to bring him whatever had to do with Gottliebsohn's guilt or innocence. But finally Glass thought he was only trying to avoid a personal responsibility.

He picked up the phone and placed that delayed call.

It took some time. Dean Wolfe was at the Institute, they said, but he missed him there, and eventually reached him just as he arrived home.

"Well, Norman," the dean said, "I'd about given up expecting a call from you. Are things going well?"

"I thought so," Glass said wearily. "I thought I had the case perfectly diagnosed. And I'm afraid I proceeded on a mistaken assumption to the point where I may have jeopardized my patient."

"Go on," the dean said, when Glass hesitated.

"I need your advice," Glass said. "But I don't know quite how to put it to you. It is privileged information, after all."

"Well, you can tell *me*," the dean said impatiently.

"I'm sorry, Dean Wolfe, but I can't," Glass said, knowing this would hurt the old man, and his relationship with him, but seeing no way out of his dilemma. "We'll have to talk around it," Glass went on slowly. "I just can't reveal certain things—when you've heard me out, I think you will understand."

The dean took in a quivering breath, and then contained his irritation. "You always were a trial to me, Norman," he couldn't resist saying, however. "What have you been up to, overidentifying with the patient again?"

Glass was shocked. Him overidentify? Him identify at all? But that was not how he pictured himself. Or how his wife pictured him either. And then he saw how accurate the old man was. That lack of sympathy he professed was only an act so he might hide from others, and therefore himself, how vulnerable he really was. And he, like his patient, searched for a personality he could be comfortable with; he, like his patient, not able to change the world, tried instead to change himself.

"Even if I have," Glass said at last, "that's not the problem."

"What *is* it then?" the dean asked, now completely exasperated.

"Gottliebsohn has been cleared of the collaboration charge," Glass said.

"Thank God for that!" the dean said, pleased for his old friend Hortsky.

"Not only that," Glass said, "it turns out that he killed a German officer before he escaped from Germany—abandoning his girl in the process; the girl was the sister of the man he killed."

"I can see where the problem lies," the dean began, after taking a moment to absorb it all; and then Glass interrupted.

"But that might not be the whole truth."

"Ah," the dean said sharply. And then he said, worried, "You think he *did* collaborate then?"

"I don't know," Glass said slowly. "I'm not sure that's even important any more. The problem is this: I think that Gottliebsohn has been telling the truth all along *as he believes it to be.* If he's lying, he's only lying to himself—but do I have any right to keep the truth, whatever it might be, from him? Doesn't he have a right to know? Besides, what if the truth should suddenly come home to him, in another dream, say; it could be absolutely shattering, couldn't it? But if the truth is that he's guilty, I could be sentencing him to his death!"

"Now calm down, Norman," the dean said in his best teacher's voice, at the same time trying to get his own wildly surmising thoughts in order. The patient was in jeopardy, he had gathered that much—but then so was the mission, if this unstable young American were to go off half-cocked.

"It's a dilemma of my own creation," Glass continued, not even hearing Wolfe's precautionary admonition. "If I hadn't made an incorrect analysis right from the start, he wouldn't be in this terrible situation now . . . Maybe," he finished desperately, "I should be taken off this case."

The dean was momentarily tempted to agree. And then he thought that if the patient was as close to breaking down as Glass had implied, that could be disastrous—for everybody concerned. "You can't run away from yourself forever, Norman," he said.

"I didn't think of it as running," Glass said, wincing at the implication.

"And you can't divorce the political aspects of this case from the patient's mental situation," the dean continued. "I know, I know," he said, to forestall an interruption, "I promised you neutrality, but now the situation has changed, by your own admission, through a mistake *you* made." The dean heard the dismayed intake of breath, but he ignored it successfully by telling himself that putting the other in a dependent condition was necessary. "But I'm not calling you on your error, I'm just trying to help you see what the realities are—difficult, you will admit, since you have kept me pretty much in the dark. Now let's fumble around in that dark for a bit. Isn't the center of your interest in the wrong place? It seems to me the *truth* you're after, whatever that may be, is more for *your* benefit than your patient's. It's *your* conscience that worries you. We're not like the medical fraternity, Norman, we don't keep a patient alive just for the medical record, not if, as appears to be the case here, his existence alive is far worse than it would be dead." The dean hesitated. "It's knowing *when* to play God that makes all the difference," he finished, finally, though it grieved him to have to say so.

The other was so quiet the dean began to wonder whether he was still on the phone.

"You think I should let it lie as it is, then," Glass said, hurt by the other's criticism.

"For the time being," the dean said. "Later, when you've all returned to Israel, when the mission business is done, bring him around to see me. We can reevaluate the whole matter—when everything's quieted down." And then the dean realized he had made a mistake.

Glass could not believe what he had just heard. His revered mentor, the one to whom he had been looking to set his own mental house in order, was pushing not for the good of a patient, but simply for delay. And that could only mean that the respected old man, former champion of the individual, lecturer on the uniqueness of the particular personality, writer on the special qualities peculiar to each human soul, had thrown in with the politicians, had opted for the society.

"Do you agree?" the dean pressed when the silence grew inordinately long. He had been unable to resist qualifying his position. He was not ready for this new world, he told himself bitterly; he had too much of the old left in him, and the terrible thing was he had possibly thrown away not only his old friend, but his young patient as well. "Norman?" the dean said. "It's almost a perfect compromise. What do you say?"

"I don't know," Glass said, agonizing over the death of still another illusion.

The dean heard that sense of loss, and sorrowed for both of them. "Look here, Norman," he said then, speaking quite softly, "I think I know how you feel. And I'm truly sorry. When you're older—I'm sorry about *that* old chestnut, too—I think you'll understand. Age and experience does poor things for us. As a favor to me, Norman, no other reason, no specious nonsense about playing God—just simply as a favor to me—don't do anything until you come back. Sam Hortsky and I are very old friends. He can be terribly damaged by all this if the mission fails."

Glass listened, and understood what motivated the old man. He did not sympathize—perhaps because, as the other had said, he was too young; and yet he could not forget all that the old man had stood for in the past; he was obligated, and he could not reject that fervent plea out of hand.

"Do you understand, Norman?" the dean asked.

Someone was knocking at the hotel door. "I understand," Glass said, and cupping the receiver, shouted, "Just a minute," and then to the dean again said, "I'll try, but I'm not promising anything."

"I don't ask for promises," the dean said. "Just for help." And without waiting for anything more, he hung up. He sat then, his head bowed with weariness and self-loathing, for a

273 / THE COLLABORATOR

very long time. When he finally went to his bed he did not bother to get undressed. He knew that he would get little sleep this night.

Glass went to his door. A bellman stood waiting patiently. "There is someone most anxious to get you on the telephone," the bellman said.

"Well, why didn't you ring me?" Glass frowned, puzzled and angry.

"We never break into conversations," the bellman said. "Your line was busy; I was sent up to inform you of the other call." The bellman smiled, turned on his heel, and was gone. Glass went to the phone, cursing the stupidity of Germans.

"Dr. Glass?" It was the rather high-pitched voice of the attorney he had worked with in Jerusalem. "This is Levin. Where the devil is Kohn? I've been trying to get in touch with him—and you too, for the past half-hour."

"He's with Gottliebsohn now," Glass said, annoyed by the man's abrasiveness. He hesitated, then saw no reason why he shouldn't have the privilege of letting this offensive fellow know. "They went out—to celebrate."

"Celebrate?" Levin exploded. "What in the world do they have to celebrate about?"

"Gottliebsohn's been cleared," Glass said.

There was a silence. "You don't say," Levin said slowly, at last. "How?"

"A German witness," Glass said. "A former commissioner of police. He was involved in a group who helped Jews get out of the country, and he said that Gottliebsohn was an important go-between. There are quite a few details, but if you don't mind, I'm tired and I don't much feel like going into them. But you should be getting a report soon, perhaps even tomorrow, and—"

But Levin had interrupted. "This commissioner of police," he said, "did he know our man personally?"

Glass became alert to something in the other's tone. "I don't know," he said cautiously. "Why do you ask that? Is it important?"

"Is it important you ask?" Levin repeated mockingly. "Let me read you something, my young American friend, and you can judge for yourself. I'm calling you from Lod airport. I've just finished interrogating Gottliebsohn's sister."

"The sister?" Glass asked, his heart sinking, fearing the worst.

"That's right," Levin snapped. "I've got the notes on it right here. She wasn't very cooperative at first—but listen for yourself. I'll read you only the pertinent parts." His tone changed, and he spoke very rapidly in a legalistic courtroom drone:

Q. There are some details connected with your brother that are still to be cleared up.

A. I knew nothing of my brother's activities.

Q. Is there some reason you object to questions about your brother, Mrs. Brankowicz?

A. Why do you suggest that?

Q. Your general attitude. Look at you. Your hands are trembling. And you left Bonn so quickly . . . wasn't it a very pleasant reunion?

A. Is that any of your affair?

Q. You are wrong to feel resentful, Mrs. Brankowicz. Please put aside your suspicions. We are only trying to help your brother . . .

A. I am not resentful. What difference does it make now in any case?

Q. Allow me to ask the questions. Why did you leave Bonn so soon?

A. I am anxious to get back to my husband.

Q. Of course. But one would think after not having seen your brother for so many years . . .

A. Did you expect us to fall into each other's arms? It was like meeting a stranger. Surely you can understand that?

Q. To be honest with you, I cannot. I believe something about that reunion was disturbing to you. Did your brother recall something to you?

A. (Silence)

Q. I need a verbal answer. Shrugs are difficult to describe in transcripts.

A. Who is this transcript for?

Q. The Secretary to the Cabinet. Your brother is quite important to us all. What upset you, Mrs. Brankowicz?

A. Only that he reappeared so suddenly after so many years. It was an emotional strain. I am not a well person, Mr. Levin, and even that doctor suggested it would be best if I returned home."

Here Levin interrupted his reading. "Is that true, Doctor?"

"Not exactly," Glass said slowly. "She asked me to let her go."

Levin laughed shortly.

Q. Tell me, Mrs. Brankowicz, you are a former inmate of a concentration camp, are you not?
A. (*Reluctantly*) Yes.
Q. How do you feel about your brother participating in a mission of this nature? Are you in favor of it?
A. (*Silence*)
Q. Please answer the question Mrs. Brankowicz.
A. (*Silence*)
Q. Please answer the question, Mrs. Brankowicz.
A. How can anyone be?
Q. Is *that* why the reunion with your brother was not as pleasant as it might have been? Because he is so important to the success of the mission?
A. What difference do *my* feelings make? We live, we die, the world goes on just the same.
Q. But it does make a difference, Mrs. Brankowicz. Many of us share your feelings. I myself am hoping that this mission fails.
A. They will not fail.
Q. They will if you cooperate, Mrs. Brankowicz.
A. I *am* cooperating.
Q. You are obviously not telling us something you know about your brother. I know it is difficult to talk about poor behavior on the part of a family member, but when so much is at stake . . .
A. What are you insinuating?
Q. Mrs. Brankowicz, I don't like to hurt you. Believe me, if there were any other way to avoid telling you what I am about to tell you now—
A. (*Interrupting*) Something about Ernst?
Q. There have been certain accusations.
A. What kind of accusations?
Q. He has been accused of collaborating with the Germans.
A. That is not true!
Q. Control yourself, Mrs. Brankowicz. Perhaps it is not true. We are trying to find out.
A. I want to call my husband.

Q. Of course. When we have finished with our discussion.

A. Please let me call him.

Q. We can be finished in a moment. All you need do is answer my question. Was your brother a collaborator?

A. (*Mumbling*) That man is not my brother!

Q. What is that you say?

A. (*Shouting*) That man is not my brother! He is an imposter!

Q. The man you met in Cologne?

A. Yes, yes, the man you all think is Ernst Gottliebsohn is not! He has fooled you all! Even me, for a time, but then it has been so long and it was difficult for me to really *look* at him, but then I began to grow suspicious—things he said, the way he referred to me, for example, things he remembered that never happened, a nickname I never had, and then I really studied him, but covertly, so no one should know, and I saw that it was not Ernst at all, but somebody else masquerading as my brother! I felt sorry for him. I could see that he truly had amnesia. He seemed so pathetic, so lost, like a child, and he was so grateful to have found someone, a relative, that I didn't have the heart to expose him. But he is not my brother! You cannot accuse my brother of collaboration, can you, when it is not even him?

Q. Who is he then?

A. I don't know. I never saw him before. Please, may I call my husband now? (*Begins to weep*) He will be so disappointed. He was so proud that my brother was such an important person."

Levin cleared his throat. "Well, Doctor?" he said harshly. "Who is he?"

But Glass had slammed down the phone. All he could think of was getting to his patient. Gottliebsohn an imposter! The half-hearted promise to Dean Wolfe, the agonizing self-doubts, the moralizing about what to do next had been made meaningless in an instant through that cruel interrogation at the airport outside Jerusalem. There was no doubt now but that Levin, as soon as he got hold of Kohn, would have Gottliebsohn arrested. And he had to get to him before that happened.

14

WHEN GLASS LEFT GOTTLIEBSOHN and Kohn in the bar, earlier, the two men rather quickly, at Kohn's urging, finished off their third drink and were making their way out when they heard Gottliebsohn being paged.

"Now what," Kohn growled, and he was impatient as Gottliebsohn took the call at a lobby phone.

It was Swartzwald. A foreboding shiver ran down Gottliebsohn's spine, though what he dreaded from the other he did not know. "Are you not alone?" the other asked.

"Never," Gottliebsohn said shortly.

"Ah, too bad," Swartzwald said. "Can you not get to be alone? I would think, after my testimony, that you would be free to come and go as you choose."

"What is it you want?" Gottliebsohn asked. Kohn looked at him curiously.

"I thought we might have a drink together," Swartzwald said. "For old times' sake."

"I would rather not," Gottliebsohn said.

"Oh?" Swartzwald said. "Now is that the sort of attitude to take with me? I suggest that you think again. A drink with me might be to your advantage."

"Who is it, Ernst?" Kohn asked, seeing the distaste in Gottliebsohn's face.

"It's the German," he said, cupping the receiver. "Swartzwald. He wants to have a drink with me."

"Well, why not?" Kohn said expansively, after a moment. If he were to live properly in his new world, he must learn to push his old antipathies aside. "He helped you, didn't he? Besides, since the headknocker faded out on us, we need someone for the third girl."

Gottliebsohn was reluctant. But he did not want to antagonize the now ebullient, tipsy Kohn. He told Swartzwald who was with him, and that he might join them at the *Weinstube*.

"It's as good a place as any," Swartzwald said, cheerful again, and hung up.

The hall was crowded and smoky. It being Saturday night, the concertina player had been joined by a pianist and a saxophonist, and couples were dancing a slow, old-fashioned fox trot in a cleared space off to one corner of the floor. It appeared they might have difficulty getting seated, but a few words from Kohn, along with the passing of money to an aproned waiter, put them at a table on a little balcony just back of the musicians.

Kohn had not spotted any of the girls. "They can't have found customers so early, can they?" he said, worried, standing up the better to look over the crowd. "You don't suppose the cops picked them up?" Then he saw Ilse dancing with an elderly man. "Look, look there, Ernst," he said, quite excited, "see the purple tam and the leather jacket? Same clothes. I hope she at least changes her underthings," and Kohn, after asking Gottliebsohn to order whiskey and a plate of hot sausage, left for the dance floor. Gottliebsohn watched him tap the older man on the shoulder, saw the two engaged in a brief but furious argument, after which Ilse said something which sent the older man away. A few minutes later Swartzwald came down the stairway entrance, and standing on the bottom step, began searching the room for them. Gottliebsohn ducked his head, hoping not to be seen. But it was no use. Kohn had somehow, in spite of his spirited interest in Ilse, seen Swartzwald, and he danced over to the German, pointing up at their table.

"Your captain likes a good time, I see," Swartzwald said,

when he arrived. He pulled up a chair without being asked. Gottliebsohn shrugged, and as the waiter came just then, gave him the order. "The same for me," Swartzwald said, when it became apparent that Gottliebsohn was not including him. "It's a poor substitute for dinner," he said, "but delicious all the same. It's what keeps us Germans fat. But not you, I see, Herr Gottliebsohn. Hard as a rock. Is the diet different in that damnable desert? You must miss all this enormously."

"I miss nothing in Germany," Gottliebsohn said.

"Is that a fact?" Swartzwald said, clucking sympathetically. "I would have thought differently. But then you have done pretty well for yourself in Israel, *nein*? A most important member of your adopted country's delegation—but a little frightening for you I would think. That was a close call in the chancellory this afternoon."

Before Gottliebsohn could respond, he saw by the look on Swartzwald's face that someone had come to their table. He turned to see Kohn and the girl.

"You remember Ilse?" Kohn asked, grinning hugely. "She's the most choosy, lucky for me. But I got there just in time. That old porker was about to hustle her out. Her two friends will join us shortly. They made contracts for only an hour."

Ilse smiled carefully at Ernst, glanced briefly at Swartzwald, and took the chair that Kohn offered.

"Of course if you're ready now, Ernst," Kohn said significantly, "you can go with Ilse. After all, this little party is in your honor. And personally, I'm hungry at the moment for food."

Gottliebsohn shook his head, and was grateful when the whiskey came. Kohn too drank his quickly, then ordered beer all around, and dug greedily into the platter of steaming sausage.

Swartzwald smiled at Gottliebsohn, though the other refused to meet his gleaming eye. Ilse refused the sausage—it was not good for the breath, she said—but accepted the offer of a drink and requested champagne. She watched Kohn attack the plate for a few moments, then turned to Gottliebsohn, who, because of Swartzwald's overbearing and somehow threatening presence, could not bring himself to eat, though he was incredibly hungry.

"Perhaps we might dance?" Ilse said to him.

He was about to refuse; then, with the others watching him, thought better of it. Kohn had been witness to his near-hysterical scene with the women before, and he did not want him to think nothing had changed—he was frantically concerned that his own behavior, with the return of his memory, be "normal."

But Gottliebsohn felt anything but normal down on the dance floor. The heat and the smoke and the closeness of this painted woman made him sweat; it was not so bad during the waltz, but the musicians began playing a fox trot, and with the pickup in tempo, he felt quite giddy.

"You are light on your feet for a big man," Ilse said, after they had made several circuits of the small floor. Her perfume was overpowering, and Gottliebsohn averted his head so the sweet reek should not completely disorder his mind. "I am glad you came back to see us," she said. Another couple bumped into them, and Gottliebsohn inadvertently tightened his arms. Before he might release that embarrassingly close grip, she had moved in tightly against him, and he could not push her away without looking foolish. "I've been worried about you, dear," she continued. "I've been thinking about how you must have felt the first night back, and I understand why you were . . . the way you were. But it's better for you now, *nicht?*"

"It's all right," Gottliebsohn said, steering her away from the little band and its whining saxophone, trying hard to find a rhythm to step to in that off-tempoed music.

"I've been following your conference in the daily papers," she said.

The band stopped and Gottliebsohn was glad of the excuse to drop his arms. But she still stayed too close to him, making no move to leave.

"You won't mind dancing another?" she asked.

"If you like," Gottliebsohn said, wanting to refuse but remembering that Swartzwald was waiting to talk "old times" with him. The music started, this time an inordinately lethargic, romantic melody, and the couples moved in a kind of dumb-show slow motion, and with arms clasped about one another, breast high, began swaying in parodies of a lovers' embrace. Ilse was doing something wicked with her stomach and hips. Gottliebsohn felt his breath coming short.

"Why don't you take your friend up on his offer?" she murmured. "It's you I like; I can tell you're a man, and besides, he makes me nervous. I haven't been with anyone at all today, if that's what's bothering you."

Gottliebsohn felt the temptation grow in him; excitement made him tremble. And then Gottliebsohn noticed that she had a peculiar way of speaking, not a lisp exactly, but rather the way she pronounced certain words, and for some reason this frightened him.

"You are not from Cologne?" he said.

"No," she said. "From up the river a few miles."

He stared at her, and reminded himself that she was young, that she could not possibly be anyone that he had ever known. But he abruptly turned and walked from the floor.

"Do you know the place?" she asked, hurrying to keep up.

He did not answer because he was not sure, and that frightened him too. Why was this girl's way of speaking more familiar to him than that of his own sister? He pushed her question away, but it was an effort, and it cost him dearly of what strength he had mustered to maintain his new-found happiness.

Neither Kohn nor Swartzwald got to his feet when he and that girl arrived back. Somehow this infuriated Gottliebsohn, but he ducked his head not to show it. Who was he to feel protective about a common whore?

"Hot down there?" Kohn asked, wiping his grease-smeared lips, amused at Gottliebsohn's red and perspiring face.

Gottliebsohn managed a smile, and then plunged his face into the stein of cold beer, taking long, thirsting swallows.

"Well, Ernst?" Kohn said, leaning back and patting his stomach. "Did the dance change your mind?"

Gottliebsohn did not answer. Kohn grinned, then lifted the bottle of champagne from the bucket, checking its contents. Ilse offered her empty glass and Kohn took it—also took her patent-leather purse, opened it, and dropped the glass inside. Then, wrapping the bottle in a napkin, he tucked it in the crook of his arm and stood up.

"We'll take it with us," he said, smiling brilliantly at her.

Ilse looked briefly at Gottliebsohn; he would not look at her. She was only momentarily reluctant; then, like the practiced professional she was, she returned Kohn's smile. But Gottliebsohn stood up with them, and both Kohn and Swartzwald looked surprised.

"You're not leaving?" Swartzwald asked, and smiled, though his face darkened.

"You stay, Ernst," Kohn commanded. "The others will be back any minute; maybe one of them can change your mind. We can all meet back here in an hour or so; you see that he enjoys himself, Commissioner."

Swartzwald nodded, and Gottliebsohn reluctantly sat back down, watching Kohn's and the girl's progress out of the hall with something like jealousy.

"Now we can relax," Swartzwald said expansively. "While the captain takes his pleasure, you and I can have a really good chat."

"What is it you want?" Gottliebsohn asked irritably, wishing the other would finally get to the point.

"I'm not sure," Swartzwald said blandly. "I did you an enormous favor, of course; I'm sure you realize that, and how difficult it must have been for me, considering that you cost me a great deal, almost my life, in fact; the Eastern front, even behind the lines, was no picnic, disgruntled people, every one of them capable of assassination if you gave them the least opportunity. But that's all water down the Rhine; I'm not rancorous, as you can see. I don't know of any favors at the moment I might ask in return. Were you aware, by the way, that Dieter Krieg talked to Herr Professor Schenke and me at some length? He found the name Lena Brunner in his aunt's files, and he was fascinated when I filled him in on some of the story. He is willing to pay a goodly sum if I help him 'research' a novel. It is a tempting offer. I've always had a penchant for the literary world. But I would have to be exceedingly careful not to spill all the beans."

Gottliebsohn stared at the other with increasing dislike. "It is nothing to me," he said finally. "Do as you like."

Swartzwald's smile disappeared. "Oh, is that so?" he

said. "And what if I should tell Herr Krieg enough to make his novel truly sensational?"

"Well, what if you should?" Gottliebsohn demanded.

Swartzwald's eyes narrowed. "Don't you think it's time to drop your act?" he said.

"My act?" Gottliebsohn repeated, dumbfounded. What was the other getting at? And then he became very frightened. He could hardly bring himself to ask the question. "Did you lie at the hearing then? You didn't believe I had amnesia . . . are you saying I *was* a collaborator . . . ?"

"Is it possible?" Swartzwald asked, looking at him now curiously. And then he began laughing. "Come on, Brunner, enough of this game. You can't throw me off with behavior like that. You must know that I recognize you."

"Brunner?" Gottliebsohn said, crouching in his chair so that he might run for it if he had to, sensing a dark truth but pushing it from him, out of his mind . . .

"Trust me," Swartzwald said. "I'll not turn you in. Not that I blame you for never letting down; it's the kind of game where it won't do to ever let anyone see your real face; your killing the Jew was bad enough; you remember how definite the orders were after Crystal Night not to have any more 'incidents.' Not that I blame you, your sister living with that bastard in defiance of all racial law, but you should have stayed to face it out, not run away like a common deserter, though I must say it was clever of you to take the Jew's identity . . ."

As Swartzwald talked on and told the truth about Lena, his sister, who had been taken to a camp, where she died, Gottliebsohn began shaking his head, as if by that naysaying gesture he could shake the truth out of his mind, blur the mental images that were beginning to come into focus, the dream, the struggle, the chase and the echoing cathedral, with that soldier, himself, in the shadows, spying on the genuflecting Jew, through the back streets, the long black-mirrored tunnel, the wet uniform, the stink of wool and of fear, the fading image in the other's eyes, the identity card blurred by the rain and his own tears, his absent family, his sister, the piano, his sister contaminated by that subhuman creature, and the creature a man, dead by his terrible hands, and him the man, him the creature, him the Jew, and he stood up, shaking his head with such force that his whole body began to twist with the force of that shake, no's tumbling from his lips in a cascade of sound, a waterfall of no's, saliva spurting with the violence of that negative emotion, neck cracking as his head whipped left to right to left again, his body not quite keeping up, twisting at the shoulders, the hips, the knees, the ankles, and his feet, until he was almost spinning, until suddenly, with a swallowed scream that he choked into silence, he froze. His mind stopped working. Those pictures that had almost come into focus blurred into unrecognizability. And he stood frightened to death, bulging-eyed, afraid that if he moved, the pictures would move and come clear, and he breathed noisily through his mouth without blinking or twitching any other muscle, only his strangled breath indicating that within that statue-hard figure a man lived, until even that panting sound like the chuff of trains faded into the distance and he was safe.

"What is it?" Swartzwald cried, astounded, cringing, afraid that the other was about to attack him. And then, when the fit had passed, and Gottliebsohn remained standing in so grotesque a position, his head twisted one direction and his body another, Swartzwald could not believe his eyes. "An epileptic?" he muttered aloud, and pushed himself to his feet to make his escape, only to be blocked by that American, Glass.

"Catatonic!" Glass moaned, taking it all in in one horrified glance. He had looked through two other beer halls before finding this one, with the passing of time growing more desperate about reaching his patient. "How long?" he demanded of the German, who seemed as rigid as his patient. "How long, damn you!" he shouted, and Swartzwald started.

"Just now," he mumbled. "It only happened as you arrived . . ."

Glass began wrestling the immobile Gottliebsohn over to a chair, trying to get that stiffening figure into a semblance of an ordinary posture. "It's all right," he pleaded. "Don't run from it. We can work it out if you'll only give us a chance . . ." He continued talking into Gottliebsohn's ear while he struggled with him, hoping to stop what he knew was the swift retreat of his patient's consciousness down into the subterranean corridors of his mind, but there was no reaction. He slapped him then; he held one hand over the other's bulging, glazed eyes, and with the other managed to strike a match and thrust it suddenly at the unseeing eyes as he took his blinding hand away; he shouted, almost screamed, into the other's ear . . . and all of it was hopeless.

"Get an ambulance here," he said to Swartzwald. The other nodded, and began to get up. "Move, damn you!" Glass shouted, and the German, though he flushed with anger, ran down the steps to the floor, shouting at a waiter to show him the phone. The crowd became aware that something was going on; now the hall was silent after a final wheeze from the concertina, and all of them were staring up at the alcove table.

By the time the ambulance came Glass had managed to get Gottliebsohn's head and shoulders facing front, and the upward arm, raised as if he were fending off a blow, lowered, but he was still rigid as death, and the attendants, after attempting unsuccessfully to move him as they normally would—his arms over their shoulders while they walked him out—instead, at Glass's suggestion, just picked him up log-like and carried him that way.

"You told him, didn't you?" Glass said to Swartzwald, who had nervously followed the little procession through the now murmuring crowd.

"Told him?" Swartzwald began, but that pretended innocence had a ragged edge to it.

"Don't pull that with me!" Glass said savagely. "You knew all along he was someone else—why didn't you tell him at the inquiry when he may have had a chance? Maybe I could have gotten him through it!"

"I wasn't sure," Swartzwald said, licking his lips. "Besides, I didn't know he was really *verrücht*, I thought it was all a pretense . . ."

"Who is he?" Glass demanded, though he was almost certain he knew, remembering that initialing of the dust on the tabletop of the apartment in Cologne. "The soldier, right?" After Levin had read him the sister's deposition, and all during the time he had been desperately hunting his patient, he had gone over in his mind everything he knew about the man posing as Gottliebsohn. He could hardly be anyone else than that stalking, uniformed figure of his hallucination.

Swartzwald nodded reluctantly. "Brunner," he said. "Kurt Brunner." He hesitated. "Will he be . . . that way . . . long?"

"He could be that way forever," Glass said, and as he said so felt on the verge of breaking down himself.

"Forever?" Swartzwald said, incredulous. "Is he paralyzed then?"

"I suppose you could call it that," Glass muttered, and turned to climb in the ambulance alongside his patient.

Swartzwald grabbed his arm. "And there's nothing you can do?"

"A few things," Glass said, unwilling to take even this brief moment for explanations. "Shock, maybe . . . he doesn't want to face the truth, or accept who he really is . . . it's easier for him this way."

"Well, he doesn't have to know it," Swartzwald said eagerly. He leaned in the door. "Can you hear me, Brun— Gottliebsohn?" he said loudly. "No one but we three need ever know. Is there any reason for others to know?" he demanded of the doctor, in a whisper.

Glass climbed inside, nodded to the waiting driver, then turned back to Swartzwald. "Every reason," he said. "He's already been found out." And he had to restrain himself from laughing wildly at the grotesque clown-like look which came over Swartzwald's face. But as he closed the doors and the vehicle pulled away, its two-noted warning horn clearing a path for them, he wondered whether he was not really laughing because he had been tempted, even now, to conspire with the German to keep Gottliebsohn's identity secret, even though he knew it was already too late.

Kohn watched Ilse put on her clothes. He was still in the bed, taking his ease with a small cigar, looking on appreciatively as she struggled to get her well-formed breasts into the brassiere.

"Come over here. I'll help," he said.

She became instantly quiet and thoughtful, then did as he asked. Kohn lowered the brassiere and began casually experimenting with her nipples. In a moment they were outthrust, long, dark, and wonderfully chewy—like licorice, he thought, as he put his teeth to them. She shivered and her skin became rough to his exploring hand. He chuckled. German girls were terrific, he thought. He had heard it argued that women were the same the world over, equally good or bad or passive or abandoned, varying only with the individual, but like all such theories based on the universality of mankind, it failed to take into account certain national characteristics. And the Germans could be expected to perform any sensual act, be it eating, torture, or sex, with great gusto.

"You're hurting," she said, but her breath was coming fast.

"Want another?" he asked.

"You said you wanted to get back to your friends," she said.

"Friend," he corrected her. "But I could be talked into another performance."

She said nothing. He laughed. "Too much for you?" She looked at him, then pulled her lace panties down over her hips.

"You have marked me," she said, showing him.

He looked at the bruises dispassionately. "I get carried away," he said. "But wasn't it worth it?"

"You are cruel," she said, and went to pull the panties back up.

He stopped her. "But you enjoyed it," he said.

"Please," she said. "You will tear them. They cost me eighteen marks."

"Didn't you?" he asked.

"Yes," she said finally.

"Well, get dressed," he said, getting out of bed and putting his own clothes on. "I do want to see how Ernst is getting on. If your friends aren't back, I'll recommend you to him myself." He took his gun from under the mattress, where he had hidden it earlier, and returned it casually to his coat.

Her friends had returned to the *Weinstube*, but Ernst and Swartzwald were nowhere to be seen. "They weren't here when you got back?" he asked of Ursula, the one with the bad teeth, who had called to them the moment they entered.

She started to shake her head and then a strange, excited

look came into her face. "You don't suppose *he* was the one?" she asked. And then she explained what had taken place.

Kohn panicked. "What table?" he demanded. "Where did it happen?" A waiter pointed up at the little balcony. Swearing under his breath, Kohn stopped only long enough to find out where the hospital was, then rushed outside and hailed a cab. He muttered to himself all during the short ride, cursing his misfortune to have been gone when it happened. Though Gottliebsohn was technically no longer in his charge, since he had, after all, been cleared, the fact that the American, Glass, had asked him to keep an eye on the other made him tremendously uneasy, and he crossed his fingers against his luck, hoping against hope that it was not nearly so serious as had been described.

But his luck was against him. Gottliebsohn, the reception nurse said, was in the suite on the third floor reserved for foreign dignitaries. And when he walked inside the anteroom, he saw that a great many people had arrived before him.

"Where have you been?" Auerbach demanded, in a scarcely contained rage.

"That will not help," Hortsky cautioned.

Kohn looked at the others: Schenke, Swartzwald, and Bettmann. What were they doing here? That premonition of disaster hardened into certainty.

"How is he?" Kohn asked uneasily.

"You left him," Auerbach continued furiously. "Why? If you'd stayed where you belonged, perhaps this wouldn't have happened . . ."

"Is he dead then?" Kohn asked, now thoroughly frightened.

"Better if he were!" Auerbach said, his voice rising, and then broke off when Hortsky stared him down.

"He is in a catatonic state, Captain," Hortsky said, running his hands through his unkempt hair. "When Swartzwald told him who he was, the shock apparently caused his mind to snap—"

"Swartzwald?" Kohn interrupted, uncomprehending. "Told him what . . .?"

"Who he really was," Hortsky said. "Gottliebsohn is not

Gottliebsohn after all, it seems. He is really . . ." The old man turned to Auerbach. "What was the soldier's name?"

"*Brunner?*" whispered Kohn, incredulous.

They all watched Kohn trying to absorb this, enjoying, in the perverse way one can enjoy disaster, the expressions of disbelief and bewilderment that chased themselves across his face, as those expressions had chased themselves across their own.

"He killed a Jew named Gottliebsohn," Hortsky said, "and was apparently so overcome with remorse that he took the fellow's identity, and immediately went on to act the part as if he had been born to it, fleeing the German persecution, fighting with the British, coming to Palestine, and so on . . ."

"He wasn't acting," Kohn said, denying it all, unable to believe it, stunned by the revelation.

"Technically, I suppose not," Hortsky said. "Our American psychiatrist says that was the reason for the amnesia. He wanted to believe that he really was the other man."

"Where is Glass?" Kohn demanded then. He felt vaguely that he'd been double-crossed, and he was not quite sure yet by whom. He intended to find out.

"In with his patient," Hortsky said.

"What're *they* doing here?" Kohn went on, indicating the Germans.

"They found out about it first," Auerbach said bitterly. "While you were playing around with a German tootsie, *neglecting your duty*, Gottliebsohn, Brunner, *whatever* his damn name is, was brought here—and they got here before we did."

"And now they're claiming custody," Hortsky added. "Can you imagine? He's been a Jew for over twenty-six years, and they're claiming him as a German!"

"Let them," Auerbach said.

"How can you say that?" Hortsky said. "He's one of us now."

"He killed a Jew," Auerbach said. "Can you imagine how that would go down, how impossible it would be for him, back in Israel—even if he recovers and *wants* to go back? It's impossible!"

"I disagree with you, Auerbach," Hortsky said.

Schenke cleared his throat. "Aren't you forgetting something?" he said. "His real name is Kurt Brunner, *nicht?* He is a German national. As such, we are obligated to keep him in our custody."

"In custody for what?" Kohn interjected. He had only been half listening, trying to make sense of it all.

"For one thing," Schenke said, almost apologetically, "he is a deserter. We could try him for that."

"But you said you made no claims on your nationals of Jewish descent!" Kohn cried, so bewildered and angered by the argument that he had forgotten who Gottliebsohn was. "He told me that personally, in his office," he said, looking to Auerbach for help.

"What do you expect from Germans?" Auerbach muttered. But everyone in that room heard him. They were all still, all staring at him, the originator of the Israeli mission to Germany. He who had come seeking an accommodation, he who had preached tolerance and understanding, had just mouthed a heartfelt prejudice. And Auerbach suddenly, instead of feeling shame, did not care a damn! He did not care even about Hortsky's sudden and obvious dismay. For too long he had kept his feelings buried, for too long he had denied his own emotional nature, and for what? All these years of planning and sacrifice only to have it rendered meaningless in a moment, and by someone as insignificant, in the larger scheme of things, as this man Gottliebsohn—or whatever his name—was really too much to bear. He knew what would happen back in Israel when they received the report about Gottliebsohn. The Cabinet would meet in emergency session, and the Interior Minister would move to recall the mission. All the others, however eager or reluctant, would agree that it was their only course. Even the Foreign Secretary would be forced to recognize the reality of a situation where a key figure on an already highly controversial mission was identified as a former German soldier, and one who had murdered a Jew at that! So what difference did it make that he had revealed so secret and deep-buried a feeling that he had almost forgotten it himself? Auerbach stood his ground and returned those startled and angry looks with equanimity.

"He is overwrought," Hortsky announced to the room at large, breaking the shocked silence.

"Do not apologize for me!" Auerbach said. And though they waited, he refused to say anything more.

"Come now, Bettmann," Hortsky said then, appealing to his old colleague, "let *us* show how to be reasonable. The man is an Israeli citizen. Let him come with us, back to where he belongs."

"Be careful," Schenke murmured warningly to his superior. "Our populace will not tolerate another show trial by the Jews. An Eichmann, yes—but not a soldier, like Brunner. Don't forget, it was not simply racial murder . . . he was avenging the honor of his sister!"

Bettmann nodded reluctantly. What Schenke said was true. Furthermore, if he was to salvage what was left of a political career out of the wreckage of these negotiations, he could not leave his enemies any more grounds to attack him. Von Haupt had submitted his resignation, but whether for his own reasons or to accommodate the Bavarian remained, thus far, unclear.

"He is, in fact, a German," Bettmann said then to Hortsky. "Nothing can change that. He must remain in his own country."

"You, of all persons, a nationalist?" Hortsky said. "We dreamed once, you and I, of an international system, where men could rid themselves of such stupid factionalisms, where the only loyalties were to mankind!"

"Those were dreams," Bettmann said.

"Think of it," Hortsky said, his voice rising, pounding his fist in his palm as the idea took hold of him. "With this man we can prove that it *is* possible for the wolf to become a lamb! The fable can be made real!"

"He is a murderer," Auerbach said.

"We will defend him then!" Hortsky thundered. "I promised to assist you in the event it came to that—remember how cleverly you got that promise from me? Well, I now hold you to your word!"

"You see?" Schenke said to Bettmann, still furious over Auerbach's earlier remark. "If we let them take custody they will crucify him!" And though he flushed when he realized what he, doctor of philosophy, had said, he clicked his teeth shut and prepared to stand his own ground.

Then the door to the inner room opened and Glass appeared, white-faced. "Are you all out of your minds?" he demanded, his voice shaking with anger. "To argue like this in a hospital room?"

They subsided, shamefaced.

"How is he?" Kohn asked in a whisper.

Glass made a helpless gesture.

"Can he hear us then?" Hortsky asked. "I assumed he was deaf to the world."

"Who can say?" Glass asked. "Perhaps he heard nothing. But what if he sensed what it is you're all saying—haggling over him as if he were an object, a thing!"

Auerbach grimaced. "And what is he then in his condition? Give us your prognosis, Doctor. Will he ever recover from this state?"

"The chances are slight," Glass admitted. He glared around the room. "Is he perhaps better off?"

"Look, gentlemen," Hortsky said, "let us allow the matter to rest in the doctor's hands for now. Meanwhile we can allow our tempers to cool overnight, and meet again tomorrow, and discuss the situation like reasonable men."

"If he doesn't recover," Auerbach said, "the whole business is academic."

"Perhaps each side can come in with alternative proposals?" Hortsky went on, ignoring him.

Everyone looked doubtful, but since it was obvious that nothing could be resolved with the patient in his present condition, they finally agreed. They filed silently out the door into the linoleumed corridor. Auerbach and Kohn walked together.

"What about the mission now?" Kohn murmured anxiously, in an aside to Auerbach.

"What about it?" Auerbach said bitterly. "We'll be lucky not to be repudiated for overreaching ourselves, accused of going beyond the original guidelines . . ." He let his voice trail off. "It was too soon," he said, as much to himself as to the other. "We're not ready for it, not in this generation—"

He was interrupted by Hortsky. "We can't let them have him," Hortsky said, in an undertone. "Can you imagine the uproar back home if we let the Germans have him?"

"You want to see him hang instead?" Auerbach demanded, in a fierce whisper.

They were shushed by the nervous Kohn, who indicated

that the Germans were attempting to overhear. Then the elevator came. Since it was small and there were five other men, Kohn had an excuse for not riding with them.

He wanted to be by himself. He wanted to think through all the ramifications of what seemed a personal failure.

15

THERE HAD BEEN AN UPROAR IN THE Cabinet, as Auerbach had predicted. The in-fighting was even more vicious than might otherwise have been the case, since the very morning in which Hortsky informed the Prime Minister by phone of Gottliebsohn's true identity, an opposition newspaper, *Haaretz*, headlined the Eisenberg denunciation. One of its reporters had gotten onto that "protective custody." As if that were not enough, pages from a projected special issue of *Haolam-Hazeh*, brought to the Cabinet meeting by the Interior Minister (who saw to it that he got advance editions of just such radical journals), carried a denial of the charges by Ruth Brankowicz, who pointed out that the accused man was not even her brother. (She had remembered *Haolam-Hazeh* as the magazine which had carried that earlier story about Kohn, and had given them an interview.) The assembled Ministers saw that nothing less than a full disclosure was possible. But there had to be a position taken by the government, and the argument ran hot and heavy as to just what that position should be.

Hortsky, who had been called by the Foreign Secretary after that extraordinary Cabinet session, had immediately summoned Auerbach to his suite; now he filled the other man in while he bustled about, getting his bags packed.

"I have to go back at once," he said, his voice pitched high in his excitement. "The Knesset meets tomorrow; I must be there for the debate. The Interior Minister is planning some sort of dramatic move; perhaps even a resignation. If that happens, his party will withdraw from the coalition. I don't think, under the circumstances, that the Prime Minister can win a vote of confidence. A new government may have to be formed."

Auerbach watched in amazement as the old man flung his clothes every which way into the open valises: that fantastic burst of energy could only mean one thing.

"And the mission?" Auerbach asked, trying to keep the dismay out of his voice.

Hortsky delayed answering until he had wrestled a suitcase shut. Then he faced the younger man, suddenly glum. "It has been recalled," he said.

Auerbach struggled to maintain his composure. Though he had expected nothing less, somehow the announcement itself, blunt, final, and irrevocable as it was, had caught him emotionally unaware, and he knew a grief so profound his heart ached. He grimaced, and began a shrug, hoping to hide how awfully he had been shaken—when Hortsky's next words drove all feeling from him.

"Except for you," Hortsky said. He gave the startled man a moment to absorb this. "You are to stay," he continued, "and work for Gottliebsohn's return. On that, there was unanimity. Even the Interior Minister agreed—"

"But of course he did!" Auerbach cried, recovering, almost beside himself now with anger at this old man's obtuseness. "He'll want to try him . . ."

"You forget that I will be there to prevent that," Hortsky said.

"How?" Auerbach asked bitterly. "Because you think they will ask you to form the new government?" His heart sank. He saw, by the old man's reaction, that he had guessed right. "And you don't think you have been out of the political wars for too long?"

"Who else is there?" Hortsky retorted. "The Foreign Secretary? The Interior Minister? Their positions are too extreme. And there is no one else of sufficient stature . . ." He hesitated, looking shrewdly at the younger man. "You? But you are too closely identified with the mission. And the mission has failed. It is not your time, Auerbach. You were ahead of your time. Now you must wait for events to catch up with you . . ."

"But you yourself agreed to the mission," Auerbach pointed out, his voice shaking, terribly upset, as the old man, like a funereal bell, tolled the death of his political hopes. "You believed in it."

"And I still do," Hortsky said. "You don't think I intend to jettison all we've worked for out of mere political expediency? No, my young friend, on the contrary. I intend to find our victory in the ashes. It's not as far-fetched as it may sound. After all, what we worked for would have had enormous benefits, moral as well as material, for all concerned. Our people are emotional, but they are reasonable, too. I intend to make an emotional appeal to their reason." He hesitated. "But to do that, I'll need your help."

"Mine?" said a completely incredulous Auerbach.

"I need Gottliebsohn as a symbol," Hortsky said. "You must accomplish that for me. You must stay and negotiate with the Germans for his release. I promise you this— succeed, and there will be another mission, not right away, mind, we must work for a proper climate, but undoubtedly in another year . . ."

"I had intended to resign," Auerbach said helplessly, aghast at what the other seemed to be saying.

"Would you be so foolish?" Hortsky said angrily. "A resignation would be an admission of failure. You pride yourself on being practical. Be practical now. If you leave under these conditions you will be withdrawing into a perhaps permanent obscurity. You will always be identified with a moral catastrophe. But if you stay, if you pull it through, if you can pull Gottliebsohn out of the fire, you can change all this into a kind of personal triumph. You are still young, as politicians go. This will be my last chance, my last opportunity to prove my beliefs." He hesitated. "Help me, Auerbach," he said, suddenly pleading. "You'll not regret it."

Auerbach grimaced, and to hide his doubts he turned away and lit another cigarette. What was he being promised? The passing on of the mantle of leadership? Yes, nothing less—*if* the old prophet succeeded in taking the reins of power himself, *if* he succeeded in imposing his mystical ideas upon the Knesset—both if's rendered precarious, if not impossible, by Hortsky's insistence upon regarding Gottlieb-sohn as a Jew. It was plain he intended to plead Gottlieb-sohn's cause in the coming debate—a symbol, as he had said, a way in which to characterize the old man's own be-liefs, a platform from which to trumpet his vision of the future. It was, in Auerbach's judgment, a dangerous if not downright impossible approach. And yet . . . and yet, as he thought about it, he saw that it was not so far-fetched as it had seemed at first hearing. Better to tackle an issue head-on than to try and avoid what was unavoidable. The old man was identified with the mission, too, and therefore with the two-faced Gottliebsohn. The Interior Minister would not sit quiet, even for Hortsky—the old man would be vig-orously, even brutally attacked. But because he truly believed that Gottliebsohn should be judged only by his con-duct as a Jew, he could bring a kind of passion to his argu-ments for a German-Jew accommodation that might be con-vincing. It was possible, Auerbach thought; he might pull it off—but only because Germans and Jews had specific need of each other, not for the moralistic reasons this visionary would give. But he just might pull it off, because they needed a moralistic reasoning to justify a materialistic act. To pull it off, however, he needed to bring Gottliebsohn back.

And what about himself? Could he bring himself once more to bury his feelings, to face the Germans as though nothing had happened, as if his outburst in the hospital room had not taken place? Of course he could, he told him-self cynically. He had not trained himself politically for so many years for nothing. He was being given another chance, albeit a slim one. How was he to convince the Germans, or the corpse-like Gottliebsohn, that he ought to remain a Jew? Still, any chance was better than none. That vision of ob-scurity which Hortsky had so casually presented was chilling.

"It seems I am an optimist," Auerbach said, not liking himself much for what he planned to do about Gottlieb-sohn, but then he had not rested easy with his conscience for a long while in any case. "I'll stay and keep the channels open. But I must warn you; in my opinion our chances for success are almost nil."

"An optimist, you say?" Hortsky said, but he was very pleased. And calling for someone to come for his luggage, he sat down with Auerbach to discuss what sort of statement should be made to the press.

Glass stayed in the hospital suite overnight, sleeping only intermittently, and then spent all of the next day working on his patient, trying desperately to bring him out of his paralytic state. The hospital offered him complete freedom to use all of its facilities, including the services of staff, and reluctantly Glass put the patient through electro-convulsive shock therapy. But it did not seem to make any perceptible difference.

Finally Glass had the somnambulant patient brought back to his room, where he might remain alone with him, hoping, though it seemed increasingly doubtful, that this stupor would be transitory, as it was in many such cases.

Like Kohn, he was bitter about his own failure. How awfully he had misled himself as well as this other, going so far in order to win the other's confidence as to acknowledge the title of Jew for himself, and even, finally, even beginning to think of himself as truly bred-in-the-bone Jewish, to the manner born, as his wife, if not his parents, had always wanted him to be, and the nearer they got to the other's past, the closer he came to understanding himself, and he began to believe that their search ran on parallel tracks, at almost the same speed. But he had not, and would never, accomplish his own breakthrough. He had a tougher emotional threshold—he thought himself apart from and not the same as other men—and if that were true, why did he sit grieving over the hiding soul of a man who so desperately wanted to be something that he was not? And for whom did he grieve, himself or the other? In searching out this other, he had learned a great deal about himself, and whether out of compassion or some deeper identification or the feeling that there was yet some final understanding to be accomplished, for the other and for himself, Glass just could not let the matter rest.

He began talking to the silent man in the bed. He sympathized with the struggle that must be going on inside the other's mind, in which two persons, Gottliebsohn and Brunner, German and Jew, victim and murderer, fought for the final supremacy, and he begged the other to let himself be helped, that only with help could he separate those conflicting personalities. Then he apologized for interfering, apologized for the physical indignities—he had no right, he said, to try and force the other's return, it was really none of his affair. His only excuse was that he meant well, he said; he did not want to lose someone whose struggle was in some way like his own, someone of whom he had grown very fond. And then he began pleading with the other to come "out," to accept the truth, to face up to reality, trying to reassure the corpse-like figure that he would not be condemned for past guilts, that his self-inflicted punishment was far more severe than anything the world could invent, that all of them, knowing the truth, were as accepting of his true identity as they had been of the false. Even Auerbach had been asking after him, he said, had called once every hour since morning. But the speech rang hollow in the small white room, and the psychiatrist became as silent and still as the patient himself.

Did he dare tell him about his conversation with Auerbach? It seemed the hapless Gottliebsohn was still in contention between opposing forces. He was not to be permitted any peace. The rise and fall of politicians and governments, of Germans and Jews, were somehow still bound to this stupefied man. As matters now stood it was a standoff. Both sides were adamant. The Germans, as Auerbach had found out in a personal, private meeting with Bettmann, would under no circumstances consider releasing the mentally ill man. But, Auerbach said, if he were to come out of his stupor and himself *choose* to become one thing or the other, then legal arguments of acquired citizenship rights versus national birth might have some validity.

Glass had angrily refused permission for Auerbach to come talk to his patient, resenting the fact that these ambitious individuals were still attempting to use him to their own purposes. He had been surprised when Auerbach had not responded in kind. That normally volatile person was strangely subdued. Auerbach had only thought, he said, that if Gottliebsohn was shamming, or if he could at least *listen* to his, Auerbach's coaxing, it might have some effect on his condition. Again Glass had refused, resenting too that charge of shamming (though he had considered the possibility himself, even so profound a "sham" would be the act of a mentally desperate man).

Finally Auerbach had retreated, saying that perhaps it was best, after all, if Gottliebsohn remained in limbo. As matters presently stood, he was at least safe. Though Hortsky had promised his protection, the eventual disposition of the case would be doubtful, to say the least. He had agreed to negotiate for the custody only because he could see no other course. But there was a limit to cynicism, he told Glass. Perhaps it would be best all around if Gottliebsohn lived out his days behind the protective walls of an asylum.

Did he mean it? Glass wondered. Or was it a devious tactic, meant to deceive Glass as to his motives? It didn't matter. Meant or not, that last remark upset Glass enormously. To think of Gottliebsohn remaining, safe or not, in his present state, was abhorrent to him. The man had a right to know what was going on, had a right to decide, insofar as it was possible, the direction of his own fate.

And so he told him finally what he had heard from Auerbach. He told him how he was the object of controversy between German and Jew, German and German, Jew and Jew. And he told him how that argument mirrored the one going on in his own mind. If he had retreated, hoping that others would make a decision for him, he was mistaken. They could not decide. They were at a stalemate. Only he could make the choice. Furthermore, once he chose, it would not only resolve his own conflicts but all those others' as well.

He did not tell him which side to choose, because, after all, he could not.

It was then Glass saw a glint of moisture in the glazed, staring eyes. He called for the staff doctor, and though the other agreed that the eyes were indeed wet, he thought it likely that the secretion of those ducts was a physical reaction only. He did not agree that the patient had understood anything.

Shortly after that Glass returned to his hotel room. He lay down on the bed fully clothed, intending to rest for only a few moments, but before he quite knew it he had fallen into a troubled sleep.

The telephone awakened him. It was dark in the room: looking at the luminous dial of his watch, Glass saw that it was ten minutes of eight. He had slept for over two hours

Still groggy, he lifted the receiver, but what he heard next brought him sharply awake.

"Is it finally you?" Kohn demanded. "You took your sweet time answering. He's taken a powder again!"

"Who's done what?" Glass asked, unbelieving.

"*Him*," Kohn said, almost groaning with anger and frustration. "They went in to try and feed him and he was gone! I was there to visit the poor bastard when they called the alarm to the reception desk—I went up to help look for him, but when I found out that he'd taken his clothes I knew it was hopeless. He's out of the building, I'm convinced of that, and I called to see if maybe he'd gone looking for you."

"Where are you now?" Glass said, now thoroughly awake.

"At the hospital," Kohn said. "You take a run downstairs and check our room. He may have headed back there. Meanwhile I'll get over there too."

Glass immediately went down to their room. The door was unlocked, and for a moment as he stepped inside he thought the other might be there, but after a quick search he saw that it was debris of Kohn's that had misled him. An ashtray was overflowing with small cigar butts, an empty bottle of schnapps lay on the stand next to Kohn's bed, which was rumpled and untidy with ashes, and the air of the room was fetid with the smell of still drifting smoke. Kohn must have lain here for hours, Glass thought, quietly getting drunk, and once again he was aware of the dark undercurrents that seethed inside that tense little man.

"Where do you think he's got to?" Kohn demanded, when he met Glass in the lobby.

"Cologne," Glass said.

Kohn thought about it, shaking his head to clear it of the drink. "He's going to look for himself all over again, isn't he?" he said. "Well, let's get after him. We've got to collar him before the Germans do."

They took a diplomatic limousine. Glass took the wheel, Kohn obviously in no condition himself, and in a short time they were speeding down the highway by the river toward Cologne.

From moment to moment he was unsure which of the two men he was. When he got on the river steamer shortly after dusk, he was Gottliebsohn, repeating the journey he had made two days before as if it had not yet occurred. But when he got off the boat, and walked the few blocks to the cathedral steps, he was Brunner, wondering why it was that the Jew, Gottliebsohn, had gone into this Catholic sanctuary. Did he dare to seek protection from a Christian God? A Lutheran himself, Brunner could not help feeling awed. He reached for his cap and was surprised to find himself already bareheaded, like a civilian. But the ominous gloom and the incense and the guttering candles took his mind from himself, and thinking he saw the slender, quick figure of his sister's lover disappearing around a pillar, he hastened after him.

He stepped into a darker shadow, watching, and then saw that he was mistaken, that prayerful supplicant was someone else. Then where had the Jew gone? Had that traitorous priest once again taken him into a confessional? He tiptoed then from box to box, listening at each, and once, hearing a murmur, he flung open the grilled door, only to be confronted by a woman's startled eyes, and he fled, darting through the shadows to the side entrance, hoping that he had lost that lurking pursuer. And as he hurried from the cathedral he was Gottliebsohn again, hastening from a conspiratorial meeting, out of that ominously echoing interior into the empty square, hunching into his coat against the mist drifting in from the river, heading toward the flat where he lived with the German woman he loved, avoiding the lighted boulevards for fear his follower would too soon pick up his trail.

But by the time he reached the apartment building he was not the followed but the follower again, and he stepped into an empty doorway across the street from that sinful building, taking up the lonely vigil that he had experienced night after long night. He stared up at his sister's apartment, seeing by those darkened windows that no one was home, and wondered for the thousandth time when the police were going to pick up that accursed Jew! And then he remembered his last conversation with the commissioner of police, when he had gone there to complain. They were not going to do anything!

"You have an exaggerated opinion of Jews," Swartzwald had told him then, contemptuously. "If you saw as many of them as I do you would realize that they are neither so fearsome or grotesque as the party makes them out to be. It is a mistake to make Germany *Judenrein;* who then will we have for our villains? They are too shrewd for their own good, true, but then how else would you have them act in a situation where their very lives may depend on shrewdness? Yes, their lives; I happen to know that the party plans to do more than just deport them. That pleases you, I suppose? It should not. If your sister marries this fellow, it may be all up with her too."

His sister, married to a Jew? He had been almost insane with fear and rage, and he had immediately gone to Gestapo headquarters to report the clandestine activities of that despicable creature, then rushed back to warn his sister. He had waited in the shadows, as he waited now, until he was certain she was alone, and then walked in on her while she was playing the piano, frightening her by his unexpected intrusion, interrupting her in the midst of that waltz by Strauss, his own favorite, and that she now played only for the other!

It had been a terrible scene. He had finally gone to the closet, tearing the Jew's clothes from the hangers, throwing hers on the bed along with her suitcase, threatening to remove her bodily from this contaminated place, and only her collapse from contemptuous anger into helpless tears deterred him. It was hopeless, he realized, and he stood like some stupid ox in the middle of the room, as if each of her sobs did not wrench at his own heart, as if he did not care for her as much as the other did. He began to rage inwardly that she, whom he had watched since she was the littlest doll, who had grown up into a talented and too beautiful young woman, should turn for love to that loathsome other, and he became outraged at her betrayal of her German blood, and sickened by the thought that she permitted one of that subhuman species to touch her, to . . . who knew to what unspeakable indignities she was subjected?

He left her without another word, took up his post in the doorway shadow, waited for the Jew to come back from God-knew-what despicable rendezvous, trying to blot out of his mind those things his sister had told him about her illicit lover, his warmth and his tenderness, his devotion, and he became half frantic with anxiety, knowing that he would have to kill, believing that if he killed with his bare hands the act of murder would somehow be pure, reminding himself that what he was about to do was in perfect keeping with the exhortations of the New Order, going over and over in his mind the tracts he had been disciplined to read until they were ingrained in his soul like catechism, and with which, despite the disdainful arguments of his sister, he was in absolute accord. The world would be a better place without Jews, he thought, anxiously peering up at those blind windows, and if he were to take his place among those who were leading Germany to new glories, it was fitting that he perform this ritualistic act.

He did not know that he was crying.

Kohn and Glass came out of the cathedral.

"Now where?" Kohn asked. He was remarkably tense. The drink had not worn off but its deadening effect had, leaving him with a miserable headache and the kind of sensitized nerve endings where he became excruciatingly aware of every light and sound and movement about him.

"The sister's apartment, I think," Glass said. "He's terribly disoriented, and he'll be trying to get back into the past. It's the past where he made the switch in identity. That's where he'll try and switch back."

Kohn nodded, and the two men began walking the same back streets and alleys they had taken before. During the long drive, Glass had explained something of what must be going on inside the man they were following. He had described for Kohn how the switch in identity had probably taken place, immediately after the killing, the enormity of the act too awful to contemplate, his mirrored image in the dying man's eyes, and how he had then taken his victim's identity, thereby destroying his own. But he had the misfortune, almost immediatey thereafter, of finding his acquired family gone, and by the action of the neighbors, he suspected himself, that new identity, in spite of the virtues given it by the sister, of having a new guilt—that of abandonment of his family, which paralleled so awfully the abandonment of his sister. Instead of being "clean," he found himself with a new and even more intolerable burden. It was to protect his new identity from his old that he insisted he was incapable of certain crimes, that he was willing to believe himself capable of murder, but not collaboration. That was why, after the incident in the cathedral, he had been so worried about who the informer might be. That was why, in Gottliebsohn's village, he had been as interested in finding out about his "character" as in the specifics of his departure. He had had the bad luck to take an identity which possessed a sister of its own, and the confusion in his mind when he confronted the other man's sister must have been incredible. Not to mention that his love for her went beyond the "normal"; his hatred of the Jew was based not only on tract, but on jealousy. And then the wild fluctuation of his search, in which it seemed increasingly evident that he was a collaborator, followed by the sudden exoneration —it was no wonder that he had gone into a catatonic stupor when told who he really was. The emotional changes were too much for him, going from the blackest of melancholies to a kind of mad exultation. There seemed no other way out. Glass suspected, too, that another reason for Gottliebsohn's psychotic retreat was the hope that he would no longer influence, one way or another, the progress of the negotiations —so when Glass had told him that his withdrawal had made him the major stumbling block to any accommodation, the countershock had been enough to bring him back and send him running away, physically as well as mentally.

Kohn asked about the Arab women. Glass pointed out that only by limiting himself to those women who could under no circumstances be related to him could he avoid an incestuous act—with either identity's sister, or her offspring, if any—which was why the hysteria over the offer of the whore to bed with him. He might have succeeded at losing his true self, Glass said, had not the hallucinatory nightmare always reminded him that deep inside, another identity struggled to reassume its rightful place. In that long speech about remembering finally who he was, ticking off all the details that had been provided for him—he might have finally, completely made the transfer, had not Swartzwald confronted him with the inescapable truth.

"The poor bastard," Kohn muttered, not quite grasping it all, but understanding enough to guess at the awful struggle that was going on in the other.

As they approached the street where the sister had lived, both men instinctively began walking more quietly.

"If he's there," Glass cautioned, "don't move in on him too fast. If he's coming out of it at all, it'll be highly tentative, and if we scare him, we're liable to drive him right back into that freeze. And this time, it could be for keeps!"

Kohn saw him first, across the street, in the shadows. He put a stopping hand on the other's chest.

"What do you think?" Kohn whispered. "Who is he?"

"I can't tell," Glass replied at last. "He could be either. He's probably trying to figure that out for himself." He turned to make the point clearer and took in his breath.

"Ernst," Kohn said, advancing across the narrow street toward the other man. "Ernst Gottliebsohn . . . it's me, Kohn. Everything's okay, Ernst . . . you're cleared of all charges. I've come to take you back!"

He heard the footsteps and the commanding voice and his name being called, and he crouched down and turned to see an ominous figure advancing on him, mouthing indistinguishable but somehow threatening words, and without a moment's hesitation he whirled and fled. Behind him hard-running footsteps echoed his own, and he put on a frantic burst of speed, and finally, just when he thought he must give up the flight and turn and confront his follower, those footsteps faded, diminished in tempo, and stopped altogether! But not taking any chances, he ducked into an alley and ran half its length before he stopped—then listened. His heart was pounding so hard it was difficult for him to hear anything else, and as that erratic pulse thundered in his ears he became wildly confused once again as to which he was, hunter or hunted.

He ran his hands hastily over his clothes—they were surprisingly dry—and he fumbled through his pockets, looking for something with which to identify himself. But his pockets were empty.

He lay his hot cheek up against cold brick and sagged against a wall, grateful for any support for his exhausted body. Slowly, as his pounding heart quieted and the flood of blood receded, he began to hear the night again. The night itself was still, but through it, in the distance, he could hear the rumble of traffic, and from the river a boat whistle hooted, and he shivered with some unexplained fear.

And then that sound, as it darkly flew into remote distances, recalled to him another equally grieving sound, the screaming of a cat, a lost soul, a mangy, yellow-eyed beast, a scream that had once been human, that had once been his sister's lover, that had once been a Jew, that had once been Gottliebsohn, before he had been murdered—by whom? He looked at his hands, so busy now massaging one another in grief and supplication, and he remembered those hands gripped, only moments before, around the surprisingly muscular neck of the other, strangling life away. Then he, unbelieving, had seen his own face mirrored in those distended, blood-reddened eyes, and had watched, incredulous, that image of himself fading as life faded, himself disappearing as the soul disappeared. He remembered letting the other go, letting him sag and drop to the pavement, standing there empty-handed in the sorrowing rain, knowing that he had lost something extraordinarily precious, but unable to remember for the life of him what it was.

"I said to be careful with him," Glass said, trembling with anger after he had caught up with Kohn.

"Who'd think a man that big could run so fast?" Kohn gasped, holding his sides.

"And calling him by the wrong name," Glass continued furiously. "What was that supposed to accomplish? You want a permanent invalid on your hands?"

Kohn's own temper flared. "That's how I know the man!" he said. "The name just slipped out!" The sweat was standing out on his face; suddenly he gagged—that exertion, after all the late hours, the drink and the anxiety, was almost too much for him. He turned into the street and was briefly sick. "Maybe I wanted him to be who we thought he was," he said weakly, wiping his mouth with his handkerchief. "Maybe I did. But can't we drop it? He may be all the way across town by now. If we're going to bring him in . . ."

"Bring him in to what?" Glass demanded, and had the satisfaction of seeing Kohn completely discouraged. But he realized that the other was right. "We can't let him run about like this," he agreed, "like some . . ."

"Lunatic?" Kohn wondered, and now Glass was the one who became subdued. "Well, where to now?" Kohn asked.

"The station," Glass said.

The tunnel was very bad for him. It was a nightmare of a tunnel, the dazzling white lights blinding him, the reflecting black tiles distorting his running shadow, reminding him of the reality of dreams, and of that deadly struggle he was having, had had, was about to have, and as his fleeing steps echoed down the long tunnel he became convinced that he would never get out alive. Did it matter? He was a shell, a man without heart or soul, a man who had been robbed of everything, including his name. But he had shown that shameless thief, had strangled him, stripped him bare, and shivering in the cold rain, flung his own wet clothes over the blank-eyed other, hastily buttoning himself against the chill, crouching for . . . how long? next the garbage pails, until the cat's scream brought him to his senses, and fumbling through his pockets he remembered who he was—and he ran out of the far side of the tunnel.

A freight train stretched out into the misting darkness. He would take the freight, he thought, trying to get his breath, the sweat stinging his eyes, and his lungs searing his insides. He would go to the very end of the tracks, and wait in the darkness for the freight to come by, then leap for a handrail, and climb to the top of the car, and ride with his family to their doom.

And then he heard the footsteps.

"There he is!" Kohn cried. He began to run. "It's me!" Kohn cried. "You don't have to run from me!"

"Come back!" Glass echoed, trying to make his voice reassuring. "You don't have to run!" But he was dismayed to hear himself hoarse and frightened.

The running figure disappeared into the misting darkness. Glass remembered how it had been for his patient before, when he had tried to run from who he was, and followed. Kohn hesitated, tired and frustrated by this never-ending chase, then began dog-trotting to catch up to the long-legged American.

They went past the end of the train and then slowed, peering into the darkness on either side of the track, looking for the hiding figure. They walked on for another fifty yards and stopped.

"He'll try and catch the train going out," Glass said, now very discouraged.

"Maybe this train isn't going anywhere tonight," Kohn said hopefully.

But the train was; they could hear the hiss of releasing

brakes, and then the slow grind of metal against metal, and sparks fired the darkness, and a wavering headlight bore down on them, and the train ground past.

They watched the engine disappear into the darkness, moving slowly, gathering momentum with a terrible, nightmare-like slowness, and then they saw him come out of the darkness and run alongside the cars.

They ran after him. "Don't do it!" Kohn cried, but he was so exhausted that he only managed an agonized gasp, and he drew his gun, intending to fire a warning shot.

The other leaped for a rung, missed, and fell, and they gained a few yards on him. But he was up again in a moment, and this time when he leaped, he caught and held on.

Kohn did not remember changing his mind. All he could think of was that his head ached and he had the taste in his throat of vomit, that the mission was finished, his own assignment botched, and that his career was being carried away from him in the person of a lunatic on a slow-moving freight. He believed that he had been genuinely fond of the man he would always think of as Gottliebsohn, and that he might have fired as much out of pity, as out of anger or frustration. But he was not really sure. All he knew was that he stopped running and lifted his gun and looked once briefly at Glass.

Glass was not sure about his own motives either. Perhaps he truly believed that this man they were chasing was better off dead, or it might have been that he hoped, at some primitive emotional level, that in killing the other his own inner conflicts would be done away with too. Whatever the reason, when he saw the gun he stopped, horrified, and while Kohn was taking deliberate aim (after that one quick glance to see if he objected) Glass thought wildly that he ought to keep running, catch up to the fleeing man (although he did not know whether he meant to escape self-knowledge by riding that train with his patient into the welcoming darkness, or to protect him from the coming shot), and he thought about knocking that gun-hand down, but he thought too about the quarreling Germans and Jews in the hospital room, and that the other had no future now that his past was revealed, and he thought that on the one hand he was duty-bound to save his patient, but that on the other hand he had no right to intrude, and while he was thinking all those contradictory thoughts he remained in one spot, frozen—and did nothing.

Kohn fired, and that superb marksman, who fired perhaps out of pity, or of anger, or of frustration, or of all three, and with the silent concurrence of his horrified companion, who was at once himself gentile and Jew, anguished and angry, victim and murderer, hit his mark for the final and most perfect shot of his bloody career, each thinking perhaps to destroy ambiguity, but Glass at least left with the sudden appalling knowledge that there are no simple identifications, knowing that for the rest of his life he had to be all things to all men, for all men are all things.

The fugitive tumbled from the moving train, rolling over and over and over again until he came to rest up against the embankment at the side of the tracks.

By the time they got to him he was dead.

ABOUT THE AUTHOR

S. L. STEBEL was born in Iowa and lived there some fifteen years before moving to California, where he attended a number of schools, including the University of Southern California under the G.I. Bill. He served in the army for three years during World War II, saw two years of combat in the Pacific, and has since traveled extensively in Mexico and in Europe. He has been the editor of a "little" magazine and of an alumni review. He has also worked as a grocery clerk, a warehouseman, in editorial production (for *Time*), as a public relations counselor, and as a principal in an advertising agency. He has done newspaper book-reviewing, and has published an occasional short story in such magazines as *Botteghe Oscure* and *Story*. His next novel, *The Gifted Ones,* a study of genius, has been in progress for the past five years.